★★★★★★★★★★★★★★★★★★★★★★★

O
K·A·P·L·A·N!
MY
K·A·P·L·A·N!

A *Carus Enviek* BOOK

BOOKS BY LEO ROSTEN

THE 3:10 TO ANYWHERE
THE *LOOK* BOOK (Editor)
RELIGIONS IN AMERICA
DEAR "HERM"
LEO ROSTEN'S TREASURY OF JEWISH QUOTATIONS
ROME WASN'T BURNED IN A DAY: THE MISCHIEF OF LANGUAGE
PEOPLE I HAVE LOVED, KNOWN OR ADMIRED
A TRUMPET FOR REASON
THE JOYS OF YIDDISH
A MOST PRIVATE INTRIGUE
THE MANY WORLDS OF L*E*O R*O*S*T*E*N
CAPTAIN NEWMAN, M.D.
THE STORY BEHIND THE PAINTING
THE RETURN OF H*Y*M*A*N K*A*P*L*A*N
A GUIDE TO THE RELIGIONS OF AMERICA
THE DARK CORNER
SLEEP, MY LOVE
112 GRIPES ABOUT THE FRENCH (War Department)
HOLLYWOOD: THE MOVIE COLONY, THE MOVIE MAKERS
DATELINE: EUROPE
THE STRANGEST PLACES
THE WASHINGTON CORRESPONDENTS
THE EDUCATION OF H*Y*M*A*N K*A*P*L*A*N

★★★★★★★★★★★★★★★★★★★★★★★★★★

O
K★A★P★L★A★N!
MY
K★A★P★L★A★N!

LEO ROSTEN

HARPER & ROW, PUBLISHERS

New York, Evanston, San Francisco, London

★★★★★★★★★★★★★★★★★★★★★★★★★★

To

"MR. PARKHILL"

after so many Waterloos

Portions of this work have previously appeared in shorter and different form in *The Return of H*Y*M*A*N K*A*P*L*A*N*, published by Harper & Row, Publishers, Inc., and in *The Education of H*Y*M*A*N K*A*P*L*A*N*, published by Harcourt Brace Jovanovich, Inc.

Designed by Janice Willcocks Stern

LIBRARY OF CONGRESS CATALOGING IN PUBLICATION DATA

Rosten, Leo Calvin, date
  O K*a*p*l*a*n, my K*a*p*l*a*n!
  (A Cass Canfield book)
  "New, completely rewritten H*y*m*a*n K*a*p*l*a*n, combining The education and The return with a new introduction."
  I. Title.
  PZ3.R73860ad [PS3535.07577]   813'.5'2   74–15891
  ISBN 0–06–013676–6

76 77 78 79 10 9 8 7 6 5 4 3 2 1

CONTENTS

WARNING

The God-fearing characters in these tales do not portray persons living, dormant or dead.

Readers who insist that Miss Mitnick or Mr. Hruska, Olga Tarnova or Casimir Scymczak, act exactly like the neighbor upstairs are hallucinating: The people in these stories *do* live upstairs, but only in the house of my imagination.

L. R.

AUTHOR'S CONFESSION

I wrote the first Hyman Kaplan story when I was twenty-four. To my joy (and everlasting pride) *The New Yorker* purchased the tale and published it as a lead "piece."

In the next two years, I wrote fourteen more stories about Mr. Kaplan and Mr. Parkhill and Miss Mitnick and the outlandish melees which exploded in the beginners' grade of the American Night Preparatory School for Adults; and these fables, too, were published in the magazine in which any author I ever met yearned to see his work printed. In 1937 *The Education of H*Y*M*A*N K*A*P*L*A*N* appeared as a book.

Twenty years later I wrote a dozen new stories about the hopeful immigrants to our shores who try—so movingly, so clumsily —to master the elementary yet baffling elements of the English tongue. I wrote these tales with an increased awareness of the agonies endured by adults, weary from long days of toil, who night after night wrestled the heartless ogres of an alien language. These stories appeared in 1959, in a volume called *The Return of H*Y*M*A*N K*A*P*L*A*N*.

Both books have remained in print, *mirabile dictu*, ever since. And scarcely a week has passed without my receiving heartwarming mail—from Bangor or La Jolla, Harvard or Dropsie College, from students, teachers, Oxford dons. Letters bearing the exotic stamps of Hungary, Egypt, Hong Kong, Turkey, even India and Japan have rainbowed my days. I learned that my books had become a favored gift to hospital patients when the Nurses Association of America sent me a heartrending plea: to place a warning wrapper around the jackets of Mr. Kaplan's

adventures (so help me God) "because some of our post-opera-
tives laugh so hard they risk breaking their sutures." I once received a letter, scrawled by a Swedish sailor on a freighter rounding the Cape of Good Hope, begging me "please don't let Mr.
Parkhill go *crazy* from Mr. Kaplan!" and a valentine from a
coin-dealer in Shanghai who told me that his grandfather, who
"talked exactly like Fischel Pfeiffer," had migrated to China
from a woebegone hamlet in Lithuania.

Please believe me when I say that I tell you all this not in
vanity, but in gratitude; and because the foregoing is needed to
explain what follows.

My publishers long urged me to combine both Kaplan books
into a single volume, adding an introduction which would
explain to readers how and why I embarked upon the unlikely
saga of a beginners' grade in an obscure night school for
adults.

> Had I actually taught in such an institution in New York? (No;
> I was a fledgling teacher in such a night school in Chicago.)
> Was there a real Hyman Kaplan? (Well, I did have one student,
> as eager as he was exasperating, who vaguely inspired the charac-
> ter—but would certainly not recognize himself in the Cortez who
> came to dominate my pages.)
> Was there a real Miss Mitnick: that sweet, shy maiden who was
> always right but never victorious? An Olga Tarnova, lost in "ro-
> montic" memories, who could wring "trogic" overtones from a
> laundry list? A Norman Bloom, Fanny Gidwitz, Gus Matsoukas?
> (Yes and no: yes, because each of these earnest souls dimly resem-
> bled someone I once knew—my uncle, a neighbor, our grocer; a
> seamstress, a spinster, an ice-cream vendor named Nicolapolous;
> no, because the differences between my models and my portrayals
> are as great as the gap between a peacock and its egg.)
> Was I Mr. Parkhill? (Alas, only in function; I have nowhere near
> the patience, kindliness and fortitude with which Mr. Parkhill is
> either blessed or afflicted. He is the product of Anglo-Saxon minis-
> ters from New England, I the child of Ashkenazic knitters from
> Lodz. He never loses faith in the possibility of teaching anyone the
> rudiments of English; I was driven to the shattering suspicion that
> some people can no more learn than pole-vault.)

Are the Kaplan stories *true?* (I certainly hope they ring true, though they never happened.)

How many of the hundreds of malapropisms, massacred idioms and outrageous "jokes" did I actually hear from the mouths of my pupils, or read in their bizarre compositions? (Four.)

Why did I use the pseudonym Leonard Q. Ross on the first stories and book? (Because I was engaged in studying the Washington Correspondents under a grant from the Social Science Research Council, and I feared the wrath of that august body should they discover I was committing humor. I had, after all, taken the vows of academe: poverty, bibliography and jargon. I salved my conscience by writing the Kaplan stories only on weekends; every weekday and night was indentured to my doctoral endeavors.

In 1963, I blithely signed a contract to combine the two Kaplan books. What could be easier? I needed to rewrite nothing, add nothing, invent no more. All I had to do was beget a seductive Introduction.

But now it is 1976, and the volume you hold in your hands is not at all a collection of tales you may already have read. It is not a simple joining of two previously published books. It is a completely new work, vastly expanded and, I think, enriched; a ripened delineation of the original characters plus a spirited brigade of new ones. It contains entirely new chapters, fresh feuds and furors in that chamber which, to Mr. Parkhill's consternation, often resembles a battlefield more than a classroom.

"But why on earth did you rewrite all of the stories?" I'm glad you asked.

To bring forth the "combined" volume, I began to reread both Kaplan books—merely to polish them, I thought, to eliminate repetitions, sharpen certain points, refine the devices of humor. I thought I might add grace notes, so to speak, amplifying a character here or heightening a fracas there, strengthening one story's opening or another's middle or yet another's ending.

I had not the faintest notion of writing a new, quite large book. Indeed, I would have rejected such a suggestion with indignation. It seemed foolhardy to change stories which had so long retained a devoted following, to say nothing of flattering benisons from critics and authors I profoundly admire. It is no small thing for a young writer to count among his fans such masters as James Thurber and P. G. Wodehouse, that finicky mandarin Edmund Wilson, or that blistering pixy Evelyn Waugh.

And yet . . . as I reread the tales I had written I was torn by discontent. The discontent soon plunged me into depression. I was ashamed to run across imprecise diction, dismayed by shakiness of structure, disgusted with myself for failing to convert a silhouette into a portrait, a smile into a chuckle, something funny into something much funnier.

The more I read, the more I fell prey to a writer's harshest despot: the dream of perfection. But the longer I read the more I found myself flooded by impulses of improvement: new ideas, new characters clamoring to be set loose in the classroom's wrangles, new thrusts and parries of repartee, fresh "touches" to add juice to the comedy. The demons of creative desire drove me not simply to polish or improve, but to re-create from the very outset.

I was possessed, I admit, intoxicated by those unpredictable surges of fantasy which are a writer's most precious resource.

I could not bring myself to strangle the newcomers who swarmed out of my reveries: a young redhead, Nathan P. Nathan, for instance, a compulsive laugher whose middle initial stood for a name which would create pandemonium among his peers; or the identical twins, Milas and Tomas Wodjik (not only identical twins but dressed identically and always seated side by side, which causes Mr. Parkhill to address his comments to neither one nor the other, but between them); or Olaf Umea, a congenital mutterer; or merciless Reuben Olansky, who is both nearsighted and farsighted; or Christian J. Fledermann, who teaches music, and bearded Isaac Nussbaum, who is a cantor.

And as these additions to my cast strode across the stage of my mind, I was lured into the newfound, tantalizing jungles of their startling pronunciation and spelling and grammar.

I have widened the role and plumbed the ruminations of Mr. Parkhill, who deserves it. I have taken the reader behind the scenes to a meeting of the night-school faculty, to witness the absurd solemnities of the principal, the nitpicking fixations of Louella Schnepfe, the pedantic jocularity of Mr. Krout, the waspish comments of Miss Higby ("Drill! Drill! *Drill! There* is the answer to our problems!"). I have even given myself the pleasure of inventing a manual on the principles of adult education, from which I occasionally quote the grave precepts of professors I am pleased to name Plaut and Samish. (They are very strict about fricative spirants.)

And I pursued Mr. Kaplan through new mazes of his lawless logic. Only after a score of sleepless nights did it dawn on me that that capricious genius loved to learn but hated to conform; his thirst for knowledge clashed with his passion for originality; he seemed to want to make the whole English language start from scratch and justify its rules anew; he converted my classroom into a courtroom. In a burst of unnerving insight it dawned on me that Mr. Kaplan came to school not to be instructed but to be consulted.

The more I reread, the more I found myself creating new episodes, new encounters with the slippery syntax and adamant grammar of our noble tongue. And in doing so, I discovered how easily a delinquent word or reckless phrase can transform proper English into hair-raising jabberwocky. I learned as never before how close to the ordinary is the laughable.

I had become captive to ungovernable fascinations. Before I realized the magnitude of my thralldom, I was lost—helplessly, deliciously lost—in writing a new book.

Now, experiences of this kind, which the Athenians called *cacoëthes scribendi*, "a mania to write," are by no means limited to authors. The delirium of re-creation has often seized poets, composers, painters. A quatrain in time may flower into a sonnet. A melody mounts into a sonata. A sketch on Hogarth's thumbnail generated a tumultuous canvas. A short story by Chekhov became a great play. Lafcadio Hearn rewrote and expanded many of his tales of Japan. Walt Whitman kept adding passage after passage to successive editions of *Leaves of Grass*.

I suppose that the central motivation which drove me to do what I did was the same impulse that led them to do what they did: the belief that one is a better storyteller at forty than he is at twenty, a surer craftsman at sixty than at thirty. A writer

xiii

learns more as he writes more; he receives new visions, perceives new subtleties of technique. He grows more sensitive to the cadences of prose, the aural resonance of a written line, the power of the active as against the passive verb, the offense of maudlin phrases and inflated sentiment. Only the mature Anatole France could end *Thaïs* with this stupendous line: "He had become so ugly that by passing his hand across his face he could feel his hideousness."

In reviewing the stories I had written in greener days, I hit upon stronger levers of narration, more effective nuances of characterization, bolder tensions in plot, those many, many-sided graces of style which create the "atmosphere" which envelops a story or electrifies a climax, the filigree of wording which can better convey emotion—whether sympathy or empathy or the catharsis of laughter.

I have been trying to write since I was eight; my first story was printed in a high school magazine when I was thirteen; and in the legion of years since then I have roamed across the spectrum of literary forms: essays, novels, biographies, melodrama, research studies, screen-plays—every form, I suppose, except poetry (or pornography). I have no hesitation in declaring that of all these molds, comedy is by far the most complex, tricky and elusive.

Take one aspect of humor: if a reader recognizes a comic intention, or spots a seed planted to sprout into jest, he is impelled to resist the writer's purpose. He will snicker, not smile; scoff, not laugh. For he has pierced the camouflage of design, seen stratagems that should pass unnoticed behind the narrative surface. No writers court disaster so surely as those who try to be funny —and fail.

Comedy requires a special slant of conception. Literary yeomen have analyzed the "psychology of humor" to death, which is not surprising: autopsies may inform the clinician, but they slaughter what is living. Even a genius like Sigmund Freud, seeking the keys to the risible, stopped with some brilliant but limited perspicuities about wit. But wit is as unlike humor as puns are unlike lyrics. Freud did not persist, perhaps because he foresaw defeat, in investigating the tenuous attributes hidden beneath the cloaks of comedy.

I like to define humor as "the affectionate communication of insight." Humor depends on characters. It unfolds from a fondness for those it portrays. Humor is not hostile. It is not superior to its players. Unlike wit, it is not corrosive; unlike satire, it is not antiseptic; unlike slapstick, it is not ludicrous; unlike buffoonery, it is not banal. Humor is a compassionate account of human beings caught in the carnival and the tragedy of living.

There are, of course, various categories of comic prose: the devastating ironies of Voltaire, the gentle humor of Jane Austen, the dry mockery of Mark Twain, the dazzling paradoxes of Chesterton, the mordant ridicule of Groucho Marx.

A species all its own is dialect. To elicit laughter instead of confusion, dialect cannot be a literal transcription of "funny talk." Nothing is more lame than a passage of mangled pronunciation recorded in accurate phonemes. Any yokel in the Ozarks can try to be a thigh-slapper by writing "We wuz shure suprized by Maw's coolinary conkokshun." The sounds are authentic enough, and enough to make me wince.

Vernacular which is reproduced precisely just demands too much effort from the reader. He must translate visual distortions into comprehensible restorations. It is sad but understandable that so few people today read, say, Finley Peter Dunne: they do not have the patience to slog through the admirable patois of "Mr. Dooley." Nor do contemporary readers seem to get pleasure from the slow, slow decoding needed to understand Josh Billings or "Abe Martin" (Frank McKinney Hubbard).

I have written enough dreadful drafts of any one of the stories in the present book to realize how infuriating it can be to try to wring laughter from dialect. After many a sterile season spent plowing this intractable field, I think I can identify its treacheries.

The central point about written dialect is that it must intrigue the reader without irritating him. Dialect must reveal what it conceals before frustration drives the reader up the wall. Dialect creates plausible deceptions, persuasive flows of expectation which must be outwitted by surprising and amusing pay-offs.

Dialect must signal a promise to the reader, even while he is puzzled, that what he does not instantly recognize will in another instant be deciphered—and crowned by delight. The reader's responses must be controlled and "cued" so that he will be enticed into reading on with the confidence that momentary bewilderment will be illuminated within a moment in sudden laughter. Dialect must transform its red herrings into angel fish before the reader drowns in despair.

Degas once said: "A picture is not what one sees but what the viewer must be made to see." That is especially true of humor.

I once illustrated the thorny obligations of dialect by citing the example of Mrs. Moskowitz, that virtuoso of the "Oy!" Were I to reproduce a typical sentence of her talk with exactitude, I would have to write "I hate the brat." But that is not at all what Mrs. Moskowitz *means.* Were I to transcribe her spoken words as "I ate the brat," which is closer to her message, Mrs. Moskowitz would be tainted with cannibalism, which is absurd (she would not dream of eating certain *animals,* much less children). I am forced to sacrifice part of the phonetic truth by transcribing Mrs. Moskowitz's sentence as: "I ate the brad." Were I to render this as "I ate the bread," which is what Mrs. Moskowitz had in mind, it would be neither funny nor faithful to her pronunciation. (Besides, if Mrs. Moskowitz could deliver that line that way, I would promote her at once to Miss Higby's grade.)

The phonetic problem becomes much more complex because the characters in my stories write differently from the way they talk. Each scholar in the beginners' grade uses two separate vocabularies. Mr. Kaplan is perfectly capable of writing "word" but he pronounces it "void." He says "sheep" when he means "ship," but he says "ship" to designate the source of wool. Even so mundane a word as "sad" will undergo mind-boggling changes in the larynxes of my flock: "sad" is vocalized as "sat," "said," "set," and even "sod." I, at least, am enchanted when Mr. Pinsky uses "fife" to name not a flute but a number, or when Mr. Blattberg regards "tan" as the numeral after nine. But Mr. Parkhill may be forgiven for wondering how the Tower of Babel moved into his classroom.

If we apply other foreign-language reflexes to the pronunciation of English, we flounder in a labyrinth of crooked mirrors. Take immigrants from Cuba or Colombia. They just cannot say "yes." They say "chess." They also transform "this" into "thees," and "with" into "weeth." My German students go mad trying to draw tongues across teeth to pronounce the English "th," but they end up saying "zis" and "zat" and "zoze" so often that Mr. Kaplan protests that they sound like hissing steam "cattles." Dutchmen gloomily try to pronounce our "th" (whether the "th" of "those" or the more energetic "th" of "throw"), but unlike Germans they vocalize "th" as "d," so our "United States" becomes their "Unided Sdades." Italians, of course, garnish English words with melodious but superfluous vowels: "I lova da landa of Spaina." And Puerto Ricans sing, rather than recite: "Thees lády has pérfume eet ees bétter as flówers."

Jewish students wander through bewildering gorges trying to arrest their habitual interchange of vowels—each of which they can easily enunciate yet treat as musical chairs. Thus, a bed becomes "bad" or a "bet" or even a "bat." A medicinal pill turns into "peel" yet an orange peel turns into "pill." The sons of Abraham convert "gone" into "gun," make a hall a "hull," and pronounce "pool" as "pull." I could only suffer along with the vocal acrobatics which confound terminal consonants: a bag becomes a "back," a rack a "rag," a wedding ring a skating "rink."

Or take the names of the countries from which my earnest students came: Russians identify their native land as "Roshah," Austrians call their homeland "Owstria," Greeks say they are "Griks," Germans call their country "Chermany." And Jewish pupils, trapped within the picturesque phonemes of their mother tongue, think "kink" the title of a monarch.

Malapropisms can daze the most alert teacher or reader: I was certainly thrown for a loop by Mrs. Yanoff's vocal disclosure that Mary's little lamb had fleas as white as snow; by Mr. Kaplan's announcement that *The Mikado* was written by Gilbert and Solomon; by Mr. Trabish's letter to a cousin in "Grand Rabbits, Michigan"; or by Nathan P. Nathan's conviction that the Norwegian author of *A Doll's House* was "Henry Gibson."

A kind reviewer in London's *Times Literary Supplement* once described me as a chap "who has carried on a lifelong affair with the English language." I would be a fool to deny it.

My love of words may be rooted in the tradition in which I grew up and the genes I inherited. My mesmerization by language owes much to the fact that my mother tongue was Yiddish, so my youth was spent in mental shuttlings between "the Robin Hood of languages" and English.

I thank my lucky stars that from the age of four I was bilingual. I had to be, in order to communicate with my parents and their friends and my cronies of the street and school. I was forced to develop facility in rapid interior translation. And when, in graduate study, I had to acquire an acquaintanceship with French and German (and a smattering of Spanish), I discovered more and more jewels in the marvelous world of words.

We say "It's Greek to me." What, then, does a Greek say? What he says is "Stop talking Chinese." Then what does a Chinese say? He says "Your words are like a Buddha, twelve feet high, whose head and feet I cannot recognize." Poles complain "I am hearing a Turkish sermon," but in the Malayalam of southwest India, the exquisite protest is "I do not even know the dried ginger of it." And Jews, who love nothing better than to mince words, dismiss foolish or confusing locutions with a crisp "Stop knocking a teapot."

It always tickles me pink (do Eskimos turn pink when tickled?) to recall that Russian physicists believed that the first atomic pile in history was built "in a pumpkin field in Chicago." That is how Muscovites translated the "squash court" in the concrete bowels of the University of Chicago's stadium: "Stagg Field." And I doubt that a Comanche turns "red" when embarrassed, or that Senegalese say they turn white when frightened.

The intricacies of language play havoc even with our faith in the universality of onomatopoeia. It seems absurd to Anglo-Saxons that dogs can bark in any way except "bow-wow" or "woof-woof." But in Japanese dogs bark "wan-wan" and in Vietnamese "gau-gau." Frogs, in Devon or Des Moines, croak; but to Bavarians their frogs go "quack-quack," which would create a severe identity crisis in American ducks. Arabs definitely hear their donkeys neigh "ham-ham," a shameless affront to Rumanians— who hear their *dogs* make that sound.

I cannot for a moment take seriously the notion that dogs, frogs, ducks, donkeys actually come in national breeds that do, in fact, produce the mishmash of sounds itemized above.

Perhaps you think that only living things create sonic rhubarbs among the nations. Then consider scissors. Surely scissors make the same sound in Lisbon as they do in Peking or Detroit? Scissors do not. Phonetic "truth" lies in hearers' ears. In America, a pair of scissors work with a "snip-snip" or "snip-snap." But to a Chinese they hiss "su-su." To a Portuguese they gabble "terre-terre." And to a Greek they screech "kritz-kritz."

If you think I have strayed from my topic, let me remind you that my beginners' grade contains a polyglot assortment of immigrants who must contend with a mystifying language into which they try to translate their own native words and phrases. Think of the dismay a foreigner feels upon being told that the sound "sh" is required for such different spellings as "*sh*immer," "pa*ss*ion," "lo*ti*on," "o*c*ean," "*s*ure," "suspi*ci*ous," "pa*ti*ent," "*ch*aperone," "ten*si*on," "con*scie*n*ti*ous," "*Sch*ick." Or that "rats" takes a closing sound quite different from "nails" ("z") or "roses" ("ez") or "daisies" ("eez").

To learn English, my students had to stop, look, listen, read— and translate. It is easy to write "translate"; but translation presents brutal barriers to understanding. Translation involves not merely the replacement of words in one language with their counterparts in another. Translation does not contend with words but with meanings. No language can be ripped from its cultural skeleton or its psychological skin.

Who, therefore, can blame Mr. Kaplan for thinking that Washington's Farewell Address was Mount Vernon? Or that the principal parts of "to die" are "die, dead, funeral"? We must ooze sympathy when Miss Clara ("Cookie") Kipnis thinks the opposite of "wet" is "fry." Or when Sam Pinsky flays the British for hounding American colonists by putting "taxis" on their tea.

A language teaches its children how to articulate what they are in fact taught to see, feel, think and hear. "Reality" is bounded by the words we learn, and only through them do we perceive the world around us. Some Polynesian tongues have no word for "time," others no names for direction. The Quechua of Peru reason that since the past can be recalled, it lies in front of them; but the future, being neither known nor capable of envisaging, obviously lurks behind them.

What all the languages (around 3,000) of our mortal breed do have in common is only function: the use of words to try to describe the swarm of impressions registered by the senses; indoctrinated values and mores; the sublime range of intelligence and imagination.

I shall never forget the moment I read this passage in Walter Nash's *Our Experience of Language:*

> In language I make . . . effigies and create ikons. In words, whispering, stumbling words, in the litter and ceaseless drift of words, I search for my identity . . . and the articulation will go on, at the heart of all experience, till at last all burdens are laid down and I need no more words, not even amen and good night.

Readers sometimes ask which part of a writer's labors gives him the most satisfaction. I, for one, find greatest pleasure in the unexpected appearance of the felicitous. In writing the present book, I cherished the deliciously appropriate names that soared out of my unconscious reservoir (surely Minnie Pilpul would be ill-served as Sybil Cohen), the ferocious *contretemps* which erupted from a matter-of-fact remark, the sudden twists and turns of plot which ensnarled Mr. Parkhill's expositions, the bedlam which howled around a routine classroom exercise.

A large portion of the "ingenuity" with which you may credit me was born not from advance intention, but from the conjunction of events neither planned nor foreseen. I cannot estimate the number of linguistic "inventions" which were not so much invented as stumbled upon. Lest this mislead you into thinking my luck was greater than my effort, please remember Claude Bernard's maxim about scientists: "Chance favors only those who are prepared."

I close with a comment I hope you will not challenge: that this new parade of stories is worth the blood, sweat, toil and delight (I never wept) I poured into the long, long journey of re-creation. Those who disagree can, of course, simply go back to the original tales from which this book surprisingly blossomed.

Leo Rosten

New York, N.Y.

★★★★★★★★★★★★★★★★★★★★★★★★★

PART ONE

1

THE RATHER BAFFLING CASE
OF H·Y·M·A·N K·A·P·L·A·N

"Mr. Aaron Blattberg."

"Here."

"Miss Carmen Caravello."

"Ina place!"

"Mr. Karl Finsterwald."

"Ratty!"

"Mrs. R. R. Rodriguez."

"Sí."

"Mr. Wolfgang Schmitt."

"Ja!"

"Yussel Spitz."

No answer.

"Yussel Spitz?" Mr. Parkhill looked up.

There was no Yussel Spitz.

A growl from Mr. Gus Matsoukas, in the back of the room, preceded the announcement: "He laft class. Gave op. Won't come back. He told me to say."

Mr. Parkhill made a note on his attendance sheet. He was not especially sorry, in all honesty, that Mr. Spitz had given up the ghost of learning. Mr. Spitz was an echoer. He had a startling need to repeat every question directed at him. If asked, "What is the plural of 'child'?" Mr. Spitz was sure to echo, "What is the plural of *'child'*?"—and offered no answer whatsoever. Even worse, Mr. Spitz had so spa-

3

cious a temperament that he often repeated questions asked of students two rows in front of him. This upset them. Many members of the beginners' grade had grumbled that their answers had been positively "crippled" by Yussel Spitz's prior requestioning.

"Mrs. Slavko Tomasic."

"Mm."

"Olga Tarnova."

"Da, da."

Besides, Mr. Parkhill thought, it was not unusual for a pupil to drop out of the American Night Preparatory School for Adults. Students came; students went. Some stayed in Mr. Parkhill's class for more than one semester; some left after only one session, or a week's, or a month's. Some enrolled because a father or mother, mate or loved one, had come to Manhattan or Brooklyn or the Bronx. Some departed because a husband's work or a wife's family drew them to another borough or another city. (Last year, a Mrs. Ingeborg Hutschner had disappeared after six weeks of conscientious attendance and commendable progress in both spelling and pronunciation; no one knew where on earth Mrs. Hutschner had gone, or why, or if she still bit her nails.)

"Miss Mitnick."

"Yes, sir," came the soft, shy voice.

And Mr. Parkhill always bore in mind that many of his students entered the portals of the A.N.P.S.A. because of the world's political upheavals: a revolution in Greece, a drought in Italy, a crisis in Germany or Cuba, a pogrom in Poland or a purge in Prague—each convulsion of power on the tormented globe was reflected, however minutely, in the school's enrollment or departures. For immigrants came to the A.N.P.S.A. not only to learn the basic, perplexing ingredients of English; they came to learn the rudiments of Civics, so that they could take the municipal

4

court's examination for that priceless, magical event: admission to citizenship.

"Mrs. Moskowitz."

"Oy."

"Mr. Kaplan."

"Here is Hyman Keplen! In poisson!"

Mr. Parkhill sighed. Mr. Kaplan baffled him. Mr. Kaplan had baffled him more than any other of the thirty-odd members of the beginners' grade ever since the very first class assignment: "Twenty Nouns and Their Plural Forms." After correcting a dozen papers, in his apartment, Mr. Parkhill came to one from which glared:

Nuns		*Pl.*
house	makes	houses
dog	"	dogies
libary	"	Public libary
cat	"	Katz

Mr. Parkhill had read this over several times. Then he put the page aside and tried to sort out his thoughts. He recalled Plaut and Samish's classic *Teaching English to Foreigners,* which again and again warned teachers not to jump to the conclusion that a student was backward, a laggard or "resistant learner," before probing to the core of whatever it was that might be *causing* the neophyte's errors. Sometimes, for instance, a slow reader needed stronger glasses, not stricter tutelage. Sometimes a poor speller was lazy, not stupid. (Spelling had nothing to do with intelligence, as the historic research of Dr. Tyler B. Ponsonby had proved.) And sometimes a pupil's errors resulted not from ignorance but from confusing *sounds:* Mr. Parkhill had noticed that some of his students said "chicken" when they meant "kitchen," and "kitchen" when they meant "chicken." The results were mystifying. He had returned to the page before him:

5

ear	makes	hear
up	"	levator
pan	"	pants

Mr. Parkhill cleared his throat. All doubt now vanished: here, clearly, was a student who, if not given prompt first-aid, might easily turn into a "problem case." Anyone who believed that the plural of "cat" is "Katz" certainly needed special attention. As for transforming nouns into nuns . . .

Mr. Parkhill had run his eye down that unforgettable page, looking for the pupil's name. There was none. That was strange: the other members of the class always wrote their names at the top of the page. But no name was inscribed on the top of this page—not in the middle or at the left- or right-hand corner.

Mr. Parkhill turned the sheet over. The name was there, all right. It was printed, not written, and in large, bold letters. They looked especially bold because each character was executed in red crayon—and outlined in blue; and between every two letters sparkled a star, carefully drawn, in green. The ensemble, as triumphant as a display of fireworks, proclaimed:

H*Y*M*A*N K*A*P*L*A*N

At the next session of the class, Mr. Parkhill had studied Mr. Kaplan with special interest. He was a plump, apple-cheeked gentleman with blondish hair and merry blue eyes, who always had *two* fountain pens clipped to the breast pocket of his jacket. (Other male pupils advertised their literacy with one.) But it was not these features that most vividly seized Mr. Parkhill's mind. It was Mr. Kaplan's smile—a bland, bright, rather charitable smile. That smile rarely left Mr. Kaplan's face. He beamed even while being corrected for the most dreadful errors in speech or

6

spelling or grammar. He seemed to take pride in both the novelty and the number of his mistakes.

Mr. Parkhill recalled the time, in Vocabulary Building, when he had been calling off new words to the class, words to be used in oral sentences.

To "duty," Mr. Pinsky had responded: "To be a good American, please do all your duty!"

Given "nickname" (a word the pupils greeted with delight), Miss Kipnis had replied: "My name is Clara, but friends are calling me 'Cookie.' "

But presented with "choose," Mr. Kaplan had beamed: "I hate to put on a pair vet choose."

And another time, in a brisk drill on opposites, with Miss Mitnick eliciting admiration for the list she daintily wrote on the blackboard:

pull	push
cry	laugh
fix	brake

and Wolfgang Schmitt winning hosannas for his forceful

work	rest
right	rong
sunshine	moonshine

Mr. Kaplan had stunned Mr. Parkhill with

milk	cream
life	debt
dismay	next June

Why, in one composition drill Mr. Kaplan had described how much he hated violins. It had taken Mr. Parkhill several damp moments to hit upon the fact that when Mr. Kaplan wrote "violins" what he probably had in mind was "violence."

Any lingering doubts about Mr. Kaplan's singular use of

7

English were resolved when he was asked to conjugate the verb "to die." Without a second's reflection, Mr. Kaplan had answered: "Die, dead, funeral."

Mr. Parkhill felt a pang of guilt. He had clearly been remiss; he had not applied himself as diligently as he should have to the case of Hyman Kaplan.

Having completed the roll call, Mr. Parkhill opened the session by announcing, "Tonight, class, let us devote ourselves to—Recitation and Speech."

A symphony of approval, punctuated by moans of dismay and groans of alarm, ascended from the rows before him. Most students enjoyed Recitation and Speech, but those who had moaned preferred writing to speaking (like Miss Valuskas, who came from Finland), and those who had groaned considered public performance of any sort out-and-out torture (like Casimir Scymczak, a plasterer from Danzig).

"Suppose we begin with Mr."—Mr. Parkhill tried to sound as if the choice was entirely spontaneous—"Kaplan."

The cherub seated in the chair he always occupied in the exact center of the front row gasped, *"Me?!"*

"Yes," smiled Mr. Parkhill. "Won't you start us off?"

"Gledly!"

"Good," said Mr. Parkhill.

"You valcome," said Mr. Kaplan.

He rose, ecstatic, stumbled over the outstretched legs of Mr. Perez (who uttered an Iberian oath), bumped the knee of Mrs. Yanoff (who hissed, "Mister, you are a fireman?!"), apologized to both colleagues with a debonair "Oxcuse," and hurried to the front of the room. Mr. Parkhill ambled to the back. (He always took a seat in the rear during Recitation and Speech.)

At Mr. Parkhill's desk, Mr. Kaplan turned to face his

peers. He placed one hand on the dictionary, as if posing for a statue, raised the other like a Roman reviewing his legions, broke into the sunniest of smiles, and in a ringing tenor declaimed: "Mr. Pockheel, ladies an' gantlemen, fallow mambers of beginnis' grate! For mine sobject I vill tell abot fife Prazidents fromm vunderful U.S.A. Foist, Judge Vashington, de fodder of his contry. Naxt, James Medicine, a *fine* lidder. Den, Ted E. Roosevelt, who made de Spenish Var a soccess. Also, Voodenrow Vilson, he made de voild safe for democrats. An' lest, mine *favorite* prazident, a *great* human bean, a man mit de hot an' soul of an angel: Abram Lincohen! . . . Denk you."

Mr. Kaplan strode back to his chair like a hero.

"That's a *speech?*" protested Mr. Bloom.

"Go-o-o-d-bye English," mourned Olga Tarnova.

"Oy!" That was Mrs. Moskowitz.

Mr. Parkhill cleared his throat. "That—uh—was very good, Mr. Kaplan—in content. But I'm afraid you made a con*side*rable number of mistakes in pronunciation."

"My!" chortled Mr. Kaplan.

"The floor is open for corrections," called Mr. Parkhill. "Anyone?"

The repairs came from everyone.

"I'm *dizzy* from so many mixed-op woids!" announced Aaron Blattberg.

"He pronounces 'v' like 'w'—and 'w' like 'v'!" proclaimed Mr. Marcus.

Miss Rochelle Goldberg advised Mr. Kaplan to monitor his sibilants with greater vigilance, "because you told us, teacher, how it is important to keep the difference between 's's and 'z's, so a 'ssss' shouldn't toin into a 'zzz,' and a 'zzz' —God fabid—into a 'sss'!"

Several of Miss Goldberg's cronies broke into applause. This caused Wolfgang Schmitt, who was sensitive about his own sibilants, to exclaim that "beans" are not human, and that the "ham" in President Lincoln's first name had been totally omitted. " 'Abram Lincohen' iss not Abra *ham* Lincollen!" was how Mr. Schmitt put it.

"Right!" boomed Mr. Bloom, his bald head gleaming.

"Bravo!" cried Miss Caravello.

"Class . . . please. . . ." Mr. Parkhill saw a tiny hand flutter in the air. "Miss Mitnick."

Miss Mitnick, by all odds the best student in the class, shyly observed, "The speaker can improve in his speaking, I think, if he maybe *listens* to the sounds he is making. Then he will say 'l*ea*der,' not 'l*i*dder,' also 'heart' not 'hot,' and '*fath*er,' which is absolutely different than '*fodd*er'— which is for horses, not humans."

Mr. Parkhill ignored the guffaw from Mrs. Tomasic and the cackle from Miss Gidwitz. "I agree with Miss Mitnick, Mr. Kaplan. You can greatly improve your *pro*nunciation by being careful about your *e*nunciation. For instance, we say 'f*e*llow students,' Mr. Kaplan, not 'f*a*llow students.' We say 'pr*e*sident,' not 'pr*a*zident,' and 'first,' not—er—'f*oi*st,' which is a wholly different word. And it's *'George'* Washington, Mr. Kaplan, not *'Judge'* Washington. Why, right there is a perfect example of why pronunciation is so important! Washington was a *general,* not a judge." (The news came as a blow to Mr. Kaplan.) "And if we pronounce it 'M*a*dison,' Mr. Kaplan, we are uttering the name of a President; but if you say, as you did—er—'M*e*dicine,' you are not pronouncing the name of a President, but something we take when we are sick."

The laughter (and Aaron Blattberg's scathing observation that James Madison never owned a drugstore) caused Mr. Parkhill to call on the next student at once.

What most troubled Mr. Parkhill was the fact that throughout the entire barrage of corrections from his colleagues, Mr. Kaplan smiled and chuckled and nodded his head in undisguised admiration. One could not tell whether he was congratulating his colleagues on their proficiency or preening himself on having hatched so many fascinating contributions to the English language. Mr. Parkhill felt distinctly uneasy.

During the weeks that followed, Mr. Kaplan's English showed no improvement. If anything, his mistakes increased in scope and were magnified by his enthusiasm. What made Mr. Parkhill's task doubly difficult was the fact that Mr. Kaplan was such a *willing* student. He adored learning. He never came to school late. He always worked hard. He knit his brows regularly, unfailingly submitted his homework on time, and never, never missed a class.

One evening it occurred to Mr. Parkhill that Mr. Kaplan might improve if he simply was encouraged to be a little less *hasty* in the answers he volunteered with such gusto. That insight was born during a lesson on parts of speech, when Mr. Parkhill asked Mr. Kaplan to "give a noun."

"Door," said Mr. Kaplan.

Mr. Parkhill remarked that "door" certainly was a noun, but had been supplied only a moment earlier, by Miss Ziev. "Can you give us another noun?"

"Another door," said Mr. Kaplan.

No, Mr. Kaplan could not be said to be making progress. Asked to name the opposite of "new," he had replied, "Second-hand." Told to construct a sentence using the word "fright" (which Mr. Parkhill *very* carefully enunciated), Mr. Kaplan responded: "I like fright potatoes more than smashed potatoes." And in an exercise on proper nouns, after the other students simply recited names (Lexington Avenue, Puerto Rico, New "Joisey"), Mr. Kaplan proudly announced, "Ohio!"

"Very good!"

It would have been better had not Mr. Kaplan added, "It sonds like an Indian yawnink."

An Indian yawning . . . the outlandish image haunted

11

Mr. Parkhill as he tossed and turned in his bed half that night.

Or take the pleasant, moon-bright evening Mr. Parkhill was running through a useful list of synonyms and antonyms: "Cheerful . . . Sad. Easy . . . Difficult. Lazy—"

"Kachoo!" sneezed Mrs. Shimmelfarb.

"God blast you," said Mr. Kaplan.

"*Mis*ter Kaplan," gasped Mr. Parkhill. "The expression is 'God *bless* you.' Why, you have confused 'bless' "—he printed BLESS on the board—"with 'blast' " and he printed BLAST right underneath. "The words, though somewhat similar in sound, are *entirely* different in meaning . . . I'm sure you all know what 'bless' means?"

"Sure!"

"Soitinly."

But the sage in the front row, scornful of lazy affirmations, gazed at the ceiling and murmured, " 'Bless' . . . 'Bl*ess*'?" His ruminations were audible in the back row. "Aha!" He beamed upon Mr. Parkhill: " 'Bless'! Dat's an okay fromm God."

Mr. Parkhill straightened his tie. "Y-yes . . . Now, what is the meaning of 'blast'?"

"Past tanse of 'blass'?"

"Oh, no, Mr. Kaplan. Goodness, no! The whole *point* lies in the difference between the short 'e' "—Mr. Parkhill placed the pointer on BLESS—"and the open 'a'!" He slid the pointer down to BLAST. "Who can tell us what this word means?"

"Is 'blast' a relation to gas?" asked Mr. Finsterwald.

"Well—er—gas can set off a blast. So can dynamite, or gasoline. But—"

"I think 'blast' is a type exploding," ventured Miss Mitnick.

"Precisely! *Very* good, Miss Mitnick. A blast *is,* in fact, an explosion."

"Blast gas," Mr. Kaplan decreed, searing Miss Mitnick with a superior glance.

Hard though he tried, Mr. Parkhill could discover no consistent pattern to Mr. Kaplan's many errors. They erupted in totally unpredictable ways and wholly spontaneous improvisations.

Take the evening the class was working on "a one-paragraph composition." Mr. Kaplan submitted the following:

> When two people are meating on the street [Mr. Parkhill noted that although Mr. Kaplan wrote "street" correctly, he always pronounced it "stritt"] on going Goodby, one is saying, "I am glad I mat you," but the other is giving answer, "Mutchual."

It had taken twelve minutes for the class to complete its autopsy on that one paragraph.

But it was in Recitation and Speech, which elicited Mr. Kaplan's greatest affection, that that intrepid scholar soared to new and unnerving heights. One night, carried away by his eloquence, Mr. Kaplan referred to America's first First Lady as "Mother Washington." Mr. Parkhill was compelled to employ all his powers of persuasion before he could convince Mr. Kaplan that although George Washington was the father of his country, that did not make Martha the *mother*.

Or take the time Mr. Kaplan followed young Vincente Perez's eulogy to Cervantes, whom he proclaimed the greatest writer "een all the world litterture." Mr. Kaplan cast a scornful eye upon Mr. Perez as he delivered a patriotic rejoinder: "Greatest authors are from U.S." The greatest and most "beauriful" American authors (he had read them, it seemed, in his native tongue) were "Jek Laundon, Valt Vitterman, an' de creator of two vunderful books for grown pipple an' boyiss: 'Hawk L. Barryfeen' an' 'Toms Oyer.' "

13

Mr. Kaplan explained that he was not conferring laurel wreaths on "Edgar Allen Pope" because that wizard had written mysteries, a genre Mr. Kaplan did not admire, nor on "Hoiman Malville," because "Mopy Dick gives more attantion to fish dan to pipple."

The whole episode had so alarmed Mr. Parkhill that he asked Mr. Kaplan to remain after class, to discuss his disastrous reversals of the open "a" and the short "e" ("A *pat,* Mr. Kaplan, is not a *pet;* nor is a pet a pat!"); his repeated transpositioning of the short "i" and the long "e" (Mr. Kaplan once advised the class to patronize only those dentists who are so skillful that they can "feel a cavity so you don't iven fill it"); his deplorable propensity for converting the hard "g" into the startling "k," and the broad "o" into the short "u" (Mr. Kaplan transformed "dogs" into "dugs," and "sucks" into "socks").

To all these earnest supplications, Mr. Kaplan responded with ardent thanks, abject guilt, and an exuberant promise to "chenge vunce an' for all all mine bed hebits!"

Plaut and Samish contained not one page about a student who wedded such willingness to such unteachability.

Everything, Mr. Parkhill feared, pointed to the likelihood that Mr. Kaplan would have to remain in the beginners' grade for an extra year. How could such a pupil possibly be promoted to Miss Higby's Advanced Grammar and Civics? The fear was strengthened in Mr. Parkhill's mind the night Mrs. Yanoff read a sentence from the textbook *English for Beginners* about the "vast deserts of Arizona." (Mrs. Yanoff, a lugubrious pupil, always wore black, though Mr. Yanoff was far from dead.) In the discussion that followed, Mr. Parkhill learned that Mrs. Yanoff did not understand the meaning of "vast"; she thought it a misprint for "best."

So Mr. Parkhill turned to the blackboard and there

printed VAST. "Well, class," he smiled, "who can tell us the meaning of 'vast'?"

Up shot Mr. Kaplan's hand.

"Yes?"

"Ve have four diractions: naut, sot, yeast, an' vast."

"No, no. That is *'west,'* Mr. Kaplan." On the board he printed WEST under VAST. "There is a *considerable* difference in meaning between these two words—apart from the fact that the first is pronounced *'v-v-v*ast,' Mr. Kaplan, and the second *'w-w-w*est.'"

This seemed to flash a new light into Mr. Kaplan's inner world. "Aha! So de void you eskink abot is *'v-v*ast' an' not *'w-w*ast.'"

"'W*e*st,'" said Mr. Parkhill, "not 'w*a*st.' You *must* watch those 'e's and 'a's!"

"Hau Kay. De void you esk is not 'w*e*st' but 'v*a*st'?"

Mr. Parkhill declared that "vast" was indeed the *"word"* for which he was *"ask*ing."

"So—" Mr. Kaplan beamed. "Ven a man buys a suit, he gats de cawt, de pents, an' de vast."

Mr. Parkhill lowered his chalk. "I—uh—am afraid you have introduced still another word."

Mr. Kaplan awaited the plaudits of the crowd.

"'V*e*st,'" frowned Mr. Parkhill, "is an article of clothing, but 'west' . . ."

And then Mr. Kaplan turned Mr. Parkhill's concern into consternation. It came during Open Questions. Open Questions was Mr. Parkhill's own invention, a half-session devoted to answering any questions his students might care to raise about any difficulties with English they might have encountered in the course of their daily work and life. The beginners' grade loved Open Questions. So did Mr. Parkhill. He enjoyed helping his flock with practical problems; he felt ever so much more constructive that way. (Miss Higby often told Miss Schnepfe, secretary to the principal of the A.N.P.S.A., that if ever there was a born Open Questions teacher it was Mr. Parkhill.)

"Questions, anyone? *Any* questions—spelling, grammar, pronun—"

Gus Matsoukas emitted his introductory growl, consulted a dog-eared envelope, and muttered his question. "For furniture: is it 'baboon' or *'bam*boon'?"

"Well, a 'baboon' is a type of—er—ape," said Mr. Parkhill, "whereas 'bamboo' is a certain wood. Bamboo is what is used in furniture. *Baboons* are—er—what you may see in a zoo. . . . Next?"

"The word 'stamp'—for putting on mail. Isn't that masculine?" asked Bessie Shimmelfarb.

"N-no," said Mr. Parkhill, and stressed the difference between the postal and the human. (Mrs. Shimmelfarb had obviously equated "mail" with "male.") "Next question?"

"What is the League of Women Motors?" Miss Gidwitz, a fervent feminist, inquired.

"The League of Women *Voters,*" said Mr. Parkhill, "is an organization . . ." His exposition led several women to applaud.

"Who was Madame Pumpernickel?" asked Oscar Trabish, who was a baker. (Mr. Trabish's occupation often affected his diction.)

"Madame *Pompadour,*" gulped Mr. Parkhill, "was a famous character in French history. She was King Louis XIV's—er—favorite. She—"

"Pompadour is a type haircut!" protested Barney Vinograd, who was a barber.

"Oh, it *is,*" agreed Mr. Parkhill at once. "The name *comes* from Madame Pompadour, who wore her hair—that way."

"Haddya like that?!" breathed Goldie Pomeranz.

"Aducation, aducation," beamed Hyman Kaplan, tendering gratitude to the wonders of learning.

" 'Merit'!" That was Mrs. Moskowitz.

"I beg your pardon?"

" 'Merit,' " Mrs. Moskowitz repeated. "Why isn't it pernonced the way it's spelt?"

Mr. Parkhill looked puzzled. "But 'merit' is spelled exactly as it is pronounced, Mrs. Moskowitz." He printed MERIT on the board. "Don't you see?"

"I see it, but I don't mean it!" Mrs. Moskowitz complained. *"That* woid I never saw in mine whole life! *I* mean, if a boy and goil are in love, they get—"

" 'Married'!" exclaimed Mr. Parkhill. "Oh, that's an entirely different word, Mrs. Moskowitz." His chalk crowned MERIT with MARRIED.

"Oy," sighed Sadie Moskowitz.

"Next question? . . . Mr. Kaplan."

Mr. Kaplan asked, "Mr. Pockheel, vhat's de minnink fromm 'A big depotment'?"

"It's 'de*part*ment,' Mr. Kaplan," said Mr. Parkhill. "Well, class, I'm sure you have all shopped in a large downtown store." A majority nodded. "Now, in these stores, if you want to buy, say, a shirt, you go to a special *part* of the store, where only shirts are sold: that is called the shirt *department.*" The quorum assented. "And if you want to buy, say, a goldfish"—Plaut and Samish approved of lightening a lesson with occasional levity—"you would go to another part of the store, where—er—goldfish are for sale . . . So, you see, each article is sold, or purchased, in a different, special place. And these different, special places are called—'departments.' " Mr. Parkhill printed DEPARTMENT on the blackboard. "Therefore, a *big* department, Mr. Kaplan, is merely a department which is large—big." He put the chalk down. "Is that clear, class?"

It was perfectly clear to the class—except, apparently,

17

Mr. Kaplan, who was blinking blankly.

"Isn't my explanation clear, Mr. Kaplan?" asked Mr. Parkhill anxiously.

"Ebsolutely! It's a *fine* axplination, Mr. Pockheel. Clear like soda-vater. Foist-class! *A* number vun! . . . But I don't unnistand vhy I hear dat void in de *vay* I do. Simms to me, it's used in anodder *minnink.*"

"There's really only one meaning for 'department.'"

"Maybe it's not 'a' big depotment but *'I* big depotment.'"

Mr. Parkhill surveyed the ceiling. "*'I* big department' does not make *sense,* Mr. Kaplan. Let me repeat my explanation." This time Mr. Parkhill enlisted the aid of a hat department, a pajama department, and "a separate part of the store where, for example, you buy—canaries, or other birds."

Mr. Kaplan hung on to Mr. Parkhill's every word; but at "canaries, or other birds," he shook his head.

"What is it that puzzles you, Mr. Kaplan?"

"Mr. Pockheel, I'm vary sorry, but I don't simm to make mine qvastion clear. So I'll give you de exect vay I hoid dat axpression . . . I'm takink a valk. In de stritt. An' I mit a frand. So I stop to say a few polite voids, like: 'Hollo,' 'Harre you?,' 'How you fill?' An' while ve are talkink, along comms somvun alse, pessink by, an' by exident he's givink me a bump. So he says, 'Axcuse me,' no? But *somtimes,* an' dis is vat I minn, he says, 'Oh, I big depotment!'"

For one shameless moment Mr. Parkhill wondered whether he could reconcile it with his conscience if he did promote Mr. Kaplan to Advanced Grammar and Civics. Another three months in the beginners' grade might, after all, be nothing but a waste of Mr. Kaplan's time.

2

MR. K·A·P·L·A·N SLAYS
THE SUPERLATIVE

Each week, Mr. Parkhill found it harder to face up to the possibility that Mr. Kaplan might have to be kept in the beginners' grade for some time to come. Promotion to Miss Higby's Advanced Grammar and Civics, at the end of the semester, seemed quite out of the question. It was folly even to think of it. (From time to time, because the idea was so tempting, Mr. Parkhill did think of it, but it was folly to cling to it.)

Every assignment Mr. Kaplan fulfilled contained some new and startling reformation of the English language. (In his most recent composition, Mr. Kaplan had written: "Each year our President gives Congriss a personal massage.") What Mr. Parkhill had to face, without shilly-shallying, was the fact that Mr. Kaplan was no ordinary pupil. Mr. Kaplan was no ordinary man, for that matter. His thirst for knowledge clashed with his passion for originality. He seemed to confuse education with imagination. Mr. Parkhill had even begun to wonder whether Mr. Kaplan's audacious innovations did not contain the seeds of a new English grammar (to say nothing of a new diction, reformed spelling, and refreshed pronunciation). Sometimes Mr. Parkhill felt that Mr. Kaplan was the apostle of an entirely new way of *thinking*.

To Hyman Kaplan, for instance, the instrument most

19

often used by plumbers is a "monkey ranch," blunders in speech are caused by "a sleeping of the tong," and the opposite of "do" is "donut." How could Mr. Parkhill blind himself to the nonpromotability of such a scholar? The man was, to put it bluntly, *sui generis.*

For two nights now, Mr. Parkhill had been fending off in his mind the fact that Mr. Kaplan would have to write his composition on the blackboard. All the names on the class roll had been ticked off except Tarnova, Caravello, and Kaplan. The rest had transcribed their homework during the week drawing to its end.

The acuteness of the class discussion had been gratifying. How swiftly had Miss Mitnick deduced that in Mr. Trabish's essay, "Hannah Lou" was not the name of a laundress, but the capital of Hawaii. How unerringly had Mrs. Slavko Tomasic caught Shirley Ziev's odd revision of Genesis: "Adam and Eve lived in the Garden of Eton." And with what scorn had not Aaron Blattberg pointed out that the "Wilhelm" twice mentioned in Mr. Finsterwald's essay must refer to an "uncle—and not, as he wrote, an 'ankle'!"

Yes, those sessions had greatly heartened Mr. Parkhill. But the composition of Hyman Kaplan was yet to be seen. It would be more accurate to say that the composition of H*Y*M*A*N K*A*P*L*A*N was yet to be seen, for even in thinking of that singular student Mr. Parkhill could not help beholding that singular signature. At first, Mr. Parkhill considered the red-blue-green starred name as a sort of trademark, or a harmless expression of pride. But lately, he had come to realize it was *much* more than that: the crayoned letters were not a name but a proclamation (in his youth, Mr. Kaplan had yearned to be "a physician and sergeant"), a symbol of individuality, a declaration of independence from the chains of the conventional. Only last week, Mr. Kaplan had given the principal parts of the verb "to fail" as "fail, failed, bankrupt."

Tonight, the fateful hour had come. There was just no way to defer Mr. Kaplan's homework further, nor cling to the hope that perhaps Mr. Kaplan would leave the room early: that loyal scholar had not once been so much as a minute late, nor left one second early.

"Miss Tarnova..." Mr. Parkhill heard himself intoning. "Miss Caravello... Mr. Kaplan... I believe it is your turn to place your homework on the board."

Carmen Caravello gave a cheerful *"Bene!"* Olga Tarnova uttered a dolorous *"Górye."* Mr. Kaplan breathed his joyous "My!"

Miss Caravello tripped to the blackboard. Miss Tarnova trudged as if on her way to the guillotine. And Mr. Kaplan passed one full board beyond Miss Tarnova's terrain, Mr. Parkhill noticed, humming a ditty of delight. Mr. Kaplan inspected several pieces of chalk, rejected them, found a stick worthy of its task, and printed:

MINE JOB
Comp. by
H*Y*

"You need not write your *name* on the board," called Mr. Parkhill quickly.

Mr. Kaplan's face was a funnel of astonishment.

"Er—to save time," faltered Mr. Parkhill.

"I got planty time," said Mr. Kaplan.

"I meant the class's time."

Mr. Kaplan blinked. "But mine name is a dafinite *pot* of mine composition."

"Oh."

Dignity restored, Mr. Kaplan completed his starry signature. The sigh with which he invested the printing of the final "N" testified to the pain he suffered in not being allowed to use colored chalks.

As Carmen Caravello sped through her assignment, and

Olga Tarnova glowered through hers, Mr. Kaplan transferred his homework from the paper which rustled in his left hand to the slate which did not flinch from his right. As he wrote, he kept his tongue in the corner of his mouth; and he executed eloquent rotations of the elbow and periodic flourishes of the wrist. But he kept his little finger genteelly extended, an aristocratic digit for whom the other four toiled. The entire elegant process was accompanied by *sotto voce* chuckles and distinct purrings of glory.

As Miss Tarnova scrawled away, her looped earrings jingled and her gaudy bracelets jangled. Mr. Kaplan stared at the offending artifacts. "Tarnova, are you wridink homevoik or givink a concert?"

The glare Miss Tarnova shot him would have slain a Borzoi. "I am womon!" she retorted.

"You sond more like an orchestra."

"Students . . ." Mr. Parkhill cut in. "There is no need to—"

"Eider she should take off or tune op her joolery," recommended Mr. Kaplan.

"Bodzhe moi!" That throaty oath, like everything about Olga Tarnova—her raven hair and satin dress, her perfumed handkerchief and sultry eyes—conveyed intimations of the time she was the toast of the Monte Carlo Ballet. (More than once had Miss Tarnova hinted that there was a time when princes of the blood, maddened by her beauty, had fought duels behind the great Casino for her favors.) *"Bodzhe moi!"*

"Are ve stodyink Rossian or English?" cooed Mr. Kaplan. "Mr. *Kap—!"*

The Slavic siren snapped her handkerchief in Mr. Kaplan's direction in silken rebuke, completed her essay, and sailed grandly back to her chair. Mr. Parkhill scanned what she had written:

My Work Now Is Millinery

I make hats. They are pretty. New shapes. All collars. Womens come from all over N.Y. to buy each other.

But millinery is not my love. It was in Ballet. Ah, Ballet, Ballet. I am sad.

O. T.

Miss Caravello completed her offering: "How Bella Bella is Roma Roma!" The celebration of Rome's beauties was not more than a hundred words long, yet managed to cram in two arches, three piazzas, and a considerable number of fountains.

Mr. Kaplan finished last, with a reluctant "Hau Kay," wiped his fingers delicately, analyzed his handiwork through narrowed eyes, nodding a benediction over his masterpiece, and returned to his chair in the stride of one preparing for coronation.

"Class, study Miss Tarnova's composition first . . ." announced Mr. Parkhill absently, for his eyes were racing across Mr. Kaplan's opus:

MINE JOB
Comp. by
H*Y*M*A*N K*A*P*L*A*N

Shakspere is saying what fulls Man is! And I am feeling the same when thinking about my job in Faktory on 38 st. by 7 av.

Why should we svet and slafe in a dark place by chip laktric and all kinds hot? For who? A Boss who is salfish, fat, driving a fency automibil?? I ask! I answer—because we are the deprassed workers of the world.

O how bad is that laktric light! O how is all kinds hot! And when I tell the Forman should be better work condittions— he hollers, "Kaplan you redical!!" Which I am not. I am only human, the same as you and me.

Mr. Parkhill's temples began to throb.

> So now I keep my mot shot. But somday will the Union win!! Then Kaplan will make the Forman a worker, and will give him the most bad stiles to cot ot! Justice.
>
> My job is a cotter mens cloths.

T-H-E E-N-D

"Well, class . . ." Mr. Parkhill could think of nothing else to say. "Let us begin with Miss Tarnova's composition . . . Who would like to start?"

Four hands popped into the air.

"Mr. Blattberg."

" 'Collars' is spelled bad," said Aaron Blattberg. "Should be 'c-o-l-o-r-s.' "

"Very good." Mr. Parkhill erased "collars" and inserted "colors." "Miss Kipnis?"

" 'Womens' is not a plural," Miss "Cookie" Kipnis observed, "but 'women,' spelled like 'men,' and without the 's.' "

"Correct!" Mr. Parkhill removed the terminal "s" from "womens." "The word 'women' is itself plural, so it needs no 's.' If you *do* use an 's,' it must be preceded by an apostrophe, this way"—he printed WOMEN'S—"which makes it *possessive,* not plural. For instance"—he tapped WOMEN'S with his pointer—"suppose we wanted to say 'women's hats' or 'women's rights'—"

"Or 'vimen's *mistakes,*' " Mr. Kaplan leered at Olga Tarnova.

"—then the apostrophe would be required. But an 's' after a word which is already plural is—er—superfluous."

The room hummed and buzzed over this increment to knowledge, but Rochelle Goldberg asked, "What means 'superfloss'? Is that big-size dental—"

" '*Super*fluous!' " Mr. Parkhill exclaimed. "That means 'not needed.' It *is* a rather—advanced word. I'm sorry. I

24

should have said that an 's' after a plural noun is not *neces-sary. . . ."*

"Thank you." Miss Goldberg reached into her purse for a gumdrop. (Miss Goldberg liked to reward her labors with a bonbon.)

"Further comments? . . . Miss Valuskas."

Gerta Valuskas observed that contrary to Olga Tarnova's unfortunate wording, the women who came to her milli-nery shop did not actually "buy each other." What they did was "buy hats *for* one and the other."

The class acclaimed the Valuskas acumen: "You right!" "Absolutely!" "Good corracting!"

"Very good, Miss Valuskas. . . . Miss Tarnova, do you understand that?"

"No."

Mr. Parkhill cleared his throat.

"Well—er—just notice. You wrote 'they' (that is, women) come to your store and—'buy each *other.'* That—"

"Maybe Tarnova sells hats an' also vimen . . ."

"Mr. Kaplan!" Mr. Parkhill said sharply. (He could hardly permit one student to accuse another of white slav-ery.) "What you should have said, Miss Tarnova, is that your clientele buy hats as presents *for* each other. Now do you see?"

"Ah, da, da," moaned Olga Tarnova.

"Any other comments? Mr. Schmitt . . ."

"I sink zat Miz Tarnova should tell us more about ze *army,"* said Wolfgang Schmitt.

Mr. Parkhill hesitated. " 'Army,' Mr. Schmitt? What army?"

"Ze Rossian army."

Mr. Parkhill frowned. "But why—"

"Because she wrote—zere, on ze board—about her work in ze military—"

"No, no, no!" exclaimed Mr. Parkhill. " 'Millinery' is not

'*military,*' Mr. Schmitt!" He wrote "military" on the board swiftly.

"Schmitt batter not show his face in de gomment districk," observed Mr. Kaplan.

The clock stood at 9:30; time was running out. Mr. Parkhill said, "Let us proceed to Mr. Kaplan's composition."

"Oy," prophesied Mrs. Moskowitz. (To Sadie Moskowitz "oy" was not a word; it was a lexicon.)

Mr. Kaplan said, "Is planty mistakes, I s'pose . . ."

"Y-yes, Mr. Kaplan. I'm afraid there are."

"Dat's becawss I try to give dip *ideas.*"

Mr. Parkhill pondered his inner resources. "First, class, one might say that Mr. Kaplan does not give us much description of his job—"

"It's not soch an interastink jop."

"—and wrote not a composition so much as an—er— editorial."

"I'm producink adi*to*rials?" rejoiced Mr. Kaplan.

"We must confine ourselves to simple exercises," said Mr. Parkhill sternly, "before we attempt political essays."

"So naxt time should be no *ideas?*" asked Mr. Kaplan. "Only plain fects?"

" 'F*a*cts,' Mr. Kaplan, not 'f*e*cts.' "

Mr. Kaplan's expression left no doubt that his wings, like those of an eagle, were being clipped.

"And, Mr. Kaplan, may I ask why it is that you use 'Kaplan' in the body of your composition? Why didn't you write '*I* will make the foreman a worker'? instead of '*Kaplan* will make—' "

"I didn't vant de reader should t'ink I am prajudiced. So I put de onfrandly remocks abot foremen like in de mot of a strenger."

Mr. Parkhill called for corrections.

A forest of hands, palms, pencils, pens, rulers, notebooks sprang into the air.

"Miss Mitnick."

Miss Mitnick had gathered a veritable bushel of errors —in spelling, punctuation, diction, syntax—and she recited them with rapid rectitude. "—and that *'mot shot,'* " she concluded, blushing, "should be 'm*outh*'—*'o-u'*—'shut' —*'u'* instead *'o.'* And that isn't a nice way to talk, besides!"

"Very good," said Mr. Parkhill.

"*Ax*cellent!" beamed Mr. Kaplan, baffling Miss Mitnick.

"Mr. Bloom . . ."

Norman Bloom fired a salvo at no fewer than eight errant words, six crippled sentences, nine deformed phrases, and two throttled infinitives, finishing the onslaught with "—and workers are depressed with an 'e' not an 'a'!"

"Bloom," chuckled Mr. Kaplan, "you soitinly improvink!"

"*I'm* improving?" Mr. Bloom protested, mopping his pate. "It's *your* composition we are discussing!"

"An' in discossink, you improvink!"

"This mon," mourned Miss Tarnova. "This *mon . . .*"

"Mr. Matsoukas."

Gus Matsoukas indignantly changed "fulls" to "fools," "cloths" to "clothes," and hotly challenged the propriety of "Justice" standing all by itself, unsupported, "in one-word-not-sentence!" No one dared challenge a Platonist where justice was at stake.

Then Miss Gidwitz declared, with some force, that Mr. Kaplan meant " '*opp*ressed,' not '*dep*ressed,' workers of the world!"

"Aren't day deprassed, too?" rejoined Mr. Kaplan.

"Mr. Blattberg?"

The massacre of Mr. Kaplan's essay neither flagged nor faltered. Mr. Blattberg blurted out a catalogue of acid rectifications. Mrs. Tomasic tendered a poisoned bouquet of praise: "Mr. Keplen has a big imagination, but look how he spelled wrong Shakespeare's name!" Even Casimir

27

Scymczak leaped into the melee, belying the complexity of his name by the simplicity of his attack: "Why Mr. Koplen writes 'chip'? Is 'c-h-e-a-p.' Why letters '*t-o*' when is '*t-o-o*' for 'also.' "

"Bravo!" gloated Miss Caravello.

And when the heated scholars had exhausted both their knowledge and their umbrage, Mr. Parkhill took over. It was astonishing how many blunders Mr. Kaplan could commit in such limited space. Mr. Parkhill altered tenses, added commas, removed periods; he changed the indirect to the direct (and the direct to the indirect) object; he pointed out that it was wrong to say "I am only human, the same as you and me" because the "I am" clearly made the "and me" redundant.

Throughout the whole fusillade, Hyman Kaplan sank into neither passivity nor despond; instead, he sighed, coughed, chuckled, closed his eyes, held his forehead, clucked his tongue, exclaimed "My!" or "Tchk-tchk!" or "Haddaya like dat?" at strategic intervals. The forehead-holding showed amazement, the cough was pure demurrer, the tongue-clucking implied self-blame, but the expletives tendered consolation to his ego.

"Finally, class, let me call your attention to an error—a very *important* error—which no one has noticed." Mr. Parkhill ran his pointer along the line which described the fate that awaited Mr. Kaplan's foreman should that heartless tyrant ever be replaced by Mr. Kaplan himself:

. . . and will give him the most bad stiles to cot ot!

"Please notice 'most bad stiles.' (That should be a '*y,*' incidentally, not an 'i.') 'Most bad,' class, is totally incorrect! There *is* a word, a common word, for 'most bad,' just as there is for the 'most' of other adjectives. It is the form called—the superlative. . . ."

"Oy," wailed Mrs. Moskowitz.

"We need not be frightened by the word 'superlative,'" said Mr. Parkhill earnestly. "We just use different adjectives—really, different forms of the same adjective—whenever we want to describe something, then want to *compare* it to another thing, and then if we want to show that it is even more so than all the other things to which we may wish to compare it!"

A new *"Oy*-y-y" indicated that Mrs. Moskowitz was not frightened but horrified.

"Notice how *simple* it is!" exclaimed Mr. Parkhill. "For example, we say that someone or something is 'tall.' . . ." He printed TALL more swiftly than he had ever printed anything on the board before. "This is the first or 'positive' form. Now, if we want to say that someone—let's call him John—is 'tall*er*' than, say, his sister"—a quickly chalked TALLER overshadowed TALL—"that is the 'comparative' form. And when we want to say that John is taller than everyone in the family, or any other group—I mean whenever we compare *more than two* persons or objects or even ideas—we say 'tall*est*'!" TALLEST promptly towered over its siblings. "And *that* form, using 'e-s-t,' is called—the 'superlative'! Do you see?"

"I *see!*" blushed Miss Mitnick.

"Yos," said Mr. Scymczak.

"My!" glowed Mr. Kaplan.

Miss Goldberg swallowed a marshmallow.

"Now, class, let us see how easy it is with other adjectives. Take—oh—'rich.' 'Rich . . . rich*er* . . . rich*est* . . .'" He paraded the wealthy trio down the board. "Or—'strong'! . . . 'Strong . . . strong*er* . . . strong*est.*'"

Rapture swept the forum; ejaculations of joy hailed the miracle of education.

"Now, isn't that easy, class?"

"Easy!" echoed Mrs. Yanoff, who rarely found anything easy.

29

"A snep!" grinned Sam Pinsky.

"You *mov*velous!" cheered Mr. Kaplan.

Mr. Parkhill was so pleased by their enthusiasm that he permitted himself a modest smile. "Let us see how many other examples *you* can volunteer."

"Sick, sicker, sickest," sang out Miss Mitnick.

"Good!"

"Dark, darker, darkest," offered Mr. Feigenbaum.

"Very good."

"Da fat, da fatter, da fa-a-atest!" trilled Carmen Caravello.

"Excellent. . . . And now, class, let me take one moment to note that there are certain exceptions—"

Groans instantly greeted the ominous "exceptions." The beginners' grade had long ago learned to fear—nay, loathe —the Exception to the Rule. It was the bane of their learning, a snake in the garden of perception. (Mr. Krout, the senior instructor in the A.N.P.S.A., once enlivened a faculty meeting by declaring that "the very *bête noir* of English is the skulking multitude of Exceptions to the Rule!" How Mr. Parkhill had admired the way Mr. Krout had put that! He admired it almost as much as he admired Mr. Robinson, the school principal, for responding: "I heartily agree, Mr. Krout. There are as many exceptions to the rule in English as there were thieves in Baghdad!" Who could forget such a simile? "But we cannot *change* the rules of grammar—nor, if I may say so, can we exile all the exceptions. . . . Carry on! That is what we all must do. Carry on!" If there was one quality Mr. Parkhill had inherited from his ancestors, it was the capacity to carry on.)

"Class," said Mr. Parkhill, "it is not as complicated as you assume. For instance, take the adjective 'good.' We don't say 'good . . . gooder . . . goodest . . .,' do we?"

"Oh, *no,"* said Miss Mitnick.

"Never!" called adamant Bloom.

30

"It's to leff!" laughed Mr. Kaplan.

"Quite so. 'Good, gooder, goodest' is ridiculous. . . . What do we say, then? 'X' is good, 'Y' is—"

"Who," demanded Mrs. Moskowitz, "is dis 'X'?"

" 'X' is just a symbol," said Mr. Parkhill, "a *sign* for, well, any name or thing. . . . So, we say 'X' is good, but 'Y' is—"

"Who is 'Y'?"

"Anodder tsymbol!" snapped Mr. Kaplan. "Fa goodness *sek*, Moskovitz, don't you onnistand a *semple*, a plain 'for instance'?"

"My had is swimming," moaned Mrs. Moskowitz.

"Your had is *dron*ink," said Mr. Kaplan. "Lat Mr. Pockheel halp you ot—"

" 'H*e*lp you *out,'* Mr. Kaplan!" Mr. Parkhill's pointer tapped the desk with resolution. "Again, please. We say that something is 'good,' " he raised his voice, "and that something is even—" He arched an eyebrow.

"Batter," yawned Mr. Trabish, ever the baker.

"Exactly! And for our *utmost* praise, when something is superior to even that which is better, we say—?"

"High-cless!"

Mr. Parkhill's pointer froze in midair. "Oh, no, Mr. Kaplan."

"Not 'high-cless'?" Mr. Kaplan could not believe his ears.

"No, Mr. Kaplan. The word is 'best.' . . . And now, to return to your phrase, 'most bad.' What is the comparative form of 'bad'? . . . Anyone? 'Bad' . . ."

"Worse," volunteered Goldie Pomeranz.

"Correct! And the superlative?"

"Also 'worse'?"

"N-no, Miss Pomeranz—although the superlative certainly sounds a *great* deal like 'worse.' You are *very* close . . . I'm sure you know the answer. 'X' is 'bad,' 'Y' is 'worse,' and 'Z' is—?"

31

"Now comes Mr. 'Z'?!" Mrs. Moskowitz's incredulity broke all bounds.

" 'Bad . . . worse . . .' and—?"

"Aha!" cried Mr. Kaplan. "I got it!"

"Good."

"De exect void!"

"Go on."

" 'Rotten!' "

The pointer fell out of Mr. Parkhill's hand. He bent down to pick it up, thoughtfully placed it on its ledge, fumbled for a stick of chalk, and printed W-O-R-S-T on the battle-scarred slate.

And all the while he was executing these movements, Mr. Parkhill's mind churned with this latest manifestation of Mr. Kaplan's exasperating originality: "Bad . . . worse . . . rotten. Bad . . . worse . . ."

The bell tolled reprieve down the corridor. What cared that mindless gong that Miss Caravello's "Bella, Bella, Roma, Roma" still glared, unhonored and uncriticized, on the board?

★ ★

3

O HEARTLESS HOMONYMS!

Ever since Mrs. Yanoff had made the extraordinary error of endowing Mary's little lamb with "fleas as white as snow," Mr. Parkhill realized that the beginners' grade was in dire need of a lesson on homonyms. Strictly speaking, "fleas" and "fleece" were not homonyms, since the words are spelled differently, not alike (as, say, "bow . . . bow," the first meaning to bend, the second linked to an arrow). "Fleas" and "fleece" are not even homophones: that is, words spelled differently but pronounced alike (as, say, "bear . . . bare").

But whatever the technical jargon (and Mr. Parkhill was extremely careful not to confuse his students with gruesome words such as homonym or homophone), there was no doubt in his mind that a lesson on words spelled alike but pronounced differently, or words spelled differently but pronounced alike, would be extremely useful.

During the next sessions of his class, Mr. Parkhill kept on the alert for some student's misuse of either a homonym or a homophone. His opportunity came when Miss Pomeranz, in an otherwise commendable composition, wrote:

He pulled off a piece of the tree's bark.

Mr. Matsoukas promptly growled, "Trees are not dogs! *Dogs* bark."

33

"Zo what do treess do, zing?" demanded Wolfgang Schmitt.

"Don't be silly," yawned Mr. Trabish. "Trees are daf an' dump."

"One moment!" Mr. Parkhill broke in. "A *very* interesting point is involved here. Miss Pomeranz used a word which has two different meanings—in fact as Mr. Matsoukas's comment tells us, 'bark' is really *two* different words, spelled exactly alike!"

Astonishment swept the synod, some of whom had never credited Miss Pomeranz with such virtuosity, and some of whom were stunned by yet another revelation of the duplicity of the English tongue.

"Two words spelled one way?" moaned Olga Tarnova.

"Loin, Tarnova, don't complain!" snapped Mr. Kaplan. "In ballet didn't you dance a dance?!"

"Precisely!" Mr. Parkhill stepped to the blackboard. "Notice, class." He printed:

BARK

BARK

"The spellings are identical. But the first 'bark' means the covering of a tree or a branch—"

"Aha!"

"—whereas the second is the sound made by a dog."

"Bow-wow!" came from Mr. Matsoukas.

"Now it's a school for *animals?!*" wailed Miss Ziev.

"Class," called Mr. Parkhill cheerfully, "I think you will all be greatly interested if we devote the rest of the session to just such words!"

"I'm already eenterested," vowed Mrs. Rodriguez.

"Goot idea!" declared Mr. Pinsky.

Mr. Schmitt called, "Zat could be ze most zuccezzful lezzon zis zemester—"

"I hear *bees* in de room," observed Mr. Kaplan.

"Mr. Kaplan! That was not necessary," frowned Mr. Parkhill.

"If Schmitt said 'necessary' it vould sond like a stimm-cattle!"

" 'Steam,' not 'stimm,' " said Mr. Parkhill severely. "And—"

" 'Cattle' for 'kettle'?!" Mr. Bloom guffawed. "Kaplan, do you boil water on a cow?!"

Laughter shook the ranks. Miss Tarnova waved her handkerchief. Mr. Blattberg was in ecstasy. How Mr. Kaplan felt, no one could tell. Whenever Mr. Kaplan was driven against a wall which neither ingenuity nor guile could surmount, he simply reasserted his dignity, arranging his features into disdain for the rabble whose indignities were beneath response from a man of honor.

"Class . . . class . . ." Mr. Parkhill's pointer finally stilled the commotion. "Please give me your full attention. I said that some words, such as 'bark,' look exactly alike and are pronounced exactly alike, but have wholly different meanings. Now, other words are spelled alike but are *pronounced* differently—" In a flash he printed:

1. COMBINE
2. COMBINE

"The first means to put together—'com*bine*,' but the second, '*com*-bine,' is an organized group—"

"How can I tell the difference?!" rasped Jacob Marcus.

"By the context," said Mr. Parkhill earnestly. "I mean the whole sentence in which the word is used. It's only a matter of becoming familiar—"

"I'll *never* be familiar!" predicted Miss Kipnis.

"Of course you will," said Mr. Parkhill. "We *all* have had to learn such—things. . . . And then there is a third group of words, spelled alike, and pronounced alike, but—"

"What?!" cried Bessie Shimmelfarb.

"Ooooo." Mrs. Moskowitz was trying to sound genteel.

"—totally different in meaning!"

"Oy!" came the diphthong of total despair.

"It's *extremely* interesting," said Mr. Parkhill quickly, and just as quickly plied chalk on board:

1. FAST
2. FAST

"Now, class, you see that both 'fasts' are spelled exactly alike. And both are *pronounced* alike. Yet"—he paused, aware that some minds would reel, much confidence crash with his words—"the *meaning* of 'Fast' Number One is entirely different from the meaning of 'Fast' Number Two, and vice ver—"

Not a crash but an earthquake shook the walls. The cries of disbelief, the howls of protest, the outraged accusations of trickery—the room rang with the piteous gabble of victims fleeing for their lives.

" 'Fast' Number One," called Mr. Parkhill above the uproar, "is wholly unlike 'Fast' Number Two because . . ."

"No!"

"Hanh?!"

Rochelle Goldberg was gobbling raisins as if they were penicillin.

"Please listen." Mr. Parkhill tapped the first "fast" with his pointer. "This means 'quick' or 'speedy,' and *this*"—he rattled the stick at the second and confounding "fast"— "means not to eat!"

Light struck Mr. Pinsky. "Like on Yom Kippur!"

"Right!" said Mr. Parkhill. "Now, note *this* pair." His winged chalk flew across the center of the board:

1. INTEREST
2. INTEREST

"The first 'interest' means to engage our attention or curiosity—"

"You—interesta—us!" sang Miss Caravello.

"Thank you. But the *second* 'interest' is what you receive for putting money in a savings bank."

"I dun't be*lieve* it!" said Mr. Feigenbaum.

"I do," sneered Mr. Kaplan.

"A bank isn't interested in interest?" bleated Mr. Wilkomirski, who often mixed things up badly.

"But how do we know if the word means interesting or a profit?" Mr. Blattberg twirled his watch chain, from which the baby tooth of his grandson dangled, in indignation.

"By the whole sentence!" said Mr. Parkhill.

"But couldn't Number One mean Number Two, and Number Two mean Number One?" demanded Goldie Pomeranz.

"Soitinly!" Mr. Kaplan hailed the horror as if it were a blessing.

"Yes, Miss Pomeranz. That's my point! By *themselves,* we cannot tell if 'Interest' Number One means 'Interest' Number Two. It's the *sentence* in which each word is used that tells us beyond doubt which meaning is right. Suppose I say, 'He interests the class.' That's very different from my saying 'He went to the bank and received the interest on his money!'"

"Thata I like," said Miss Caravello.

"Splandid axemple!" said Mr. Kaplan.

"There's *no* way of mistaking the meaning of 'Interest' Number One and 'Interest' Number Two in *those* sentences, is there?"

"No!"

"Never!"

"It's the sentence, not the woid!" blushed Miss Mitnick.

"Exactly. And here is a final example!" Mr. Parkhill stepped to the right end of the board cheerfully, thinking that in teaching as in life, goblins seen are goblins slain. He printed:

1. SWALLOW

2. SWALLOW

The third pair of homonyms refanned the fires of chaos.

"Too much!"

"Not fair!"

"I'll—ne-ver—agree!"

This time Mrs. Moskowitz's "Ooo-oy!" was the wheeze of a woman about to become a corpse.

"But this is a rather *amusing* example," Mr. Parkhill put in lightly. (Plaut and Samish never tired of encouraging teachers to inject humor into workaday tasks.) " 'Swallow' Number One is a movement in the throat—this way . . ." He produced a monumental ingurgitation. "But 'Swallow' Number Two is a bird!"

"Why," objected Mr. Pinsky, "can't 'Swallow' Number *One* be a boid and 'Swallow' Number *Two* be a—" He almost dislocated his Adam's apple.

"Oh, they can!" exclaimed Mr. Parkhill. "That's very good, sir. It is the way we *use* the words which tells us the difference. For instance, 'She swallowed the ice cream' tells us instantly that 'swallow' means"—he swallowed— "whereas 'She saw the swallow' tells us that she saw a bird! Do you see how *completely* the meaning is conveyed by the whole sentence?!"

"Absolutely!"

"No doubts!"

"Mr. Pockheel is a ginius!" proclaimed Mr. Kaplan.

Mr. Parkhill placed the chalk (how quickly it had become a stub) into the trough on the ledge. "Well, class, see how much we have accomplished!"

Joy reigned, albeit confined.

"Qvastion!" It was Mr. Kaplan.

Mr. Parkhill braced himself. "Y-yes?"

"I unnistand avery single pot you axplained so fine. Still, vun point bodders me. . . ."

38

Mr. Parkhill wiped the chalk dust off his fingers. "Y-yes?"

"Suppose I use a santance wit' 'Svallow' Number Vun an' *also* 'Svallow' Number Two?"

Mr. Parkhill frowned. "I fail to see—"

"Vell," asked Mr. Kaplan, "ken't a svallow svallow?"

Mr. Parkhill's head began to ache.

"Stop!" bawled Norman Bloom.

"Shame . . . shame . . ." knelled Miss Tarnova.

"I think I leave this class!" announced Mr. Scymczak.

"*I* thinka I'll taka poison!" glowered Carmen Caravello.

"Mr. Kaplan happens to be right," said Mr. Parkhill. "One *can* use a sentence with both meanings. Er—'I saw the swallow swallow the seed,' for instance, or 'Why can't the swallow swallow?' "

"Next Keplan will want a word with *three* meanings!" warned Aaron Blattberg.

"Aren't tweens enough, Koplan?" snorted Mr. Perez. "Treeples you want, yet? In English are no—"

Mr. Parkhill did not know what to say. English does, of course, contain quite a number of triple homonyms (or homophones, for that matter). He would have been delighted to take his pilgrims through the enticing guises of that one syllable which is identical for "air" and "heir" and "err." He visualized a board on which glowed:

> We breathe *air.*
> To *err* is human, to forgive divine!
> A child is an *heir.*

Why he could even have conjured up a sentence with a delightful triple-decker:

> The *heir erred* when he left the lawyer's office for a breath of *air!*

"I think we had better leave the three-meaninged words for a later session," he heard himself saying. "Perhaps near the—very end of the semester."

There was no point in pushing fate too hard. He had survived the passage between Scylla and Charybdis. But Poseidon's trident had fearful prongs. . . .

"Please turn to page sixty-one of our text. . . ."

Sometimes Mr. Parkhill wished he had become a teacher of arithmetic.

4

THE ASTOUNDING BIRTH OF NATHAN P. NATHAN

"Mr. Aaron Blattberg."

"Right here!"

"Miss Fanny Gidwitz."

"In place."

"Mr. Matsoukas."

"Ugh!"

"Mr. Nathan P. Nathan."

"Yes, *sir!* Ready and willing!"

Mr. Parkhill looked up, smiling. He rather liked young Nathan P. Nathan. This was only Mr. Nathan's third appearance in the beginners' grade. He had not registered until six weeks after the fall session had begun. But that was not unusual. The American Night Preparatory School for Adults prided itself upon its adaptability.

Nathan P. Nathan surely was no newcomer to our shores. He spoke fluent English. He used idioms with ease and colloquial phrases with abandon. He did not flinch before the wayward vernacular which tormented so many members of the beginners' grade, nor the baffling locutions which plunged so many into despair.

Everyone in the class liked Mr. Nathan. He was an energetic redhead, no more than twenty-three or -four, bubbly in manner, swift of speech. And Mr. Nathan laughed. He always laughed. He seemed to be the happiest young man on earth. His was an infectious laugh. Even Hyman Kaplan, who did not wear his heart on his sleeve, chuckled with comradely pleasure when Nathan P. Nathan laughed.

One more characteristic distinguished Mr. Nathan from all the other members of the class. He wore nothing over his sweater, no matter what the temperature outside. (The sweater had two yellow stripes running down the right side, and a thick, chenille "C.N.S." on the left pocket: the initials stood for "Cholisk's Net Sharks," the name of Mr. Nathan's basketball team, which was emblazoned *in toto* on the back.) Young Nathan always removed that sweater the moment he entered the classroom. He sat soaking up knowledge, with the utmost elation, in a short-sleeved shirt. Beneath and beyond those shortened sleeves, biceps the size of potatoes bulged, muscles of such pleasing size and grace that they were often eyed in sidelong yearning by Miss Tarnova.

The one thing that puzzled Mr. Parkhill about Nathan P. Nathan was that he never did homework. He always gave a plausible excuse: "I worked overtime"; "My uncle was sick"; "I had to visit my sister in Patchogue." And Mr. Nathan always found some reason not to go to the blackboard when his name was called: "My wrist is sprained"; "My corns are killing me!"; "I strained last night my back in basketball." (Mr. Nathan would no more think of skipping a basketball game, in the Lefkowitz League, than Miss Goldberg would think of renouncing her Milky Ways. He had the highest absentee record in the grade, and Miss Schnepfe, in the principal's office, had written him—and Mr. Parkhill—several severe notes about it.)

Now, it was the third Recitation and Speech exercise of the semester. Mr. Parkhill had devoted the preceding session to Dangling Participles. But to his students, Recitation and Speech constituted an ordeal far greater than dangling participles, because of the intensely personal character of Recitation, its demands on the poise, the confidence, the sheer recuperative speed of a lone pupil exposed to public dissection. The class was merciless when it came to criticizing a student's performance in Recitation and Speech.

The evening had opened rather well, with Mr. Wolfgang Schmitt's speech on Goethe, whose poems ("in ze orichinal Cherman") Mr. Schmitt extolled as second to none. "Cookie" Kipnis had followed Mr. Schmitt with a lively anecdote involving a *contretemps* whilst "shopping at Gimpel's," which she patronized when not loyal to "Mazy's." Miss Gerta Valuskas had recited a moving poem in Finnish, which she translated with elocutionary gestures that held her peers in thrall. (But since no one in the class knew a word of Finnish, there was no telling how accurate Miss Valuskas's translation really was—and no point, therefore, in criticizing her English version.) Mr. Finsterwald had presented what seemed an eloquent eulogy to Holland—until a reference to Beersheba made it dawn upon his mystified colleagues that Karl Finsterwald was talking not about Holland but the Holy Land.

Suddenly, Mr. Parkhill decided to call upon Mr. Nathan. He smiled invitingly as he said, "Mr. Nathan, don't you think it's about time *you* addressed us? I mean," he swiftly added, "if you feel up to it."

"I'm fit as a fiddle and happy to oblige," laughed Nathan P. Nathan.

The announcement elicited surprised "Ah"s and pleased "Oh"s and Mr. Kaplan's benedictory, "Good boy! Ve all stend besite yoursalf!"

Mr. Nathan laughed once more. His red head bobbed toward the front platform, which he reached with the leap of a hurdler. (He certainly was a healthy young man.) "Hello, folks, hello!" trumpeted Mr. Nathan. "I will talk

43

short and to the point. My name is Nathan P. Nathan and I am twenty-four years old and I was born on a train—"

A gasp escaped Mrs. Yanoff.

"—by my mother, an anagel, God bless her memory—"

"Aleha ha-shalom." Mr. Pinsky honored the departed.

"—and my father was a furrier in Odessa but he ran away to Turkey and then Engaland, where he met and got married to my mother, God bless her, and I started school in New York but we were poor so I had to stop in the six garade and go to work to help out and give every penny to my mother, a woman a saint, now in heaven—"

"She should rest in peace," called Mrs. Shimmelfarb.

"—and my first job was pushing carts in the garament distarict, then packing bundles for a boss a *murderer,* and now I stuff pillows. I push in them kapok, *piles* of kapok, eight hours a day and half-day Saturday—"

"Shame," hissed Mr. Marcus, who was extremely pious.

"—but I don't mind as the pay is good and all the guys at work are peachy. And now I come to school because—well, because even if you think my talking of English sounds good—"

"Like an American-born!" cried Miss Gidwitz.

"—I don't *read* so good, and my spelling is from hunger. So I want to learn to read and spell my father should be paroud of me. I hope every other cripple in this room will also learn perfect. Thank you, ladies. Thank you, gentlemen. Thank you, Mr. Parakhill." Laughing, dancing like a boxer, his short sleeves fluttering, the exuberant young man bounced back to his seat.

"Vunderful spitch!" cried Mr. Kaplan.

"Oh, Mr. *Nathan,*" breathed Miss Mitnick.

"Bravo!" sang Carmen Caravello. *"Bravissimo!"*

"A plashure!" crowed Mrs. Moskowitz, for once forsaking the shades of Cimmeria.

"Mr. Nathan, that was excellent—" began Mr. Parkhill, but Hyman Kaplan, heretofore unrivaled for ebullience,

44

turned to bubbling Nathan and declaimed: "I don't care if you vere born in a sobvay, boychik, you made a spitch you should be prod! But don't call de cless 'cripples.' Dat's not nice. Say better 'greenhorns.' Still—"

"Mr. Kap—"

"—congradulation, Nat'an P. Nat'an! Congradulation, class, we should have soch a student! Congradulation to de school, an Amarican-born should comm here! Cong—"

There was no telling how many persons or institutions Mr. Kaplan intended to congratulate, for the recess bell was trilling like a nightingale.

The post-recess comments on Mr. Nathan's oration were (at least, so they started) as brief as they were generous.

"It was a wonderful speech," blushed Miss Mitnick, "although you don't have to say 'anagel' for 'angel,' or 'garade' for 'grade.' "

"Mr. Parkhill is not Mr. Par*a*khill," Miss Ziev primly observed.

"Why give each word free syllable?" sulked Gus Matsoukas.

"It's a habit," laughed Nathan P. Nathan.

"Change it!" snapped Mr. Blattberg.

"I learned it from my *father*. He talks like that."

"Then don't change! Respact your father!" called Mr. Pinsky. "It won't hoit the language."

"How old is your papa?" asked Mrs. Tomasic hopefully.

"Class—" Mr. Parkhill started. "I think—"

"Where was thees train going?" piped Vincente Perez.

"*Which* tren?" asked Miss Schneiderman.

"Thees train he was born on eet!"

"I don't know," laughed Mr. Nathan.

The room was thrown into consternation.

"*You don't know where you were borned?!*" moaned Mrs. Moskowitz.

45

"No one did tell you if you are an Englisher, a Sviss, even a Toik?" asked Mr. Vinograd.

"Class—"

"Nobody *knew*," pealed Nathan P. Nathan. "We were in a big hurry. My father took the first train he could throw the whole family on."

"In which *contry?*" appealed Miss Gidwitz.

"Canada."

"Canada?!" gulped Mr. Scymczak, who confused it with Australia.

"So he's not an American!" Miss Goldberg's disappointment was so great that she ate two squares of butterscotch.

"So he's a Canadian!" called Mr. Kaplan. *"I* should be so locky!"

Mr. Parkhill drummed on the table many times before he could calm the heated forum. "Class, I do think we should return to the *English* aspects of Mr. Nathan's recita—"

"Isn't being a nativer more important than he puts in extra syllables?" That was Norman Bloom, prickly as ever.

"Well—"

"Nat'an P. Nat'an," Mr. Kaplan suddenly blurted, "vhat does it say on your birth stiff-ticket?!"

" 'Cer*tifi*cate,' Mr. Kaplan, not 'stiff—' "

"I haven't got a birth ceratificate," laughed Mr. Nathan.

"What?!"

"No!"

"A scendal!"

"Ain't you ashame?"

Sympathy for young Nathan mingled with reproaches to the authorities in Washington, Ottawa, and several wholly uninvolved capitals.

"It's a *crime* America shouldn't give a boith paper to a baby who was born—"

"How do we know he wasn't born in *Alaska?*" demanded Mr. Blattberg. "How do you know he ain't an Eskimal?"

"Our train didn't go through Alaska," laughed Mr. Nathan. "We carossed Niagara Falls. And that's when I was born."

A camel playing the bagpipes would have caused no greater sensation.

"On Niakra Falls?! One of de world's natural wonderfuls?!"

"You got born on a *britch?!*" exclaimed Mr. Pinsky.

"Class—"

"Did you see it?"

"Don't be a silly!" scoffed Mrs. Moskowitz, a veteran of two parturitions. "He wasn't *born* in time to see—"

"Ladies—"

"Maybe he was!" crooned Olga Tarnova. "Maybe his forst look on worrld was Niogora Falls!"

"I couldn't see for a month!" beamed Mr. Nathan.

"Maybe just a peek out the window?" pouted Miss Tarnova.

Mr. Nathan rocked with delight. "You have to remember that I don't know if I was inside or outside my mother when we carossed the Falls!"

"Omig*ott!*" mourned Mr. Feigenbaum.

"That's true," said Mrs. Yanoff.

"Sod, sod," moaned Olga Tarnova.

"Class—"

"Vait!" Mr. Kaplan leaped to his feet, clutching one lapel in the manner of Daniel Webster. "Nat'an P. Nat'an, hear mine voids! *T'ink!* T'ink vary hod, vary careful! Exectly vhere—"

"Mr. Kaplan—"

"—did you breed in your vary foist brat?"

"In the middle of the bridge," bubbled Mr. Nathan.

Astonishment grappled with disbelief amongst the confused geographers. The room rocked between horror and incredulity.

"Ladies . . . Gentlemen . . ."

"You could be a citizen of a *britch?!*" gasped Mr. Kaplan.

"Poor Mr. Nathan," sighed Miss Mitnick.

"A bridge is not a country!" protested Miss Valuskas. "Everyone has to be born in a *country!*"

"I didn't choose it," laughed Mr. Nathan.

"Some people are born on boats!" blurted Mrs. Yanoff. "My brother's Sammy fell don on de dack—"

"My seester was born eeen a airaplane!" exclaimed Mr. Perez.

"Class—"

"Stop!" boomed Mr. Bloom. "Ain't we all jumping on conclusions? How does the rad-had *know* his first brath of air was on that train? He was just born! Probly cryink like crazy. Who *told* him he began to breed on a bridge in the middle of—"

"The conductor," grinned Mr. Nathan.

"A *condoctor?!*" Mrs. Moskowitz could not believe her ears.

"Maybe de condoctor made de delivery!" exclaimed Mr. Kaplan.

"No," laughed Nathan P. Nathan. "My mother did it alone."

"Alone?!"

"No doctor? No noises?"

"Hows about your *fadder?*" asked Mr. Kaplan. "He didn't tell you? He vas prazant!"

"My father fainted. The minute my mother's labor pains began."

"So conzolt your mother!" blared Mr. Blattberg.

"He can't, dummy! Did you forgot she pessed avay?"

"Aleha ha-shalom," incanted Mr. Pinsky.

"Class, I *must* insist that we drop this entire line of— discussion!" Mr. Parkhill rapped the knuckles of both hands on his chair until they throbbed. "However fascinating the question of Mr. Nathan's birth may be—and

48

I should be the last to deny it is a—most intriguing case—
I think we should return to our studies! Let us go back to
Mr. Nathan's recitation. Look at any mistakes you wrote
down at the time—or any improvements you care to suggest."

It was not easy to wrench adults, absorbed in an extraordinary nativity on the bridge over Niagara Falls, back to
trivial missteps in enunciation—especially since the recitation of Nathan P. Nathan had displayed such a stellar
range, such a fluent command of so spacious an English
vocabulary, that any member of the class would gladly
have changed places with him.

"Who would like to start us off all over again?" asked Mr.
Parkhill. "Mr. Trabish?"

Mr. Trabish, having dozed throughout the whole drama
of Mr. Nathan's mobile delivery, was jabbed in the ribs by
Mr. Scymczak, only to ask, "What time is it?"

Mr. Parkhill frowned. "Mrs.—Shimmelfarb?"

Mrs. Shimmelfarb said, "I don't like that Mr. Nathan
called his boss a murderer!"

"He was a crook also," laughed Mr. Nathan. "He went to
jail!"

"Miss Gidwitz?" said Mr. Parkhill swiftly. (Who knew
what a furor Mr. Nathan's past employer might cause?)

"In Mr. Nathan's fest speech, he said 'guys,'" said Miss
Gidwitz, "instead of 'boys,' 'men,' or 'other workers.' The
word 'guys' is sleng!"

"Quite so," said Mr. Parkhill. "'Guys' is slang—"

"I *like* slang," beamed Mr. Nathan.

"*I* like *'shlemiel'* but I don't say it in the class!" said Mrs.
Yanoff.

"What means *'shlemiel'?*" growled Mr. Wilkomirski.

"Class! . . . Miss Pomeranz?"

"Mr. Nathan spoke very, very nice, with good words all
over," sighed Miss Pomeranz. "But I think he should not

49

make a whole speech one-two-three, using such long sentences!"

"They were very good sentences," ventured Miss Mitnick.

"But he should stop at least for periods!" complained Miss Pomeranz. "And he should *wait* for commas, semicolons, and so for."

"That is a very helpful suggestion," said Mr. Parkhill. "Mr. Nathan, you do have a tendency to run your sentences together."

"Agreed!" Mr. Nathan chuckled. "That's why I'm in school. I never learned about stopping for periods, or waiting for commas, because at home we all talk so fast you can't get in a word hatch-wise."

"Er—it's 'edge-wise,' not 'hatch-wise,' " said Mr. Parkhill.

" 'Edgewise'!" exulted Mr. Nathan. "Already I learned!"

"Nat'an!" called out Mr. Kaplan, who had been silent for a good four minutes. "Did you aver vote?"

"Sure."

"You *voted?*"

"Why not? I'm an American."

"How do you know you're not a Nigerian?" scoffed Mr. Bloom.

"I'll esk de qvestions," said Mr. Kaplan. "Nat'an, to vote you got to give full ditails—"

"I did."

"So vhere dey esk 'Place of Birth,' *vhat did you put don?*"

"Pullman."

This brought new pandemonium into the room.

"Pullman!"

"Is that a city?"

"In U.S.?"

"A state?"

50

"Mr. Pockhall," intoned Miss Tarnova, "is there soch a place?"

Mr. Parkhill said, "I think that when Mr. Nathan said 'Pullman' he meant that he was born on a Pullman *train.*"

"Fa goodness sek!"

"Trains have *names?*" blinked Mr. Schmitt.

"Well, the individual cars in a train do," explained Mr. Parkhill. "They are often named after an American hero, or an Indian tribe—"

"Hindyans had trains?" gaped Mrs. Yanoff. "I thought they had only horses and toupees!"

" 'T*e*pees,' not 'tou—' "

"So dat's vhy his name is Nat'an P. Nat'an!" cried Mr. Kaplan. "De 'P' is for 'Pullman'!"

"Right!" laughed Mr. Nathan.

"So Nat'an P. Nat'an vas telling de ebsolute troot," declaimed Mr. Kaplan. "He vas born in a Pullman! He also *sad* he vas born dere. He jost laft ot de article 'a.' "

"No tricks!" boomed Mr. Blattberg. *"Is* there a rill place called Pullman? Or is the American government giving citizenship to *beds* and wagons—"

"Class!" Mr. Parkhill's voice ascended with force from the stand on which the unabridged dictionary—rarely consulted—reclined. He had been consulting the gazetteer. "Yes! There is a city named Pullman! It is in the state of Washington. And there *was* a suburb of Chicago named Pullman, where the sleeping-car Pullman coaches were originally manufactured!"

"Hooray!" cried Mr. Kaplan. "Nat'an P. Nat'an is no liar! In fect, he has a choice! Born in Chicago—"

"He's too young!"

"—or Vashington! I vote for Vashington!"

Mr. Nathan was shaking with jubilation. "I agree. I did. When I voted the first time, which was last year, and they asked of me, 'Where were you born?' I said 'Pullman.' The

51

lady clerk said, 'Ah, in the state of Washington. That's where my husband comes from.' I didn't deny."

"Good for you!"

"Smart!"

"So she asked if I had a birth certificate."

"Oh!"

"No!"

"What you *did?*"

Mr. Nathan laughed. "I said my father had my birth certificate, which is true. But I told them he was back in Canada, which he was at that time, working in the rush fur season."

"Not so fast!" stormed Mr. Blattberg. "Nathan was very clever—but I say it's not ligal! A boy born on a train, over vater, not on the dirt and soil of U.S.—"

"Doesn't a baby born on a train have *rights?*" cried Mr. Kaplan. "Is a child a box garlic? Ve—"

"Mr. Kap—"

"—ve have a Constitution! If Nat'an P. Nat'an vas born *vun inch* insite our borders—"

"Kaplan siddon!" fumed Norman Bloom.

"Kaplan, kip on!" called loyal Pinsky.

"Nat'an," continued Mr. Kaplan, "just enswer vun point: Did you ritch insite U.S. in time you should be a *born citizen?*"

"That's what no one knows," laughed Mr. Nathan.

"Class—"

"Soch a chence to miss. By vun minute—de most, maybe hefenarr!" ("Heffenarr" was Mr. Kaplan's way of designating thirty minutes.)

"Class, I hate to end this discussion!" announced Mr. Parkhill. "But it is almost time to leave. I—want to add just a few comments to Mr. Nathan's recitation. You said, if I remember correctly, 'my talking of English.' Would it not be better to—"

"De enswer!" cried Hyman Kaplan. "I got de enswer! Nat'an—"

"Mr. Kap—"

"De train you vere on! T'ink! Vas it goink tovard de U.S. or tovard Canada?"

Mr. Nathan was so pleased that he slapped his thigh. "We were coming from Canada, so we were going to America!"

"Dat's all! Dat's inoff! Ve'll appil to de Supreme Cawt if ve nidd to!" Never had Hyman Kaplan been so magisterial. "A train goink *to* a place minns dat de pipple on dat train got on axpactink to *go* to dat place! So if you vere born *bifore* you pessed across de border of Canada, dat vould be too bed, a tarrible mistake! But if you *pessed* Canada and vere movink *tovard* de U.S., your modder and fodder ebsolutely axpacted you vould be born on Amarican soil! *Axpactink* is de point! It shows—"

It mattered not that the bell had rung while Mr. Kaplan was still approaching the American border; no one had heard, much less heeded, it.

"—*you are a citizen becawss you vere born in U.S.A.!* Congradulation, Citizen Nat'an P. Nat'an!"

Mr. Nathan was laughing and shaking and holding his sides. "Mr. Kaplan, you are a peach. An okay guy! I'll tell my father."

"Keplen is a born lawyer!" proclaimed Mr. Pinsky.

"Did you say 'lawyer' or 'liar'?" howled Norman Bloom.

"Dipands on who he mant," said Mr. Kaplan.

The bell was still belling authoritatively as the congregation swept out of the room, babbling and excited, Nathan P. Nathan in the center of the congratulatory throng. Miss Mitnick tiptoed along the edge, blushing. Someone shouted, "This was the most intarasting class we ever had!"

"Denk you," said Mr. Kaplan.

53

Mr. Parkhill sank into his chair. The room was blessedly quiet. Slowly, he took off his glasses. He rubbed his eyes. He was exhausted.

He was also confused. How in the world could he have known that a prosaic Recitation and Speech drill would turn into the stormy case of Kaplan *vs.* the U.S. Bureau of Immigration?

5

THE FIFTY MOODS
OF MR. PARKHILL

Mr. Parkhill entered the classroom at 6:30, a full hour before the class would begin. He would have entered even earlier, but Mr. Janowitz, the school "custodian," was absolutely adamant about sweeping the floors and washing down the blackboards.

Mr. Parkhill could hardly wait (as he had to, in the corridor) to get to those blackboards. The moment morose Mr. Janowitz said, "Is finish," Mr. Parkhill hurried in. He took his "WORK" folder out of his briefcase and approached the gleaming slates. He was rather excited as he lifted a stick of fresh chalk. (Mr. Janowitz distributed fresh, full pieces of chalk along the ledges at the beginning of each week—and only at the beginning of each week, ever since Mr. Robinson had reproached the faculty: "The amount of chalk we are all using is enough to build the white cliffs of Dover!" Not many principals could put things as graphically as that.)

This was the dawn of a new week. Throughout the entire weekend, one idea had driven all others out of Mr. Parkhill's mind. . . . In capital letters, Mr. Parkhill swiftly printed, on the top of the board at the far left:

55

He balanced the folder in his left hand and, smiling, transcribed:

1. We *move.*
2.   "   *are going to move.*
3.   "   *are moving.*
4.   "   *moved.*
5.   "   *did move.*
6.   "   *had moved.*
7.   "   *had been moved.*
8.   "   *shall move.*
9.   "   *shall be moving.*
10.   "   *shall have moved.*

Mr. Parkhill stepped to the next board.

11. We *shall have been moved.*
12.   "   *will move.*
13.   "   *will be moving.*
14.   "   *will have moved.*
15.   "   *will have been moved.*
16.   "   *may move.*
17.   "   *may be moving.*
18.   "   *may have moved.*
19.   "   *may have been moved.*

Now Mr. Parkhill stepped one board farther to the right.

20. We *can move.*
21.   "   *can be moving.*
22.   "   *can have moved.*
23.   "   *can have been moved.*
24.   "   *could move.*
25.   "   *could be moving.*
26.   "   *could have moved.*
27.   "   *could have been moved.*

28.   "   *might move.*
29.   "   *might be moving.*
30.   "   *might have moved.*
31.   "   *might have been moved.*

Mr. Parkhill moved to the next blackboard.

32. We *ought to move.*
33.   "   *ought to be moving.*
34.   "   *ought to have moved.*
35.   "   *ought to have been moved.*
36.   "   *should move.*
37.   "   *should be moving.*
38.   "   *should have moved.*
39.   "   *should have been moved.*

Mr. Parkhill paused, rubbing the numbness out of his forefinger, then resumed writing on the blackboard in the corner, at right angles to the three he had filled:

40. We *will move.*
41.   "   *will be moving.*
42.   "   *will have moved.*
43.   "   *will have been moved.*
44.   "   *must move.*
45.   "   *must be moving.*
46.   "   *must have moved.*
47.   "   *must have been moved.*
48.   "   *have to move.*
49.   "   *have to be moving.*
50.   "   *have to have been moved.*

Exhilarated, and slightly exhausted, Mr. Parkhill placed the depleted chalk in the trough. Fifty examples! His eyes scanned them swiftly, and not without pride. *Fifty* examples! Mr. Parkhill rather wished that Mr. Robinson would drop into the classroom tonight, as he sometimes did, on one of his unannounced rounds of inspection.

Fifty examples—and, Mr. Parkhill reflected, he had not

even included "We have got to move" or "We have got to be moving" or even "We have got to have been moved!" He had not included them because he wholeheartedly agreed with that telling passage in Plaut and Samish:

> . . . newcomers to our shores are often discouraged, and sometimes severely depressed, by *an over-dose of examples.* Just as a seasoned physician administers a measured amount of even the best medication to a patient, knowing the dangers which may attend a larger (even fatal) quantum of medicaments, so the teacher must guard against that exuberance which tempts him, no less than the physician, to use a "shotgun" where prudence dictates *"satis superque."* Indeed, enough is often more than enough!

Fifty examples . . . Mr. Parkhill hoped he had not been carried away by his optimism. This was not at all the employment of "a shotgun," which sprays many identical bullets at one target. Each example on those blackboards was different from its companions; each was a case in its own right; each stood on its own feet and asserted its own exact meaning. How, Mr. Parkhill reassured himself, could a true survey of tenses and moods omit the pluperfect, for instance, or turn a deaf ear to the subjunctive? And what better way was there to show his students how marvelous, how rich and various and supple, are the resources of the language they strove so valiantly to master?

Fifty examples . . . They stretched across all the boards in the room. They stood arrayed, sound and confident, like —well, like fine soldiers on a parade ground. Mr. Parkhill smiled. His misgivings dissolved. He straightened his vest.

A peculiar sound, as from someone being strangled, caused him to turn. He had not heard the student come into the room. It was Mr. Scymczak. But Mr. Scymczak was not in his usual seat (on the aisle, third row). Mr. Scymczak was leaning against the wall, the color of an artichoke.

58

"Good evening," smiled Mr. Parkhill.

No comprehensible syllable interrupted the noises of asphyxiation. Mr. Scymczak's hat was clutched in one hand, his textbook hung inert from the other.

"Mr. Scymczak . . ."

Hoarse rattlings breached the gates of those bloodless lips.

"Mr. Scymczak!" exclaimed Mr. Parkhill in alarm.

The plasterer from Danzig rolled his eyeballs and, with either a sob or a whimper, staggered out of the room.

"Mr. Scymczak! Please! Don't go—"

All Mr. Parkhill heard was shoes clattering down the corridor. He sank into his chair. What on earth . . . He rather *liked* Mr. Scymczak. Could it be that—

"Goot ivnink!" a cheerful tenor sang out.

Mr. Parkhill glanced up. "Oh. Good evening, Mr. Kaplan."

Mr. Kaplan waved his hand with customary éclat and strode, humming, to his undisputed throne in the center of the front row. He sat down, placed his composition book on the arm of the chair, arranged his pencils and crayons, and brightly glanced at the board. The next thing Mr. Parkhill knew, Hyman Kaplan was sliding down his seat, the smile seeping off his lips.

"Mr. Kaplan! What's wrong?"

The stricken scholar gurgled. His head rotated as his glassy eyes traversed Moods 11 through 19.

Suddenly, Miss Higby poked her head through the open doorway. "Mr. Park—" She did not complete the name. Never before had Mr. Parkhill seen such an expression on Miss Higby's features. She looked as though she had just been embalmed. She was not looking at him. She was goggling at the blackboards.

Quickly, Mr. Parkhill said, "I thought I'd give the class a thorough overview of the many tenses and moods—"

59

"Fifty?!" gasped his colleague.

"—to demonstrate the remarkable range—"

"You have! Oh, you *have!*" And without another word, Miss Higby dropped a pink memo on his desk and bolted away.

Mr. Parkhill frowned. He leaned back in his chair. The clock on the wall sounded like a trip-hammer beating on brass. The expression on Washington's noble lithograph seemed to have curdled; the countenance of merciful Lincoln appeared to have turned aghast.

Mr. Parkhill cleared his throat. He glanced at Mr. Kaplan, who was almost horizontal in his chair. "Er—Mr. Kaplan—" To his annoyance, Mr. Parkhill's voice was hoarse.

Mr. Kaplan's hearing was no more alive than his posture.

"Mr. Kaplan," said Mr. Parkhill more loudly.

The recumbent figure quivered.

"Mr. Kaplan, may I ask you a—candid question?"

The candidate for a candid question thrashed about as if extricating himself from a straitjacket, the activity changing the color in his cheeks from none to a shade of oatmeal.

"Mr. Kaplan, do you think—please be honest!—that I have—er—overdone the examples?"

"Dey are amazink . . ."

"Thank you. But do you think I have given too many?"

Mr. Kaplan blinked. He gulped. He started to produce a gurgle when the door opened and Rochelle Goldberg, as pert as she was plump, materialized in the doorway.

"Goldboig, don't faint!" cried Mr. Kaplan.

"Huh?"

"Don't look on de boards!"

That was all Miss Goldberg needed to turn to the blackboards.

"Miss Goldberg—" began Mr. Parkhill. "I—Miss Goldberg!!"

60

Miss Goldberg had not fainted. She had not even reeled. All she had done was drop her jaw, her books, her handbag, and a bag of jellybeans. (Why Miss Goldberg had chosen this particular evening to lay in a restorative stock of jellybeans, instead of her customary nougats, caramels, or Hershey "Kisses," Mr. Parkhill knew he would never know. He could not help it if *"Deus est qui regit omnia"* flashed into his mind.) Those infernal oblates splattered across the floor and bounded around like Mexican jumping beans: yellow, pink, white, brown. . . .

Mr. Kaplan cried, "I varned you!" and fell to his knees. So did Miss Goldberg. Mr. Parkhill could hardly refuse to join them in the imperative task. The three of them scrambled about snatching at the confections, which were rolling around on the floor and under the chairs as if the classroom were a pinball machine.

"Excuse me, oh"—poor Miss Goldberg was stammering —"I'm vary sorry—"

"It's quite all right," said Mr. Parkhill.

"Even I hev eccidents," Mr. Kaplan admitted.

"I'm so embarrassed!"

"You need not be, Miss Goldberg. Not at *all*—"

"Naxt time, drop gum," advised Mr. Kaplan. "Gum don't bounce arond like mobbles."

"It's not *polite* to chew gum in class," bleated Miss Goldberg.

"It's not polite to make Mr. Pockheel sqvash colors all over his pants!"

Mr. Parkhill's knees were indeed acquiring the hues of a sticky palette. "Oh, don't mind that. I should have sent this suit to the cleaner's months ago."

At last the floor was cleared by six strong hands. Mr. Parkhill rose, smiling bravely. Mr. Kaplan rose, glancing sourly at Miss Goldberg, who rose, announcing, "I have to go to the ladies' room."

"Please come back," said Mr. Parkhill.

"Duty is duty!" scowled Mr. Kaplan.

Miss Goldberg was halfway to her refuge.

"Well..." Mr. Parkhill began dusting his trousers, then wiping the stickiness off his hands. "As I was saying, before this unfortunate interruption . . ." He paused. "I have a feeling I placed too much on those boards!"

Mr. Kaplan sighed.

Mr. Parkhill blurted, "Do you think it would be wise to remove—"

"De nombers," said Mr. Kaplan.

"I beg your pardon?"

"Take avay all de nombers."

Mr. Parkhill knit his brow. "You think I should erase all of the *numbers?"*

"Positively. If Moskowitz—just take a 'for instence'—gats vun look at a nomber like *fifty,* she'll have a hot atteck."

"Oh." Mr. Parkhill adjusted his spectacles. "I suppose I *could* omit the numbers after, say, forty—"

"I soggest all de nombers."

"All of the numbers?" echoed Mr. Parkhill in pain.

"All."

"But—"

"Mr. Pockheel," said Mr. Kaplan with a certain patience, "look. If you take a boy for a valk, you don't say, 'Let's valk fife miles.' De kit vould say, *'Vhat?!* Fife miles? I ken't!' So you say, 'Let's take a valk—a nice valk, maybe a *long* valk. . . .' "

Mr. Parkhill stepped to the board without a word. He made a series of powerful down-strokes with the eraser, expunging ninety-one numerals within nine seconds. "Yes, that *is* better . . . Uh—I shall be happy to have any other suggestions, Mr. Kaplan."

Mr. Kaplan beamed. "It's an honor."

"After all, you are more—objective than I can be."

"I don't *objact!* You a vunderful titcher! It's not my place—"

"I mean, you can see the—total impression in a way I cannot. You can see the woods as well as the trees! What else would you do?"

Mr. Kaplan made an apologetic twitch. "I don't vant to sond like a student knows batter den Mr. Pockheel . . ."

"Speak frankly, please!"

The sage closed one eye. "I also vould cot ot a bushel of all dose exemples."

"That *many?*"

"More than many! Wholesale!"

"Oh . . . Which examples would you erase?"

Mr. Kaplan rubbed his chin. "In voibs, vhat does de beginnis' cless nidd? Just de prazant tanse, de pest, an' de future. Dat's enof for a lifetime!"

Mr. Parkhill tried to repress his dismay. "You mean you would erase all of the tenses except past, present, and future?!"

"Mit' plashure."

"But so many of the other tenses—and moods—are so valuable!"

"Bendages are weluable, too," mused Mr. Kaplan, *"if* you are bliddink. But if you are not bliddink, iven in a finger, vhy bendage op de whole hend?"

Mr. Parkhill gazed with falling affection and failing pride upon that impressive aggregation: the staunch "shall have"s, the bold "shall have been"s. He felt awful. "But if I erase all of the examples except—"

"Prazant, pest, future."

"—there will remain—only three sentences!"

Mr. Kaplan shrugged. "So? De hongry don't nidd a benqvet. Sometimes a sendvich is batter den a fist!"

"I think you mean 'feast,' Mr. Kaplan, not 'fist.' "

"Denk you."

Mr. Parkhill turned to the blackboard. "Can't we leave more than just three sentences? Just a few others? I mean, the most necessary—"

"Vhich vuns?"

"Well, 'We are moving,' for instance. That is *very* important! And 'We *will* be moving.' And—"

"Dose," agreed Mr. Kaplan, "are weluable."

"I do think we should retain those!" said Mr. Parkhill earnestly.

"Agreet," said Mr. Kaplan.

With broad, sweeping strokes of the eraser, and sad sinkings of regret in his heart, Mr. Parkhill wiped out every syllable he had written on the five boards. He exchanged eraser for chalk, and as Mr. Kaplan made little clucks of approval, wrote:

> We move.
> " are moving.
> " moved.
> " were moving.
> " will move.
> " will be moving.

Mr. Parkhill placed the chalk against his lips, concentrating. "That certainly is simpler. . . ."

"It's movvelous! . . . Now put in nombers."

"Numbers?"

"Ufcawss!"

"But I thought you criticized the numbers—"

"I objected to de *nomber* of nombers. Now are only six. Bifore vere *fifty!*"

"But—"

"Fifty makes dizzy. But *six?* Dat gives de cless *hope!"*

Mr. Parkhill placed "1, 2, 3, 4, 5, 6" on the board.

Not until the session was over that night (the lesson went extremely well) did Mr. Parkhill remember to read the pink sheet Miss Higby had handed him so long—so very long—ago.

To The Faculty

In my remarks of the 17th inst., I stressed the need for drastic economy in the use of chalk. I neglected to point out that a reduction in the amount of chalk used on our blackboards will effect a corresponding economy in the wear-and-tear of our erasers!

I trust every member of the faculty will henceforth bear this in mind!

Leland Robinson
Principal

6

MR. K·A·P·L·A·N
WRESTLES THE "W"

Mr. Parkhill was troubled about "v"s and "w"s. For weeks he had known that something would have to be done about them—something drastic. For of all the peculiar mispronunciations his fledglings inflicted upon the English language, their blithe replacement of "v"s with "w"s and "w"s with "v"s was perhaps the most unnerving.

Mr. Parkhill realized that for some of his students, the speech habits of a lifetime were almost impossible to change: for instance, Mr. Kaplan said "fad" when he meant "fed" and "dad" when he meant "dead." He said "bad" when he meant "bed," but "bet" when he meant "bat." He used "full" when he meant "fool," and "pool" when he meant "pull." What particularly perplexed Mr. Parkhill was why Mr. Kaplan persisted in exchanging vowels *each of which he could enunciate with ease.* It was baffling.

Mr. Parkhill could understand the complex reasons for the wayward pronunciation of immigrants; after all, his students were adults, adults whose lips, tongues, teeth and larynxes had long been molded to vocalize their native phonemes. Such habitual reflexes, even the most tenacious teacher could rarely change, only regret.

Nor was Mr. Kaplan the worst offender. Take a line Mr. Pinsky had recently uttered: "He felt a pain in his hat."

That was improper dentalization; Mr. Pinsky simply let his tongue linger on his central incisors for a "t" instead of snapping right back for a "d." Or consider the speech habits which mangled so straightforward a monosyllable as "six" into:

"seeks"	(Mr. Trabish)
"zix"	(Mr. Schmitt)
"sex"	(Miss Tarnova)

Sometimes Mr. Parkhill wondered whether Miss Tarnova's pronunciation was rooted in her libido rather than her Russian.

Mr. Parkhill felt the most profound sympathy for refugees who had to reshape their lives, even more than their speech, in a new land, a land where, to their preconditioned ears, butter is spread on "brat," corn is eaten on the "cop," potato chips are picked out of a "back," and "coughing cake" is found in any decent bakery. Why, in one recent oration, Mr. Kaplan had praised a radio operetta he rashly called "Madman Butterfly"; worse, he had named the creators of that masterpiece as two Englishmen named "Gilbert and Solomon." And in an exercise on proper nouns, Mr. Kaplan had stated that Washington's Farewell Address was—Mount Vernon.

But sympathy is no substitute for pedagogy: Mr. Parkhill's task was to teach, not commiserate. He often told himself that the road to learning is harder for the pupil than the preceptor—for the latter is doubly rewarded: *Doce ut discas!* "Teach that you may learn." How true that was; and how it fortified one's strength in the trying hours.

Take the fricative spirants. What difficulties Mr. Parkhill had suffered because of fricative spirants! His classroom was a very charnel house of mismouthed "f"s and "v"s ("Vrankly, I lof to eat vish") and sometimes the room sounded beset by a blizzard of transposed "s"s and "z"s.

67

("Zelma broke the sipper on her zkirt.")

Or take the maddening "th." Mr. Parkhill often marveled over what happened when a student failed to respect the tiny but *enormous* difference between the "th" of "this" and the "th" of "throw." That might seem academic to people not engaged in teaching English; but it meant that pupils often converted a choice ("either") into an anesthetic ("ether").

Students from Germany practically wore their tongues out trying to pronounce that voiced fricative; yet, after months of effort, Mr. Schmitt had to settle for "Zanks" whenever he wanted to say "Thanks," and Mr. Finsterwald "truce" when what the poor man meant was "truth."

There was no end to the troubles hidden in the hard-hearted fricatives. Why, years ago a Mrs. Freda Gottschalk had electrified the class by confessing that she liked movie scenes in which the actors kissed mice. That, at least, is what it sounded like, and what precipitated a furious argument. The wrangling ended only when an alert student exclaimed, "She likes to see them kiss the *mouth,* not the 'mouse'!"

Or take the forward or trilled "r" as against the throat-born "r." (Plaut and Samish were particularly shrewd about that.) The voicing of "roar" or "rare" is child's play to those who have heard English spoken since their childhood; but had that childhood been spent in Budapest or Odessa, say, the "r"s would sound like gargling. (For fully four weeks after she had entered his fold, Mr. Parkhill thought Mrs. Moskowitz had a speech defect, when she was simply stranded at a phonetic frontier.)

Students from Cuba or Brazil *sang* rather than spoke English, Mr. Parkhill often said. They delivered a sentence in most melodious cadence: "I *go* to *store* to buy cof-f*ee.*" The charming lilt was soothing to the ear, but fouled-up the code of comprehension.

Hispanic students said "thees" for "this" and "Djou" for "you." A Mrs. Rodriguez (or a Mr. Perez) would probably never learn how to pronounce "just" except as "zhust."

One night, a newcomer from Venezuela had held the class spellbound with his tale of a fortune-teller on a ship at sea—concluding, "No one did know where thees ztrange dark womon was come from."

The class was dumbfounded, until Mr. Parkhill cried: "Gypsy! *That's* what you meant. Not 'shipasy'!"

Yes, there was no end to the changes which the children of foreign cultures could ring on English. Mr. Parkhill had never forgotten Cornelius Hoogenhagen, from Holland, who simply could not vocalize the name of his adopted country in any way but "Unide Sdades." All of Mr. Parkhill's ingenuity failed to lure Mr. Hoogenhagen into relinquishing his native, sacred "d"s. He remained glued to "died" for "tide" and "delighded" for "delighted." Mr. Parkhill knew *Fortuna fortibus favet*—but not in pronunciation.

Another term, Mr. Parkhill had had to cope with Miss Antoinette Duvrier, who nearly went crazy trying to capture the lawless stresses of English words. Miss Duvrier could not *believe* the difference between "*ad*dress" as a noun and "ad*dress*" as a verb; she went blind before the chasm that separated "*in*sult" from "in*sult*"; and she virtually turned to putty the night Mr. Parkhill tried to teach her the important distinction between "*con*vict" and "con*vict*."

Miss Duvrier did not return to the class for a week. When she did, Mr. Parkhill was so pleased that he promptly gave the class a little exercise in shifting stresses: "*pro*test"—"pro*test*" ... "*reb*el"—"re*bel*" ... "*des*-ert—de*sert*." Whereupon Miss Duvrier picked up her reticule and left the room. Rumor had it that she had moved to Quebec.

Sometimes, Mr. Parkhill felt like Sisyphus; often he could not make up his mind *where* to concentrate his instruction; but he was verging more and more to the view that it was the vampire "v" and the waffled "w" which presented the most immediate challenge to his ingenuity.

During one recess, Mr. Parkhill sought the advice of Miss Higby in the faculty lounge. Miss Higby, who was a veteran of adult education, looked considerably younger than her years. Her complexion was fair, her cheeks pink, and the hair coiled upon her head was strawberry. Miss Higby was a teacher of unflinching temperament. She snapped out her sentences with the rapidity of a machine gun. Mr. Parkhill often envied Miss Higby her fearlessness, though he was sometimes troubled by her certitude.

"Miss Higby," Mr. Parkhill had come right out and said, "I am quite concerned about 'v's and 'w's!"

Without a second's hesitation Miss Higby proclaimed that no speech imperfection had given *her* so many sleepless hours as "the voiced fricative and labiodental consonant." (She was an M.A. from Teachers College.)

"My students just don't seem to be *interested* in altering their 'w's," frowned Mr. Parkhill.

"Nor their 'v's, Mr. Parkhill. Let's not gloss over those 'v's!"

"Oh, I *don't,*" said Mr. Parkhill.

Miss Higby tapped her temple. "Drill!"

"I beg your pardon."

"I said, 'Drill.'. . . Drill, drill, drill! That's the only way to cure lazy lips and stamp out careless habits!"

Mr. Parkhill adjusted his glasses. The last time he had tried a rigorous drill, in an exercise on hyphenated words ("hodge-podge," "helter-skelter"), Miss Kipnis had come up with "Willy and Nelly" (for "willy-nilly"), whereas Mr. Finsterwald had contributed "tops and turkey" (for "topsy-turvy").

"In any case," bristled Miss Higby, looking Mr. Parkhill straight in the eye, "their 'v's and 'w's should be improved, if not mastered, before you promote them to my grade!"

There was no mistaking her innuendo.

"Oh, I agree," said Mr. Parkhill. "I just wonder *how* one can—" The bell summoned them back to their duties before Mr. Parkhill could conclude, "—teach old dogs new tricks."

As he was entering his classroom, Miss Higby sang out from her own doorway: "Drill! *Drill!*"

"Thank you," said Mr. Parkhill. He wished Miss Higby would be a bit less militant about things. Her hair, at such times, seemed on fire.

Mr. Parkhill did not by nature like to discipline others; but once his sense of responsibility dictated a course of action, there were no bounds to his perseverance. The very next time an opportunity arose to grab the enunciation of "v"s and "w"s by the horns, Mr. Parkhill did not sidestep it.

During an exercise on vocabulary, Mr. Kaplan, asked to give a sentence containing the word "value," replied, "Vell, ven ve walue a t'ing, ve are villink to—"

"Mr. Kaplan!"

Mr. Kaplan stopped dead in his tracks. "I didn't findish."

"You didn't 'fin*ish*,' not 'fin*d*ish.' I want to comment upon your enunciation."

A guard reported for duty in Mr. Kaplan's left eye.

"Your 'v's and 'w's, Mr. Kaplan. You did not pronounce one of them correctly!"

"Not *vun?*"

"Not *one,*" winced Mr. Parkhill.

Mr. Kaplan simulated an attack of asthma.

"What *you* said was something like this." Mr. Parkhill cleared his throat. "'Ven *ve w*alue a thing, *ve* are *v*ill—'

and so on. You pronounced each 'w' as if it is a 'v,' and the 'v' as if it is a 'w'!"

Not with gloom or rue did Hyman Kaplan accept this reprimand. Instead, he sighed sheepishly, "Mine dobble-yous is tarrible, Mr. Pockheel, an' mine 'v's is a shame. Still, I'll try to awoid mistakes—"

" 'A*void*! There it is again!"

Mr. Kaplan recoiled. "I'm gaddink voise an' voise."

" '*Worse* and *worse*!' " exclaimed Mr. Parkhill, a tinge of desperation in his tone. (He saw no point in confronting "gaddink" at a time like this.) "Class, do you see what I mean?"

The class displayed no doubts whatsoever about what Mr. Parkhill meant.

"Kaplen toins everything opside-don!" declared bald Bloom.

"Kaplin, give an inch!" begged Mrs. Shimmelfarb.

"This mon, this mon," croaked Olga Tarnova.

"Mr. Kaplan is not the only student," added Mr. Parkhill, "who commits this error . . ."

"By me is a 'v' like a knife in de mout," confessed Mrs. Yanoff.

"*Kill* me and I couldn't pronounce a 'w'!" proclaimed Wolfgang Schmitt. "In Cherman, ve alvays say 'v' vhen is printed 'w'!"

"So go beck to Joiminy," suggested Mr. Kaplan.

"Now, now." Mr. Parkhill tapped the desk with his pointer. "I know it seems difficult, but each of you really *can* conquer the—er—'v'-'w' habit. Even if you enunciate other consonants correctly, you—"

"What's 'consoments'?" asked Mr. Matsoukas.

Mr. Parkhill studied his knuckles. "Mr. Matsoukas, don't you remember our lesson on vowels and consonants?"

"No."

"Well"—Mr. Parkhill debated his next move—"we

72

haven't time to go into it thoroughly again, Mr. Matsoukas, but just to touch on the highlights: 'a,' 'e,' 'i,' 'o,' 'u,' and sometimes 'y' are vowels. All the other letters in our alphabet are called *con*-so-nants."

"I thought consoment is a soup," scowled the waiter from Athens.

"That's 'con*sommé*,' Mr. Matsoukas! Do you see how important pronunciation is?"

"Eesn't consonants what you have in a frand?" inquired Vincente Perez.

"That's 'con*fid*ence,' Mr. Perez! . . . Returning to 'v' and 'w,' we *must* train our lips to distinguish one from the other!"

"I know," mumbled Mrs. Tomasic—who, as it happened, never used "v"s for "w"s, only "w"s for "v"s. ("I will learn with wim and wigor," that Croatian once promised.)

"To me are 'w's like teffy-epples," grieved Mr. Vinograd.

Mrs. Moskowitz's "Oy!" conveyed an omnibus confession of fricative sins.

"Mine Gott!" Mr. Kaplan could contain himself no longer. "You vill all give Mr. Pockheel hot-failer!"

" '*W*ill,' not '*v*ill.' "

"*I* never say 'vill,' " smirked Mr. Finsterwald, "day or night."

"You hear how you slip?!" retorted Mr. Kaplan.

"Class, there is no reason to quarrel! Now, please. Watch my lips." Mr. Parkhill wet his lips. "First, I shall pronounce the 'v' sound." He opened his mouth, put his upper teeth on and overlapping his lower lip, took a deep breath, and was just about to emit a vivid "vvvvvv" when a sneeze from Mr. Scymczak shattered the spell.

Mr. Parkhill closed his mouth.

" 'Scooz," mumbled Mr. Scymczak miserably.

"Again, class. Notice: I place my upper teeth"—he tapped his upper teeth—"on my lower lip"—he tapped his lower lip—"and *push* my breath out to—"

"Kachoo!" sneezed poor Scymczak again.

Mr. Parkhill forced a smile onto his lips. "Watch my teeth. Ready . . ."

"Skimzek, hold *beck!*" cried Mr. Kaplan.

Mr. Parkhill turned to the blackboard. Perhaps it would be wiser to start with the "w" sound. He printed:

WE

" 'We,' " said Mr. Parkhill. "To pronounce this *very* common word, I round my lips this way"—he rounded his lips into a zero—"and say 'ooo.' O*oooo . . .*"

The class was bewitched.

"Will you all do that, please? Everyone. Round lips . . ." Thirty-odd students, puckering sixty-odd lips to encirculate thirty-odd mouths, looked as if they had swallowed alum. "Now, *without moving your lips,* simply expel your breath—'oooo'!"

Not a single lip moved as a ghostly "Ooooooo . . ." moaned through the room.

"Good! Now I shall say 'eeee.' Watch, please." Mr. Parkhill drew his lips far apart, clenched his teeth, and said, "Eeee . . . *eeee* . . . Class?"

The beginners' grade bared their teeth and blew forth a mistral of "Eeeee"s.

"Splendid!" said Mr. Parkhill. "Let's take the 'oooo' again. Round mouths . . . firm lips . . . expel. . . ."

"Oooo," crooned the resolute chorus.

"Excellent. Now—lips apart, teeth together . . ."

"Eeeee . . ." keened the ardent scholars.

"Perfect!" smiled Mr. Parkhill. "Now let's put the two sounds *side by side*—this way." Mr. Parkhill rounded his lips. " 'Oooo.' " He bared his teeth. " 'Eeee.' "

They echoed: "Ooooo. . . . Eeeee . . . !"

"And *now,*" said Mr. Parkhill eagerly, "we put the two sounds closer, thus: 'Oooo-eee.' "

"Oooo-ee ee!"

"And if we *join* the two sounds, this way—'oo-ee,' 'oo-ee' . . ." his legion quivered with excitement "—we will pronounce a perfect 'WE'!"

"We!"

"We!"

"We!"

The first person plural whirled around the walls as if the celebrants were on a merry-go-round.

"Horrah!"

"I did it!"

"Me, too!"

"You *hoid?!*"

They were beside themselves—grinning, chortling, reeling on the heights of Parnassus. For they had, *mirabile dictu*, pronounced perfect "w"s. They had wrung the baffling and elusive secret from the voiced labial open consonant, which need never again strike terror in their hearts.

Mr. Parkhill was delighted, visibly, unashamedly delighted. "Again! *'We.'* "

"Oo-*ee!*" sang Miss Mitnick.

"Oo-ee . . . oo-*ee!*" wheed Oscar Trabish, as if it were New Year's Eve.

"Fine!" exclaimed Mr. Parkhill.

"W*ohn*derful," crooned Miss Tarnova.

"Look, look," cried Mr. Pinsky. *"Ooee, oo ee!"*

"Mr. Pockheel is a ginius!" rhapsodized Mr. Kaplan. "A ragular ginius!"

"And again," called Mr. Parkhill. "Please face each other, so that you can *see* how it is done."

All through that happy chamber, students faced each other, rounding their lips, baring their teeth, pronouncing mellifluous "ooo-ee"s.

"Excellent, class! Perfect. You *see* how simple it is? Now, the very same use of your lips and teeth will pronounce perfect 'w's in *any* word!" He printed

on the board. "The same way, class. First, 'ooo' . . . then 'er.'
Then together, 'ooo-*er'*—'*ooo*-er'—which becomes 'were'!
All together . . . 'Ooo-er'—'were'!"

"Ooooo-*er,*" came one great gust. "Were!"

"Ooooo-*ait,*" called Mr. Parkhill. "Wait!"

"Ooooo-ait. *Wait!*"

"Ooooo-ish. *Wish.*"

"Ooooo-ish," they echoed, *"wish!"*

"Will . . . warm . . . woman . . ."

The "w"'s rolled out in euphonious rondo.

"Want . . . winter . . . wake . . ."

Strong "Ooooo"'s began each word; teeth flashed as lips
flew back to send another word starting with "w" winging
toward the stars.

"Now, let's try a whole sentence!" Mr. Parkhill's chalk
flashed across the board. The first part of the sentence he
devised was a stab in the dark, but the second was sheer
inspiration:

> While we were waiting with William West, we were won-
> dering where Walter White was.

"Ees plenty 'w's!" exclaimed Mr. Perez, who tended to be
literal-minded.

"Planty?" cried Mr. Kaplan. "Ha! Peratz, is *all* dobble-
yous! If Mr. Pockheel gives dobble-yous, he gives *dobble-
yous!*"

"Oy," faltered Mrs. Moskowitz.

Mr. Parkhill wiggled his pointer cheerfully. "You'll see
how simple it is to pronounce that sentence! Take it slowly.
Miss Kipnis."

Miss Kipnis rose, swallowed, reconnoitered the sentence
sprayed with "w"'s like a scout expert in detecting am-
bushes, then, as Mr. Parkhill's pointer touched each word,

76

maneuvered her mouth around the fourteen "w"s ("Oo-ile oo-ee oo-ere oo-aiting oo-ith oo-illiam—") with not a single blunder.

"Congradjulations, Cookie!" cried Mrs. Shimmelfarb.

"T'ree chiss fa Kipnis!" exulted Mr. Kaplan.

"*Splen*did!" smiled Mr. Parkhill. "Next—" Mr. Kaplan was waving his hand furiously. "Miss Tarnova."

Miss Tarnova stood up, dabbing her perfumed handkerchief at her feverish lips, surveying the fearful stretches of "While we were waiting with William West, we were wondering where Walter White was," and bravely plunged forth. On the sixth "w" she stammered; on the ninth she turned pale; on the eleventh "w" she gulped; on the thirteenth she wailed, "No more! I go later."

Mr. Kaplan blared a call to the colors: "Tarnova, don't give op de sheep! Remamber Kipnis!"

Miss Tarnova fluttered her lashes, sniffed at a scent from Araby, rounded her mouth, and corraled the last "w" in that resplendent sentence.

"*Ex*cellent!" exclaimed Mr. Parkhill.

"Hau Kay," conceded Hyman Kaplan. (Olga Tarnova did not deserve "t'ree chiss": she had shown cowardice under fire.)

"Next—" Mr. Parkhill glanced around the room.

Everyone wanted to be next, their waving hands a veritable field of wheat in a wind.

"Er—"

Mr. Kaplan's hand was wig-wagging like a signal at a railway crossing. "Mr. Pockheel! Mr. Pockheel!" The man looked as if he would burst right there and then if denied his moment in the sun.

"Mr. Kaplan . . ."

Up rose the complete semaphore. "Hau *boy!*"

"Mr. Kaplan," Mr. Parkhill said earnestly, "be careful. Speak slowly. And remember, keep those lips round!"

"Arond itch dobble-you my mot is goink to make a detour! 'Oooooo' den 'eeee' . . . Hau Kay!" He flung his head back and charged. "Ooooo-ile! Ooooo-ee! Ooooo-ere! Ooooo-aiting . . ." The class was on the edge of their chairs. "Ooooo-ith ooooo-illiam ooooo-est—"

"Good, Mr. Kaplan!"

"—oo-ee ooo-ere ooo-ondering ooo-here ooo-alter ooo-ite ooo-as!"

"Perfect, Mr. Kaplan!"

"Bella, bella!"

Mr. Pinsky slapped both cheeks in homage, with a triumphant "Pssh!" thrown in for good measure.

"You see, class?" Mr. Parkhill laughed. "That's all there is to it! Now, if you will only *practice*—drill, drill, drill—"

"Prectice?" Mr. Kaplan's voice rang out. "Fromm nah on, ve vill voik vit dobble-yous till ve vouldn't iven vhisper vun void vitout—"

Mr. Parkhill did not hear the rest of that gallant pledge. Mr. Parkhill did not even see Mr. Kaplan. A black curtain had dropped over his eyesballs.

78

MR. K·A·P·L·A·N
AND THE HOBO

Despite Mr. Kaplan's distressing diction, his wayward grammar, his outlandish spelling, Mr. Parkhill was determined to treat him exactly as he treated every other pupil. Just because Mr. Kaplan referred to rubber heels as "robber hills," or transformed a pencil sharpener into a "pantsil chopner," was no reason to deny him equal time in class activities. (Mr. Parkhill's resolution *had* weakened a bit when Mr. Kaplan gave the opposite of "inhale" as "dead.")

Now Mr. Kaplan stood at the front of the room, right next to Mr. Parkhill's desk, smiling, primed to address his colleagues (whom he somehow treated as disciples) for three minutes of Recitation and Speech. (It often amazed Mr. Parkhill that three minutes could be so long.)

"Please speak slowly," said Mr. Parkhill. "Remember, it isn't how fast you talk, Mr. Kaplan, or—how much you crowd into your recitation. . . . Strive for accuracy, simplicity, directness. And enunciate as distinctly as possible."

The beam on the face of the cherub broadened.

"And watch your 'e's and 'a's! You tend to use one for the other quite—er—carelessly."

"I'll be so careful, Mr. Pockheel," the champing novice promised, "you'll positively be soprize!"

" 'Surprised,' Mr. Kaplan. . . . And, class, feel free to inter-

79

rupt, if you have a correction, at any time." Allowing the class to cut in on a speaker had proved a real boon to Recitation and Speech. It not only kept the listeners on their toes; it made the reciters particularly careful. There was, after all, a certain stigma attached to being corrected by a student, instead of by Mr. Parkhill. "Very well, Mr. Kaplan. You may begin."

Pride stiffened Mr. Kaplan's stance, nobility suffused his demeanor. Mr. Kaplan loved to recite. He loved to write his homework on the board. In fact, he loved any chance to be the center of attention. Now he narrowed his eyes, shot his cuffs, and gazed into the empyrean. "Ladies an' gantleman —I s'pose dat's how I should aupen op—"

" '*Op*en *u*p,' " said Mr. Parkhill.

"*O*pen *u*p," agreed Mr. Kaplan. He waved a gesture worthy of a cardinal. "In mine spitch tonight, becawss it's Rasitation an' Spitch time—"

" 'Sp*ee*ch,' Mr. Kaplan," Mr. Parkhill interpolated. "And '*my* speech,' not 'mine' speech."

"So I'll talk about mine—no—*my* vacation!"

Mr. Parkhill, pleased, nodded.

Mr. Kaplan, delighted, nodded back. "So is de name fromm my sp*ee*ech: 'My Hobo.' My hobo is—"

"Your *what?*" gaped Fanny Gidwitz.

"My hobo."

"No such woid!" shouted Mr. Bloom. (Whenever Norman Bloom sensed a departure from the orthodox, he charged that there was "no such woid.")

"No?" murmured Mr. Kaplan. "Maybe you *pos*itif?"

"There *is* such a word, Mr. Bloom," Mr. Parkhill put in hastily, "but, Mr. Kaplan, are you *sure* the word you mean is—uh—'hobo'?"

"Aha! So dere *is* soch a void!" Mr. Kaplan shriveled Mr. Bloom with scorn. "Vell, I *t'ink* I minn 'hobo,' Mr. Pockheel. My hobo is hikink—hikink in de voods, on de heels,

80

op an' don montains, all kinds hikink. Vhenever is a fine day, mit sonshinink—"

"He means 'hobby'!" exclaimed Miss Mitnick.

"Hobby?" yawned Oscar Trabish, awakening from his customary doze.

"So I'll say 'hobby.'" Mr. Kaplan acknowledged the emendation with a generous inclination of the head. "Vun point for Mitnick." He braced his shoulders. "De sky! De sonn! De moon! De stoss!—"

"'Stars'!"

"De clods! De frash air in de longs! De gress onder de fit! De sonds from beauriful boids—"

"'Beautiful birds,'" Mr. Parkhill cut in anxiously. "And it's 'sounds,' not 'sonds.'"

"—de sounds from beautiful birds, and bees, an' gless hoppers—all, all are pot fromm de vunderful vunders fromm Netcher!"

"'Nature,'" pouted Miss Valuskas.

"'Wonders' not 'vunders,'" sulked Vincente Perez.

"'Grasshoppers,' not 'glass' hoppers," gibed Mr. Marcus.

These petty alterations did not deter Hyman Kaplan. "An' do ve humans rilly appreciate? Are ve taking edwantage? Ha! No!" (Miss Mitnick, at whom the bard was glaring as if she were personally responsible for man's indifference to the out-of-doors, lowered her head.) "Dat's vhy I'm making such a hobby fromm hiking . . . Ladies an' gantleman! Have you vun an' all, or even saparate, falt in your soul dose trees, dose boids, de gress, de bloomers, de—"

Titters from two ladies and one outraged "Bloomers?!" forced Mr. Kaplan to halt, hand arrested in midair.

Mr. Parkhill cleared his throat. "What word are you using, Mr. Kap—?"

"All kinds."

"But you used one word—"

81

" 'Bloomers!' " blurted Mrs. Moskowitz. "That woid ain't nice in mixed company! Also bloomers come from ladies' stores, not nature!" As a matron, Mrs. Moskowitz could speak out where maidens of the class felt too genteel to object.

"I think he means 'flowers,' " Miss Mitnick shyly ventured.

"Don't mix op two languages, Keplan!" blared Mr. Blattberg, swinging his vest chain, from which his grandson's baby tooth dangled.

Mr. Parkhill, who had thought that "bloomers" came from a misconstruction of "to bloom," suddenly realized that *Blumen* were flowers in Mr. Kaplan's native tongue.

"So podden me, Moskovitz, t'anks a million, Mitnick, an' I take beck 'bloomers,' Blettboig, and put in 'flars.' "

" 'Fl*ow*ers,' " sighed Mr. Parkhill.

"I love dem! I also love to breed frash air. An' I *love* to hear de leetle boids sinking—"

" 'Sin*ging!*' You *must* watch your 'k's and 'g's."

" '*Sink*ing' boids?" jeered Norman Bloom. "Kaplen, boids are not *fish!*"

The caustic thrust did not trouble the troubadour. "An' ven dose boids are sin*ging,* den is Mama Netcher commink ot in all kinds gorgeous!"

Mr. Parkhill rubbed his temples. *Epea pteroenta:* winged words—but on such ailing wings . . .

"Lest veek, I took my vife ot to de contry. I said, 'Sarah, you should take a vacation. Just slip, eat, valk aron' in Netcher. Stay in bad how late you vant itch mornink.' "

" '*Ea*ch mornin*g.*' "

"But my vife! Did she slapt late? No. Did she valk aron'? Saldom. Who ken change de life's times hebits of a poisson vun-two-tree? . . . Avery mornink my Sarah got op six o'clock, no matter vhat time it vas."

An explosion rocked the hall of learning.

"Mistake!"

"Mish-mosh!"

"Cuckoo!"

"I'll *die!*"

"Class . . . *class!*" pleaded Mr. Parkhill. "We *must* restrain ourselves! If you have a correction—yes, Miss Mitnick?"

Flushed but firm, Rose Mitnick responded, "How can Mr. Kaplan say Mrs. Kaplan got up every morning at six o'clock *'no matter what time it was'?*"

Laughter shook the faded walls.

"You right, Miss Mitnick!"

"Whoever heard such a silly?"

"With this mon, many mistakes are as sand on a bitch," Olga Tarnova gloated.

"Tarnova," lofty Kaplan inquired, "are you complainink or explainink?"

"Koplin!" railed Gus Matsoukas. "You should give *thanks* to Miss Mitnick!"

"I'll send her a talagram."

"Miss Tarnova iss right!" howled Wolfgang Schmitt.

"So give her a madel."

"Class—"

"Give an *inch,* Mr. Kaplen," wailed Bessie Shimmelfarb. "Give an *inch.*"

"I'm making a speech, not a ruler," rejoined the purist.

"Class! Let us confine our attention to the point at issue. Mr. Kaplan, I—I'm sure you didn't quite mean what you said in your last passage."

"Vhich pot?"

"Miss Mitnick," said Mr. Parkhill, "please repeat your point."

"I said that giving the exact t-time, six o'clock," Miss Mitnick stammered, "and *then* saying 'no matter what time it is'—that's impossible!"

Mr. Kaplan surveyed Rose Mitnick from Olympus. "Maybe for *som* pipple, it's umpossible. But *my* vife voke op so oily in de mornink she got op six o'clock no matter vhat time it vas!"

Miss Mitnick's expression was heart-rending. "But, Mr. *Kap*lan, if—"

"Don't be a stubborn, Kaplen!" bellowed Mr. Bloom. "If it's six o'clock, you *do* know what time it is, no?! So how can you say—"

"Aha!" cried Mr. Kaplan. "You make de same mistake Mitnick! Pay batter attention to my *minnink*. My vife is fest aslip. It's six o'clock. Hau Kay. She gats op. So does *she know vhat time it is?* Vould *you* know it's six o'clock if *you* are fest aslip?!"

Mr. Bloom ranted, Miss Mitnick whimpered, Mr. Pinsky sang "Pssh!" and slapped his cheek in tribute to his idol.

"*Mr.* Kaplan!" Mr. Parkhill repressed his desperation. "You are evading the point. If you state the exact time, then it is simply incorrect to add 'no matter what time it was.' That is a flat contradiction!"

Mr. Kaplan's smile ossified for a second, then recovered its aplomb. "If it's a *conter*diction, it's not just a mistake. Bloom, do you onderstand dis important difference?"

Mr. Bloom protested such shameless sophistry. Miss Goldberg choked on a lozenge. Miss Mitnick bit both her lip and her pencil in frustration. (Poor Miss Mitnick: ever correct, never victorious.)

"Koplan," croaked Olga Tarnova. "They should sand you to Siberia!"

"Dis is not a class in geography," observed Mr. Kaplan.

"*Mr.* Kaplan!"

The orator had flown back into rhapsody: "How many you city pipple aver saw de son rizink on a fild? How many you children from Netcher smalled de frash gress in de mornink, all vet mit dues? How many—"

84

No one would ever know how many "how many"s Mr. Kaplan still had in reserve, because the bell pealed in the corridor. The Cicero of the beginners' grade froze, hands in midair.

"That's all for tonight," said Mr. Parkhill. Only strength of character made it possible for him to conceal his relief.

Mr. Kaplan bowed to the cold-heartedness of time. "So dat must be de and fromm de speech of Hyman Keplen!"

And Mr. Parkhill saw the name. It was absurd, of course, utterly preposterous; but through some peculiar transmutation of sound into sight, Mr. Parkhill seemed to behold the name of Mr. Kaplan just as Mr. Kaplan always printed it: H*Y*M*A*N K*A*P*L*A*N. How could a man pronounce his name in red and blue and green?

Mr. Parkhill sat quite still, frowning his perplexity, as the class filed out.

MR. K·A·P·L·A·N,
EVER MAGNIFICENT

Only after considerable soul-searching, plus the encouragement of Miss Higby (who was, after all, a blooded veteran of adult education), did Mr. Parkhill decide to introduce the beginners' grade to a new subject: writing letters. No instruction, surely, was more likely to benefit his pupils, or be put to swifter use outside the schoolroom.

So, one pleasant evening, as the long twilight bathed the walls in saffron, Mr. Parkhill opened the session by explaining the proper form and structure of personal letters: where to write the home address, where to place the date, how to phrase the salutation, how to word the final greeting. Rarely had his flock been so attentive; never had they displayed such eagerness to explore new terrain.

Now, the first fruits of Mr. Parkhill's tutelage glowed on the blackboards. Six happy students had transcribed the assignment: "A letter to your husband or wife, a relative or friend." Miss Mitnick had composed an *excellent* letter (as Mr. Parkhill had been confident she would) inviting her sister to a surprise party for one Lily Edelcup. Mr. Bloom had written a cousin in Los Angeles, Calif., describing a memorable Sunday of fun and frolic at Coney Island. Mr. Trabish had written to a friend in "Grand Rabbits," Michigan. Mrs. Rodriguez had reported her impressions of a New York subway ride to her mother in San Juan: "fast, but hot, noise, speet, durt, crazy." Mrs. Moskowitz had lolled in sweet fantasy by pretending she was vacationing in an elegant hotel in "Miami, Floridal," and reminded her husband, back home in Brooklyn, to be sure "the pussy gets each morning frash milk." (Mrs. Moskowitz was so devoted to "the pussy" that she repeated the admonition four times, which left insufficient room for a description that could do justice to the scenic beauties of Miami.) Mr. Kaplan—as Mr. Parkhill scanned the last letter on the board, his larynx knotted.

"It's to mine brodder," Mr. Kaplan explained.

Mr. Parkhill nodded absently.

"He lives in Varsaw."

"Mmh."

"Maybe I should rid *alod* de ladder," its author delicately suggested.

" '*Let*ter,' Mr. Kaplan, not '*lad*der.' "

"Aha! So maybe I ken rid de *let*ter. . . ."

"N-no, I'm afraid we won't have enough time."

Mr. Kaplan sighed, lamenting the heartlessness of Father Time.

"Class, please study Mr. Kaplan's letter carefully. . . ."

From their oaken, one-armed chairs, the company of scholars focused fiercely on the blackboard. Miss Mitnick quickly began making notes. Mr. Blattberg looked offended. Mr. Pinsky feasted on his hero's creation, then slapped his cheeks with ecstatic "Tchk! Tchk!'s." Mr. Matsoukas, demoralized by Mr. Pinsky's adoration, leaned far forward, as if the decreasing of distance would sharpen his critical faculties. Mrs. Moskowitz cast not a glance at the board; instead, she fanned her cheeks, exhausted. (The vicarious excitements of that evening had been too much for Mrs. Moskowitz: an invitation to a surprise party, a thrilling day at Coney Island, a ride on the Far Rockaway subway—it had been a veritable Mardi Gras for Sadie Moskowitz.)

And Hyman Kaplan sat in his chair as if on a throne, his

countenance proud, his indulgence spacious, his modesty fraudulent. He conducted a sidelong surveillance of those privileged to behold his handiwork, then gazed brightly at Mr. Parkhill. . . . Anxious little lines had crept around Mr. Parkhill's face when he first had scanned Mr. Kaplan's letter; naked disbelief possessed the leader's countenance as he read the epistle again:

> 459 E 3 Str
> N.Y.
> New York
>
> Octo. 10
>
> HELLO MAX!!!
> I should tell about mine progriss. In school I am fine. Making som mistakes, netcheral. Also doing the hardest xrcises like the best students the same. Som students is Blum, Moskowitz, Mitnick—no relation Mitnick in Warsaw.
> Max! You should absolutel come to N.Y. and belong in mine school!

(It was at this point, envisaging another Mr. Kaplan in the beginners' grade, that dismay invaded Mr. Parkhill's eyes.)

> Do you feeling fine? I suppose. Is all ok? You should begin right now learning about ok! In America you got to say ok all the time. Ok the wether, ok the Prazident, ok the bazeball, ok the foot we eat.

(At this point, consternation covered all of Mr. Parkhill's features.)

> How is darling Annie? Long should she leave!
> So long.
> With all kinds entusiasm,
>
> Your animated brother
> H*Y*M*I*E

Mr. Parkhill turned to his flock. He tried to clear his throat, but succeeded only in coughing. "Has—everyone finished reading?"

The heads bobbed up and down like eager robins. That, at least, was encouraging. But the whispered chortles and mordant leers, the sly exchange of winks and grins and giggles, augured neither moderation nor mercy in the discussion that loomed ahead.

"Let us begin. One at a time, please. Who would like to start?"

The air turned into a palisade: pens, pencils, rulers, hands, fingers sprang up, and even a comb, swinging.

"Er—Mrs. Tomasic."

"Shouldn't 'N.Y.' be *after* 'New York'?" Mrs. Tomasic blurted. "So 'New York' should be on top of?"

"Good!" cackled Mr. Marcus.

Mr. Parkhill made the change on the board. "Mr. Finsterwald?"

"In all places is 'mine' positively wrong!" proclaimed Karl Finsterwald. "It should be 'my,' 'my,' 'my'!"

"Bravo!" trilled Carmen Caravello.

"Quite right," said Mr. Parkhill. "Mr. Kaplan—this really applies to everyone—you *must* learn the basic and important difference between 'my' and 'mine.' 'My' is an adjective; 'mine' is a pronoun—and is *never* used with a following noun!" On the board he swiftly chalked:

This is my towel.

"That," said Mr. Parkhill, "uses 'my' as an adjective. *But—*" Beneath the sentence, which seemed to have hypnotized Mr. Scymczak, Mr. Parkhill wrote:

This towel is mine.

"Here, 'mine' obviously refers to 'my towel.' So the first sentence would be altogether wrong if it read: 'This is *mine* towel.' . . . Is that clear?"

"Poifick!" affirmed Mr. Kaplan.

"Is the same also true with 'his' and 'her'?" asked Miss Pomeranz.

"Well . . ." Mr. Parkhill paused unhappily. "The adjective 'his' may be used both ways." He wrote:

> This is his toothbrush.
> This toothbrush is his.

"How*ever*, in the case of the pronoun 'her,' we have an unusual case—"

"Ooy!" Mrs. Moskowitz's morale melted like butter the moment "unusual" or "exception to the rule" emerged from Mr. Parkhill's lips.

"—because 'her' . . ." Quickly Mr. Parkhill scribbled:

> Her hat is yellow.
> The yellow hat is hers.

"—becomes 'hers.' "

"No sanse," mumbled Mr. Scymczak.

"It's really not difficult," said Mr. Parkhill, "once you learn a few—"

"English don't stond still!" mourned Olga Tarnova. "In Rossian—"

"To return to Mr. Kaplan's letter . . . Further corrections?"

" 'Progress' is not with 'i,' " declared Miss Mitnick, "but with *'e,'* and 'some' needs at the end an *'e.' "*

"Very good . . . Mrs. Yanoff?"

"From the spelling of 'absolutel' I could *die!*" exclaimed the lady in black.

"Why?"

"It's spelled bad."

"How should it be spelled?"

"I don't know."

"Som corractor," snapped Mr. Kaplan.

Mr. Parkhill emended the word in contention.

"Vhy 'exercise' hass no 'e' before 'x'?!" demanded Wolfgang Schmitt.

" 'Baseball' weeth a *'z'?!"* Young Vincente Perez, a fleet shortstop, was outraged.

"Who puts a 'z' in 'president'?" bristled Miss Valuskas.

The corrections came fast and furious: the absurd spelling of "weather," the butchered abbreviation of "October," the erratic tenses of verbs, the flagrant distortion of "Are you feeling fine?" into *"Do* you feeling fine?"

"Keplan has crimitted so many mistakes," shouted Mr. Feigenbaum, "we could make a whole book examples wrong English from that letter!"

"It's a mish-mosh!" blustered Mr. Blattberg. "Every type, size and amont of!"

"Yos," rumbled Mr. Matsoukas. "Give exomples!"

Norman Bloom swooped in from the sidelines with examples. "Kaplen means 'Long should she *live*'—not 'Long should she *leave,'* which means 'Go away from here!' and is a tarrible way to talk about a sister-on-law!"

His cohorts gave Mr. Bloom an ovation.

"He even—*spelled—wrong—my—name!"* fumed Mr. Bloom, his indignation making it clear that this was the most intolerable of Mr. Kaplan's errors.

"Shame!" foamed Olga Tarnova. "To spell wrong a mon's name! Koplon, Koplon . . ."

"Is in my name double 'o,' not 'u'! I ain't like *som* Blooms!" With this restoration of the honor of the House of Bloom, its scion sneered at his nemesis.

"Goot fa you!" sang Mr. Kaplan, bewildering his adversaries. "Bloom, you gattink batter an' batter to spit so many mistakes."

91

" 'Spot' so many mistakes!" exclaimed Mr. Parkhill.

Mr. Bloom's bald scalp prickled in confusion.

Mr. Kaplan half rose. "I give formal congradulation to Norman Bloom for his improvink in English!"

"That's nice," observed Mrs. Shimmelfarb.

" 'Nice?' " retorted Mr. Pinsky. "Mr. Keplen is *big!* Only a big men edmits small mistakes!"

"For that Kaplin desoives credit," chimed in "Cookie" Kipnis.

Mr. Bloom looked flabbergasted. Mr. Kaplan's manly gesture was not pure gallantry, for it diverted attention from his blunders to Mr. Bloom's progress. In consequence, Mr. Bloom did not know whether to feel flattered or irate. Vanity squelched umbrage. "Thank you, Kaplen!"

"My plashure, Bloom," murmured Machiavelli.

Mr. Nathan burst into laughter.

Mr. Parkhill, realizing why the preceding fusillade had made no dent in Mr. Kaplan's self-esteem (the man had merely been busy loading his weapons), lowered his pointer. "Any more corrections?"

Miss Mitnick flushed. " 'N-e-t' in 'natural' should be 'n-a-t,' with no 'ch' and a 'u,' not an 'e.' And we eat *'food,'* not 'foot'!"

Mr. Blattberg shook with spring giggles. "A foot is for walking, not itting!"

"Also, a small 'ok' is wrong," continued the hawk-eyed damsel. "Should always be 'O.K.' with capitals and periods, because 'O.K.' is an abbreviation."

Mr. Kaplan fashioned the most debonair of smiles. (What was he planning now? Mr. Parkhill wondered.) "Good, Mitnick."

Strengthened by virtue, Miss Mitnick rode to an unseen abyss. "Finally, *three* exclamation points after 'Hello Max'?! You are wrong."

"Aha! . . . Vhy?"

"B-because one exclamation point is plenty!"

"Podden me, Mitnick," crooned Mr. Kaplan. "Your odder corractinks vere fine, Hau Kay—an' I minn Hau Kay mit capitals an' periods. But I soggest you riconsider your remocks abot t'ree haxclimation points. . . ."

"Mr. Kaplan," said Mr. Parkhill firmly, "Miss Mitnick is entirely right. If you feel that you *must* use an exclamation point"—he was guarding himself on all sides—"then one is certainly sufficient."

"For de vay I'm fillink abot mine brodder?!" In that deadly riposte, sublime in its simplicity, Mr. Kaplan virtually accused Miss Mitnick of (1) familial apathy, and (2) trying to undermine the powerful love between blood brothers.

"Not so fast, Kaplen!" Mr. Bloom rushed to Rose Mitnick's defense. *"Three* exclamation marks?!"

"Mex is my *favorite* brodder," declared Mr. Kaplan.

"I don't care if he's your favorite mother!" raged Mr. Bloom.

"My mother isn't 'he,' an' besites she ken't rid English."

"Red harring!" stormed Mr. Blattberg. "Get back to your brother—"

"For a favorite brodder you vant *vun leetle* haxclimation point?" Mr. Kaplan retorted. "Ha! Dat I give to *strengers!"*

Mr. Blattberg howled, Miss Mitnick whinnied, Mr. Bloom turned apoplectic, and Rochelle Goldberg swallowed two nougats.

"Class—"

"Keplen could be right!" opined Sam Pinsky. "A brother desoives more exclamation points than a stranger!"

"I agree," said Miss Gidwitz.

"Class—"

"Then how about the word 'entusiasm'?" Miss Mitnick protested. "It is spelled without 'h'! And is 'With all *kinds* enthusiasm' a way to end a letter?!"

"Vell," Mr. Kaplan admitted, "maybe 'entusiasm' is

spalled wronk; but not de vay I'm *us*ink it. Because *I* write to my brodder *mit real entusiasm!*"

The implication was clear: Rose Mitnick was one of those ingrates who, corrupted by the wealth of the New World, would let her brother starve overseas.

"*Mr.* Kaplan!" Mr. Parkhill could bear no more. "I—"

"I love my brother more than you!" charged Gus Matsoukas.

"So give him a samicolon," shrugged Mr. Kaplan.

"Kaplan, give an *inch!*" wailed Bessie Shimmelfarb. "Give an *inch!*"

He waved off an invisible mosquito.

"But, Mr. Kaplan—" Miss Mitnick tried one final plea for reason. "Take that word 'animated.' 'Your *animated* brother, Hymie?' Isn't *that* wrong?"

"Yes," said Mr. Parkhill flatly. "'Animated' is quite out of place!"

Mr. Kaplan squinted sincerely. "I looked op dat void in de dictionary. It minns 'full of life.' Vell, I falt planty full of life vhen I was wridink to Mex."

Miss Mitnick collapsed.

"That is *not* the point," said Mr. Parkhill severely. "We say that someone has an animated manner, or we say, 'The music has an animated refrain.' But—"

Mr. Kaplan's orbs widened. "Ken't you fill enimated onless you play music?"

"—one just does not say 'your animated *brother*'!"

Applause rattled from the anti-Kaplan cabal; gloom enveloped Mr. Kaplan's grenadiers.

"There is a better word to convey your—feelings in your final greeting," Mr. Parkhill swiftly added. "How about— 'fond'? 'Your *fond* brother—er—Hyman'?" (His lips refused to form "Hymie.")

"'Fond'?" Mr. Kaplan closed his eyes, referring this moot point to his Muse. "'Fond' . . ." he whispered. "'Your fond brodder, Hymie.'" He shook his head, all regret.

94

" 'Fond' is a fine void, Mr. Pockheel—but it don't have enough *fill*ink."

"Then what about 'dear'?! 'Your *dear* brother'—and so on."

Once more Mr. Kaplan went through the process of interior consultation. " 'Dear' . . . 'dear' . . . 'Your dear brodder, Hymie.' " He grimaced. " 'Dear' is too *common*. . . ."

"Then what about—"

"Aha!" cried Mr. Kaplan. "I got it! Fine! Poifick! *Soch* a void!" His smile could have lighted a village.

"Yes, Mr. Kaplan?"

"Give it," urged Shirley Ziev.

"Tell!" begged Sam Pinsky.

" 'Megnificent!' " said Hyman Kaplan.

The class sat dumfounded. " 'Your magnificent brother, Hymie.' " It was the stroke of a master.

All heads turned to Mr. Parkhill. He cleared his throat.

"N-no, Mr. Kaplan. I'm afraid 'magnificent' is entirely inappropriate."

The parting bell pealed down the hall. The beginners' grade rose as one, gathering up foolscap, notebooks, pencils, even as they affirmed their loyalties; some branded Mr. Kaplan a brazen "shop-shooter," others praised so inspired and independent a spirit. Nathan P. Nathan, who so loved life that he never took sides, soothed Miss Mitnick by laughing as he patted her hand. "It's only a lesson, Rose. Next time you'll trap him!"

The last to depart were Messrs. Pinsky and Kaplan.

"Keplen," grinned Mr. Pinsky. "Tonight, you vere tremandous! Where you hoid such a wonderful woid?"

" 'Megnificent,' " Mr. Kaplan savored the lilt of those syllables. "A *beautiful* void. . . ."

"Believe me!" burbled Mr. Pinsky. *"Splan*did. Onusul! But how you found it?"

"By *dip* tinking."

9

THE NIGHT OF THE MAGI

When Mr. Parkhill noticed that Miss Mitnick, Mr. Bloom, and Mr. Kaplan were absent, and heard a mysterious humming beneath the ordinary sounds which preceded the start of a class session, he realized that it was indeed the last meeting of the year, and that Christmas was but a few days off.

Every grade in the American Night Preparatory School for Adults each year presented a Christmas gift to its teacher. By now, Mr. Parkhill was quite familiar with the ritual. Several nights ago, there must have been a concerted dunning of those who had not yet contributed to the collection. Now the Gift Committee was probably engaged in last-minute shopping in Mickey Goldstein's Arcade, debating the propriety of a pair of pajamas, examining the color combination of shirts and ties, arguing whether Mr. Parkhill, in his heart of hearts, would prefer fleece-lined slippers to onyx cuff links.

Mr. Parkhill cleared his throat. "We shall concentrate on spelling tonight."

The students smiled knowingly, stealing glances at the three empty chairs, exchanging sly nods and soft chuckles. Mrs. Moskowitz directed a question to Mrs. Tomasic, but Mr. Blattberg's fierce "Shah!" murdered the words on her very lips. Rochelle Goldberg reached for a chocolate, giggling, but swallowed the sound instead of the sweet the moment Mr. Perez shot her a scathing rebuke.

"We shall try to cover—forty words before recess!"

Not one stalwart flinched.

Mr. Parkhill always gave the class a brisk spelling drill during the last session before Christmas: that kept all the conspirators busy; it dampened their excitement over what would soon transpire; it involved no speeches or discussion during which the precious secret might be betrayed; above all, a spelling drill relieved Mr. Parkhill from employing a rash of ruses to conceal his embarrassment. "Is everyone ready?"

A chorus worthy of *Messiah* choraled assent.

"The first word is—'bananas.'"

Murmurs trailed off, smiles expired, as "bananas" sprouted their letters on the arms of the chairs.

"Romance . . ."

Pens scratched and pencils crunched as "romance" joined "bananas."

" 'Fought,' the past tense of 'fight' . . . *'fought.'* " Now all brows tightened (nothing so frustrated the fledglings as the gruesome coupling of "g" and "h") while the scholars wrestled with "fought."

"Groaning . . ." Mr. Parkhill heard himself sigh. The class seemed incomplete without its stellar student, Miss Mitnick, and bereaved without its unique one, Hyman Kaplan. (Mr. Kaplan had recently announced that Shakespeare's finest moments came in that immortal tale of star-crossed lovers, "A Room in Joliet.")

"Charming . . . horses . . ." Mr. Parkhill's mind was not really on charming horses. He could not help feeling uneasy as he envisaged what soon would occur. The moment the recess bell rang, the entire class would dash out the door. The committee would be waiting in the corridor. The class would cross-examine them so loudly that Mr. Park-

97

hill would get a fairly good idea of what the present was. And as soon as the bell pealed its surcease, the throng would pour in from the corridor, faces flushed, eyes aglitter, surrounding one member of the committee (the one carrying the Christmas package) to conceal the fateful parcel from their master's view.

The class would come to order with untypical celerity. Then, just as Mr. Parkhill resumed the spelling lesson, the chairman would rise, apologize for interrupting, approach Mr. Parkhill's desk, place the package upon it, and blare out the well-prepared felicitations.

Mr. Parkhill would pretend to be overwhelmed by surprise; he would utter a few halting phrases. His flock would smile, grin, fidget until the bravest among them would exclaim, "Open it!" or "Look inside the present!" Whereupon, Mr. Parkhill would untie the elaborate ribbons, remove the wrapping from the box, lift the top, and —as his students burbled with pleasure—he would pluck the gift from its cradle, exclaiming "It's *beau*tiful!" or "I shall certainly put *this* to good use!" or (most popular of all) "It's just what I wanted!"

The class would burst into a squall of applause, to which he would respond with renewed thanks and a stronger counterfeit of spontaneous thanksgiving. (It was not always easy for Mr. Parkhill to carry off the feigned surprise; it was even harder for him to pretend he was bowled over by pleasure: One year the committee, chairmanned by Mr. David Natkowitz, had given him a porcelain nymph—a pixy executing a fandango despite the barometer in her right hand and the thermometer in her left.)

As Mr. Parkhill's remarks concluded, and the class's "Don't mention it!"'s and communal fervor trailed off, the spelling drill would resume and the session would drag on until the final bell.

"Accept . . ." called Mr. Parkhill. "Notice, please, the

word is 'accept' ... Not, 'except'; be careful everyone; listen
to the difference: except ... 'Cucumber ...' "

And after the final bell rang, the whole class would cry
"Merry Christmas! Happy New Year!" and crowd around
him with tremendous smiles to ask how he *really* liked the
present, advising him that if it wasn't just right in size and
color (if the gift was something to wear), or in shape and
utility (if something to use), Mr. Parkhill could exchange
it! He didn't *have* to abide by the committee's choice. He
could exchange the present—for anything! That had been
carefully arranged with Mickey Goldstein in person.

This was the ritual, fixed and unchanging, of the session
before Christmas.

"Nervous ... goose ... violets ..."

The hand on the wall clock crawled toward eight. Mr.
Parkhill tried to keep his eyes away from the seats, so
telling in their vacancy, of Miss Mitnick, Mr. Bloom, and
Mr. Kaplan. In his mind's eye, he saw the three deputies
in the last throes of decision in Mr. Goldstein's Arcade,
torn by the competitive attractions of an electric clock, a
cane, spats, a "lifetime fountain pen." Mr. Parkhill
winced. Twice already had "lifetime" fountain pens been
bestowed upon him, once with a "lifetime" propelling pencil to match. Mr. Parkhill had exchanged these indestruct-
ible gifts discreetly: once for a woolen vest, once for a fine
pair of earmuffs. Mr. Parkhill hoped it wouldn't be a fountain pen.

Or a smoking jacket! He had never been able to understand why the committee, in his second semester at the
A.N.P.S.A., had decided upon a smoking jacket. Mr. Parkhill did not smoke. He had exchanged it for a pair of fur-
lined gloves. (That was when Mr. Goldstein told him that
teachers were always changing the Christmas presents
their classes gave them: "Why don't those dumbbells
maybe ask a teacher some questions in advance they could

99

get a *hint* what that particular teacher really *wants?*" Mr. Goldstein had been quite indignant about such foolhardiness.)

"Pancakes . . . hospital . . . commi—" In the nick of time, as a dozen apprehensive faces popped up, Mr. Parkhill detoured disaster: *"—ssion.* Commission! . . ."

The clock ticked away.

Mr. Parkhill called off "Sardine . . . exquisite . . . palace" —and at long last the bell trilled intermission.

The class stampeded out of the room, Mr. Pinsky well in the lead. Their voices resounded in the corridor and floated through the open door. Nathan P. Nathan was playing a harmonica. Mr. Parkhill began to print "Bananas" on the blackboard; he would ask his pupils to correct their own papers after the recess. He tried to shut his ears to the babbling forum outside the door, but the voices chattered like shrill sparrows.

"Hollo, Mitnick!"

"Bloom, what you chose?"

"Ees eet for wear?"

"So what did you *gat,* Keplen? Tell!"

Mr. Parkhill heard Miss Mitnick's "We bought—" instantly squashed by Mr. Kaplan's stern "Mitnick! Don't say! Averybody comm *don* mit your voices. Titcher vill hear soch hollerink. Be soft! Qviet!" Mr. Kaplan was born to command.

"Did you bought a Tsheaffer's Fountain Pan Sat, guaranteet for life, like *I* said?" That was Mrs. Moskowitz. (Poor, dear Mrs. Moskowitz; she showed as little imagination in her benefactions as in her homework.)

"Moskovitz, mine *Gott!*" The stentor was Kaplan. "Vhy you don't use a lod spikker?! Cless, lat's go to de odder and fromm de hall!"

The voices of the beginners' grade dwindled as they márched to the "odder and" of the corridor, rather like the

100

chorus in *Aida* (which, in fact, Mr. Nathan was playing, off-key) vanishing into Pharaoh's wings.

Mr. Parkhill printed "Horses" on the board, then "Accept . . . Except," and he began to practice the murmur: "Thank you . . . all of you . . . It's just what I wanted!" Once he had forgotten to say "It's just what I wanted!" and Miss Helga Pedersen, chairman of the committee that year, had been hounded by her classmates well into the third week of January.

It seemed an hour before the gong summoned the scholars back to their quarters. They poured in *en masse,* restraining their excitement by straining their expressions, resuming their seats with simulated insipidity.

Mr. Parkhill, printing "Cucumber" on the board, did not turn to face his congregation. "Please compare your own spelling with mine—"

Came a heated whispering: "Stand *op,* Mitnick!" That was Mr. Kaplan. "You should stend op, too!"

"The *whole* committee," Mr. Bloom rasped.

Apparently Miss Mitnick, a gazelle choked with embarrassment, could not mobilize the fortitude to "stend op" with her comrades.

"A fine represantitif *you'll* gonna make!" frowned Mr. Kaplan. "You t'ink is for *my* sek I'm eskink? Mitnick, stend *op!*"

"I can't," whinnied Miss Mitnick.

Mr. Parkhill printed "Violets."

"Lest call!" barked Mr. Kaplan. "Come op mit me an' Bloom!"

The anguished maiden's eyes were glazing. Even Mr. Nathan's cheerful "Rosie!" fell on paralyzed ears.

"Class . . ." began Mr. Parkhill.

A clarion voice cut through the air. "Podden me, Mr. Pockheel!"

It had come.

101

"Er—yes?" Mr. Parkhill beheld Messrs. Bloom and Kaplan standing side by side in front of Miss Mitnick's chair. Each was holding one side of a long package, wrapped in green cellophane and tied with great red ribbons. A pair of tiny hands, their owner hidden behind the box, clutched the bottom of the offering.

"De hends is Mitnick," explained Mr. Kaplan.

Not for a second did Mr. Parkhill avert his gaze from the tableau. "Er—yes?"

"Lat go," Mr. Kaplan whispered.

The hands of Mitnick disappeared.

The diminished committee advanced with the parcel. Mr. Kaplan's smile was celestial; Mr. Bloom's nostrils quivered. Together, the staunch duo thrust the package toward Mr. Parkhill's chest as Mr. Kaplan proclaimed: "Mr. Pockheel, is mine beeg honor, as chairman fromm de Buyink-an'-Deliverink-to-You-a-Prazent Committee, to prezant you mit dis fine peckitch!"

Mr. Bloom dropped back two paces (it resembled the changing of the guard, so well had it been rehearsed) and stared into space.

Mr. Parkhill stammered, "Oh, *goodness*. Why, thank—" but Mr. Kaplan rode over his words: "Foist, I have to say a few voids!" He half turned to the audience. "Mitnick, *you still got time to join de committee!*"

The maiden was inert.

"She fainted!" cried Mrs. Yanoff.

This was not true.

"She is stage-fried!"

This, despite the solecism, was true.

Mr. Kaplan shook his head in disgust and re-faced Mr. Parkhill, smoothed a paper extracted from his pocket, and read: "To our dear titcher (dat's de beginnink): Ve are stendink on de adge of a beeg holiday. Ufcawss, is all kinds holidays in U.S.: holidays for politic, holidays for religious, an' *plain* holidays. In Fabruary, ve got Judge Vashington's boitday—a *fine* holiday. Also Abram Lincohen's, iven batter. In July comms, netcheral, Fort July, de boitday of America de beauriful. . . . Also ve have Labor Day, Denksgivink (for de Peelgrims), an' for victory in de Voild Vide Var, Armistress Day."

Mr. Parkhill studied his chalk. "Thank—"

"Make an *end* awreddy," growled Mr. Bloom.

Mr. Kaplan scorned impatience at such a moment. "But arond dis time year, ve have a *different* kind holiday, a spacial, movvellous time: Chrissmas. All hover de voild are pipple celebraking. Becauss for som pipple is Chrissmas like for *odder* pipple Chanukkah—de most secret holiday fromm de whole bunch."

(" 'Sacred,' Mr. Kaplan, *'sa*cred.' ")

"Ven ve valkink don de stritts an' is snow on de floor an' all kinds tarrible cold!" Mr. Kaplan's hand repelled winter's tribulations. "Ven ve see in all de chop-vindows dose trees mit rad an' grin laktric lights boinink . . . Ven de time comms for tellink fancy-tales abot Sandy Clawss—"

(*"Fairy* tales . . .")

"—flyink don fromm de Naut Pole on rain-emimals, an' climbink don de jiminies mit stockings for all de lettle kits. Ven ve hear de beauriful t'oughts of de tree Vise Guys, chasink a star on de dasert to Bettelheim."

(*"Mis*ter Kaplan!")

"Ven pipple saying, 'Oh, Mary Chrissmas! Oh, Heppy Noo Yiss! Oh, bast regotts!'—den ve *all* got a varm fillink in de hot, for all humanity vhich should be brodders! Ve know *you* got de fillink, Mr. Pockheel; *I* got de fillink; Caravello, Matsoukas, iven Mitnick"—Mr. Kaplan was not one to let perfidy go unchastised—"got dat fillink!"

"*I* feel my feet dying," muttered Mr. Bloom.

"An' vat do ve call dis fillink?" cried Mr. Kaplan. "De Chrissmas Spirits."

103

(" 'Spir*it,*' Mr. Kaplan, 'spir—' ")

"Now I'll prezant de prazent."

The class leaned forward. Mr. Parkhill straightened his shoulders.

"Because you a foist-cless titcher, Mr. Pockheel, an' ve all oppreciate how you explain de hoddest pots gremmer, spallink, pernonciation, vhich ve know is planty hod to do mit greenhorns, ve all falt you should gat a semple of our —of our"—Mr. Kaplan turned his page over hastily—"Aha! —of our santimental! So in de name of de beginnis' grate of Amarican Night Priparatory School for Edults, I'm pre- zantink de soprize prazent to our vunderful titcher, lovely Mr. Pockheel!"

(" *'Beloved,'* Mr. Kaplan . . .")

A hush gripped the chamber.

Mr. Parkhill tried to say, "Thank you, Mr. Kaplan . . . Thank you, class . . ." but the phrases seemed so time-worn, so shorn of meaning, they stuck in his throat. Without a word, he untied the big red ribbon, unfolded the green cellophane wrapping, lifted the cover off the package, fumbled with the inner maze of wrapping. He raised the gift from the box. It was a smoking jacket. A black and gold smoking jacket. Black velvet, the lapels a lustrous gold. On the breast pocket, an exotic ideograph sparkled. And a dragon was embroidered all across the front and back; its tongue flickered across the sleeves.

"Horyantal style," Mr. Kaplan confided.

Mr. Parkhill coughed. The room seemed very warm. Mr. Bloom was peering over Mr. Kaplan's shoulder, mopping his bald head and clucking like a rooster. Mrs. Moskowitz sat stupefied. Moist-eyed Olga Tarnova moaned from the depths of one of her many passions.

"Th-thank you," Mr. Parkhill succeeded in stammering. "Thank you—all of you—very much."

Mr. Bloom blared, "Hold it op everyone should see!"

Mr. Kaplan turned on Mr. Bloom. *"I'm* de chairman!"

Rose Mitnick was bleating.

Miss Goldberg cracked a pistachio nut.

"I—I can't tell you how much I—appreciate your kindness." The dragon, Mr. Parkhill noted, had green eyes.

Mr. Kaplan beamed. "So plizz hold op de prazent all should see."

Mr. Parkhill raised high the jacket for all to behold. The symphony of admiring "Oh!"s and "Ah!"s was climaxed by Mr. Kaplan's ecstatic "My!"

"It's—beautiful," said Mr. Parkhill.

"Maybe you should toin arond de jecket," suggested Mr. Kaplan.

As Mr. Parkhill revolved the jacket slowly, the dragon writhed in the folds.

"A voik of art!" sang Mr. Pinsky.

"Maybe ve made a mistake?" whispered Hyman Kaplan.

"I beg your pardon?"

"Maybe you don't smoke. Mitnick vorried abot dat. But I sad, 'Uf *cawss* a ticher smokes. Not in cless, netcheral. At home. At least a *pipe!'* "

"No, no, you didn't make a mistake. I do—occasionally— smoke. A pipe!" Mr. Parkhill cleared his larynx. "Why— *it's just what I wanted!"*

The class burst into cheers.

"Hooray!" laughed Mr. Trabish.

"I knew it!" boomed Mr. Blattberg, whirling his grandson's tooth.

"Hoorah," growled Gus Matsoukas.

"Bravo!" chimed Miss Caravello.

"In Rossia we song in all the chaurches," droned Olga Tarnova. "On differont day but."

"Vear it in de bast of helt!!" cried Mr. Kaplan.

"Thank you, I will. Class, you have been most generous. Thank you."

"You welcome!" came the congregation's response.

It was over.

Mr. Parkhill started to fold the dragon back into its lair. Mr. Bloom marched to his seat, acknowledging the praises due a connoisseur who had participated in such a choice. But Mr. Kaplan stepped closer to Mr. Parkhill's desk.

"Er—thank you, Mr. Kaplan," said Mr. Parkhill.

The chairman of the committee shuffled his feet and craned his neck and—why, for the first time since Mr. Parkhill had known him, Mr. Kaplan was embarrassed.

"Is anything wrong?" asked Mr. Parkhill anxiously.

Sotto voce, so that no ears but Mr. Parkhill's could hear it, Mr. Kaplan said, "Maybe mine spitch vas too long, or too *formal*. But, Mr. Pockheel, avery void I sad came fromm below mine heart!"

For all the unorthodox English, thought Mr. Parkhill, Mr. Kaplan had spoken like one of the Magi.

10

THE SUBSTITUTE

Sleet slithered down the windows. The room smelled of wet coats, drying above the radiators, and soaked hats and damp mufflers, dangling from pegs along the side wall, where many rubbers crouched and galoshes glared like brass-eyed gnomes. Dripping umbrellas, some open, some closed, were propped along the back wall, beneath the lithographs of Washington and Lincoln that flanked the forlorn panes.

It was a nasty night, a night of soaked shoes, raw throats, sniffles and snuffles and sudden sneezes. A fourth of the chairs were empty, their occupants at home. So was Mr. Parkhill.

At his desk and in his stead, a young Substitute, bubbling with missionary zeal (it was only the second time he had been summoned to "fill in" for an indisposed teacher), was addressing the beginners' grade.

Actually, the Substitute had taken his stand in *front* of Mr. Parkhill's desk. (Any graduate student in Education knows that standing in front of a desk creates a closer rapport than standing behind it; one is more effective, psychologically, posed before instead of behind the site of authority. As for sitting in the *chair* of the teacher for whom you are a proxy, that is "an insensitive beginning," Plaut and Samish warned the unwary, "for it converts the

107

substitute into an usurper. To take command so brusquely is to offend some students' loyalty—and may even arouse the resentment of others."

Plaut and Samish had gone on, in their masterful chapter called "Emergency Pitfalls," to ordain:

A desk is more than a desk. It is a lectern, a pulpit, even a dais. Let no teacher forget that if he adopts the demeanor of a judge, he transforms a classroom into a court—in which his comments become verdicts, his sentences *sentences.*

No one ever put that better.

"—and so, unfortunately, Mr. Parkhill shan't be with you tonight. But I shall do my best—"

"Teacher is sick?" gasped one woman.

"Mr. Parkheel is *home?"* gulped another.

"Lat's hope it's not seryous!" intoned the gentleman in the exact center of the front row.

"Oh, I'm sure it's nothing more than a cold." The Substitute spread an emollient smile.

"Vunderful!"

"Mr. Parkhill told me he will surely be back on Monday, Mr.—?"

"Keplen."

"—Mr. Kaplan."

*"Hy*man Keplen."

"Hyman Kaplan," the tutor echoed, examining this pupil with curiosity. He beheld a pleasant, plump gentleman with twinkling blue eyes, blondish hair, and an elfin, debonair manner. A debonair elf was something the young Substitute had never before encountered. And when the elf smiled, as he was doing now, he took on the radiance of a cherub.

Mr. Kaplan, for his part, was appraising Mr. Parkhill's replacement. "Should be taller," noted Mr. Kaplan (the young man *was* shorter than Mr. Parkhill), "and more skinny" (an odd cavil, considering the fact that Mr. Kaplan was considerably weightier), "an' he should at *list* have more hair on his chiks!" (*That* critique was valid, for the surrogate lacked hirsute jowls.)

"I can assure you all," the Substitute continued, "that Mr. Parkhill will rejoin you fit as a fiddle."

"Mr. Parkhall plays the *feedle?*" exclaimed a matron in black.

"No, no," the Substitute exclaimed. "That's just a way of saying he will come back in perfect health!"

"Ufcawss," said Mr. Kaplan.

"Aman," added a voice from the rear.

"That takes a load off!" declared a mustached male.

"Sir," the Substitute said at once, "I believe you mean 'That takes a load off *my mind*'!"

"He sad 'Sir' to a *student?*" a swarthy brunette asked her neighbor.

"Vary polite," the neighbor whispered back.

"Well, class, suppose we follow Mr. Parkhill's schedule tonight and—"

Up rose the hand of Mr. Kaplan.

"Yes?"

"Podden me, but ken ve know *your* name?"

The Substitute flushed boyishly. "Oh, I *am* sorry. My name is Mr. Jennings."

From the expression on Mr. Kaplan's face, the name belonged to a Choctaw. *"Chann*ink?" he echoed.

"No, no. *Jen*nings." The instructor stepped to the blackboard; his chalk sped through J-E-N-N-I-N-G-S.

"Aha!" Mr. Kaplan nodded sagely. *"Chenn*ink! I t'ought you said *'Chann*ink!' "

"N-no, sir, I'm quite sure I said *'Jen*nings.' "

"Mr. Jenninks," announced Mr. Kaplan, "valcome! An' don't be noivous."

The startled Substitute gulped. "Uh—thank you . . . *Well,* according to Mr. Parkhill's instructions, we should devote ourselves to Open Questions. I am told you all keep notes, during the week, of all sorts of questions you intend to raise in class. If you will refer to them now, for *just* a few minutes. . . ."

Notebooks, tablets, scraps of paper, even a small box and two envelopes emerged from folders, purses, briefcases, and one basket. But Mr. Kaplan, to Mr. Jennings's discomfiture, consulted no record at all. Instead, he tilted his head to one side, closed both eyes, and whispered in a tone audible to one and all, "So ve stot Haupen Qvastions! . . . T'ree points. Foist, esk abot 'A room goink arond.' "

"I beg your pardon?" put in Mr. Jennings. "I didn't hear what you were saying."

Mr. Kaplan opened one optic organ. "I vasn't *say*ink, I vas *t'ink*ink."

"Oh, I'm sorry."

"Don't mantion it." Mr. Kaplan returned to vocal rumination. "Qvastion number two: Esk abot 'so-an-so.' "

Mr. Jennings's ears began to itch.

"Number t'ree, de *big* qvastion, esk—"

"Let us begin," called Mr. Jennings. "We shall recite in order, starting with—with the gentleman at the end of the back row, please." (That would leave Mr. Kaplan almost to the end.)

"De lest row *foist?*" cried Mr. Kaplan, a man betrayed.

"Shall we commence?" Mr. Jennings asked. "Mr.—?"

"Scymczak. Casimir Scymczak." The owner of this formidable name ran a hand across his crew-cut, sniffled, apologized, and inquired which was correct in refined company: to lift peas to one's mouth with a knife, spoon, or "fog."

"Well, now." Mr. Jennings merrily explained the difference between a fork and a fog. The explanation was so

110

vivid that three pupils jeered at Mr. Scymczak.

Miss Rochelle Goldberg, who was next (she seemed to be chewing licorice), sought help with the spelling of "Tsintsinnati," where her brother lived. "I looked already five times in my dictionary, but there is no 'Tsintsinnati'!"

"Ah, *well,*" Mr. Jennings reassured her, "I'm afraid a dictionary will not help if you look in the wrong place. From the way you pronounced the name, I sus*pect* you looked under 'Ts'!"

"How did you *know?*" Miss Goldberg marveled.

"Goldboig should look under 's'!" advised Mr. Kaplan. " '*Sin*cin—' "

"No, no, Mr. Kaplan! 'S-i-n-' is not at *all* where the young lady should have looked. 'Cincinnati' begins with a 'c' . . ." He wrote the name on the board. "Next?"

A Mr. Karl Finsterwald declared that he was perplexed by when to use "beside" and when to use "besides."

"That's an *extremely* interesting question," said Mr. Jennings and analyzed the distinction, which stunned Mr. Blattberg.

Miss Gidwitz was in a quandary about the differences between "loan," "borrow," "lend," and "ask for cradit."

Mr. Jennings breezed through this thicket with such alacrity that the class rewarded him with "Ah"s and "Oh"s and one resounding "Aha!" of approbation (from Mr. Kaplan).

Mr. Oscar Trabish raised a rather puzzling query: "Why in a t'eater do they sell salami?"

"Hanh?" bawled Mr. Bloom.

"Vhere?!" demanded a homemaker.

"In t'eater, last vik-end!" yawned Mr. Trabish.

"Salami . . . ?" Mr. Jennings frowned. "In a *the*ater?"

The guffaw from Wolfgang Schmitt brought one and all erect. "I did zee zat show! It vass not salami; it vass 'Salomé'!"

Hilarity replaced mystification as the scholars grasped the magnitude of Mr. Trabish's howler: Miss Kipnis's giggle almost developed into hiccoughs, Mr. Perez's snorts swept two loose pages off the arm of his chair, and Mrs. Tomasic laughed so hard she had to readjust her dentures.

" 'Salomé!' " exclaimed Mr. Jennings.

"Salami is meat with garlic," indignant Tarnova intoned. "But Salomé donced with savon veils ond chopped off John Baptist's neck."

Mr. Trabish turned red and slumped into the refuge of slumber.

"Next . . . Miss—?"

"*Mrs.* Yanoff," puffed a lady all in black, who proceeded to inquire whether there wasn't something queer about the interrogative: "What time did you *came*, dollink?"

Mr. Jennings was ever so glad to deal with that. He demonstrated why "did came" was bad English, just as "did ate" or "did ran" would be. "You see, class, the 'did' serves to convert the next verb into the past tense!" He went even further, expatiating on how "do" and "did" function as invaluable auxiliaries to a verb ("Do you play tennis?" "Did he telephone the doctor?"), and how, in a different context, the tenses of "to do" provide unique emphasis ("She *did* strike the postman!" "You *do* believe in God!").

The class, which had seen Mr. Parkhill plow this very pasture a dozen times before, sent bright nods and gay murmurs to bolster Mr. Jennings's morale. "Notice how adding a 'do' or a 'did' to a *question* lends *much* greater force than if we had no 'do's or 'did's at our disposal!" A shudder shook the synod at the thought of such a calamity. "For example: *'Did* he kill the lion?' *'Do* you like turnips?' *'Does* the weather report predict showers?'!"

It pleased Mr. Jennings no end to notice how absorbed the class remained throughout the disquisition: how few coughed or wheezed or shuffled their feet; how many took notes with those special smiles and private chuckles which testify to the pride of comprehension. "Suppose we try a few sentences—or questions—to illustrate these points! Anyone?"

"She *did* learn to tangle?" blurted Miss Ziev.

"Tang*o*," said Mr. Jennings. "Very good."

"*Did* he anlist in the French Foreign Luncheon?" called Mr. Pinsky.

"The French Foreign *Leg*ion!" Mr. Jennings, aghast, kept encouragement glued to his lips.

"Did he did his shempoo?" sallied Mrs. Moskowitz.

"No, no, Mrs. Moskowitz. The first 'did' makes the second 'did' incorrect. It's: 'Did he *do*—or take—his shampoo?' "

At this point, it occurred to Mr. Jennings that for the past fifteen minutes Mr. Kaplan had not uttered a word. He had raised not one question, answered not one invitation to supply an example. He had not even scoffed at a single volunteer's offering. Throughout the entire give-and-take that swirled around the interrogative or emphasizing aspects of "did," Hyman Kaplan remained as indifferent as a clam, except once, when he moved in his chair with undisguised impatience.

"Next."

The next gentleman was Gus Matsoukas, who asked whether "doodle" was an American type of noodle. This sent one yeoman into hysterics and another into a chant: " 'Doodle-*noodle*? Noodle-*doodle*'?!*"

"Well, sir," replied Mr. Jennings, ignoring the levity, "a 'doodle' is an aimless scribble, marks made when one is dawdling or day-dreaming. This sort of thing." On the board he chalked some scrawls and scratches, a cryptic fez, a bristling pretzel. *"These* are doodles."

"They look like chop suey," said Mr. Kaplan.

"Y-yes—and that is an interesting association, Mr. Kaplan, because although chop suey does not contain *noodles,*

113

so far as I know, chow mein contains a good many!"

"Is thees teacher a *cook?*" gasped Mrs. Rodriguez.

"*I* like chop suey!" announced Mr. Bloom.

"Stick on de point," coldly cut in Mr. Kaplan. "Matsoukas esked a qvastion an' he desoives a straight enser." He proceeded to ask it. "Matsoukas, do de Griks like soup?"

"Yos."

"So *you* like soup?"

"Yos."

"Mr. Kap—"

"You like different type *objeks* in your soup? Like rice? Peace? Domplings?"

"No."

"You like *noodles* in soup?"

"Mr. Kap—"

"No."

"Aha!" The inquisitor struck home. "So you *do* know vhat noodles are!"

"Mr. Kaplan!"

"So what's all crazy marks on blackboard??" Matsoukas demanded.

Mr. Kaplan waved airily. "Dose are boo-boos, not noodles. Mocks mitout minnink, ven your mindt is on *doodles.*"

"*I* never make doodles!" the Athenian glowered.

"So anjoy noodles."

"*Gentle*men . . . class . . . !" Mr. Jennings had never dreamed that Open Questions could turn into guerrilla warfare. "Let our lesson proceed! Mrs . . . ?"

"Moskowitz. Sadie L. Moskowitz, Mrs." The corpulent dowager, who had never heretofore so much as hinted that an initial decorated her name, went into a repertoire of heaves and hoves before inquiring why "quiet" was sometimes spelled "q-u-i-t-e."

"Oh, those are *entirely* different words. Let me explain." Mr. Jennings did, but saw that Mrs. Moskowitz was bewildered by subtle discriminations. He hurried ahead. "Mr. . . . ?"

"Perez. Vincente Perez. Why we put 'e' on the end of 'tease'? Mr. Parkhill told us 's' to make the plural of *'tea.'* "

"But *'tease'* with an 's-e' is a word which has no relation whatsoever to 'tea' or 't-e-a-s' *without* an 'e.' " Mr. Jennings printed the crucial words on the board:

TEA

TEAS

TEASE

The exclamations would have done justice to the Aurora Borealis. So pleased was Mr. Jennings by such enthusiasm that before he fully realized what he was risking, he called upon Mr. Kaplan.

The man rose, his smile approaching ecstasy. No other student had risen, but there was something altogether fitting about Mr. Kaplan's elevation to address the forum. A rustle (of anticipation? of daggers being unsheathed? of armor buckling?) skimmed across the room. "Ladies an' gantleman an' Mr. Channink, who is doing soch a fine jop in dis emoigency—"

"Stop the *spitches!*" scowled Mr. Bloom.

"Enof!" growled Stanislaus Wilkomirski.

Mr. Kaplan heeded not the varlets. "Avery place I go, I am vatchink, listenink"—Mr. Kaplan narrowed his eyes to lend authenticity to "vatchink, listenink"—"for t'ings I should esk in cless durink Aupen Qvastions."

All this, Mr. Jennings discovered, was but overture.

"So de foist qvastion I esk is: Vat's de minnink fromm 'A room is goink arond'!"

" 'A *room* is going around?' " Mr. Jennings's face fell.

"A room is goink arond."

"Oy!" bassooned Mrs. Moskowitz. "Is dat a cuckoo!"

"*Som* qvastion!" chortled Sam Pinsky, slapping one cheek.

" 'A room is going around,' " re-echoed Mr. Jennings, in a delaying maneuver. "Well, the meaning of the words is simple, Mr. Kaplan. But I find the phrase—somewhat exceptional." Inspiration suddenly brightened his downy cheeks. "Of course, if one were dizzy, or faint, or *drunk*" (in Education 403, Professor Mullenbach had told his trainees never to mince words), "then one might say, 'I feel *as if* the room is going around.' "

Norman Bloom snickered. "Still an' all, a crazy quastion!"

"Mine dear Bloom," murmured Mr. Kaplan, "only crazy *pipple* esk crazy qvestions."

"*I'm* crazy?!" bridled Mr. Bloom. "*You* are—"

"Mr. Kaplan," Mr. Jennings quickly put in, "perhaps you could tell us where—I mean, in what circumstances you heard that phrase."

"Gledly. I hoid it fromm Mr. Skolsky (dat's de man livink opstairs) abot Mrs. Nalson (dat's de femily livink *don*-stairs). Mr. Skolsky told me, 'You know, I t'ink Mrs. Nelson vants a divorce!' So I esked, netcheral, 'How you know?' So Mr. Skolsky enswered: '*Avery*body's sayink dat. A room is goink arond.' "

" 'A *rumor's* going around!' " cried Mr. Jennings. "Oh, yes, of course! Why, that's an *excellent* phrase. Indeed, it uses an interesting word: 'rumor.' Let me explain that: 'rumor' refers to—"

Mr. Kaplan shot arrows of triumph at Norman Bloom, who was beating his fists on his thighs, and a superior leer at Mrs. Moskowitz, who seemed to have fallen into a manhole.

After Mr. Jennings had defined and illustrated "rumor," Mr. Kaplan beamed: "My! A *fine* axplination."

"Your next question?"

"I hoid an axpression, it sonds fonny. *Fonny*"—Mr.

Kaplan steered a warning glance toward Mr. Bloom—"not crazy . . . Vhat's de minnink frommm 'a so-an'-so'?"

Mr. Jennings stared at Mr. Kaplan miserably. " 'A so-and-so'?" he repeated cautiously. "That phrase is heard quite commonly, but it really is—well, it's a way of not using—profanity." Mr. Jennings paused, hoping some comment would come to his rescue. His hopes died in the silence. "Well, class . . . let me see. . . ." He wondered how he could explain profanity without using it. "Profanity means—cursing, swearing, using not nice language."

"Mr. *Kap*lan!" Miss Mitnick caught her breath in horror.

"Shame," hissed Olga Tarnova, "shame!"

Rochelle Goldberg fortified her modesty with a marzipan.

"Let me put it this way, class. Suppose Frank, say, wants to say something nasty—"

"Who's 'Frank'?" asked Mrs. Moskowitz.

Mr. Jennings wiped his palms. *"Any Frank. I used the name only as an example."*

"Like 'X' an' 'Y,' Moskovitz," flashed Hyman Kaplan. "You forgot awreddy Mr. Pockheel's smot exemples 'X' an' 'Y'?!"

"I don't like 'X' and 'Y' *and* also Frank!"

"You don't like 'i' before 'e' except after 'c'!"

"Have a hot, Mr. Kaplin!" wailed Mrs. Shimmelfarb. "Give an *inch . . .*"

"Class . . . listen. Suppose someone—anyone"—Mr. Jennings lunged on—"wants to say something not nice about someone else—"

"He should sharup!" blurted Mr. Blattberg, touching his grandson's baby tooth as if to preserve its innocence.

"An' soppose he has to svear?!" cracked Mr. Kaplan.

"Mr. Kap—"

"Dat's de exect problem Mr. Channink is tryink to halp us ot mit! If a man vants to svear—"

"He should bite—his—tong!" retorted Miss Ziev.

"Efter he svears he ken bite his tong!" decreed the master.

"Give an *inch,* Mr. Kaplan," pleaded Mrs. Shimmelfarb. "Give an inch!"

Stern Kaplan rebuffed the apostle of compromise. "De essantial problem Titcher is tryink to axplain is how to svear by *not* svearing!"

"Precisely!" said Mr. Jennings. "That's a—forceful way of putting it." *Let* the faces of Mr. Kaplan's foes drop or darken: his ingenious elucidation had saved the day. "Someone who does not want to employ offensive or vulgar language *can* say, 'He's a so-and-so!' instead of—" Too late did young Jennings realize he had gone too far. "Instead of—"

The students leaned forward tensely.

"Instead of—" Mr. Jennings floundered.

"Low-life! Bum! Goot-fa-nottink!"

"Yes, Mr. Kaplan! Exactly!" Mr. Jennings almost choked with gratitude. "That's *precisely* how 'a so-and-so' is used!"

"Ah!"'s of admiration ululated down the ranks, but Mr. Bloom protested, "That still doesn't make Kaplen's quastion polite! *We have ladies in the room!"*

"Ve also have *lights,"* parried Mr. Kaplan, "so does dat minn ve should naver mantion sonshine?"

"Mein Gott!" railed Wolfgang Schmitt.

"Don't split a hair!" fumed Mr. Marcus.

"An *inch,"* begged Bessie Shimmelfarb, "for once, give—"

"Ladies! Gentlemen!" the Substitute shouted. "Do let us observe decorum!"

Decorum was alien to both the vocabulary and the ground rules of the embattled partisans. Miss Tarnova rushed to support Mr. Bloom's *politesse* with poisoned glares at Mr. Kaplan. Mr. Scymczak rallied to the Kaplan

118

banner with a counterthrust: "In class should be frenk and honest on all times!" Mrs. Rodriguez blared, "No dirt in clean houses!" To which stout Pinsky, his voice breaking into a falsetto, retorted, "If Keplen didn't ask, *how would you know it's doity?!*"

"Let Kaplon siddon!" shouted Karl Finsterwald.

"Kaplin, hooray!" rejoined Miss Ziev.

Miss Goldberg must have consumed two Tootsie Rolls during the melee, and Miss Mitnick was wringing her hands in futile offers of propitiation. (Mr. Nathan P. Nathan was not there to cheer her with laughter. He was, at that very moment, dribbling a basketball around "Pepi" Martino of the Canarsie Buckets.)

"Please! *Class!* Can we not respect one another's—" Mr. Jennings might just as well have been home with a cold, too.

"Keplen shouldn't bring street talk into class!" blazed Mrs. Tomasic.

"Shame, shame, Koplon!"

"Aha!" Mr. Kaplan's defiance resounded. "Tarnova, in education is no 'shame-shame' qvastions! Only ashamt *brains* make ashamt minninks!"

"Zat iss not zufficient excussess!" howled Wolfgang Schmitt.

"I hear bomble-bees," observed Mr. Kaplan.

"We are here to learn *nice* English!" protested "Cookie" Kipnis.

"Ve are here to loin averyt'ing!" rang out redoubtable Kaplan.

"Ooooy!"

And just when new attacks on Mr. Kaplan's indelicacy collided with fresh defenses of his purity of purpose, the cause of all the pandemonium raised an imperious hand. "I apolochize. It's all mine fault. I vas wronk!"

Tiberius himself could have received no swifter submis-

119

sion. Mr. Kaplan apologizing? Hyman Kaplan confessing he had erred? Down sank the contesting banners. Stilled were the combatants' voices. Passion oozed into murmurs.

"Yas, I made a beeg mistake!" Mr. Kaplan admitted. "De type 'so-an'-so' I hoid vas not de type 'so-an'-so' ve should make so many oguments abot."

"Watch for a trick," warned Mr. Vinograd.

"I dun't believe mine iss!" said Mrs. Yanoff, who had uncommonly large ears.

"It's no trick," sighed Mr. Kaplan. "It's a plain misondistendink. Listen. Here is vhat heppened. Lest vik, I mat Banny Kovarsky. A frand. Not a *close* frand, like fromm de old contry; still, a nice man. . . . Vell, Banny looked tarrible. His chiks pale. His ice sed, doll, mitout a spockle. His axpression vas like a man pulled ot of vater vhere—God fahbid—he could dron."

So bewildered was Mr. Jennings by the succession of solecisms, and so hypnotized by the unfolding tale, that he forgot all about his duty and corrected not one excruciating pronunciation.

"So I sad, 'Kovarsky, you look like you vaiting for an operation!' So Kovarsky pulled don his mot, silent. 'How you *fill*?' I esked. He sight, 'I vas seek. Not *dyink*. Seek.' So I continue, 'Bot now you fine?' He vent, 'Mnyeh.' So I looked on him mit full sympaty." Mr. Kaplan illustrated his sympathy by spreading wide his arms. " 'Banny, tell me de troot!' " his voice rang out. " 'How you fill *now*?' An' how did Kovarsky answer? Like dis: 'Not jompink, but not in a coffin.' Dat Kovarsky! He is de type if you esk 'Vat time it is?' saz 'Maybe four o'clock, maybe fife.' In vun brat, Kovarsky can say 'Yas,' 'No,' 'Maybe' an' 'Vhy esk?'!"

"Enof awreddy!" boomed Norman Bloom.

"Make the *end!*" groaned Mr. Matsoukas.

"Tolstoy wos foster with *War and Peace!*" sneered Miss Tarnova.

Mr. Jennings roused himself. "Do—come to the point."

Mr. Kaplan dropped both hands wide to appease the multitude. "So efter all dis hammink and hawkink fromm dat *shlemiel* Kovarsky, I dimanded, rill lod: 'Stop bitink arond bushes! Do you fill *normal*? Do you fill *rotten*? Enswer!' . . . So how did he enswer? He sad, 'I fill so-and-so'!"

"You mean 'so-*so*'! " cried Mr. Jennings. "Not 'so-*and*-so.' Of course! 'So-so!' That means not well, but not ill; not happy, but not gloomy. Just—it's an *ex*cellent colloquial expression—'so-so'!"

"Aaah," beamed Mr. Kaplan.

"Psssh!" psshed Mr. Pinsky, slapping both cheeks.

Mr. Bloom mopped his forehead, babbling.

The bell knelled in the corridor. At once the shoal of students surfaced, chattering and gossiping, wrestling into raincoats, snatching galoshes, fluttering umbrellas. It was pouring outside.

Mr. Jennings stood quite still, thinking. He wondered if he would ever forget that astounding evening. How could he report it, in all its flavor and tumult, to Professor Mullenbach? . . . He sat down and swiftly scrawled notes. He might have remained at Mr. Parkhill's desk for an hour had not a man with a mop and pail called from the doorway: "Mister, you expect to sleep here all night?"

"Oh. I'm sorry."

"Time to close."

"Yes, of course."

The man scratched his chin. "Young man, you feel all right?"

"What? . . . Certainly!" Mr. Jennings broke into a sweat; he had tottered on the very brink of replying, more accurately, "So-so."

11

MR. K·A·P·L·A·N'S
UNSTAINED BANNER

It seemed only logical to Mr. Parkhill that, having introduced his students to the pitfalls of the Personal Letter, he should initiate them into Business Communications. Indeed, business letters could prove even more useful to the beginners' brigade: they might want to apply for a job or complain about a bill—or things of that sort.

For some time now, Mr. Parkhill had held off tackling Business Letters; but when he studied his outline for the remaining weeks of the semester, he realized that the schedule was becoming exceedingly crowded. It was foolhardy to delay any longer. *"Tempus* does *fugit* swifter than one realizes!"* was what he concluded.

"The general form of a business letter follows that of the personal letter," said Mr. Parkhill briskly. "It, too, requires your home address, the date, a salutation, a final greeting—or, as some call it, 'the complimentary close.'" He went on to explain that the business letter was, of course, more official in mood; that the address of the person or company to whom one wrote had to be placed on the left-hand side; that both salutation and final greeting were formalized—the former being "Dear Sir," "Dear Sirs," or "Gentlemen," and the latter "Yours truly," "Yours very truly," or "Very truly yours." Mr.

Parkhill described Business Letters with considerable patience.

All had gone well, very well, so well that Mr. Parkhill held high hopes for the homework he had assigned: "A Short Business Letter." Now six students were transcribing their chore on the blackboard. Miss Valuskas, commendably ambitious, was applying for a position as secretary to the president of the zoo. (Miss Valuskas was admired by all her colleagues for her familiarity with animals.) Mr. Feigenbaum was ordering "1 dozen shirts size 15" from the emporium he called "Orbox." Mr. Norman Bloom, the soul of efficiency, was inscribing a note to "S. Levin, Jobbers," curtly reminding them that they owed him $217.75 for merchandise "lust in transit." (The debt was fictitious, of course: Mr. Bloom made pockets for Never-Leak Raincoats.) Miss Fanny Gidwitz was chalking a polite order to "Alexanger" for a sport coat and "pair gloffs" she wished delivered "C.O.T."

At the corner of the room, next to the door, Hyman Kaplan was stationed. Sheer incandescence adorned Mr. Kaplan's smile this evening, and something of Rembrandt distinguished his posture. The blackboard might have been a canvas, for Mr. Kaplan kept his left hand behind his back as he stepped back and forth, eyes narrowed, in periodic appraisal of the wonders his right hand transferred to the slate from the notebook propped on the blackboard's ledge. Both the smile and the stance made Mr. Parkhill uneasy. No sooner had Mr. Kaplan completed his business letter than Mr. Parkhill's eyes raced straight through it:

459 E. 3. Street
New York
Janu. 8

Joseph Mandelbaum
A-1 Furniture Comp.
741 Broadway
New York
NY
USA
Dear Sir Mandelbaum—

Sarah and me want to buy a refrigidator. Always she tells me "Hymie, our eyes-box is terrible. Old. Leeking." This is true.

Because you are in furniture, I am writing about. How much will cost a refrigidator? It must not have a short circus. The 1 we have, brakes a fuze each time I close the door. I told Sarah "Do not full around with laktricity!"

So please xamine your stock. If your eye falls on a bargain pick it up.

Very Truly Wating,
H*Y*M*A*N K*A*P*L*A*N
(Address on Top)

P.S. Best regards from Sarah:

With all kinds fond fillings,
H*Y*M*I*E

When the last member of the platoon left the board, Mr. Parkhill said, "I think we had better take Mr. Kaplan's letter first." (Customarily, recitations started at the *left* side, but Mr. Parkhill determined to face the worst first.)

"Me *foist?*" Mr. Kaplan was transmogrified.

"Yes."

"My!" By the time Mr. Kaplan reached the board his smile was supernal. "Ladies an' gantleman, in dis lasson I falt—"

"Mr. Kaplan," Mr. Parkhill broke in, "just read your letter. There is no need for an—er—introduction."

Only Mr. Kaplan's pride in being first sustained him in so crushing a rebuff. "Podden me." He turned to the letter. " 'Dear Sir Mendelbum . . .' "

"Holy mackinel!" exploded Norman Bloom. " 'Dear *Sir* Mandelbum'?"

"Maybe he iss in the Houze of Lords," snorted Wolfgang Schmitt.

"Kaplan, look noble!" laughed Mr. Wilkomirski.

Mr. Parkhill tapped his pointer rapidly. "Let us hold all comments until Mr. Kaplan has finished."

Mr. Kaplan's squint at Mr. Bloom would have cowed an Apache. " 'Dear Sir Mendelbum,' " he repeated. " 'Sarah vants to buy a refrigidator.' "

"Hanh?" came through Mr. Finsterwald's adenoids.

"He means a refrigi*make*r!" called Miss Pomeranz.

"Eet weel break *don* as soon he opens the door!" predicted Mrs. Rodriguez.

" 'Always she tells me "Hymie . . ." ' " Deaf to the bleatings and protestations of the *hoi polloi,* Mr. Kaplan read on in the cadence of dignity. He uttered the final words with regret. " 'Wit all kinds fon fillings, Hymie.' " His features simulated modesty. "Dat's de and."

"Thonk God," crooned Olga Tarnova.

"Good-*bye* English!" croaked Mr. Blattberg. (Mr. Blattberg had begun to foretell the death of English whenever Mr. Kaplan began *or* finished a recitation.)

"Class," said Mr. Parkhill, "everyone will have a chance to comment. But let me begin by asking Mr. Kaplan—do you think that that is—er—strictly a *bus*iness letter?"

"It's *abot* business . . ."

"But certain phrases, quite *personal* passages, the final greeting—" Mr. Parkhill paused. "I shall ask the class to comment. Who would like to start off?"

Everyone wanted to start off: Mr. Bloom was rolling his

eyes as wildly as his hand was punching the air; Miss Valuskas had *both* hands raised; Mr. Matsoukas was muttering cryptic emendations; Mrs. Tomasic's ruler was whirling around like a windmill.

Mr. Parkhill rejected the bloodthirsty; experience warned him to steer clear of vehemence at the outset. He glanced around . . . and happily beheld the small, still palm of Rose Mitnick, at whom Nathan P. Nathan was winking incentive.

"Miss Mitnick!"

"In my opinion," the sedate maid blushed, "Mr. Kaplan's letter is not a business one. Because in a business letter, you don't tell your wife's first name. And you don't send 'best regards.' And 'all kinds fond feelings' is only for *personal* letters!"

"Maybe dis is a *poissonal* business ladder?" crafty Kaplan murmured.

Miss Mitnick, startled for but an instant, demolished the sophistry. "No, Mr. Kaplan. I think it is *wrong* to give family facts in a business letter! It's not the business of a company to know what a wife is saying to a husband, or a husband to a wife!"

"Very good, Miss—"

"Mitnick," warned Mr. Kaplan, "you forgat to *who* I wrote—"

"That has nothing to do with it," Mr. Parkhill cut in. "Miss Mitnick is entirely right. One doesn't discuss personal details or family affairs in a business communication—which is, after all, to an organization, to strangers."

"Mendelbum," sighed Mr. Kaplan, "is mine oncle."

Twenty-eight throats uttered twenty-eight outcries, which roused Mr. Trabish out of somnolence and into bewilderment. Mr. Pinsky crowed "Psssh! Psssh!" over the cunning of his chieftain. Poor Miss Mitnick, the color of wax, bleated. Mr. Nathan, forfeiting affection for the moment, erupted loud laughter.

"*Mr.* Kaplan!" exclaimed Mr. Parkhill. "*If* that letter *is* really addressed to your—er—uncle, then it should not be called a business communication in the first place!"

"Vell, I edmit dat fect boddered me, too," conceded Mr. Kaplan. "If I am buyink a refrigida—"

" 'Refrigerator'!"

"—a refrigerator, buyink *is* business. Dat's vhy in de foist pot fromm de ladder—"

" '*Let*ter,' Mr. Kap—"

"—I wrote cold, formal, stock-op." Mr. Kaplan elevated his nose to illustrate "stock-op." "But den, I falt it is time to show som family *fillink.* An oncle is an oncle! So I put don 'bast rigotts from Sarah—' "

"And is 'best regards' right for a business letter?" stammered Miss Mitnick.

"It's *spalled* right," parried Mr. Kaplan.

"Koplon!" howled Olga Tarnova.

"A *trick!*" fumed Norman Bloom.

"Give an inch, Mr. Kaplan, give an *inch,*" wailed Mrs. Shimmelfarb.

"He won't give an *ounce,*" grinned Mr. Pinsky.

"He avoids the ezential izue!" seethed Wolfgang Schmitt.

"His 'Yes' is 'Maybe' and his 'No' is 'Who cares?' " stormed Mr. Blattberg.

Mr. Parkhill rapped the pointer on his desk with certitude. "Mr. Kaplan . . . the objections are well taken. As Miss Mitnick put it, quite correctly, you cannot *combine* two forms. Either you write a business letter or you write a personal letter!"

Mr. Blattberg chortled, Mrs. Tomasic snickered, Miss Caravello applauded with rapture.

Mr. Parkhill warned Mr. Kaplan that in the future he write personal letters only to friends or relatives, and business communications to total strangers. "Now let's turn to the other mistakes—of which, I may say, there are many."

"The mistakes by Kaplen are like customers at a fire sale!" cried Norman Bloom. " 'Sarah and me' should be 'Sarah and I.' And 'eyes-box'?! Phooey! 'I-c-e' means 'ice'; 'e-y-e-s' means *'eyes.'* One is for seeing, the other for freezing!"

No sally of Oscar Wilde's ever elicited greater mirth.

Miss Ziev crowed that "leaking" was spelled wrong. Karl Finsterwald added, "And so is 'examine.' " Miss Valuskas remarked caustically that there should be no capitals after "very" in "Very truly" and cast doubts on the legitimacy of "Very Truly Waiting," adding: "Also a mistake in its spelling, for is missing 'i.' " Mr. Marcus was all irony as he intimated that Mr. Mandelbaum was probably wise enough to read Mr. Kaplan's address without being told to look for it in "Address on Top." Even stolid Mrs. Yanoff leaped into the autopsy. "I know one thing," she said, smoothing her black dress. "A circus is with alephants, clons, and flying tepees. So you can't put a circus in a refrigerator, not even a *'short* circus'!"

"You don't know abot laktric," charged Mr. Kaplan.

"Electric, gez, even cendles!" Mrs. Moskowitz dived into the lists. "A soicus won't fit insite an ice-box!"

"Maybe de kind *you* minn," began Mr. Kaplan, "bot—"

Mr. Parkhill rapped the desk firmly. "You don't mean 'short *circus,'* Mr. Kaplan. You mean 'short *circuit.'* " He wrote both words on the board. " 'C-i-r-c-u-i-t,' Mr. Kaplan, not 'c-i-r-c-u-s.' They are entirely different words!"

"De resamblance is remockable," observed Hyman Kaplan.

Mr. Nathan doubled over.

"I see another mistake!" called Miss Mitnick. "In Mr. Kaplan's letter is the line: 'If your eye falls on a bargain, pick it up.' " Flushed, Miss Mitnick repeated: "If your *eye* falls on a bargain pick *it* up!"

Hilarity convulsed the arena: laughs, hoots, taunts; jeers

128

of derision danced among caterwauls of scorn.

Mr. Parkhill was puzzled by Mr. Kaplan's airy acceptance of such rank ridicule; then he noticed that the smile Mr. Kaplan smiled was as close to revealing an ambush as any smile can be.

"An' vhat's wronk, Mitnick?" asked Mr. Kaplan. "Vhat's de exect mistake?"

"You don't *zee*?" cracked Mr. Schmitt.

"N-no . . ." grinned Mr. Kaplan.

Mr. Bloom, who should have been warned by Mr. Kaplan's blithe demeanor, now crowed like a rooster. " 'If your *eye* falls on a bargain please pick *it* up?' 'It?' The *eye?!!*"

Then Mr. Kaplan struck. "Mine oncle," he said, "has a gless eye."

Mr. Bloom's jaw fell apart. Mrs. Moskowitz collapsed. Miss Mitnick whinnied. Mr. Nathan was choking in elation. Olga Tarnova gasped Russian maledictions. Mr. Pinsky cried, "Ginius! Keplen is an ebsolute ginius!"

And Mr. Kaplan's smile was as serene as a child's, deep in a dream of glory. He had routed an ignoble legion. He had demolished his petty foes. Once again he had snatched victory from the very teeth of defeat. His honor, unstained, waved above him like a pure white banner.

12

THE DEATH OF
JULIUS CAESAR

It was Miss Higby's idea. (At least, Mr. Parkhill reflected, it had all started that way.) One night in the faculty lounge, Miss Higby remarked how unfortunate it was that students came to her class wholly unaware of the *finer* side of English, of its beauty and grandeur, of (as she put it) "the glorious heritage of our literature." "There is no reason on earth," Miss Higby had blurted, "why the beginners' grade might not be introduced to a *taste,* at least, of Longfellow or Tennyson or—even Shakespeare!"

Mr. Parkhill could not deny that there was much to be said for Miss Higby's point of view. His pupils *were* adults, after all; they had come to our shores from lands renowned for poets and scholars and men of letters; and many a fledgling in English referred, on occasion, to some classic of European literature. Mr. Matsoukas, for all his cryptic grunts and saturnine moods, sometimes tossed off names from the *Iliad* with considerable fervor. Miss Tarnova (who could wring lurid overtones from a telephone number) rarely let slip by a chance to extol Tolstoy or Gogol or Lermontov. Wolfgang Schmitt, who had gone halfway through a *gymnasium* in Ulm, once delivered an impassioned testimonial to great Thomas Mann. ("Who said he vas a voman?" Mr. Kaplan had scoffed.) And any number of others in the beginners' grade had seen one or another production, in their native tongue, of *Hamlet* or *The Cherry Orchard, Cyrano de Bergerac* or *A Doll's House* (whose author had unfortunately been identified by Nathan P. Nathan as "Henry Gibson").

Apart from Miss Higby's effusive recommendation, Mr. Parkhill realized that his students had been studying English for some time now; they had added *hundreds* of words and phrases to their vocabularies; they had reached a level of familiarity with their new tongue which few teachers would have thought possible when the term began.

"Poetry will alert your class to more precise enunciation," Miss Higby had gone on to say, "and may even attune their ears to the subtleties of English inflection!" (Miss Higby, whose master's thesis was on Coventry Patmore, *loved* poetry.)

Mr. Parkhill had remarked, "I just wonder whether my beginners may not feel a bit beyond their depth—"

"Nonsense!" Miss Higby promptly retorted. "As Plaut and Samish dis*tinct*ly state in their final chapter. . . ."

That was the crowning argument. No one teaching English to foreigners could fault a fiat from the magisterial opus of Plaut and Samish.

So it was that when he faced the class the next Tuesday night, a beautiful night, soft and smelling of spring, Mr. Parkhill produced his portable Shakespeare. The love Miss Higby felt for poetry in general was nothing compared to the love Mr. Parkhill bore for Shakespeare in particular. (How many years was it since he had played Polonius at Amherst?)

"Tonight, class," Mr. Parkhill smiled, "I am going to try a little—experiment."

Thirty heads swung upward. Sixty eyes turned guarded. The beginners' grade had learned to regard Mr. Parkhill's innovations with foreboding.

"We shall take a little excursion into poetry—great poetry—from the greatest master English has ever known. . . ." Mr. Parkhill delivered a little sermon on the special beauty of poetry, its charm and precision and economy, its revelation of the loftiest thoughts and emotions of mankind. "I think this will be a welcome relief, to all of us, from our—er—run-of-the-mill exercises!" The approving nods and murmurs heartened Mr. Parkhill no end. "So . . . I shall write a famous passage on the board. I shall read it for you. Then, as our Recitation and Speech exercise, you will give short addresses, using the passage as the—springboard, as it were, for your own interpretation: your own thoughts and ideas and reactions."

He could not remember the last time an announcement had so roused the rows before him.

"Bravo!" sang Carmen Caravello.

"How my mohther did lof Heinrich Heine," sighed Mr. Finsterwald.

Miss Mitnick blushed, mingling pride and wonder. Mr. Bloom clucked—but rather cagily. Mrs. Rodriguez wrinkled her nose: *her* last foray into loftiness was a speech praising Brooklyn Bridge. And Hyman Kaplan, the smile on his face more salubrious than ever, showered Mr. Parkhill with expressions of admiration, whispering: "Poyetry. Now is poyetry! My! Must be som progriss ve makink!"

"The passage," said Mr. Parkhill, "is from Shakespeare."

A bolt of lightning could not have electrified the room more than did the magic of that name.

"*Shakes*peare?!" echoed Mr. Perez. "Eee-ai-ee!"

"The greatest poet from English?" gasped Miss Ziev.

"Imachine!" murmured Mr. Kaplan. "Villiam Jakesbeer!"

" '*Shakes*peare,' Mr. Kaplan, not '*Jakes*beer'!"

Mr. Parkhill took a fresh stick of chalk to write the passage on the board in large, crystal-clear letters:

> Tomorrow, and tomorrow, and tomorrow
> Creeps in this petty pace from day to day,
> To the last syllable of recorded time;
> And all our yesterdays have lighted fools
> The way to dusty death.

"Be*au*riful!" glowed Mr. Kaplan.

>   Out, out, brief candle!
> Life's but a walking shadow, a poor player
> That struts and frets his hour upon the stage,
> And then is heard no more; it is a tale
> Told by an idiot—

"True; sod, but true," moaned Olga Tarnova.

>   —full of sound and fury,
> Signifying nothing.

The hush of consecration muffled that mundane chamber. Open mouths and suspended breaths, gulps of awe and gapes of reverence edified the eyes that drank in the deathless phrases of the immortal bard. Even Nathan P. Nathan sat solemn.

Mr. Parkhill cleared his throat. "I shall read the passage aloud. Please listen carefully; let Shakespeare's words—I know some are difficult—sink into your minds . . . 'Tomorrow, and tomorrow and tomorrow . . .' " Mr. Parkhill read very well; and this night he endowed each word with an eloquence even Miss Higby would have admired. " 'Out, out, brief candle!' " Miss Mitnick's face was bathed in wonderment. " 'Life's but a walking shadow . . .' " The brow of Gus Matsoukas furrowed. " 'It is a tale told by an idiot . . .' " Mr. Kaplan's cheeks were incandescent. " '. . . full of sound and fury . . .' " Mr. Trabish's eyes were shut. (Mr.

133

Parkhill could not tell whether Mr. Trabish had surrendered to the spell of Shakespeare or the arms of Morpheus.) " '. . . signifying nothing!' " Miss Goldberg fumbled for a jellybean.

"I—shall read the passage once more." Mr. Parkhill's voice was so loud and clear that it roused Mr. Trabish from his coma. " 'Tomorrow, and tomorrow, and tomorrow . . .' "

After Mr. Parkhill completed that incomparable passage, he surveyed his congregation gravely. "I am sure there are words, here and there, which some of you may find—uh—difficult. Before I call upon you to recite, please feel free to ask—"

Freedom of inquiry erupted within the instant. Mrs. Tomasic asked if "petty" was the diminutive of "pet." (Mr. Parkhill could scarcely blame her for asking if it could be used for her neighbor's "small white rabbi.") Wolfgang Schmitt asked why "frets" lacked a capital "f." (The meticulous butcher thought "frets" was the Americanized form of "Fritz.") Mrs. Shimmelfarb wondered whether "creeps" was a variation of "creaks." Miss Gidwitz, who was exceedingly clothes-conscious, asked if "fury" was the "old-fashion" way of spelling "furry" (her new coat was a beautiful "tweet" with "a furry collar").

Each of these queries Mr. Parkhill explained with patience. " 'Petty' means trivial, mean, or—not worthy, as in 'Jealous people tend to be petty.' . . . 'Frets,' Mr. Schmitt, means to be impatient, showing discontent, as in 'She frets because her train is late!' . . . 'Creeps,' Mrs. Shimmelfarb, means to move slowly, *very* slowly; for instance, 'A turtle *creeps* through the grass.' . . . And 'fury,' Miss Gidwitz, denotes a powerful emotion, not an animal's—er—hide. . . . Anyone else?"

Up stabbed the finger of Casimir Scymczak. "Why," he mumbled, "is no 'l' in word 'pace'? Wrong spalled?!" Mr. Parkhill saw in a flash that Mr. Scymczak was confusing motion with location. "The spelling is entirely correct: you see, *'pace'* is in no way related to *'place.'*" Mr. Parkhill found, to his surprise, that he was beginning to perspire. "'Pace' means the rate or speed of movement, as 'The soldiers marched at a brisk pace,' or 'The cars moved in slow, respectful pace to the cemetery.'"

This saddened Mr. Scymczak.

"Are we ready now, class?"

"No!" came from sultry Miss Tarnova. "Did Shakespeare steal that whole idea from Dostoevsky?!"

Before Mr. Parkhill could nip this delusion in the bud, Mr. Kaplan wheeled around. "Are you *crazy?* You talkink about *Jakes*beer!"

*"Shakes*peare, Mr.—"

"I'm sick an' tiret hearing soch chipp remocks. Lat's begin recitink!"

Mr. Parkhill wiped his palms. (He felt rather grateful to Mr. Kaplan.) "Very well, class . . . Miss Caravello."

Miss Caravello lunged to the podium. "Da poem isa gooda!" she proclaimed. "Itsa have beautiful wordsa, *bella*, lak great musica anda deepa, deepa philosophy. Shakespeare isa lak Alighieri Dante, da greatest Italiano—"

"Vhat?!" bristled Mr. Kaplan. "Shakesbeer you compare mit Dante? *Shakesbeer?!* Ha!"

"Mr. Kaplan, Miss Caravello is merely expressing her opinion."

"Dat's not an opinion, it's a crime! How ken she compare a ginius like Shakesbeer mit a dantist like Dante?!"

"Dante wasa no dentist!" fumed Miss Caravello. "He—"

"He didn't iven stody *teet?*" purred Mr. Kaplan.

Miss Caravello blazed an execration from her homeland and shot back to her seat, gibbering calumnies worthy of Juvenal. Mrs. Shimmelfarb soothed her with sympathy. Miss Goldberg offered her a sourball.

Mr. Parkhill felt dizzy.

"Corrections, anyone?"

Aside from Mr. Trabish's sleepy remark anent Miss Caravello's tendency to add the vowel "a" to any word in sight, and a gritty observation from Mr. Perez that *"bella"* was a foreign word "and we supposed dzhust to talk English!" criticism expired.

The next speaker, Mrs. Yanoff, began, "This pome is full high meanings." Her eyes, however, were fixed on the floor. "Is hard for a person who is not so good in English to catch all. But I like."

" 'Like'?!" flared Mr. Kaplan. "Batter *love,* Yanoff! Mit Shakesbeer must be *love!*"

"Mr. Kaplan . . ."

Mrs. Yanoff staggered through several skittish comments and stumbled back to safety.

Next came Norman Bloom. Mr. Kaplan groaned. Mr. Bloom was as brisk, bald, and emphatic as ever. Only his peroration was unexpected: "But Shakespeare's *ideas* are too passimistical. I am an optimist. Life should be with hope and happy! . . . So, remember—this is only a poem, by a man full of gloomy! I say, 'Mr. Shakespeare, why don't you look for a silver lining on the sonny side of each street?' "

"Bloooom!" bawled anguished Kaplan. "You forgat how *honist* is Shakesbeer! He is a passimist because *life* is a passimist also!"

"Not *my* life!" sneered Mr. Bloom.

"You not dad yat," observed Mr. Kaplan, not without regret.

Nathan P. Nathan caterwauled.

"Gentlemen!" Mr. Parkhill was growing quite alarmed. It was clear that Mr. Kaplan had so identified himself with Shakespeare that he would not tolerate the slightest disparagement of his alter ego. How harness so irate a champion? How dampen such flames of grandeur? Perhaps the best course (Mr. Parkhill stifled many misgivings) was to call on Mr. Kaplan at once.

After pointing out several flaws in Mr. Bloom's syntax, and the thoroughly improper use of "gloomy" as a noun, Mr. Parkhill said, "Mr. Kaplan, you—er—seem to be bubbling with so many ideas, perhaps you—would prefer to recite?"

The smile that spread across Mr. Kaplan's countenance rivaled a rainbow. *"Me* next?" The innocent blink of surprise, the fluttering lashes of unworthiness—rarely was modesty so fraudulent.

"Yes."

"Now comes the circus!" announced laughing Nathan. "Rose, get ready all your penecils and all your paper!"

"Go, Keplen!" grinned Mr. Pinsky.

"Trobble, trobble," moaned Olga Tarnova.

"For God's sek, talk *briff!"* growled Mr. Blattberg.

"Give him a *chence!"* snapped "Cookie" Kipnis.

"Oyyy," forecast Mrs. Moskowitz.

Mr. Kaplan rose with dignity, slowly, affecting the manner of one lost in unutterable profundities. In stately stride he mounted the platform. He clutched his lapels à la Daniel Webster. Never had the plump figure appeared so lordly, or displayed such consciousness of a rendezvous with history. He surveyed the ranks before him, thoughtful, silent, deliberating how to clothe majesty in words fit for commoners.

"Omi*god!"* blared Mr. Blattberg.

"So *talk!"* glowered Mr. Matsoukas.

"You are waiting for *bugles?"* taunted Miss Valuskas.

Mr. Kaplan ignored the carping crowd. "Fallow lovers of fine literature. Edmirers of immortable poyetry."

" 'Immor*tal,' "* Mr. Parkhill put in. (He would not have been surprised if Mr. Kaplan had launched into "Friends, Romans, countrymen . . .") "And it's *'po*-etry,' not *'poy-*

etry.' If you will try to speak more slowly, Mr. Kaplan, I'm sure you will make fewer mistakes."

Mr. Kaplan inclined his head graciously. "So I'll begin over . . . Ladies an' gantlemen . . . Ve hoid fine spitches by odder mambers of de cless abot dese vunderful voi—*wor*ds from Shakesbeer. Vell, are you sarisfite?"

" 'Satisfie*d'*!"

"Not me. I am ebsolutely not sa*ti*sfite. Because to me dose movvelous *wor*ds on de blackboard are not *wor*ds! Dey are jools! Poils! Diamonds!"

"Psssh!" crowed Mr. Pinsky.

"T'ink abot it, cless. T'ink *bilow* an' *arond* dose ectual phrases Shakesbeer put in de mot of—of who? Dat's de important point! *Who is talkink?* A man mit a tarrible problem lookink him in de face. Try to remamber how dat man, Julius Scissor, himsalf falt—"

"Mr. Kaplan! It was *not* Julius—"

The eulogist heard him not. "—on dat historical night! Because in dose movvelous *wor*ds on dis simple bleck-board"—he flung out his right arm, as if from under a toga, pointing to the fateful passage—"Julius Scissor is sayink—"

"Mr. *Kap*lan! That passage is from *Macbeth!"*

Hyman Kaplan stopped in his tracks. He stared at his master as if at his executioner. *"Not* from *Julius Scissor?!"*

"No, no!"

Mr. Kaplan gulped. "I vas sure—"

"The passage is from *Macbeth,* Mr. Kaplan. And it's not Julius 'S*cis*sor'—but Julius C*ae*sar!"

Woe drowned the once lofty countenance. "Excuse me. But isn't a 'seezor' vhat you cottink somt'ink op mit?"

"That," said Mr. Parkhill, "is '*sci*ssor.' You have used 'Caesar' for 'scissor' and 'scissor' for 'Caesar'!"

"My!" Mr. Kaplan was marveling at his virtuosity.

Mr. Parkhill stood shaken. He blamed himself for not

having announced at the very beginning that the passage was from *Macbeth.* "Mr. Kaplan, may I ask what on earth made you think that the passage is from *Julius Caesar?*"

"Because I see it all before mine two ice! De whole scinn —just like a movie. Ve are in Julius's tant. It's de night bafore dey making him Kink fromm Rome. So he is axcited, netcheral, an' he ken't slip—"

" 'Sleep.' "

"—so he's layink in his bad, t'inking: 'Tomorrow an' tomorrow an' tomorrow. How slow dey movink. Dey practically cripp. Soch a pity de pace!' "

Before Mr. Parkhill could protest that "petty pace" did not mean "Soch a pity de pace!" Mr. Kaplan, batteries recharged, had swept ahead: "An' he t'inks: 'Oh, how de time goes slow, fromm day to day, like leetle tsyllables on phonograph racords of time.' "

"Mr. Kap—"

" 'An' vhat abot yastidday?' esks Julius Scissor. Ha!" Mr. Kaplan's eyes blazed. " 'All our yastiddays are only a light for fools to die in de dost!' "

" 'Dusty death' does not mean—" But no dam could block that mighty flood.

"An' Julius Scissor is so tiret, an' vants to slip, so he hollers, mit fillink, 'Go ot, go ot, short candle!' "

Mr. Parkhill sank into a chair.

"So de candle goes ot." Mr. Kaplan's voice dropped to a whisper. "Still, pracious slip von't come to Julius. Now is bodderink him de whole idea fromm Life. 'Vhat is Life altogadder?' t'inks Julius Scissor. An' he gives his own soch an enswer!—de pot of dat pessitch I like bast!"

" '*Pas*sage,' " groped Mr. Parkhill.

" 'Life is like a bum actor, strottink an' hollerink arond de stage for vun hour bafore he's kicked ot! *Life?* Ha! It's a pail full of idjots—' "

"No, *no!* A *'tale'* not a *'pail'*—"

139

" '—full of funny sonds an' phooey!' "

" 'Sound and fury!' " cried the frantic tutor.

" 'Life is monkey business! It don't minn a t'ing! It single-flies nottink!' . . . Den Julius closes his ice fest"—Mr. Kaplan demonstrated Caesar's exact ocular process by closing his own "ice"—"an' drops dad!"

Silence throbbed its threnody in that hall of learning. Even Miss Tarnova, Mr. Blattberg, flighty Miss Gidwitz sat magnetized by such eloquence. Nathan P. Nathan was holding Miss Mitnick's hand. Miss Goldberg sucked a mint.

Mr. Kaplan nodded philosophically. "Yas, Scissor, great Scissor, dropped dad, forever!" He left the hallowed podium. But just before he took his seat, Mr. Kaplan added this postscript: "Dat vas mine idea. But ufcawss it's all wronk, because Mr. Pockheel axplained how it's not abot Julius Scissor altogadder." A sigh. "It's abot an Irishman by de name MacBat!"

It seemed an age before Mr. Parkhill reached his desk, and another before he could bring himself to concentrate on Mr. Kaplan's memorial. For Mr. Parkhill found it hard to wrench his mind back to the cold world of grammar and syntax. Like his students, he was still trying to tear himself away from that historic tent outside Rome, where "Julius Scissor," cursed with insomnia, had pondered time and life, and philosophized himself to a strange and sudden death.

Mr. Parkhill felt distinctly annoyed with Miss Higby.

13

VOCABULARY, VOCABULARY!

"Vocabulary!" Mr. Parkhill thought. "Above all, I must help them increase their vocabularies."

He was probably right. What the students in the beginners' grade most needed, what they could put to instant use, was a copious supply of words: English words, words for naming ordinary objects, asking simple questions, describing everyday experiences. If one weighted the respective merits of vocabulary and, say, spelling, as Mr. Parkhill had spent many an hour doing, one would be forced to decide in favor of devoting more time to the former than the latter. However basic spelling is (and to Mr. Parkhill nothing was more basic) it is nonetheless not so pressing *outside* a classroom to adults who do little actual writing in their daily work and life.

"After all," Mr. Parkhill had put it to Miss Higby, "one does not need to know how to *spell* English in order to use it!"

"Our students certainly prove that," Miss Higby had replied.

What about grammar? Mr. Parkhill had spent an entire weekend debating the comparative importance of vocabulary and grammar. What he concluded was that for newcomers, vocabulary must be given priority over grammar. His pupils needed words, phrases, idioms to which gram-

141

mar could be *applied.* Of what use is grammar, after all, until one had the words to use that grammar on? Grammar without words was like—well, like a useless skeleton. And one needed the word "skeleton" before one could even say what a skeleton *is.*

"Words are the basic *bricks,"* he said to Miss Higby, "whereas grammar is the building."

Miss Higby gazed at him in admiration. "Have you just made that up, Mr. Parkhill?"

"I think so."

"But that's very *good!"* exclaimed Miss Higby. "Why, it's more graphic than anything in Plaut and Samish!" (That was just about as high praise as anyone could receive from Miss Higby.)

What about pronunciation? There certainly was a strong, strong case to be made for pronunciation. (Only last Tuesday, Mr. Hyman Kaplan had waxed lyrical about such favorite foods as "rose beef, cinema toast, and pie à-la-Moe.") Mr. Parkhill often toyed with the unhappy idea that correct English pronunciation might simply be beyond some of his fledglings' capacities.

Take the "th" sound. What could appear so simple? Yet Mr. Wolfgang Schmitt had spoken German for so many years before coming to the American Night Preparatory School for Adults that his tongue-and-teeth coordination were frozen into patterns which just could not pronounce the "th" except as "s." (In one recitation, it was impossible to know whether Mr. Schmitt was discussing "themes" or "seams.") Other students would never be able to pronounce the "th" except as "z." (It had unnerved Mr. Parkhill to hear Mr. Finsterwald describe a political rally in which "zree zousant zroats" had acclaimed the speaker.) Or take Mr. Kaplan. Mr. Parkhill sighed. (He had fallen into the habit of sighing whenever Mr. Kaplan invaded his ruminations.) Mr. Kaplan was a willing, diligent student.

Yet, despite Mr. Parkhill's persistent lecturings about the need to exercise care in pronouncing words, Mr. Kaplan had recently said of the Mayor of New York that he showed a fine set of teeth "vhenever he greens." Another time, so deceived could Mr. Kaplan's *hearing* be, when asked to use "heaven" in a sentence, he had replied: "In sommer, ve all heaven a fine time."

At that moment, Mr. Parkhill had spotted an important linkage between vocabulary *and* pronunciation: to teach one could produce the side-effect of *teaching the other, too!* Mr. Parkhill had scarcely been able to sleep, one night, so full was his mind with the methods he would employ to teach his flock vocabulary in such a way that they would see the crucial difference between, say, "these" and "seize"—or even between "box" and "bucks." (It was terribly confusing to have a student talk about money all the while Mr. Parkhill thought he was referring to deer.)

Vocabulary! The last shred of doubt vanished from Mr. Parkhill's mind. He could hardly wait for the evening to come.

". . . so tonight I shall call off a list of words, simple, *useful* words, words which you will find helpful in your daily life. I shall assign three words to each of you. Write three sentences in your notebook, using each word in a separate sentence . . . Miss Valuskas? Yes, you certainly may use your dictionary . . . When you are finished, go to the board and copy your sentences."

The class seemed quite pleased by vocabulary. Miss Mitnick's self-effacing pallor changed to one of pink eagerness. Mr. Bloom announced public approval: "I like vocabulary!" Mrs. Moskowitz even prepared her notebook without a single prophetic "Oy!" Young Mr. Nathan chuckled. And Mr. Kaplan opened his box of crayons, smiled a solar smile, turned to a fresh page in his notebook

143

and, long before Mr. Parkhill even reached his name in the alphabetical roll, printed:

VOCAPULARY

(Prectice in Book. Then Go to Blackb. and putting on.)

by

H* Y* M* A* N   K* A* P* L* A* N

Mr. Parkhill called off the words: "Mr. Blattberg: 'sugar . . . camera . . . breakfast. . . .' Mr. Bloom: 'bicycle . . . delicious . . . policeman. . . .' "

The beginners' grade heaved into action. Brows furrowed, chins were stroked, heads scratched, dictionaries riffled. "Mr. Kaplan, your words are: 'pitcher . . . fascinate . . . university.' "

Mr. Parkhill noticed that Mr. Kaplan's thinking process involved closing one eye, cocking his head to one side, pronouncing each word to himself, then, emerging from his interior caucus, testing the word in a sentence in a whisper that could be heard with ease anywhere in the room. " 'Pitcher . . . pitcher . . .' " Mr. Kaplan murmured. "Is maybe a pitcher for *milk?* Could be. . . . Is maybe a pitcher on de vall? Also could be. Aha! So is *two* minninks! Exemples: 'Plizz put milk in de pitcher.' Or 'De pitcher hengs cockeye.' "

Suddenly it dawned on Mr. Parkhill that Mr. Kaplan's soliloquy was not a mannerism but a stratagem: for as he murmured a sentence with one eye closed, he watched Mr. Parkhill out of the eye that was open. The man was trying to discern from his teacher's expressions which interpretation of "pitcher" would be acceptable! Mr. Parkhill froze his features into neutrality.

Soon, four students trooped to the blackboard, transcribed their sentences and returned to their seats. When Mr. Kaplan finished his three sentences, he glanced proudly toward Mr. Parkhill (who, pretending to scruti-

144

nize the blackboard, was unconsciously watching Mr. Kaplan out of the corner of *his* eye) and hurried to the front of the room.

"Well," said Mr. Parkhill after the boards could take no more chalking, "let's start at—er—this end. Mr. Bloom."

Norman Bloom read his sentences with crisp authority.

1. She needs a *bicicle.*
2. The soup is *delicious.*
3. Last Saturday, I found a *policeman.*

"Excellent!" said Mr. Parkhill. "Are there any questions?"

There were no questions.

"Any—uh—*corrections? . . .* Mr. Bloom spelled one word incorrectly."

There were no corrections either. So Mr. Parkhill changed "bicicle" to "bicycle," pointing out the amusing difference between a cycle and an icicle. ("My!" Mr. Kaplan exclaimed.) The exercise marched on.

On the whole, things went surprisingly well. Except for young Mr. Nathan's misuse of "chorus" ("She sings in the school chores") and Mr. Blattberg's unfortunate twisting of "tan" ("one, two, three . . . nine, tan"), the students' sentences were quite good. Vocabulary was proving a decided success.

"Next . . . Mr. Kaplan."

Mr. Kaplan rose. "Mine foist void, ladies an' gantleman an' Mr. Pockheel"—Mr. Kaplan would be crushed if denied his introductory fanfare—"is 'pitcher.' I am usink it in dis santence: 'Oh, how beauriful is dis pitcher.' "

Mr. Parkhill hesitated. "Er—Mr. Kaplan, the word I gave you was 'pi*tch*er,' not 'pi*ct*ure.' "

"Mr. Pockheel, dis void *is*—"

"No, no. When you say, 'Oh, how *beautiful'* are you not in fact talking about a pi*ct*ure?!"

145

Mr. Kaplan consulted his Muse. "If you *pay* enough for a pitcher it's as beauriful—"

Mr. Parkhill winced. He had been gulled: Hyman Kaplan had straddled both words through a canny use of one. "Read your next sentence."

"De sacond void," declaimed Hyman Kaplan, "is 'fessinate'—an' believe me dat is a planty hod void! So is mine santence: 'In Hindia, is all kinds snake fessinators.' "

"You are thinking of snake *charmers,*" said Mr. Parkhill.

"Snek *'chommers'*? In mine dictionary I couldn't find 'fessin—' "

"That's probably because it's spelled with an 's-*c*-,' " Mr. Parkhill explained; and (before anyone could blurt "Why?") went on: "Suppose you try the word in another sentence. 'Fascinate' in its active sense means to attract, to interest greatly; or, if one *is* fascinated, it means to *be* intensely interested or attracted to . . ."

"Hau Kay." Mr. Kaplan took thought and said, "You fessinate me."

Mr. Parkhill asked Mr. Kaplan to read his last sentence.

"Mine toid void is 'univoisity.' "

"That should be 'my'—not 'mine'—'th*ir*d w*or*d is univ*er*sity'!"

But Mr. Kaplan had already launched into his crowning sentence: " 'Elaven yiss dey are married, so is time for de tvalft univoisity.' "

"Mistake!" chirped Miss Mitnick. "Mr. Kaplan mixes up two words. He means *'anni*versary,' which comes each year. But 'university' is a college—the highest college!"

"Good for Rose Mitnick!" called Miss Pomeranz.

"Very good, Miss Mitnick," said Mr. Parkhill. "Do you see the difference, Mr. Kaplan?"

Mr. Kaplan, who had listened to Miss Mitnick with courtly sufferance, wrinkled his nose.

"Try another sentence using 'university.' "

"Som pipple didn't have iven vun day's aducation in a *univ*oisity"—Mr. Kaplan's glance at Miss Mitnick was withering—"but still, efter elaven yiss marritch dey have deir tvalft *ann*ivoisery!"

Miss Mitnick bit her lip. Mr. Nathan winked at her, with some effect.

"Keplen never sorrenders!" crowed Mr. Pinsky.

"He never gives an *inch!*" wailed Bessie Shimmelfarb.

"Oy!" scowled Mrs. Moskowitz.

"Next student."

Throughout the remaining recitations, Mr. Kaplan sat strangely silent. He did not bother to comment on Mrs. Yanoff's spectacular misuse of "guess" ("Turn off the guess"). He did not so much as take a side-swipe at Carmen Caravello's unfortunate use of "omit" ("The child omits a cry"). He let pass even Casimir Scymczak's egregious use of "hoarse" ("He hollers until his troat feels like a horse").

Throughout the lively discussion each of these solecisms triggered, Mr. Kaplan kept a cryptic smile glued to his lips. It was obvious that in his sensitive soul smoldered the memory of humiliation at the hands of Rose Mitnick.

Mr. Parkhill felt uneasy. "Miss Mitnick, I believe you are last . . ."

Miss Mitnick rose, blushing, and in a tremulous timbre read: " '*Enamel* is used for painting chairs.' "

Out rang Mr. Kaplan's voice: "Mistake by Mitnick!" It was more like a battlecry than a notification. "Ha! Mit *enimals* she is painting chairs?! Mit monkeys—or pussy-cets—"

"The word is 'e*na*mel'!" said Mr. Parkhill, severely. "Not 'animal.' Miss Mitnick is absolutely right."

Mr. Kaplan looked as if he had been stabbed in the back.

"Good for Miss Mitnick," laughed Mr. Vinograd.

"Shame, shame, Mr. Koplon!"

147

So profound was Mr. Kaplan's mortification that he allowed Miss Mitnick's reading of her next sentences to go unchallenged. (There was, in truth, little anyone *could* challenge in Miss Mitnick's, "Oh, how men are selfish in every *century.*" Or in her wistful, "I wish I could play any *piano.*")

Miss Mitnick's final sentence was a *tour de force:* "In English movies, we see that the prisoner stands in a courts *dock.*"

"Mistake by Mitnick!" cried Mr. Kaplan.

Mr. Parkhill tried to head him off. "There should be a certain punctuation mark, Miss Mitnick, in 'courts.' . . ."

"Dat's not my mistake!" Mr. Kaplan was aggrieved.

"I—" flushed Miss Mitnick. "I—forgot to put the apostrophe betwin 't' and 's'!"

"Exactly!" Mr. Parkhill chalked the sign of the possessive. "Very good, Miss Mitnick."

"Still not my mistake!" declared Mr. Kaplan. "De void 'dock' is used wronk!"

"Not at all! Miss Mitnick has used 'dock' in one of its perfectly proper uses. In England, those accused of a crime do stand on a raised platform, which is popularly called the—er—'dock.' "

"I am t'inkink abot Americans."

"Well, Mr. Kaplan, there *is* a more—familiar American usage. Can you use 'dock' that way, Miss Mitnick?"

Miss Mitnick floundered in cerebration.

Miss Ziev went to the ladies' room.

"Anyone . . . ?" asked Mr. Parkhill.

"I like roast dock," said Mr. Kaplan.

"No, no, no! That word is 'd*u*ck'! There is all the difference in the *world,* Mr. Kaplan, between a 'dock' and a 'duck'!" Mr. Parkhill placed "dock" and "duck" on the board with a decisiveness that matched his speed. "You *see* how important enunciation is, class? Mr. Kaplan is

148

confusing the 'u' sound with the 'o' sound—just as he does when he pronounces 'bog' as—er—'bug'! If we learn to speak carefully, we will be helped to spell correctly. And vice versa!"

Mr. Kaplan looked woebegone. Mr. Marcus looked blissful.

"Notice once more the word I gave Miss Mitnick. It is not a hard word, class." Mr. Parkhill tapped each letter with his pointer. " 'D-o-c-k' . . . Now, anyone?"

Anyone, alas, became no one.

"Let me give you a hint, class. Each of you, in coming to America, had *direct experience with a dock.*" Mr. Parkhill paused. "Now is that clearer? *Think,* class."

The class fell into a frenzied search of memory. (Mrs. Moskowitz, reliving her seasickness, searched no further.) Mr. Perez scratched his scalp to stimulate his powers of recall. Miss Goldberg enlisted the aid of a piece of peanut brittle. Mr. Pinsky, who was scanning a comic book, made no response at all. And Mr. Kaplan, desperate to make the dramatic, redeeming kill, rummaged through his associations in frantic whisperings: " 'Dock' . . . Commink to America . . . old boat . . . big wafes . . . seeink lend. . . ."

They were getting nowhere. Miss Kipnis kept wrinkling her brow in vain. Oscar Trabish had slid into slumber. Mr. Norman Bloom apparently forgot all about "dock" (he was, in fact, recalling a pinochle game on the S.S. *Potovski,* in which he had won four and a half dollars) and mopped his bald dome.

"I'll make it even easier," blurted Mr. Parkhill. "Where did your boats land?"

"Alice Island!" beamed Hyman Kaplan.

Mr. Parkhill frowned. "You landed at *E*llis, not *A*lice, Island. But in discussing the word 'dock' *I* meant specifically—"

An ululation of pure joy ascended. "I got him! Ufcawss!

149

'Dock!' Plain an' tsimple! Ha!" Mr. Kaplan shot a scathing arrow at Rose Mitnick. "I'm soprise a student like Mitnick shouldn't know a plain void like 'dock.' I got de enswer! Mr. Pockheel—"

How Mr. Parkhill wished that some other student—any other student—would volunteer. His glance swept the ranks. "Miss Valuskas?"

Miss Valuskas looked limp.

"Mrs.—Shimmelfarb?"

Mrs. Shimmelfarb looked haggard.

"Mr. Matsoukas?"

Mr. Gus Matsoukas was totally deaf to Mr. Parkhill's words; he seemed hypnotized by Mr. Kaplan's hand, which was wig-wagging like a metronome.

Mr. Parkhill confronted the inevitable. "Very well . . . Mr. Kaplan."

The man from "Alice Island" said, "Hello, *Doc!*"

Even while shaking his head frostily to inform Mr. Kaplan that he had gone wildly astray once more, Mr. Parkhill thought, "Vocabulary. Above all, we *must* increase their vocabulary!"

14

CAPTAIN K·A·P·L·A·N

Mr. Parkhill was not at all surprised when the first three students delivered orations on "Abraham Lincoln," "Little George and the Sherry Tree," and "Wonderful America," respectively. During the month of February, the classrooms of the American Night Preparatory School for Adults throbbed with patriotic fervor, and the passionate *amor patriae* usually welled well into March.

The cause was simple: Mr. Robinson, the school principal, could never allow the birthdays of Lincoln and Washington to pass uncelebrated. On each of these hallowed occasions, the entire student body crowded into Franklin Hall (that Benjamin Franklin's nativity went uncommemorated was something Mr. Parkhill always deplored) for a solemn ceremony.

At the Lincoln assembly, each year, Mr. Robinson delivered a tribute entitled "The Great Emancipator." ("His name is inscribed on the tablet of history, in letters of eternal gold!") After that, the star student from the senior class delivered a pithy oration, which Mrs. O'Hallohan had edited. Then Miss Higby recited Walt Whitman's "O Captain! My Captain!" No one could elocute "O Captain! My Captain!" the way Miss Higby did, and each time she finished, the students shook Franklin's walls with their ovation.

For the Washington convocation, the order of things was much the same: Mr. Robinson's address was entitled "The Immortal Father of Our Country." ("First in war, first in peace, first in the hearts of his countrymen—yes, but far more than that! His name will forever burn in the hearts of true Americans, old *or* new, a glowing ember, a glorious reminder of his deathless achievement!") The star student's speech usually eulogized "Crossing the Delaware" or mourned "The Terrible Winter at Valley Forge." Then Mr. Krout would recite the words of "The Star-Spangled Banner" in his most solemn manner. The ceremony ended with faculty and students together singing "My Country, 'Tis of Thee."

So dramatic were these rites that for weeks afterward, each year, every teacher in the A.N.P.S.A. was deluged with essays on Lincoln or Washington, speeches on the Gettysburg Address or the Declaration of Independence, even poems, odes and ditties on Lincoln *and* Washington. Night after night, the classrooms echoed the historic phrases: "1776," "Honest Abe," "Bunker Hill." Miss Schnepfe, Mr. Robinson's assistant, dubbed the annual rites "The Ides of February and March." (Sixteen years under Mr. Robinson certainly had sharpened Louella Schnepfe's wit.)

Now, a full week after the successive convocations, the beginners' grade still luxuriated in tributes to their new-found heroes. The next-to-last student to face the class was Carmen Caravello. "I will spik ona man joosta lak Georgio Washington—great Giuseppe Garibaldi!"

After the torrent of benisons to Washington and Lincoln, Mr. Parkhill felt a surge of relief. It was short-lived.

"Garibaldi! Firsta in war, also in peace, *per primo* in da heartsa alla countryman!"

The scholars scarcely stirred. They were sated. Wolfgang Schmitt twiddled his thumbs. "Cookie" Kipnis dipped into Miss Goldberg's cache of "monkey nuts," Mr.

Trabish dozed so thoroughly that he might just as well have been in Mexico.

"Eacha letter isa *burn* (lak Mist' Robinson say): da 'g,' da 'a,' da 'r,' da 'i' . . ." Miss Caravello articulated the letters of Sicily's liberator with zeal. Mrs. Yanoff yawned.

Mr. Parkhill noticed that Mr. Kaplan, on his pre-empted throne in the center of the front row, had been sighing, twitching, coughing or snorting throughout the preceding orations. That was odd. For Mr. Kaplan to display ennui where Washington and Lincoln were concerned boded no good; Mr. Kaplan was yet to deliver his own ruminations.

"Anda I find out thata Giuseppe Garibaldi, *Comandante* of *Cacciatori delle Alpi,* he liveda here ina U.S.!"

Mr. Kaplan sat up, narrowing both eyes.

"He wasa working asa maker ofa candles!"

Mr. Kaplan's eyebrows doubled his disbelief.

"Anda I find out Garibaldi—wasa *citizen U.S.A.!* So— Horray, Georgio Washington! *Viva* Giuseppe Garibaldi! *Viva, viva, viva!"* With that triple display of chauvinism, Carmen Caravello flounced back to her seat.

Miss Mitnick breathed, "Oh, Carmen!"

Nathan P. Nathan patted the breathless eulogist on the back, but winked, renewing fealty, at Miss Mitnick.

"Da, da," moaned Olga Tarnova. "We should more respact great mon from *all* nations . . ."

"Thank you, Miss Caravello," said Mr. Parkhill. "That was very—thought-provoking. . . . Now, class, comments . . . ?"

Karl Finsterwald cited Miss Caravello's customary garbling of the past and present tenses. Gerta Valuskas criticized Miss Caravello's habit of attaching melodious "a"s right and left to English words which recoiled from them. Harry Feigenbaum suggested with steely rectitude that the proper phrasing was "foist *in* war, foist *in* peace, foist *in* the hearts his countrymen."

153

"Correct . . . right . . . quite so," said Mr. Parkhill. "Any more?"

The scornful tenor of Hyman Kaplan sliced through the air. "How can enybody compare a Judge Vashington mit a Gary Baldy? Ha!"

"Fathers of a country are alla same!" retorted Miss Caravello. "Heroes! Greata men!"

"*Candy* makers?" leered Mr. Kaplan.

" 'Can*dle,*' Mr. Kaplan, not '*candy*'!" Mr. Parkhill hastily intervened. "Miss Caravello happens to be right. It is a little-known fact that Garibaldi did work as a candlemaker . . . Any further comments? Very well; our final speaker is—Mr. Kaplan."

"Can't we skip him?" hissed Mr. Bloom, *sotto voce.*

"Oy," agreed Mrs. Moskowitz, *a priori.*

"Never!" cried Mr. Pinsky, *con brio.*

Deaf to both foe and friend, Mr. Kaplan strode frontwards. He turned to the divided tribunes, delicately buttoned his coat, made a slight bow to Mr. Parkhill, shot his cuffs and sang out: "Fallow petriots!" He paused for a fraction of a moment. "Judge Vashington! Abram Lincohen! Jake Popper!"

"Er—Mr. Kaplan," said Mr. Parkhill anxiously, *"please* watch your pronunciation. It's *'George'* not *'Judge'* 'Washington,' not *'Vashington.'* And 'Abra*ham* Lin*coln,'* not 'Abram Lin*cohen.'* " (Mr. Parkhill could think of nothing to say about Jake Popper, of whom he had never heard.)

"Hau Kay," conceded Hyman Kaplan. "So foist abot *Jaw*dge Washington. Ve—we all know abot his movvellous didds. How, beink a leetle boy, he chopped off all de cherries on a tree so he could enswer, 'I kennot tell a lie, Papa. I did it mit mine leetle hatchek.' "

" 'Hat*chet,*' not 'hat-*check*'!"

"Hat*chet.* . . . But ve shouldn't forgat more important

fects abot dis vunderful hero! *Jaw*dge *W*ashington vas a ravolutionist, fightink for friddom, friddom against de very bed Kink of England—"

" 'Kin*g*—' "

"—Kin*g* Jawdge Number Tree, dat no-goot autocrap who—"

" 'Auto*crat'!*" Mr. Parkhill was aghast.

"—who vas iven puddink stemps on *tea,* so it tasted tarrible! An' *Jaw*dge *W*ashington trew dat whole bunch tea in de vater fromm Boston Hobber, but he vas smot so he drassed op like a Hindian!"

"He was *not* in Boston, nor disguised as—" Mr. Parkhill might as well have been addressing a Zulu. The entire class hung on to Mr. Kaplan's orison: even vengeful Bloom, sullen Tarnova, prickly Blattberg—all seemed hypnotized by Mr. Kaplan's dramatic revision of history.

"My! Vas Jawdge a hero. Foist-cless! . . . Vun night in de meedle a frizzing vinter, he lad his loyal soldiers across de ice in a canoe—"

"*Mr.* Kap—"

"—because he knew he vould cetch de British an' all deir missionaries—"

" '*Mercen*aries'!"

"—foolink arond, not mit deir minds on duty! So *W*ashington von de var!"

" '*W*on the *w*ar!' " loud and clear went unheeded.

"So de pipple sad, 'Jawdge, you our hero! Our rill lidder! Ve love you! You should live till a hondrit an' tvanty yiss old! Ve elact you Prazident de whole U.S.A.' So he vas elacted—anonymously—"

Mr. Parkhill's " 'Un*an*imously' " drowned in the rolling wave of words.

"—an' like Mr. Robinson sad, before de whole school, 'In *W*ashington's name is itch ladder like a hot piece coal, boinink ot his gloryous achivmants!' " Mr. Kaplan embroidered the achievements with an imperial sweep of his arm.

"You *must* speak more slowly," protested Mr. Parkhill. (He could not forget that Lincoln and "Jake Popper" were yet to come.)

"I'll try." The noble sigh, the gracious inclination of the head—who could deny that though Hyman Kaplan's body was in the beginners' grade, his soul was in Carnegie Hall? "So now I toin to Abra*ham* Lincollen. Vat a human man. Vat a naubel cherecter. Vat a hot—like *gold!* Look, look!" Mr. Kaplan flung a finger toward the wall where a lithograph of the Great Emancipator reposed. "Look on dat sveet face! Look on dose ice, so sed mit fillink. Obsoive his mot, so full goodness. See his high forehat—showink tremandous *brens!*" Mr. Kaplan's searing glance at Miss Caravello suggested that brains were not Garibaldi's strong point. "Look on dat honest axpression! I esk you: Is it a vunder averybody called him 'Honest Abie'?"

" 'Honest Abe'!" Nathan P. Nathan laughed like a hyena.

The Cicero of the beginners' grade answered his own question. "No, it's no vunder. Lincollen vas a poor boy, a voodchopper, a rail-splinter. But he made de Tsivil Var." (Mr. Parkhill wiped his dampening brow.) "Oh, my, den came terrible times! Shoodink, killink, de Naut Site U.S. aganst de Sot Site U.S. Blecks aganst vhites, brodder fightink brodder . . . An' who von? *Who?* Ha! Abraham Lincollen!" Thrice did Kaplan nod. "So he decidet all bleck pipple should be exectly like vhite! Ufcawss, Lincollen couldn't change deir collars—"

" *'Col*ors,' not—"

"—de blecks still stayt bleck. But *free* bleck, not slafe bleck! Citizens, not kettle. Americans, true-blue, no metter how bleck. An' Lincollen gave ot de Mancipation Prockilmation: 'All men are born an' createt in de same vay!' So he vas killed!"

156

Mr. Kaplan paused, heavy of heart and funereal in manner. The eyes of Fanny Gidwitz glazed before him. The eyes of Sam Pinsky shone star-struck. Rochelle Goldberg fumbled for a gumdrop.

"So maybe you vonderink, 'Vat's all dis got to do mit Jake Popper?' " Their expressions testified to the fact that Mr. Kaplan had taken the question right out of his colleagues' mouths. "I'll axplain. Jake Popper also vas a fine man, like Abe Lincollen, mit a hot like gold. Ve called him 'Honest Jake.' "

Mr. Schmitt began to strangle.

"Jake Popper vasn't a beeg soldier like *W*ashington. He didn't make a Valley Fudge—"

" *'Forge*'!"

"—or free any slafes. . . . Jake Popper owned a dalicatessen. An' in dat store the poorest pipple, pipple mitout a panny, could alvays gat somting to itt."

" *'Eat*'!"

"Jake Popper vas ebsolutely a frand to de poor. He did a fine business—on cradit. So averybody loved him . . . Vun day, Honest Jake vas fillink vary bed. He had hot an' cold vaves on de body by de same time—vat doctors call a fivver—"

" *'F*e*ver*!' " pleaded Mr. Parkhill.

"—so averybody said, 'Jake, lay don in your bat, take it izzy, rast. But did Honest Jake lay don in his bat? Did he take it izzy—"

" *'Ea*sy.' "

"—an' rast? Not Jake Popper! He stood brave behind de conter in dat delicatessen, day an' night. He said, 'I got to soive mine customers!' Dat's de high sanse *duty* he had!" Whether from throat strain or emotion, hoarseness entered Mr. Kaplan's voice. "Oh, sed, sed, sed, to play mit halth for de sek of odders. . . . So dey had to call a doctor, and he came an' said, 'Mr. Popper, you got bronxitis!' So

157

Jake vent into his bat. An' got *more* seeck. So de foist doctor insulted odder doctors—"

"You mean *con*sulted'—"

"—an' dey took him to Mont Sinus Hospital—"

" 'Mount Sinai'!"

"—vhere dey fond Jake Popper had double demonia! So dey gave him spacial noises—"

" '*Nur*ses'!"

"—an' from all kinds madicine de bast, iven oxenjin tants, he should be able to breed. An' dey gave him blood confusions—"

" '*Trans*fusions'!"

"—an' dey shot him in de arm he should fall aslip, mit epidemics. An' efter three long dace and nights, Honest Jake Popper pest avay." The mention of death brought a hush sufficient to turn the classroom into a cemetery. Miss Mitnick lowered her head. Mr. Nathan tried to look glum. Mrs. Rodriguez fingered her crucifix. "So in Jake Popper's honor I'll recite a pome—like Miss Hikby did de same vit 'O Ceptin, my Ceptin!' " Mr. Kaplan lifted a paper from his pocket, raised both his head and the sheet high, and, as Mr. Parkhill sought solace in the ceiling, declaimed this benediction:

> "O hot! hot! hot!
> O de bliddink drops rad!
> Dere on de dack
> Jake Popper lies,
> Fallink cold an' dad!"

Celestial wings fluttered over the American Night Preparatory School for Adults; unseen angels mourned the grandeur that was Popper.

"Isn't dat beauriful?" sighed Mr. Kaplan.

Mr. Parkhill managed to find his voice. "Thank you, Mr.—"

158

But Mr. Kaplan was adding, "Vun ting more, so de cless shouldn't fill *too* bed abot Jake Popper. It's awreddy nine yiss since he pest avay!"

An invading giraffe would have caused no greater sensation.

"Hanh?!" howled Karl Finsterwald.

"Nine *year?!*" shouted Gus Matsoukas.

"Gentlemen—"

"Cookie" Kipnis shot Mr. Kaplan the furious look of one whose emotions had been cruelly exploited. Mr. Scymczak resorted to a Polish oath. Olga Tarnova moaned, "This mon . . . this *mon!*" Young Nathan was beating his thighs in glee.

"An' I didn't go to de funeral." With this extraordinary addendum, Hyman Kaplan, head bent in mourning, returned to his seat.

The class was in an uproar. They bellowed, they hooted, they protested a climax which negated all that had preceded it.

"He didn't went to *funeral?!*" Mrs. Yanoff could not believe anyone so cold-hearted.

"Oooy!"

"He did not even attand the soivices?!" boomed Mr. Bloom.

"I complain!" complained Mr. Perez.

"Class—"

"A shame, a scendel!"

"An insult to the dead!"

"Order, *please—*"

Mr. Blattberg's outrage was so great that it paralyzed his larynx, but this did not prevent him from twirling his gold chain with such vehemence that his grandson's baby tooth struck Miss Schneiderman on the elbow.

Suddenly Miss Valuskas demanded, *"Why you didn't go to the funeral?!"*

"Yas!"

"Enswer!"

"Som frand!"

"This is one excuse I'm dying—excuse the expression—to hear," bubbled Mr. Nathan.

"Class! I think—"

No one ever heard what Mr. Parkhill thought, for Mr. Kaplan had risen, stilling the carpers with one tolerant hand. "You all right to esk. Bot connsider de rizzon." His face was a study in both humility and nobility. "Jake Popper's funeral vas in de meedle of de veek. I sad to minesalf, 'Keplen, to go or not to go? Dat is de qvastion. Remamber, you are in America. So *t'ink* like an American!' So I t'ought. An' I didn't go, because I remambered dat fine Yenkee provoib: 'Business bafore plashure!' "

Pandemonium availed the mob nothing.

15

THE FEARFUL VENGEANCE
OF H·Y·M·A·N K·A·P·L·A·N

Mr. Parkhill wondered whether he had not been a bit rash vis-à-vis idioms. Idioms are, obviously, of crucial importance in English—or in any other language, for that matter. Was it not Aristotle who called idioms the very foundation of style? . . . Good style, Mr. Parkhill reflected sadly, was a distant dream for the beginners' grade; but idioms—idioms were an immediate necessity and an obstacle to progress.

As Plaut and Samish had so well put it:

> Idioms present a particularly difficult challenge to the teacher of English, since they are expressions, often colloquial, whose meaning may differ radically from the meanings of the separate words they employ. Hence, idioms may be both peculiar and exasperating to foreigners unfamiliar with their uniqueness.

Small wonder, then, that Mr. Parkhill had come to regard the idiom as a perverse creature, a goblin who played hob with his students' comprehension. "Is there anyone whose heart does not sink upon first encountering an idiom in a new tongue?" Mr. Parkhill once blurted to Miss Higby. "Why, idioms are like messages in code!"

"Coded messages?" Miss Higby had given him an odd look. "I never thought of it that way. . . ."

But a conscientious teacher *had* to think of it that way. How else explain "She gave him the cold shoulder"? Or "He walked me off my feet"? Or (Great Scott!) "He's going to the dogs"? The more he thought of it, the more Mr. Parkhill saw no way of postponing a lesson on idioms any longer.

So it was that on this gloomy, windswept night, he spent fifteen full minutes explaining to the beginners' grade what idioms are, how they grow, how they convey special, vivid ideas. He had illustrated his lecture with many a fascinating example. And now his students were going to the board, in groups of five, to transcribe the assignment: "Three short sentences, using an idiom in each."

The exercise was not proving altogether successful. Try though Mr. Parkhill did to gloss over the facts, he could not deny that idioms teetered on the brink of disaster.

Mr. Marcus, for example, had adorned the slate with:

> It will cost you free.

That, to Mr. Marcus, was an idiom.

Mrs. Tomasic had submitted only one sentence, so depleted was her morale by the complexity of the assignment:

> Honestly is the best policy.

Mr. Vincente Perez was groping in the right *direction,* at least, when he concocted:

> By 2 in the PM the job will be as good as down.

But Carmen Caravello had been driven delirious, it would seem, by idiom's drastic demands. How else explain:

Dont beet donkeys
Dont beet monkeys.
Dont hit babys (or members of family!)

Yes, it had been a trying—a most disappointing—night for Mr. Parkhill. He braced himself to confront the homework to the right of Miss Caravello's. Three lines loomed before him under a sort of marquee:

3 SENT. AND IDIOTS
by
H*Y*M*A*N   K*A*P*L*A*N

"Mr. *Kap*lan," said Mr. Parkhill, in horror, "the word is 'idioms,' not 'idiots'!" With uncharacteristic severity, he wiped IDIOTS off the slate and printed IDIOMS in its stead.

"My!" beamed Mr. Kaplan. "Som difference fromm vun lettle latter."

"There certainly is—as we have seen in many of our spelling drills. Why, just recall the consequences of misusing one *vowel,* in the test I gave the class Wednesday."

Up went the hand of Mr. Matsoukas. "I was not here Weddnesday. What was?"

Mr. Parkhill studied his chalk for a moment. "The exercise showed how important it is to watch every letter in your spelling; for one change, one addition, can make a world of difference." He cleared his throat. "I shall not be able to repeat *all* of last Wednesday's drill—"

"I work overtime Weddnesday," muttered Mr. Matsoukas.

"—but here are several examples." In a clear space on the board, Mr. Parkhill wrote:

sat
set
seat

163

sit
sot

"I theenk a nicer example ees 'hat,'" announced Mrs. Rodriguez.

"Very well." Mr. Parkhill wrote a column parallel to the one he had just completed:

hat
heat
hot
hoot
hit
hut

"*My* faworite was 'batter'!" chirped Miss Ziev.

"Yes," Mr. Parkhill nodded, "that *was* an effective example," and he wrote:

batter
better
bitter
biter
butter

"Good lesson," grunted Mr. Matsoukas.

"Good? It vas voit a million dollis!"

"Thank you, Mr. Kaplan. For more examples, see pages eighty-one through eighty-four of our text, Mr. Matsoukas. And I suspect we shall find similar—er—errors as we go along . . . Now, Mr. Kaplan, please read us your idioms."

Mr. Kaplan rose. "Ladies an' gentleman an' Mr. Pockheel. T'ree santences I vas wridink—"

"Can't you even *read* without a speech to Congress?" demanded Mr. Blattberg.

"—on de bleckboard." (Mr. Blattberg lived in limbo, as far as Mr. Kaplan was concerned.) "I tried in dis axercise to—"

Mr. Parkhill tapped the blackboard with his pointer.

164

"You—there is nothing to *explain,* Mr. Kaplan. Just read your sentences."

"I back your podden," sighed the penitent. "So—mine foist santence . . ." Mr. Kaplan read it:

1. He's nots.

Mr. Nathan fell off his chair.

Mr. Parkhill adjusted his glasses. "That is *not* an idiom, Mr. Kaplan. That's—slang."

The paling of his rosy features left no doubt that Mr. Kaplan had put his heart and soul into "He's nots."

"He's nots!" crowed Mr. Bloom. (It wasn't clear whether he was mocking Mr. Kaplan's sentence or describing his mental condition.)

"Ve hear many pipple usink dose exect voids!" Mr. Kaplan protested.

"It does not matter how many people say it, Mr. Kaplan. Besides, you spelled the word—er—'nuts' wrong."

"I dit?"

"It's 'n-*u*-t-s,' not 'n-*o*-t-s.' " Mr. Parkhill printed N-U-T-S on the board. "There, Mr. Matsoukas, is an excellent example of what I was stressing just a moment ago!"

Mr. Kaplan looked mortified. "Mine sacond santence. . . ." The second sentence was, if anything, more astonishing than the first:

2. Get the jams. By hook or cook!

"Is that English or Chinese?" jeered Mr. Blattberg.

"I think Mr. Kaplan meant 'gems,' not 'jams.' " Mr. Parkhill erased the latter and wrote the former.

" 'Jem' is for puttink on brat!" crowed Mrs. Moskowitz. "A 'gem' is for charity bells—"

" *'Balls,'* Mrs. Moskowitz. But let us get back to the idiom. 'By hook or cook' is *almost* correct, but—class, what is wrong?"

"Should be 'by hook *and* cook!' " sallied Miss Goldberg.

165

"That," said Mr. Parkhill glumly, "would only make it worse."

Miss Goldberg revived herself with a Life Saver.

"I think it should be, 'By hook or *crook,*'" blushed Miss Mitnick—at Mr. Nathan.

"Exactly! Thank you, Miss Mitnick. . . . '*Crook,*' Mr. Kaplan, not 'cook.'"

"I t'ought a 'crook' is a boiglar—"

" '*Bur*glar.' "

"—a chitter—"

" '*Cheat*er,' Mr. Kap—"

"—a plain, low-don tiff!"

" 'Thief'!" Mr. Parkhill's throat was getting dry. "The word 'crook' can mean any—or all—of those things; but the phrase 'by hook or by crook' means to use any means whatsoever to—er—get the gems."

"Iven like a crook!"

"But you wrote '*cook,*' Mr. Kaplan, not 'crook'!"

Mr. Kaplan cocked his head. "Som cooks are crooks, an' some crooks are cooks."

"*Mein Gott!*" howled Wolfgang Schmitt.

"Don't choppa hairs!" flashed Miss Caravello.

"He *kills* me!" gasped Nathan P. Nathan.

"Mr. Kaplan"—Mr. Parkhill was wrestling with both astonishment and displeasure—"read your last sentence."

Mr. Kaplan read it with alacrity:

3. Hang yoursalf in reseption hall, please.

"God's almighty!" whooped Norman Bloom, which triggered a giggle from Miss Gidwitz and a guffaw from Mr. Vinograd.

"*Koplan* ees nuts!" laughed Vincente Perez. "Weeth a 'u'!"

"Class . . ."

"Read that idiom again!" grinned "Cookie" Kipnis. "I love it!"

166

"Heng—yoursalf—in—resaption—hall—plizz," stout Kaplan repeated.

"I dun't be*lieve* it!" cackled Miss Pomeranz.

"I *do,*" leered Mr. Finsterwald.

"Oy," oyed Mrs. Moskowitz.

Above these savage indictments, Mr. Parkhill managed to call, "Class, quiet!... Mr. Kaplan, examine that sentence carefully. Pay special attention to the object of the verb 'hang' and you will see why the sentence struck the class as being so—funny."

"Hmmnh." Mr. Kaplan pursed his lips, wrinkled his brow, closed one eye, and searched for the treacherous source of his colleagues' pleasure.

"Nu, Kaplan?" gibed Norman Bloom.

"Aha! Should be kepitals on 'resaption hall'!"

The Bloom-Moskowitz-Blattberg entente rocked in rapture: "Cuckoo!" "Absoid!" "Som gass!"

"No, Mr. Kaplan," said Mr. Parkhill, " 'reception hall' is not a proper noun, hence does not require capital letters. It is the *meaning* of your sentence that's at fault. 'Hang *yourself* in the reception hall,' Mr. Kaplan? Is that—er— what you say to your guests?"

"I try to make mine gasts fill at home."

Mr. Bloom brayed, " 'Hang *yoursalf*'? Som host!"

"If soitin pipple came to mine house," murmured Hyman Kaplan, "dat vould be exectly vhat I vould say!"

"Oy!"

"Shame!"

Mr. Nathan was in hysterics.

"Mr. Kaplan!"

When only ten minutes remained in the night's allotted span, Mr. Parkhill put the class through a vigorous spelling drill. (Of all time fillers, spelling drills were the safest.) "Restaurant . . ."

The class inscribed varying versions of "restaurant" on

the pages before them—all of the class, that is, except Mr. Kaplan. He wrote nothing. He sat with his arms folded.

"Chocolate . . ."

Lids lowered, Mr. Kaplan retreated into that inner world in which his steadfast Muse resided.

"Bungalow," called Mr. Parkhill.

Mr. Kaplan might just as well have retired to a monastery.

"Accident . . . skip . . . lettuce . . ."

Mr. Kaplan opened his eyes. On the pad before him, he now crayonned aimless scribbles and scratches, doodles and hatches.

"Shampoo . . ."

A faint smile formed on Mr. Kaplan's lips.

"Mystery . . ."

Mr. Kaplan unscrewed his fountain pen. He was humming.

"B-basement . . ." Mr. Parkhill faltered.

Mr. Kaplan propelled his pen across the paper with startling speed.

"Hurricane . . ."

Mr. Kaplan chuckled, dotting an "i," crossing a "t."

With but a moment remaining before the large hand on the clock over the door reached 10, Mr. Parkhill announced the last word loudly: "Confess! . . ."

So fleeting, so secretive was Mr. Kaplan's smile that Mr. Parkhill could not help but think of Mona Lisa.

At her post in the principal's office, alert Miss Schnepfe pressed the button which tintinnabulated the final bell.

The students stood up and packed up for their trek home. The room became a sonic jumble of friendly chatter, closing briefcases, snapping rubbers. The class filed past Mr. Parkhill's desk to drop off their exercise papers. "Good night"s—some hearty, some weary—rent the air. Mr. Kaplan's farewell was uncharacteristically blithe: "Ontil ve mit agan . . ."

Mr. Parkhill wiped his hands.

When all had gone, he took his attendance report to Mr. Robinson's office.

"Good attendance?" asked Miss Schnepfe.

"Oh, yes. Only three absent." Hastily, he added, "Mr. Trabish is in the hospital, I believe. Appendicitis."

"Tell him to cut it out!" Miss Schnepfe flung her head back, cackling in glee. (No one enjoyed her own wit more than Miss Schnepfe: Mr. Krout was sure that she tippled.)

"Good night."

It was chilly outside. The city was swathed in bleakness. Mr. Parkhill wrapped his muffler tightly and hurried to the subway.

No sooner did he find a seat than he opened his briefcase and began to scan the pages on which his students had written the spelling test. Miss Mitnick had done *very* well, as usual. Mr. Bloom had managed to scale the heights of an 85! Young Mr. Nathan had outdone himself, except for "shampoo," which, given his athletic inclinations, he had rendered as "champoo." Mr. Scymczak had misspelled only eight out of fifteen words—a superior performance for Casimir Scymczak. Mrs. Moskowitz . . . poor Mrs. Moskowitz; she was still confusing English with some other, unrevealed language.

The next paper was blank. Mr. Parkhill frowned. Some student had turned in an empty page by mistake. Mr. Parkhill turned the paper over, to pass on to the next one, but beheld a conglomeration of scrawls, numbers and tic-tac-toes: there was even an unfinished ear and an American flag, executed in colors. Firmly, Mr. Parkhill wrote on top of the page: "Mr. Kaplan: Please submit your spelling drill!"

He was about to proceed to Miss Caravello's offering, when something caught his eye. Words had been written around those vagrant hieroglyphics. Mr. Parkhill adjusted his glasses and looked closer:

169

Critsising Mitnick
is a picnick.

Natan P. Natan,
For what are you waitin?

Bloom, Bloom
Go out the room!

Olga Tarnova
Is crazy all over.

Mrs. Moskowitz,
By her it doesn't fits
A dress—size 44.

It was a fearful vengeance which Mr. Kaplan, defeated but unbowed, had wreaked upon those who had tried to besmirch his honor.

16

MR. K·A·P·L·A·N SLASHES A
GORDIAN KNOT

"Tonight," said Mr. Parkhill, "we come to our semester's end—and thus to our final examination."

It was not really necessary for Mr. Parkhill to go through the formality of a final examination. He well knew, weeks before the end of a term, which members of the beginners' grade deserved to be promoted to Miss Higby's Advanced Grammar and Civics, and which students, by even the most generous measure of achievement, would have to be "held back."

Mr. Parkhill *hated* to hold any student back. The night before a final examination he would toss and turn in bed, trying to justify the possible promotion of "borderline cases": a student such as Mr. Marcus, for example, who had worked very hard, improved his spelling, reformed his grammar, but still deformed his diction. (Asked for an oral sentence using "denounce," Mr. Marcus had burbled, "I have trouble with verbs, but never de nouns.") Or a pupil as wayward as Mrs. Rodriguez, whose Hispanic ear just was not attuned to English sounds. (In one composition, Mrs. Rodriguez had written: "Today, I heard a funny choke.")

Mr. Parkhill often fell asleep only after forcing himself to think about students he could promote without the slightest moral qualms: Miss Mitnick, for example: there

171

was no shred of doubt in Mr. Parkhill's mind that Miss Mitnick was ready for Miss Higby's tutelage. Or Wolfgang Schmitt. True, Mr. Schmitt's pronunciation of "th"s as "zzz"s begged for alteration, yet this in no way affected the excellence of his spelling, the soundness of his syntax, the range of his vocabulary. Mr. Schmitt would surely pass. Or Gerta Valuskas. Why, Miss Valuskas should be ready for *graduation* from the American Night Preparatory School for Adults in several years. Or Nathan P. Nathan. He spoke English so fluently, but played basketball so often; Miss Schnepfe would raise a frightful rumpus over so errant an attendance chart—much more than over Mr. Nathan's aberrant spelling or absent punctuation.

But upon awakening from his slumbers, Mr. Parkhill would go right back to worrying about the pupils he would be forced to disappoint. Mrs. Moskowitz, for example. By no stretch of either hope, faith or charity could Mrs. Moskowitz be given the cherished "Passed." (Only last week, Mrs. Moskowitz had defined "absolute" as "won't salute.")

Or Gus Matsoukas. Mr. Matsoukas's English was as unnerving as his mutterings. In a recent exercise on new words, the immigrant from Greece, given "ponder," had growled, "Every night I clean with toot ponder."

Or Mr. Kaplan. Mr. Parkhill winced. (Mr. Parkhill had come to wince whenever he thought of Hyman Kaplan.) That intrepid scholar was surely the most diligent and determined soul in the class: he never missed a lesson; he never grew discouraged; the smile of optimism, of undaunted aspiration, rarely fled those cherubic features. But Mr. Kaplan's English still shuttled between the barbaric and the unheard of. His spelling remained eccentric, his grammar deplorable, his pronunciation—there was only one word to describe Mr. Kaplan's pronunciation: hair-raising. (Were one to accept Mr. Kaplan's usage, "grin" is a color, "pitch" a fruit, and a "kit" anyone under twenty-one.)

In all fairness, Mr. Parkhill reminded himself, Mr. Kaplan *had* shown commendable improvement in ever so many zones: "because" was certainly an advance over "becawss," and "singink" was certainly better than "sink-ink." But so much of Mr. Kaplan's English remained to *be* improved that the hills of his progress shrank before the mountain of his errors.

One could only marvel over Mr. Kaplan's uncanny capacity to resolve one problem by creating another. On Tuesday, for instance, Mr. Kaplan had implored his classmates to avoid any foods or agitations that cause "high blood pleasure." In an exercise on comparative adjectives, he had submitted, "Cold, colder, below zero." In a quite routine review of gender, Mr. Kaplan had ordained that "opera" was masculine but "operetta" feminine. And (the very recollection made Mr. Parkhill pale) Mr. Kaplan believed that the bravest of American frontiersmen was "Daniel Bloom."

Sometimes Mr. Parkhill wondered whether it wasn't unfair to try to clamp the chains of conformity on so unfettered an intelligence.

The time had come. The last exam was at hand. "Please clear the arms of your chairs of everything except paper, pens or pencils."

Up rose the hand of Mr. Pinsky.

"Yes?"

"Is allowed to hold bladders?"

It took Mr. Parkhill a moment of acute distress to figure out what Mr. Pinsky meant. " *'Blotters'!* Oh, yes, Mr. Pinsky. If you are using ink, you certainly may hold on to your—er—blotters. Is everyone ready?"

Rueful nods, brave smiles, resigned suspirations—all testified to the momentous inquest ahead. Many a mouth went dry; many a heart beat faster. In the eyes of some students glowed visions of Advanced Grammar and Civics;

173

in the eyes of others—well, life had taught them not to elevate their expectations. Down the waiting ranks, pens and pencils poised like falcons. Miss Mitnick's hair was disarranged. Miss Tarnova inhaled a restorative scent from the Orient. Mr. Nathan looked as if he had just put two free throws through the hoop. Miss Goldberg swallowed raisins.

"The first part of our examination will be a combined spelling-vocabulary test," said Mr. Parkhill. "Write a sentence—a short sentence—using each of the words I shall call off. Is that clear?"

The "Oy" of Mrs. Moskowitz suggested that it was too clear.

"Very well . . . Our first word is—'knees.' " Mr. Parkhill paused and repeated, " 'Knees,' " buzzing the terminal fricative as if it were "z."

The class attacked "knees." Mr. Kaplan leaned back, closed his eyes, and sought aid from his guardian angel. " 'Neez,' " he whispered. " 'Neez' . . . a fonny void . . ." He opened one eye to monitor Mr. Parkhill's reaction to the soliloquy yet to come. "Aha! Has *two* minninks. . . . Vun, a piece of a lag. . . . Two, mine sister's daughter is mine nee—"

"Mr. Kaplan," frowned Mr. Parkhill, "you are disturbing the class."

"I back you podden." The injured air signified that Mr. Kaplan could not think clearly if forbidden to whisper to himself.

" 'Heat' . . ." Mr. Parkhill wished Mr. Kaplan would not look as if he were David robbed of his slingshot. " 'Heat.' "

" 'Heat,' " Mr. Kaplan automatically echoed, then caught himself; he pressed his lips together and, in melancholy mufflement, wrote a sentence using "heat."

" 'Pack' . . . 'excite' . . . 'throat.' "

Mr. Parkhill announced each word slowly, allowing a

174

full minute to elapse before he uttered the next syllables; and he articulated each word with the utmost precision. ("Excite" he repeated three times.)

So well did Mr. Parkhill time his recitation that he called the last of the thirty test words a good forty seconds before the recess bell tinkled. He waited for a few laggards to complete a sentence using "Adorable."

"The first part of our examination is over," he declared. "Please hand in your papers."

Relief swept the beleaguered ranks. Students rose, stretched, rubbed their temples, massaged their fingers, handed in their pages and ambled into the corridor—to share and compare, describe and debate the sentences they had manufactured. Their voices were very loud, and Mr. Nathan was playing "Yes, Sir, That's My Baby" in the lower register of his harmonica.

Mr. Parkhill began to scan the papers. Miss Mitnick had, as usual, done excellently. Mrs. Yanoff seemed to have struck disaster with "throat," for she had written several sentences, scratched them out, and in panic settled for "He throat the ball." Mr. Parkhill came to the paper headed H*Y*M*A*N K*A*P*L*A*N:

1. My brother's girl is my *neece* and has two *neez*.
2. I *heat* him on the head, the big fool.
3. When we buy potatos we buy potatos by the *pack*.
4. In theatres is the insite, the outsite, and the *exite* (in case Fire).

Mr. Parkhill read no further.

At 8:40 the bell clanged an end to recess; the victims rumbled in for the completion of their ordeal. Some looked worried, some confident, some tense. Miss Mitnick looked happy, for Nathan P. Nathan was holding her hand. Mrs. Moskowitz and Mr. Kaplan entered side by side. Common adversity had oiled the waters of their enmity. Mrs. Moskowitz was moaning, "I'm *sha*king, Mr. Keplan."

Mr. Kaplan waved with aplomb. *"Stop* de shakink. Kip high your had! Dis pot vill be a *snep!"*

The dolorous matron sighed. "I wish I had your noives."

Mr. Kaplan graciously inclined his head. "If you fill blue, remamber det vunderful song: 'Heppy Dace Is Here Vunce More!' " As Mr. Kaplan sat down, he tossed a final bone of encouragement across the tiers: "Moskovitz, don't give op de sheep!"

Mr. Parkhill tapped the desk sharply. "Well, class . . . the second part of our examination will be a one-page essay— on any topic you wish!"

The falling of faces advertised to the quicksand of the assignment.

"A whole paitch?" gasped Bessie Shimmelfarb.

"Any topic?" quavered Mr. Scymczak.

Mr. Kaplan rallied the faint of heart. "I like any sobjeck!"

"Keplan . . ." moaned Mrs. Moskowitz, in an S.O.S.

Mr. Parkhill cleared his throat. "I must request that you do *not* talk to each other." He looked squarely at the knight in the center of the front row. "No prompting, please, to *or* from another student!"

Mr. Kaplan winced. Mrs. Moskowitz looked as if her arm had been cut off.

"Class, you will have ample time to reread your one-page compositions carefully, as I trust you will, to correct errors in spelling, to watch your capital letters, to rewrite. . . ." He strolled down the aisle.

The silence of concentration swathed the beginners' grade as its constituents searched for topics within the compass of their capability. Miss Caravello stared at the picture of Lincoln on the wall, seeking first-aid from that compassionate countenance. Mr. Finsterwald muttered a cryptic appeal to austere Washington. "Cookie" Kipnis pressed her fists against her temples to intensify her concentration. Mr. Trabish was either cogitating or napping (since he was not snoring, it was hard to tell). The Misses Valuskas and Mitnick had long since begun writing. Mr. Nathan was charting an out-of-bounds stratagem before committing it to prose.

Soon the congregation was scribbling away: Mr. Perez breathing Iberian cues, Mr. Schmitt hissing Germanic props, Miss Goldberg consuming one jellybean after another to stoke the furnace of cerebration.

Mr. Parkhill stopped next to Mrs. Moskowitz, who was fanning her cheeks with her notebook.

"Is anything wrong?" he whispered.

Mrs. Moskowitz raised a haggard face. "I ken't t'ink of a sobject!"

"Well—er—why not try 'My Ambition'?" ("My Ambition" had always proved *very* popular.)

Mrs. Moskowitz went limp. "Who has embition?! I have hot flashes."

"Then—how about 'My First Day in America'?"

"My foist day I broke my wrisk."

Mr. Parkhill felt miserable. "Er—then suppose—"

A whistling wafted through the air, its refrain unmistakable: "Heppy Dace Is Here Vunce More."

"Mr. Kap—"

The whistling stopped; but it was replaced by disembodied whispers: " 'Should Ladies Smoke?' . . . 'Is Dere a God, Ectual?' . . ."

"Mr. Kaplan!"

But the subversive communication had been consummated.

"I'll write about a *qvastion!*" croaked Mrs. Moskowitz.

Mr. Parkhill moved on.

"Podden me, Mr. Pockheel."

Firmly, Mr. Parkhill shook his head. "No question."

"Is no qvastion," said Mr. Kaplan. "De room is too varm. Should I aupen a vindow?"

"Oh."

Mr. Kaplan rose, "aupened" a window, and returned to his chair. At once, Miss Gidwitz, on his left, put her mouth close to his ear.

"No whispering, please . . ."

Mr. Kaplan stood up again. "I batter close de vindow. Is on Gidvitz a cold graft."

He had lowered the window before Mr. Parkhill could say, " 'Draft,' Mr. Kaplan, 'd'raft.' "

Mr. Parkhill felt relieved, yet a bit sad, when the terminal bell—the last angelus of the season—chimed. (Only once, in all her years at the American Night Preparatory School for Adults, had Miss Schnepfe not pressed the bell button in the principal's office exactly on time. *That* night, classes had continued a full eight minutes after 10 P.M., because a mouse had scurried around Miss Schnepfe's office. The guardian of the bells jumped up on her chair and shrieked like a banshee. Fortunately, Mr. Robinson entered, took in the crisis at a glance, chased the mouse out by waving his hat and crying "Whoosh! Whoosh!," and pressed the button himself. . . . How Mr. Krout had regaled the faculty, the next night, remarking that Mr. Robinson was a wizard when it came to smelling a rat!)

The ringing pring rolled down the corridor. The beginners' grade collected their artifacts. They crowded up to Mr. Parkhill's desk to hand in their papers and bid him adieu. They behaved like any class in any school whenever a semester ends: some cheerful, some wistful, some grieving the cessation of learning, some welcoming the free nights ahead. Each pupil shook Mr. Parkhill's hand; each bade him farewell.

"Good-bye and good luck in anything that should hap-

178

pen to you!" was Mr. Bloom's hearty adieu.

Miss Mitnick curtseyed. "Every lesson was a real pleasure!" Her cheeks turned as pink as petunias. "I learned so much. I want to come back."

"Perhaps you'll be with Miss Higby in the fall," smiled Mr. Parkhill.

"I don't *want* to change teachers!" bleated Miss Mitnick, and fled.

"Me, too!" laughed Mr. Nathan.

Mr. Scymczak ran a hand across his crew-cut and blurted hoarsely, "You teach good, good. Thanks."

"Thank you, Mr. Scymczak."

Miss Caravello simply sang out, *"Arrivederci!"* and soared off on wings of deliverance.

Mr. Matsoukas's syllables of departure were not more comprehensible than his habitual mumbles.

Mr. Pinsky chuckled, "Another sizzon! Work findished! Thank you. *Shalom!"*

Miss Ziev's swan song smothered in a fit of coughing.

Throughout these fervent valedictories, Hyman Kaplan hovered on the edges of the throng proudly. He might have been Mr. Parkhill's mentor, savoring the praises to his protégé.

Olga Tarnova took Mr. Parkhill's hand in both of hers, jangling her bracelets, as she crooned, "Thonk you, thonk you. In Rossian we say, *'Sposibo, sposibo.' "* She bent so low that Mr. Parkhill feared she was about to kiss his knuckles; then she crouched. Mr. Parkhill, alarmed that she would kiss his shoes, exclaimed, "Miss Tar—!" but it turned out that Miss Tarnova had merely dropped her scented handkerchief, which, recovered, waved a gaudy exit.

Mrs. Rodriguez said, "I don't theenk I come back—"

"I hope you will," said Mr. Parkhill.

"Thees means I *failed?!"* cried Mrs. Rodriguez.

"Oh, no. I just meant I hope you'll return to—"

"That means I failed!"

"No, no—"

"Rodriguez!" cut in Mr. Kaplan. "Pull yourself altogadder!"

Wolfgang Schmitt had marched up, stiffened, and declaimed: "Not in all my time in Chermany, I did haff zuch exzellent teaching!"

"In Joiminy, they shouldn't say 'Chermany,'" observed Mr. Kaplan.

And so it went: Miss Goldberg wiping her fingers of chocolate before shaking her master's hand ("A *mil*lion thenks!"), Vincente Perez blurting a mystifying, "My house ees your house!," Mrs. Moskowitz, liberated from bondage, burbling moist incoherences.

Now they were all gone—all save Hyman Kaplan, who approached the desk.

Mr. Parkhill adjusted his glasses. *"Well,* Mr. Kaplan . . ."

Mr. Kaplan shook hands. He turned to cast one last, fond glance across the empty tiers, around the blackboards, over the whole jousting ground on which so many battles had raged: Kaplan versus Mitnick, Kaplan versus Bloom, the Kaplan-Pinsky-Trabish phalanx breaching the Blattberg-Tarnova-Caravello flanks. . . . "Soch good times ve had in dis room!" sighed the warrior. He shook off reverie and strode to the door—from which he waved as if he (Mr. Kaplan) was on a ship and he (Mr. Parkhill) was seeing him off on a historic voyage. "Don't vorry," said Mr. Kaplan. He passed through the portal.

Mr. Parkhill wondered what on earth made Mr. Kaplan say a thing like that. He began to fill his briefcase: the class records, the students' exam papers. He riffled them out of curiosity. The titles fluttered before him: "The Stateu of Liberty," "A Sad Night in Hospital," "Should be a Panelty

for Murdering?" (That was surely Mr. Kaplan's offering—
no, it was Mrs. Moskowitz's; but it certainly owed all to Mr.
Kaplan's advice.)

Mr. Parkhill stuffed the lot into his case and picked
up the remaining batch: "My Children Make Me a
Happy Life," "How We Beat the Manischewitz Rockets,"
"I Like Ice Cream!," "Thinking About." He winced. He
read the title again: "Thinking About." Mr. Parkhill
could not prevent himself from raising that sheet above
the rest.

"THINKING ABOUT"
(Humans & Animals)
by
H*Y*M*A*N K*A*P*L*A*N

1.

Sometime I feel sad about how people are living. Only
eating, working, sleeping. No *thinking!*

(Mr. Kaplan's spelling certainly had improved.)

These people are like enimals the same, which don't use
one pot of their brans. Humans should not be like enimals.

(Mr. Parkhill modified his opinion of Mr. Kaplan's spelling.)

Now we are having the good-bye exemination. Mostly
will the class write a story. But I ask, Why must allways be
a story? Mr. P. must be sick and tied up from reading storys,
storys, storys.

Kaplan, *Be a man!* No story. Tell better about *thinking*
something. Fine. Now I am thinking.

(Mr. Parkhill sank into the chair.)

2.

In resess, some students asked if is right to say "Its Me" or "Its I" (because maybe we will have that question *after* resess.) "Its Me" or "Its I?" A very hard question, no? Yes. But it isnt so hard if we *think about!*

I figgure this way: If sombody is in the hall and makes knok, knok, knok on my door—I holler, netcheral, "Whose there"?

Comes the answer "Its me."

Som answer! Rotten!! Who is that Me anyho? Can I tell? No! So is "Its Me" a bad way to anser "Who is it?"

Again is knok, knok, knok. Again I holler "Whose there"? Now comes the answer "Its I."

Is that an anser?! Crazy! Who is that I?? Can I (Kaplan) tell?? Ha! Umpossible!

So is "Its I" also no-good, an anser that isnt an *anser!*

So it looks like their *is no good anser!* But—(Turn around paige)

As Mr. Parkhill turned the page "around" (Mr. Kaplan had interpreted "a one-page essay" with characteristic generosity) he reflected that put that way, the puzzle of "It's Me" or "It's I" was practically a Gordian knot.

3.

But must be *som kind good anser!* So how can we find it??? BY THINKING ABOUT.

(Now comes how Humans are more smart then Enimals!)

4.

If *I* am in the hall and make knok, knok, knok, and I hear from insite (insite the room) sombody hollers "Whose there"?—*I* anser, "Hyman Kaplan!"

Aha! Now is plain, clear like gold. No chance *enyone* in U.S. will mix up a Me, I, You, Who? Ect.

This shows how by *thinking* Humans are making big advences on enimals.

This I call Progriss.

T-H-E E-N-D

A postscript climaxed this dazzling demonstration of pure reason:

To Mr. P.

ps.

I dont care if I dont pass. I just *love* the class.

★★★★★★★★★★★★★★★★★★★★★★★★

PART TWO

1

THE PRODIGAL S·O·N

"Miss Mary Atrakian."

"Yes, sor."

"Olaf Umea."

"In place!"

"Mr. Stanislaus—uh—Wilkomirski."

"I am."

"Mrs. Minnie Pilpul."

"Likevise."

Mr. Parkhill did not call the roll in alphabetical order because he was trying to familiarize himself with the new faces, matching each face to a name in the order in which the members of the class had selected their seats.

"Miss Lola Lopez."

"*Sí!*"

"Mr. Vasil—Hruska? Is that right? The 'H,' I take it, is silent. . . ."

Mr. Hruska was silent, too. In fact, there was no Mr. Hruska. "My name is Olansky!" protested the burly man with very thick glasses at whom Mr. Parkhill was smiling. "Reuben Olansky."

"Oh, I *beg* your pardon. Where is Mr. Hruska? Mr. H-r-u . . ."

Spelling did not produce Mr. Hruska. Mr. Parkhill put an "X" after the name. A crisp "✓" on Mr. Parkhill's attendance sheet signified that the student was present, a reluctant "X" that he or she was not. Sometimes, of course, a student came in well after the class session had begun, in which case Mr. Parkhill simply circled the "X." That meant the student had arrived late. (Miss Schnepfe, in the principal's office, was a stickler about such things. She *hated* tardiness.) "C. J. Fledermann."

"*Ja.*"

"Isaac Nussbaum."

"Here is Isaac Nussbaum."

Mr. Parkhill glanced up. Mr. Nussbaum certainly was there, a little skullcap on his thick hair, a fine, full beard foresting his cheeks and chin. (Mr. Nussbaum was a cantor.)

"Peter Ignatius Studniczka . . ."

Mr. Parkhill tried to call the names cheerfully. But he did not feel cheerful; he felt depressed. It was only the second night of the fall term, and a new term always brought with it fresh promise—new personalities, new problems, new challenges. Yet here and now, a brief forty-eight hours after the season's advent, Mr. Parkhill found himself possessed of melancholy, a melancholy deepened by surprising nostalgia. . . . Last year's names, last year's faces. . . . Ah, that *had* been a beginners' grade. . . .

"Miss Rochelle Goldberg."

"A pleasure." (She amplified the pleasure with a caramel.)

Well, at least some of the old flock had returned.

"Mr. Milas Wodjik."

"Oxcuse, the name is 'Vodjik,' not 'Wodjik'!"

"Oh, thank you." Mr. Parkhill nodded pleasantly. (It was not often that a student corrected a teacher's pronunciation in the American Night Preparatory School for Adults.)

"Mr. Tomas Wodjik."

188

"Ho huh."

Mr. Parkhill gave Mr. Tomas Wodjik a smile as friendly as the one he had given Mr. Milas Wodjik—but longer scrutiny. He could not tell one Mr. Wodjik from the other. They were twins. They were identical twins. To make things worse, they dressed exactly alike—blue suits, striped shirts, brown knit ties—and sat side by side. (When they had first appeared before Mr. Parkhill, handing him their registration cards, Mr. Parkhill had reached *between* them; he would have to check his glasses.)

"Mr. Lucca Barbella."

"Presente!"

"Miss Kipnis . . ."

"Hello."

"Mr. Nathan P. Nathan?"

"Yes, *sir!* Ready!" came that buoyant laugh.

"Mrs. Yanoff . . ."

"Who alse?"

For some reason, a phrase kept running through Mr. Parkhill's mind: *Où sont les fleurs d'antan?* "Where *were* the Blooms of yesteryear?" Mr. Norman Bloom, rumor had it, had forsaken the temple of learning to toil for a raincoat manufacturer in Passaic, N.J. (What a fierce classroom debater Mr. Bloom had been!) Promotion had advanced the superior scholars—Wolfgang Schmitt, Mr. Finsterwald, Gerta Valuskas, Harry Feigenbaum—to the golden pastures of Miss Higby's Advanced Grammar and Civics. Mr. Jacob Marcus had captured the heart of a comely divorcee and moved, it was said, to a bucolic cottage in Far Rockaway by the sea. Mrs. Tomasic had moved with her husband, Slavko, to Bridgeport. Gus Matsoukas had returned to Greece. Vincente Perez had transferred to a school much closer to his lodgings in the Bronx. Miss Carmen Caravello had gone to Italy "for *piccolo* vacation to see family" (a postcard had informed Miss Mitnick), but the powerful hold of family, friends and the Mediterranean sun had been too much for Miss Caravello to reject once more. ("O, I love my madre, padre, sister Angelina who is in convent," the postcard of Mount Vesuvius erupting had informed Mr. Parkhill. "Also I am in Love!" Miss Caravello had sworn never to return to the *"manicomio* of N.Y.")

And Mr. Kaplan? . . . Mr. Parkhill sighed. He always sighed when he remembered Mr. Kaplan. No one knew what had happened to him. Some said he had lost his job, others that he had lost his voice. Mr. Pinsky believed that Mr. Kaplan was planning to run for Mayor.

"Mr. Blattberg."

"Good evnink!" A third grandson's baby tooth flashed on the watch chain Mr. Blattberg proudly twirled.

"Miss Mitnick."

Mr. Parkhill was *very* glad that Miss Mitnick was back. She was a student any teacher would like—so conscientious, so intelligent, so shy. This wisp of a maiden, offered richly deserved promotion to Miss Higby's grade, had surrendered to panic, tearfully confessed to not feeling *"ready"* for such a dizzying elevation, and pleaded with Mr. Parkhill to be allowed to remain in his fold for one more season. So had Nathan P. Nathan. It was a tribute, in a way. . . .

"Miss Tarnova."

Returned, too, was Olga Tarnova, with her cobalt hair, her earrings and bracelets, her sultry moans and grand manner—a faded Cleopatra, floating down a Slavic Nile. *"Da, da."* Sometimes, Mr. Parkhill thought Miss Tarnova could wring tragedy from the multiplication table.

"Mr. Trabish."

Oscar Trabish yawned, as bakers are wont to do.

"Mrs. Moskowitz."

"Oooo." Mrs. Moskowitz had been making heroic efforts to curb her "Oy!"'s for more Americanized "Ooo"s.

190

"Miss Ziev."

Miss Ziev was somewhat subdued. Her marriage to Mr. Andrassy, in Mr. Krout's class, had been delayed by the death of his grandmother. The fact that his grandmother was in Budapest had only lengthened Mr. Andrassy's mourning.

"Mr. Pinsky."

Mr. Pinsky, a little more merry, a little less chubby, was ensconced directly in front of Mr. Parkhill, in the chair in the exact center of the front row. That was where Mr. Kaplan had always roosted. (How could one forget the place from which that intrepid spirit had referred to the Generalissimo of Nationalist China as "Shanghai Jack"?)

Mr. Parkhill put the attendance sheet to one side. "Well, class." He smiled upon them in his most reassuring manner. "Your homework, the first assignment of the semester was—'My Life.'" The first assignment was always "My Life"; the second might be "My Vacation" or "My Job" or "My Ambition"; but the first was always "My Life." Nothing so swiftly enlisted the interest of Mr. Parkhill's novitiates, so rapidly soothed their anxieties and bolstered their morale, as the simple invitation to recount the story of "My Life."

"Miss Lopez, will you please go to the board and transcribe your composition? . . . Mr. Olansky . . . Miss Tarnova . . ." He called off four more names.

They trudged to the blackboards in the single file of the doomed, seven of them: one groaned, two sagged, three sighed, one shuddered. But all advanced to confront their fate. Then they strung themselves along the boards as if deploying for combat. Brows furrowed, lips tightened, papers rustled; then sticks of chalk rose like lances. A few coughs of apology, a few moans of uncertainty, and white letters began to form words that bravely marched across the slate.

Mr. Parkhill strolled down the aisle to the back of the

room, as he usually did when the boards were being used. He turned to watch his pilgrims.

Tiny Miss Lopez was standing on tiptoe as she committed her life to the board. Mrs. Yanoff kept wiping her brow as concentration exacted its toll. Olaf Umea muttered. (Every class Mr. Parkhill had ever taught seemed to contain one born mutterer: Gus Matsoukas, who had sought no friends and tendered no confidences, as befitted a Greek among barbarians, had been the mutterer of last year's beginners' grade. Now it was Olaf Umea.) Mr. Oscar Trabish unbuttoned his sleeve to accelerate the circulation in his writing arm. Mr. Reuben Olansky, who seemed to be both far-sighted and near-sighted, kept adjusting his bifocals—the better to stare at his work or glare at Miss Tarnova, on his right. Olga Tarnova . . . her bracelets jangled as she wrote, and she fell into throaty mewings whenever she lifted chalk or pen. From time to time, Miss Tarnova dabbed a lacy handkerchief at her nostrils.

Mr. Parkhill noted how respectful was the silence fallen upon the seated. The tick of the big clock on the wall, stern Washington on one side, sad Lincoln on the other, cast soft punctuations of time in the air. . . . This was a docile class. In *last* year's class, Mr. Parkhill could not help ruminating, chattering or teasings or storm signals would long since have appeared—from Mr. Bloom, as he pounced upon some blunder hatched on the board; or from Miss Valuskas, whose Finnish pencil used to stab upward at the first sign of error; and certainly from Mr. Kaplan as he "t'ought" about some profound point. Mr. Kaplan had always thought out loud—either to consult his private Muses, of whom he had a copious supply, or to grant his colleagues the privilege of participating in his priceless cerebration. (One night, Mr. Kaplan gave the principal parts of "to eat" as "eat, ate, full." On another, asked to use "knack" in a sentence, Mr. Kaplan had declaimed: "Bloom gives me a pain in the knack.")

Nostalgia wrapped Mr. Parkhill in its shroud. He started to open the back window when, quite without warning, the door flew open. A gust of air swept in from the corridor as a clarion voice proclaimed: "Hollo, averybody! Grittings!"

Twenty-six heads turned as one.

"Valcome to de new sizzon! Valcome to beginnis' grate!"

"Oy!" gasped Mrs. Moskowitz as of yore.

"I dun't believe it!" cried Mrs. Shimmelfarb.

"Lookit who's here!" rejoiced Mr. Pinsky.

"Holy smoky," frowned Mr. Isaac Nussbaum, who had but recently immigrated from the Holy Land.

Mr. Parkhill did not have to turn to identify the voice that had trumpeted "Grittings!" He could not mistake that enunciation, that supreme (if unwarranted) aplomb, that blithe, triumphant spirit. Besides, what other student would bid "Valcome!" to those who, enjoying prior residence, should clearly have welcomed him? Mr. Parkhill knew only one man who entered a classroom as if come for coronation.

"Mr."—his eyes found the ebullient entrant—"Kaplan. Well, well, Mr. Kaplan!"

It *was* Mr. Kaplan, proud, undaunted, a knight returned to the field of glory. He looked a whit more debonair, a mite more euphoric. He was sunburned, which so accented the natural luminosity of his skin that a light seemed to be shining under his apple-shaped cheeks. And he was freckled! How odd. Mr. Kaplan, the very epitome of urban civilization, freckled. For one absurd moment, Mr. Parkhill thought the freckles were shaped like stars, so that Mr. Kaplan's countenance advertised his name as he always wrote it—the letters in red, outlined in blue, the stars green: H*Y*M*A*N K*A*P*L*A*N. Mr. Parkhill repressed this foolish fantasy.

"Hollo, Mr. Pockheel! Harre you?" Mr. Kaplan was beaming. "Oh, I'm so heppy to see you I ken't tell abot!" Mr. Parkhill found himself shaking Mr. Kaplan's hand somewhat numbly. "You lookink fine! Foist-cless! A-Number-Vun!"

"You—er—look fine yourself." Mr. Parkhill cleared his throat. "Just splendid."

"I *fill* splandid."

"I—I'm glad to see you back, Mr. Kaplan."

"I'm besite you mit joy!"

Mr. Parkhill started to say "It's 'I'm beside *myself,*' Mr. Kaplan," but it was too late: Mr. Kaplan had turned to address his classmates: "Fallow students in beginnis' grate, ve vill voik togadder! Ve vill slafe! Ve vill *loin!*" He raised an imperial finger to the heavens. "Vun for all an' all for vun an' de whole kitten cadoodle for Mr. Pockheel!"

"Welcome home, Napoleon," said Mr. Blattberg bitterly, touching his amulet, the watch chain from which his heirs' baby teeth glittered.

Mr. Kaplan's gaze swept across subversive Blattberg, whom he did not deign to answer. "Ah, Mitnick! An' Nat'-an P. Nat'an! Bote still in beginnis' grate?! A plazent soprise. . . ."

The fawn, flushed out of her thicket, stammered, "H-hello, Mr. Kaplan."

Mr. Nathan laughed.

"I soggest for dis toim, Mitnick—"

"Do take a seat," said Mr. Parkhill hastily.

Mr. Kaplan strode to the chair in the center of the front row. "Pinsky."

Mr. Pinsky chortled, "Keplen!"

"I believe you occupy mine sitt." Mr. Kaplan said it without the slightest tinge of displeasure, but in the manner of a lord of the realm, asserting eminent domain.

At once, Mr. Pinsky gathered up his textbook, his notebook, his pencils, and slid into the seat beyond. He appeared honored to surrender the hallowed place, a shield-bearer who had been holding the castle keep against upstarts.

194

"Thot mon," moaned Miss Tarnova, shooting a poison-ous glance at her enemy, "is a davil!"

"Now, class . . ." Mr. Parkhill quickly called.

The students at the board had so been beguiled by the fanfare that attended Hyman Kaplan's entrance that they had abandoned their autobiographies. They were giving the prodigal son ripe smiles, if friend, or frigid salutations, if foe. Those who were neither friend nor foe, like the Messrs. Wodjik, seemed paralyzed.

"Let us get back to our work," said Mr. Parkhill. "Mr. Kaplan will be with us for quite a while."

"Alvays," murmured Mr. Kaplan.

The image of Mr. Kaplan in the front row forever, un-changed, unchangeable, caused Mr. Parkhill to wince.

As the seven at the board returned to their labors, Mr. Kaplan took one of his fountain pens out of his outer breast pocket, narrowed his eyes, scanned the titles on the board with lightning dispatch, cocked his head to one side, whis-pered "Aha! So is de homevoik abot pest livink!" and began scribbling on an envelope furiously. Mr. Parkhill won-dered what on earth he had seen to make him start scrib-bling away so *soon.*

"Let us finish, Blackboard . . ." (Mr. Parkhill won-dered why in the world he, like other teachers, fell into the habit of characterizing students by their location. "Blackboard . . ." that was silly. He did not call the rest of the class "Chairs.")

The seven completed their transcription, returning to their seats with alibis and apologies. There was merit in their unconfidence.

Miss Lopez, ignoring the possessive adjective "my," had forsaken her life for a "Story of Life." Stanislaus Wilk-omirski, bored by his past, had expatiated on "My Wife" instead of "My Life." Miss Tarnova, true to Mother Russia, had addressed herself to "Life. Death. *What They*

Mean???" Mr. Umea had composed a confessional which consisted of but three trenchant lines:

> Come N.Y. since 6 years.
> Work in lather belts.
> Marry. feel nice in morning.

Mr. Parkhill did not glance at the other compositions. He was quite disappointed. "Let us take Miss Lopez's work first. Corrections?"

At once Lola Lopez lowered her head; she looked like a sparrow. Her colleagues sat silent.

"Mistakes?" asked Mr. Parkhill lightly.

No critic stirred.

"We need not feel so—er—shy, class. We *learn* from our mistakes. . . . Anyone?"

No one.

Mr. Parkhill looked hopefully toward Miss Mitnick. Miss Mitnick blushed. He glanced toward Mr. Fledermann. C. J. Fledermann was sharpening his pencil. Mr. Parkhill smiled at Nathan P. Nathan, who winked back, but volunteered nothing.

Now, Mr. Parkhill gazed encouragingly at Rochelle Goldberg, but Miss Goldberg was unwrapping a caramel. Mr. Kaplan? Mr. Kaplan was still scribbling away on that precious envelope, which he had split open to double its area. What *had* gotten into the class tonight?

Bereft of participants, Mr. Parkhill corrected Miss Lopez's homework himself. And he proceeded to rectify the other autobiographies with speed. He seemed in a hurry.

Another batch of students was sent to the board. "Mrs. Pilpul. . . . Peter Studniczka . . ."

Suddenly Mr. Kaplan's splayed envelope wig-wagged in the air. "Mr. Pockheel! Mr. Pockheel!" The man's smile was as spacious as it was seductive. "Ken I go, plizz?"

Mr. Parkhill averted his gaze. "We are doing our *home*-work, Mr. Kaplan. You were not here when I assigned—"

"I jost findished it! In dis exect spot!"

Mr. Pinsky exclaimed "Pssh!" and slapped both cheeks in awe.

Mr. Nathan laughed. "He will *kill* me!"

"You—uh—wrote your autobiography *here?*" asked Mr. Parkhill.

"De whole voiks!" Mr. Kaplan leaped from his seat to the board, seized a piece of chalk and, before Mr. Parkhill could protest or demur or dissuade, printed:

Hyman Kaplan
by
H*Y*M*A*N K*A*P*L*A*N

The title hypnotized Mr. Parkhill. How had Mr. Kaplan decided where to place the stars? In the first "Hyman Kaplan"? That would imply that it was the *idea* of Mr. Kaplan, not the real Mr. Kaplan, that was all-important. In both "Hyman Kaplan"s? That would suggest a split personality. But putting the stars only in the second "Hyman Kaplan," as Mr. Kaplan had done—that, Mr. Parkhill had to concede, was masterful: for it emphasized Kaplan the man, not Kaplan the subject; Kaplan the creator, not Kaplan the concept.

Mr. Parkhill forced his eyes away from Mr. Kaplan's composition to scan the work of his companions at the board. Mr. Blattberg was copying an epic entitled "Who I am!" Miss Kipnis was baring her soul in a saga called, somewhat mysteriously, "Riga 47." (It turned out that "Riga 47" referred to the city and zone of "Cookie" Kipnis's nativity.) Most surprising was the composition, if that was what it was, of Peter Ignatius Studniczka; he had poured the story of his life into a skeletonic mold:

Moth. & Fath.	Mary & Frank
broth.	6
sist.	<u>3</u>

broths & sists	9
dead	2 (sist.)
Wife	No
childs	not
job	bottel washr
want be	Bottel Boss

Mr. Parkhill turned his back to the board. He waited for them all to finish, and he heard them return to their seats, one by one. "Let us begin with"—he took a deep breath—"Mr. Kaplan." Only then did he summon the fortitude to confront the full flowering of Mr. Kaplan's soul:

Hyman Kaplan
by
H*Y*M*A*N K*A*P*L*A*N

First, I was born.
In Kiev, in old contry. (Moishe Elman, famous on fiddle, was also coming from Kiev.)

"Notice the sentence structure, class," said Mr. Parkhill absently. (His mind was not on sentence structure at all: it was wrestling with the impeccable logic of "First, I was born.")

My father had the name Joe but freinds were calling him Yussel. My mother had the name Ida, but I called her Mama. Netcheral.

"Watch for errors in spelling," intoned Mr. Parkhill.

Also was 4 brothers and sisters. Avrum, Mireleh, me (my name was Hymie), Becky. Behind Becky came Max. That Max! He is tarrible smart. He got a wonderful mamory, only he forgats.

"Pay attention to the *meaning* of the sentences," Mr. Parkhill called resolutely.

198

Came bad times (plenty) so I took 5 year to get my Visa and saled to wonderful U.S. Took 10 days, and sick also 10 days. I falt sure is allready "Goodbye, Hyman Kaplan!"

"And note the quotation marks!" Mr. Parkhill blurted in alarm.

In N.Y. I am heppy. But not 100%. So I am coming to school. To learn. All. I am full all kinds embition. My mottol is—"Kaplan, GO HIGH!!"

                    T-h-e   E-n-d

"The end . . ." Mr. Parkhill studied the floor; he knew it was only the beginning.

Hummings and buzzings and *sotto voce* gloats passed across the scholars' ranks, as they did whenever Mr. Kaplan displayed his prose.

Mr. Parkhill tapped his pointer on the desk. "Now, class. . . . Corrections."

They leaped to the onslaught with gusto. Mr. Blattberg denounced Mr. Kaplan for mutilating four entirely innocent words: " 'freinds . . . contry . . . mamory . . . embition.' " Miss Atrakian deplored the lawlessness of Mr. Kaplan's verbs, which wandered from the present to the participial without a shred of respect for the past. Mr. Fledermann exclaimed: "This man makes *backwarts* hiss quotation points! Front ones are back ones, and back ones are dizzy!" (A chorus fit for Berlioz praised C. J. Fledermann for this subtle observation.)

Miss Ziev remodeled one sentence with scorn and removed two periods with contempt. Even Molly Yanoff, smoothing her eternal black frock, caught Mr. Kaplan in flagrant error: "Who *don't* call a Mama 'Mama'? So is that 'but' after 'Ida' foolish, I think, no?" Mr. Hruska (who had entered without fanfare) grunted that "mottol" should be "motel." As for Reuben Olansky, this new Hector smote Achilles in both heels, firing scathing salvos at the malapropisms Hyman Kaplan had spawned and voicing condo-

199

lences to the diction he had massacred.

"Hyman Kaplan by H*Y*M*A*N K*A*P*L*A*N" bled.

As Mr. Parkhill's chalk raced across the board—correcting, deleting, transposing, replacing—he could not help observing that the entire class, so subdued but half an hour ago, was bursting with vitality. Whatever you might say about Mr. Kaplan, his presence could resuscitate a corpse.

"Any more mistakes?" Mr. Parkhill asked buoyantly.

Miss Mitnick stammered, "In the composition I think are mistakes also in *meaning!*"

"Good," grinned Mr. Nathan.

"Prosidd, Mitnick," Mr. Kaplan murmured, turning inscrutable.

"Should not be a musician in this homework!" Demure Miss Mitnick, who had suffered so many wounds in confrontations with Hyman Kaplan, was careful to address this statement to Mr. Parkhill: "Why does Mr. Kaplan put Mischa Elman in the story of his own life?"

"I like his playink," smiled Mr. Kaplan.

"Hanh?!" wheezed Mr. Olansky. "That's a *reason—?!*"

"No. It's a decision!"

"Oh boy!" Mr. Pinsky slapped his thigh in elation.

Miss Mitnick had begun to whinny, which so alarmed Stanislaus Wilkomirski that the gallant Pole dashed to befriend her. "No, not right!" he protested. "Is *not* got a place in your life—like lady say!"

"I vant Moishe Elman in mine life," said Mr. Kaplan. "In *your* life put Paderewski."

Mr. Wilkomirski fled the field.

"Stop!" cried C. J. Fledermann, riding in Wilkomirski's stead. "I happen to be a music teacher!"

The appearance of Gabriel could have generated no greater acclamation. "A *teacher!*"

"In our class!!"

Isaac Nussbaum surmised: "He must be high educated," and stroked his beard in homage.

"Elman's name was 'Mischa,' not 'Moishe'!" snapped Christian Fledermann.

"It dipands on who's prononcink," said Mr. Kaplan.

"Mr. Kap—"

Suddenly, Miss Tarnova cried, "From *my* homeland came Tchaikovsky, Borodin—"

"Also Resputin," crooned her nemesis.

"Rachmaninoff! Moussorgsky!"

"Crazy Kink Piter."

"Stravin—"

"Miss Tarnova—" Mr. Parkhill cut in, realizing that Miss Tarnova could go on all night cataloguing Russia's immortals, and Mr. Kaplan his roster of maniacs. "Suppose we get on with our *correc*tions."

Up shot the hand of Reuben Olansky. "I see an *important* piece of mish-mosh!"

Mr. Kaplan wheeled around to face this new peasant.

"What kind of *sanse,*" Mr. Olansky inquired acidly, "is in a student who can write—right there"—he thrust an accusatory forefinger at the board (unfortunately he was lunging at Miss Kipnis's memoir, so askew was his vision) —"that 'Max had a wonderful memory, only he forgets'?! Isn't that ridiculouse?"

The Philistines rocked in merriment.

"That's like saying a man is fat but skinny!" boomed stern Olansky. "A millionaire but poor!"

The chamber shook with hilarity.

"Good for Olansky!"

"Brilliant rizzoning!"

"Ooo Kaplan!" jeered Mrs. Moskowitz, disciplining her diphthong.

"Vouldn't you say—'poor Kaminsky'?" purred Mr. Kaplan.

"*Who?*"

"Why Kaminsky?!"

"Class! . . . Mr. Kaplan . . ." Mr. Parkhill's palms were perspiring. "Mr. Olansky is quite right. I fail to see your point about—er—"

"Kaminsky."

"—Mr. Kaminsky."

Mr. Kaplan shrugged. "Harry Kaminsky is a furrier on mine block. He has t'ree odder stores. The man is a malted millionaire, an' still—"

"*Multi*-million—"

"—he's in hospital, mit hiccups! Sofferink tarrible! So vouldn't even Olansky say 'Poor Kaminsky'?"

A storm rattled the walls.

"A treek!"

"Kaminsky is *rich,* not poor!" shouted Mr. Hruska.

"Rich and sick, not *poor* and sick!" blushed Miss Mitnick.

"That guy is a whiz-bank!" chortled Mr. Nathan.

"Class, *class!*" Mr. Parkhill's pointer was pounding an admonitory tattoo. "Mr. Kaplan, your example does *not* refute Mr. Olansky. 'Poor millionaire,' as you used it, is just a—colloquial way of putting it. You call him 'poor' to show sympathy, not to describe his—er—wealth. Let us stick to Mr. Olansky's criticism of your statement about your brother: that is, that he has a wonderful memory, but forgets. That, Mr. Kaplan, is a flat contradiction!"

"Ahh," leered Hyman Kaplan.

"*What's with this 'Aah?'*" demanded Reuben Olansky. (He could hardly be blamed for not knowing that Mr. Kaplan considered a contradiction an achievement, not an error.)

"Mr. Kaplan," frowned Mr. Parkhill, "that statement is not—logical!"

"Not *logical?*" Mr. Kaplan reeled. For Mr. Kaplan to be

accused of illogic was tantamount to Titian's being charged with color-blindness.

"Give an inch, Mr. Kaplan, give an *inch,*" pleaded Bessie Shimmelfarb.

Instead of yielding an inch, Mr. Kaplan raised a ruler. "Vhy is it not logical?"

Miss Mitnick exclaimed, "How can your brother have a wonderful memory if—as you say—he *forgets?*"

Mr. Kaplan eyed her with infinite pity. "My brodder Mex heppens to possass a movvelous mamory—"

"But you yourself admit he forgets."

"Occasionally."

"But if he f-forgets—"

"Mex is only human."

"—either he has a *good* memory, and remembers, or a *bad* memory, and forgets!" Miss Mitnick's state was heart-rending.

"Correct!" called Nathan P. Nathan.

"Koplon is tropped," intoned Olga Tarnova.

"Give Mr. Keplen a chence!" sputtered faithful Pinsky.

Mr. Kaplan crossed the Rubicon. "Mine dear Mitnick," he murmured, "I regrat your pars of rizzoning. . . . *Is* a mamory eider good or bed? Is a day eider boilink or friz-zink?" His glance impaled Reuben Olansky. "Is Life so tsimple? Is Man so cotton dry?"

" 'Cut-and-*dried.*' "

"Batter *t'ink* abot dis, Olansky! T'ink *dipper,* Mitnick!" Mr. Kaplan illustrated how to "t'ink dipper" by narrowing only one eye whilst cauterizing his inquisitors with the other. "Fects are fects! Foist, my brodder has a vunderful mamory! Like a policeman! But—*sometimes* Mex forgats. So does dat minn he doesn't have a movvelous mamory *ven ve jost agreet he did?!*"

It was outrageous. It was grotesque. It made sophistry ashamed of itself. And it plunged the classroom into pandemonium. Mr. Olansky bellowed protestations. Mrs. Pilpul was seized by vertigo. Mrs. Moskowitz complained of hot flushes. Miss Mitnick verged on tears. (Poor Miss Mitnick: once more right, yet once more routed.)

"God alsmighty!" roared two Wodjiks as one.

"Denk you," said Mr. Kaplan.

"Class—"

"*Cu*ckoo! *Cu*ckoo!" Miss Goldberg dived for a chocolate cream.

Christian J. Fledermann was so speechless that he put his head in his hands and brayed.

"Kapalan belongs in the *movies!*" caroled Nathan P. Nathan.

"He belongs in prison!" raged Mr. Blattberg.

Mr. Parkhill's rapping pointer and loudest voice quelled the broil and babble. "Ladies! Gentlemen! Attention, everyone!" The tumult subsided. "We must not let ourselves be—carried away. Criticism does not require quarreling. Let me return to the point at issue." He looked squarely at the man who had (once more) set off an explosion. "Mr. Kaplan"—Mr. Parkhill made no effort to exclude asperity from his tone—"you have simply twisted the facts! You have evaded the excellent objections raised by Mr. Olansky and Miss Mitnick. They are absolutely right. *You* are absolutely—in error!"

Mr. Kaplan looked crestfallen. The Mitnick-Olansky-Tarnova platoon preened in satisfaction.

"Let me retrace the argument step by step." Mr. Parkhill conducted his autopsy with merciless strokes. He *could* not permit Mr. Kaplan to employ such chicanery. He would not let reason be smothered by casuistry. He had seen his bravest, brightest scholars fall before Mr. Kaplan's blunderbuss. . . . Mr. Parkhill split Mr. Kaplan's offending sentence into two clearly opposed parts. He slashed the *non sequitur* to ribbons. He exposed the assertion *a priori* and deposed it *a posteriori*. *This* time, only the second night out on the new term's voyage, Mr. Parkhill was determined that Mr. Kaplan not be allowed to wiggle out of error by outrageous sophistry.

And an odd thing happened. Even as he chastised his most intractable pupil, Mr. Parkhill felt nourishing juices course through his veins. For the priceless spark of life, the very heart of learning, had been revived in what, but half an hour ago, had been a dull and listless congregation.

As he revealed each cunning nuance of the pettifoggery with which Mr. Kaplan had confounded his adversaries, Mr. Parkhill caught himself feeling grateful that Hyman Kaplan—nay, H*Y*M*A*N   K*A*P*L*A*N—had come home again.

CHRISTOPHER C. K·A·P·L·A·N

To Mr. Parkhill the beginners' grade was more than a group of adults yearning to learn English. He took a larger view of his responsibilities: to Mr. Parkhill the school was an incubator of Citizens. To imbue men and women from a dozen nations with the meaning of America—its dramatic past, its precious traditions, its noblest aspirations— this, to Mr. Parkhill, was the greater work to which he had dedicated himself.

So it was that on the eve of any national holiday, Mr. Parkhill opened the class session with a little excursion into American history. In the spring, it was Decoration Day that enlisted his eloquence. In the fall, it was Thanksgiving. (He always regretted the fact that the Fourth of July, grandest holiday of them all, fell in a month when the school was not open.) And this Monday night in October, on the eve of Columbus Day, Mr. Parkhill began with these ringing words: "Tonight, class, let us set aside our routine tasks for a while to discuss the man whose historic achievement our country will commemorate tomorrow."

Expectancy welled up in the air.

"To this man," said Mr. Parkhill, "America owes its very beginning. I'm sure you all know whom I mean—"

"Jawdgie Washington!" Isaac Nussbaum promptly guessed.

"No, not 'Georgie'—*George*—Washington. I was referring to another—"

"Cortez?" asked Lola Lopez. "Ricardo Cortez?"

"That's a moom-picture actor!" Nathan P. Nathan could hardly contain his laughter.

"N-no, Miss Lopez. It was *Hernando* Cortez who—er—came somewhat later than the historic figure to whom I—"

"Paul Rewere!" cried Oscar Trabish.

Mr. Parkhill adjusted his glasses. Mr. Trabish had formed a peculiar psychic union with "Paul Rewere": he had already written two rhapsodic compositions and made one speech of tribute to his beloved alter ego. (The written eulogies had been named "Paul Revere's Horse Makes History" and "Paul Revere: One by Land, Two by Beach." The speech had been announced by Mr. Trabish as "Paul Rewere! Why He Wasn't Prazidant?" He had been quite indignant about it.)

"Not Paul 'Rewere,'" sighed Mr. Parkhill. "It's a 'v,' Mr. Trabish, not a 'w.' You *spell* it correctly, but you replace the 'v's with 'w's—and the 'w's with 'v's—when you speak. . . . Class, let's not just guess. What *date* is tomorrow?"

"Mine boitday!" an excited tenor sang out.

Mr. Parkhill ignored that. "I'll give you a hint." He smiled hintfully. "Tomorrow is October twelfth. And on October twelfth, in the year 1492—"

"Dat's mine *boit*day! October tvalf! I should live so! Mr. Pockheel, honest to Gott!"

It was (but why, oh why, did it have to be?) Hyman Kaplan.

Mr. Parkhill took a deep breath. "Mr. Kaplan," he asked warily, "is October twelfth—*really* your birthday?"

"*Mis*ter Pockheel!"

Mr. Parkhill felt ashamed of himself.

"Keplan is too old to have bird-days!" scowled Mr. Nussbaum, stroking his beard.

207

"October tvalf I'm born; October tvalf I'm tsalebratink!" retorted Mr. Kaplan. "All mine *life* I'm hevink boitdays on October tvalf. No axceptions!"

Mr. Parkhill said, "Well, well. That *is* a coincidence." He cleared his throat. "I'm sure we all wish Mr. Kaplan many happy returns."

"Heppy retoins!"

"Good lock!"

"You should live to a hondret!"

Messrs. Olansky and Fledermann sat silent, questioning whether Mr. Kaplan's longevity was an unalloyed blessing.

Mr. Kaplan acknowledged the felicitations: a beam, a little bow, a trio of "Denk you"s.

By this time, Miss Mitnick had conquered her shyness enough to call "Congratulation."

"That goes for me!" laughed Mr. Nathan.

"Mitnick." Mr. Kaplan inclined his head. "Nat'an."

"However," Mr. Parkhill raised his voice, "the particular *historical* event we shall commemorate tomorrow pertains to—Christopher Columbus. For it was on October twelfth, 1492—"

"*Colom*biss?" Mr. Kaplan's rapture burst its seams. "Christ*over Colom*biss?!"

Excitement seized the beginners' grade.

"Columbus!"

"Columbia Day," breathed Olga Tarnova. "Ah, Colombos. . . . Romohnteek."

"Colombus discovert America!" cried Mr. Pinsky, as if he had just discovered Columbus.

"Oy!" No one could groan a "What?" or moan a "Why?" with one-tenth the significance Sadie Moskowitz put into her "Oy"s. She was the Niobe of the beginners' grade.

"Yes, class, on October twelfth, 1492—"

Mr. Trabish dropped a sneer in the general direction of

Isaac Nussbaum. "And you said George Washington! Heh!"

"*You* sad Paul Rewere! Phooey!"

"Phooey!" echoed Mr. Hruska.

"On October twelfth, 1492—" Mr. Parkhill tried again.

"By me could every day in the year be something about Paul Rewere!" proclaimed Oscar Trabish.

"And by *me* is our first Prezident worth ten men on a horse!" retorted Isaac Nussbaum.

Lucca Barbella cried, *"Bravo!"*

Miss Goldberg reached for a sourball.

"On October twelfth, 1492"—Mr. Parkhill's tone brooked no ignoring—"Christopher Columbus discovered a new continent! Setting sail in three small ships—"

A hush gripped the grade as Mr. Parkhill launched into the deathless saga of Christopher Columbus and the brave little armada that challenged the unknown. He spoke slowly, impressively. (It was not often he was afforded material of such majesty.) And his novitiates, caught in the drama of that great and fearful voyage, hung upon every syllable. "The food ran low. Water was scarce. Rumors of doom—of disaster, of fatal reefs or fearful sea monsters—raced through the frightened crew. . . ."

Shirley Ziev leaned forward to sigh into Mr. Kaplan's ear: "You are lucky, Mr. Kaplan. Born the same day Columbus did."

Mr. Kaplan was in the world of dreams. He kept whispering "Christover Colombiss" to himself, transported. "My!" He closed his eyes. "October tvalf I'm arrivink in de voild, an' October tvalf Colombiss picks ot for discoverink a new world. . . . Dastiny!"

"Mutiny faced Christopher Columbus," Mr. Parkhill intoned with feeling. "His officers begged him—"

"My boithday is Motch toity," sighed Miss "Cookie" Kip-

209

nis in envy. "Not even a soborb was discovered Motch toity!"

Mr. Kaplan comforted desolate Kipnis. "Ufcawss, Colombiss discovert a *long* time bifore Keplen iven breeded."

"October twalf is October twalf!" cried ever-loyal Pinsky.

Mr. Kaplan allowed the mantle of history to fall upon his shoulders.

Mr. Parkhill, upon whom the Ziev-Kipnis-Pinsky symposium had not been lost, described the geographical illusions of Europeans in 1492, the belief that the world was flat as a plate, the mockery to which proud Columbus had been subjected. He traced the ironic confluence of events through which two continents had been named after Amerigo Vespucci.

"Dey are called Naut an' Sot America by *mistake?*" exclaimed Mr. Kaplan, doubting his ears, and at once answered his own question with an indignant, "By mistake!" It was clear he would never forgive Vespucci.

Mr. Parkhill proceeded with determination, recounting the crisis of that immortal voyage, three tiny ships on an ocean infested, in men's minds, by demons of the deep. He extolled the fortitude of the captain who would not turn back. He described the awful night when Columbus prayed for God's guidance once more, and decided that unless land was seen the next morn he would turn back. . . . And when Mr. Parkhill whispered, "And then a voice from the crow's-nest cried 'Land! Land!' " gasps of relief vied with gulps of gratitude in the transfixed grade. A tear rolled down Miss Mitnick's cheek. When Mr. Parkhill described the landing on Bahamian soil, Miss Tarnova inhaled the scent of her kerchief and Miss Atrakian suppressed a sob. And when their earnest shepherd said, "And because Columbus thought he was really in India, he called the natives Indians . . ." the amazement of his flock surpassed description.

"Vun mistake on top de odder!" cried Kaplan.

"Dey called *Hindyans* by mistake?" gasped Mrs. Moskowitz. Mrs. Moskowitz could not believe that of history.

"Yes, Mrs. Moskowitz, Indians—by mistake."

Mr. Kaplan shook his head. "Dose poor Indians."

Miss Lopez fingered her beads.

Mr. Parkhill hurried on to the role of Ferdinand and
Isabella. Just as he was about to complete *that* absorbing
tale, Mr. Kaplan announced, "Ectual, ve ain't iven Amaricans!"

Mr. Parkhill paused. " 'Actual*ly,* we *are*n't *e*ven Am*er*-
icans,' Mr. Kaplan. There is no such word as 'ain't.' "

"*A*ctual*ly,* we all Colombians!" A demand for justice—
long overdue—burned in Hyman Kaplan's eyes.

"Now you're talking!" called stout Pinsky.

Mr. Parkhill turned the class over to Miss Mitnick for
General Discussion. This was an innovation on Mr. Parkhill's part. General Discussion was very popular with his
students, and a fruitful exercise to boot; and it was particularly productive when he delegated one of the more
competent pupils to lead it. None excelled Rose Mitnick in
ability. Whether she was as pleased as she was nervous, as
she stumbled up the aisle, no one could say; that she was
as pale as a turnip, no one could deny.

Mr. Parkhill took a seat in the back of the room, as he
always did during General Discussion (or Recitation and
Speech). Miss Mitnick mounted the platform on which Mr.
Parkhill's desk stood, her cheeks incarnadined, passing a
trembling hand across her trembling hair. She lowered
herself in Authority's chair. Mr. Nathan laughed encouragement; Mrs. Yanoff applauded; the widow Pilpul called,
"Don't be ascared!"

That, of course, trebled Miss Mitnick's trepidation. Eyes
glazed, she stammered: "F-fellow s-students . . ."

"Spik netcherel," whispered Hyman Kaplan.

"Thank you—"

"You velcome."

"—it is an honor and also a p-privilege to open, by Mr. Parkhill's own choosing, General D-discussion!"

"Oh, Rose Mitnick!" moist-eyed Moskowitz breathed.

"Mr. Parkhill has told us the wonderful story of Columbus. So maybe we—his students in beginners' grade—should begin with paying s-special attention to . . ." Miss Mitnick struck the keynote for the rest of the evening with a touching tribute to explorers in general and Columbus in particular. She ended her tribute with what Mr. Parkhill thought was a most deft comparison of Columbus and Admiral Byrd. "Both men found new worlds for humanity!"

"Edmiral *Boyd?*" Mr. Kaplan promptly echoed in disdain. "Who is dis all-of-a-sodden hero?"

"He discovered the South Pole!" exclaimed Miss Mitnick.

"Him you compare mit Col*om*biss?!" Astonishment joined umbrage in Mr. Kaplan's tone. "An Edmiral *Boyd?!"*

"It's '*Ad*miral *Byrd,*' " Mr. Parkhill called.

"He was a kind of modern Columbus," Miss Mitnick blurted. *"He* also went to a new continent—"

"Vhat kind continent? Only snow, ice an' funny pigeons!"

" '*Pen*guins!' "

"But he was the *first* one," Miss Mitnick started, "who—"

"Somvun vas foist to make popcorn, so do ve have a holiday in his honor?!"

"I'll *die!"* choked Nathan P. Nathan.

"Mr. Kap—"

"Admiral Byrd was a *hero!"* cried Rose Mitnick. "He did discover the whole South Pole!"

"Som discoverink!" sniffed Mr. Kaplan, dismissing all of Antarctica.

"Stop!" boomed Reuben Olansky, his lenses magnifying

212

his ferocity. "South Pole is very important!"

"Ha! Averyvun *knew* dere vas a Pole in de sot!" Mr. Kaplan said. "All Edmiral Boyd did vas go dere!"

Miss Mitnick turned amber, Mr. Fledermann turned blue, and Bessie Shimmelfarb pleaded, "Give an *inch,* Mr. Kaplan, give an *inch.*"

"Kaplan, are you *crazy?*" Mr. Blattberg flung a sentiment concurred in by many.

"He is not normal," opined Mr. Nussbaum.

"An' Edmiral Boyd *vas?* To go t'ousants of miles to a place vhere all you can do is prectice frizzink?"

"Class—"

Mr. Olansky was so furious that he turned his back upon Mr. Kaplan and addressed scathing protestations to the side wall: "Minerals. . . . Panguins. . . . An achievement for *Science.* . . . Koplan turns it all hopside down!!"

"I," murmured Mr. Kaplan, "don't say 'hopside' for 'opside.'"

Mr. Nathan howled.

"Gentlemen . . ." Mr. Parkhill chided them. "Please. . . . Proceed, Miss Mitnick."

Miss Mitnick, who had been biting her lip and fluttering her hands, reshouldered her duties. "In *spite* Mr. Kaplan's remark that everybody *knew* was a South Pole and Admiral Byrd only went there, we all agree he was a big hero. He soffered terrible things for humanity: cold, icebergs, alone below zero—"

"Edmiral Boyd vent mit all modinn conveniences!" cried Mr. Kaplan.

"Yos!" blurted Tomas Wodjik, to everyone's surprise.

"He even spent money for hitting goils!" affirmed Milas Wodjik.

The by-now tautened nerves of the scholars snapped into smithereens.

"Lie!"

213

"Shame!"

"Take back those woids!"

It took the hasty intervention of Mr. Parkhill, from the back row, to clarify the confusion (in which he, too, floundered). Tomas Wodjik explained that when his twin, Milas, an expert electrician but maladroit speaker, had said "hitting goils" he meant Admiral Byrd had been supplied with "heating coils."

"Oh migott!" croaked Mr. Nussbaum.

"Heating coils?!" Nathan P. Nathan slapped Mr. Pinsky's back in jubilation.

"Some cless," sighed Mr. Kaplan.

"Gentlemen! Class. . . . Thank you, Mr. Wodjik. I'm glad you explained that." Mr. Parkhill was more than glad; he was overjoyed. The thought that Admiral Byrd had spent government funds to smuggle girls to the South Pole so that he could flagellate them at his leisure was too dreadful to contemplate. "Miss Mitnick, please resume the discussion."

As Miss Mitnick made noises of strangulation, Lucca Barbella erupted: "Is only da one Cristoforo Colombo! Is only da one Amerigo Vespucci! Is noa one lak—befora, behinda!" To Mr. Barbella, beyond any peradventure of doubt, Columbus and Vespucci, wholly Italian titans, would never be matched, much less outshone. Admiral Byrd, he said flatly, was merely a "copying cat."

"Right!" beamed Mr. Kaplan.

"Class . . ."

Miss Mitnick tapped Mr. Parkhill's desk tearfully. "Order. . . . The discussion must go farther. . . . Who would like to ask the floor?"

Olaf Umea demanded the floor, and took it before Miss Mitnick could give it to him. "Columbus was a great man! No doubts about!" Columbus was indeed worth all that Mr. Kaplan and Miss Mitnick had claimed for him. But, Mr.

214

Umea glowered, how could any student of history consider Columbus more than a vapid descendant of the greatest explorer of them all: Leif Ericson? (The Viking, it turned out, was born no more than a handful of kilometers from the birthplace of Olaf Umea.)

"Boit*days* are more important den *boitplaces!*" Mr. Kaplan promptly proclaimed.

The advocate from Scandinavia blustered and muttered, "And don't even *mention* that Vestpucci, a liar—"

"No, no!" shouted Mr. Barbella. "Amerigo Vespucci was born in Italia also!"

"So was Marcus Polo," retorted Mr. Kaplan, "an' he got lost in Chinaton!"

"Class—"

"Diavolo! Assassino! Bugiardo!"

"Are ve salabratink Colombiss Day or making spaghetti?" asked Mr. Kaplan.

"Anyone else wants the floor?" entreated Miss Mitnick. "Mr.—Nathan?!"

Nathan P. Nathan was wiping tears from his eyes. "No, thanks, Rose."

"Miss Goldberg?" pleaded Miss Mitnick.

"Zln mb thnks," came through Miss Goldberg's taffy-coated mouth.

"Mr.—"

"—Keplen," completed the name's owner helpfully.

"*Any*one! The floor is absolutely *open,*" Miss Mitnick announced, but denied her offer by keeping her eyes where Mr. Kaplan's could not possibly meet them. *"Any*body can talk."

No one but her arch-enemy seemed willing to talk.

"Mr. Wodjik?!" asked plaintive Miss Mitnick.

Milas Wodjik hemmed as Tomas Wodjik hawed.

"Mrs. Pilpul?"

The widow gulped in the negative.

215

"Lest call for volunteers!" panted Miss Mitnick.

Up rose the sole volunteer. "Foidinand an' Isabel. Ha!" Mr. Kaplan sat down.

Uneasy murmurings swept through the tiers.

Miss Mitnick stammered, "I didn't c-catch."

Mr. Kaplan made gracious allowance for Miss Mitnick's impediment. "I sad, 'Foidinand an' Isabel—Ha!"

"Why he makes ha-ha on royalties?!" cried "Cookie" Kipnis.

"Thot mon is mod . . . mod," moaned Miss Tarnova.

"Mr. Kap—"

"Exaplain to Miss Mitnick!" Mr. Nathan demanded, grinning.

"Describe your exact meaning dose remocks!" the voice of Aaron Blattberg rang out. (Such clarity and persistence had made Aaron Blattberg a crackerjack shirt salesman on Avenue B.)

Mr. Kaplan smiled, silent and inscrutable.

"Koplan wants to explain, or Koplan wants to take back?" fumed Mr. Olansky, addressing the ceiling.

"Y-yes, Mr. Kaplan," called Mr. Parkhill. "I do think the class is entitled to *some* explanation—"

"All of a sodden he makes fun Foidinand Isabel!" protested Mrs. Moskowitz. "Not even saying 'Axcuse'? Is this a way to tritt kinks and quinns?!"

The frontal attack stirred the royalists into action.

"Talk, Kaplan!"

"You got the floor."

"Tell awreddy!"

"Mr. Kaplan . . ." Miss Mitnick quavered.

In response to the public demand he had cunningly created, Mr. Kaplan rose once more. "Ladies, gantleman, Mr. Pockheel, chairlady . . ." Miss Mitnick lowered her lashes. "Ve all agree dat Colombiss's joiney vas vun of de most movvelous t'ings aver happened in de voild." Nods,

216

clucks, grunts (however reluctant). *"T'ink* abot dat treep
. . . jost *t'ink.* Viks an' viks Colombiss vas sailink—sailink
t'rough tarrible storms, lighteninks, tonder. T'rough vafes
as high as de Umpire State Buildink. Fodder an' fodder
Colombiss vent—not afraid, not belivink in monasters of
de dip, crossink dat onchotted ocean, not yildink to t'rets of
ravolution fromm his screws." The new Herodotus paused
to let the awesome data sink home. "Vell, my frands, in *vat
kind boats* did Colombiss made dat vunderful voyitch?"
His eyes became slits. "In strong, fency boats? In plazant
accommodations? No! In leetle, teentsy vassals. Chizz-
boxes! Sheeps full of likks! Boats full of doit, joims, vater
commink in! *Som* boats for discoverink Amarica!" Mr.
Kaplan's indignation curdled the air. "An' dats vhy I'm
sayink, *'Shame* on you, Foidinand! *Shame* on you, Isabel!'"
The bright blue eyes flashed. "Couldn't dey give a man like
Colombiss batter transportation?"

"Shame!" cried sympathetic Pinsky.

"Olé, Columbus!" cried Miss Lopez, upon whom had just
dawned the debt Iberia owed Columbus.

"Foolish talk," muttered Olaf Umea, visualizing the
rude craft of Leif Ericson.

Now the opposition buckled on its armor.

"Lat the past alone!"

"Isabel *liked* Columbus!"

"Maybe in 1492 Koplan could manufacture a S.S. *Quinn
Elizabat?"* Mr. Olansky asked the side wall acidly.

A storm of retorts, taunts, defenses and disclaimers
rolled across the contentious ranks. Mr. Pinsky shouted
that Mr. Kaplan was absolutely right; C. J. Fledermann
snarled that Mr. Kaplan was demented. Miss Atrakian reminded Mr. Kaplan that Queen Isabella was not an interior decorator for a navy. Mrs. Moskowitz announced
that she was having palpitations. Mr. Nathan tried to en-
courage Miss Mitnick with energetic winkings, but the

wan moderator, staggering under the burdens of arbitration, wailed, "Mr. Kaplan, *please*. The ships Ferdinand and Isabella gave Mr. Columbus were f-fine for that *time.*"

"For de *time?*" thundered Hyman Kaplan. "But not for de *man!*"

"But in those days—"

"A ginius like Colombiss should have averyting fromm de bast!"

"Oh, *gott!*" croaked Mr. Blattberg.

"Kaplen, give an *inch!*" pleaded Bessie Shimmelfarb.

"Right is right!" rejoined the sage. "I don't mashure de troot on a ruler!"

Miss Tarnova moaned, "Mr. Koplon is no gantlemon."

"He's a born lawyer!" blared Nathan P. Nathan.

Mr. Parkhill rose hastily. "Class, I think—"

"Colombiss desoived batter den a *Senta Maria*, a *Nina* an' a *Pintele!*" Mr. Kaplan declaimed, hacking left and right in behalf of his birth-mate. "Ven a man stotts ot to discover Amarica—"

"But Columbus didn't go out to discover a specific *place!*" Miss Mitnick protested.

"No?" Mr. Kaplan's mien dripped pity even as his tongue dripped honey. "Vhat did he go for? *Axercise?!*"

"I mean"—poor Miss Mitnick thrashed about in throes of desperation—"I mean that Columbus didn't *know* there was a continent in the middle Atlantic Ocean! Columbus just went out—"

Mr. Kaplan tendered her a forbearance laced with contempt. "Colombiss just 'vent ot'? . . . Vhy, dear Mitnick? Vhy did he vent ot?"

"To—to discover!"

"Vhat to discover?"

Miss Mitnick bleated, "Just—to *discover.*"

Mr. Kaplan surveyed the heated ranks, tolerant, nodding, the picture of patience contending with naïveté. "Colombiss just vent; he just vent to discover," he repeated. *"Just* to discover!" He glanced toward heaven, lamenting the limitations of human perspicacity. Then, face dark, he struck. "Som pipple t'ink dat if a man goes ot to mail a letter, he only *hopes* dat *maybe* he'll find a mailbox!"

"Stop!" howled Mr. Olansky, smiting his forehead.

"Oooy!" protested Sadie Moskowitz.

"Is-there-no-law-against-such-a-travesty-of-reasoning?" was all but inscribed on Mr. Umea's flabbergasted features.

And now the battle soared—with shouts and cries and accusations; with righteous assaults on the Kaplan logic, and impassioned defenses of the Mitnick virtue. Mr. Fledermann sputtered that Mr. Kaplan had pulled an unfair rabbit out of an illegal hat; Mr. Pinsky rejoined that C. J. Fledermann was too superficial to comprehend the profundity of Mr. Kaplan's ratiocinations. Mrs. Yanoff charged that Mr. Pinsky was nothing but a "Kaplan coolie"; Mr. Barbella averred that Mrs. Yanoff was but a myrmidon of Mitnick. Mr. Blattberg warned everyone that Mr. Kaplan would drive him crazy; "Cookie" Kipnis alleged that Mr. Blattberg's mental condition predated exposure to a man of Mr. Kaplan's stature. In a spate of scuffles on the sidelines, Mr. Wilkomirski blubbered, Mrs. Shimmelfarb pleaded, Miss Atrakian ranted, Mr. Trabish woke up, and the brothers Wodjik—shipwrecked—wandered in fraternal disorientation. As for Nathan P. Nathan, he was in convulsions. (Mr. Nathan seemed allergic to partisanship, so corruptible was he by entertainment.)

"Class!" Miss Mitnick implored them. "Please, every person!"

Mr. Parkhill was hurrying to his post in alarm.

Miss Goldberg, trying to dislodge a sourball she had misswallowed during the melee, began to both gag and gasp, "Slep my beck! Slep my beck!"

219

Mrs. Pilpul slapped her back just as the bell trilled in the corridor.

The bell went "Thrring!" and "Prring!" and "Thrrang!" but so ensnarled was the multitude in conflict that no one hearkened.

High above the furor, Mr. Parkhill called, "Dismissed! Class! That will be all!" He proclaimed it with total authority but inner misgivings.

For Mr. Parkhill could not help feeling that General Discussion had not been at all successful this evening. Yet how could he have known? . . . If only Columbus had discovered America on October eleventh! . . . If only Hyman Kaplan had been born on October thirteenth. . . .

3

THE DREADFUL DREAM
OF MR. PARKHILL

It was a splendid evening. The moon washed the city with silver, flowing down the proud spires into the pockmarked streets.

Mr. Parkhill consulted his watch. Forty minutes before he was due to meet his class. He had indulged in a rather heavy dinner (he did love Brown Betty); it would do him good to walk. He tucked his briefcase under his arm and set off. . . .

At this very moment, he reflected, from a dozen diverse outposts of the vast and clamorous metropolis, his students, too, were wending their way to the school to which they came with such eagerness and from which they expected so much. Miss Mitnick was probably subjecting her homework to yet another revision on the Fourteenth Street bus. (What a salutary student Miss Mitnick was!) Peter Studniczka was no doubt on the BMT, mumbling over his battered copy of *1,000 Words Commonly Misspelled.* (Sometimes Mr. Parkhill wondered whether Mr. Studniczka was as much influenced by the columns in which the words were spelled right as he was by the columns in which they were spelled wrong.) Miss Tarnova was most likely thinking up Open Questions on the Lexington Avenue subway as she brushed her long eyelashes with mascara. (Mr. Parkhill often wished Miss Tarnova would pay as much attention to her conjugations as she did to her cosmetics.) Mr. C. J. Fledermann was no doubt flexing his reflexes by drilling himself on irregular verbs. Miss Lola Lopez had no doubt attended Mass by now, and Nathan P. Nathan—Mr. Parkhill wondered what gremlins accounted for that young man's tireless jubilations, or his habit of winking, or his compulsion to augment words, from time to time, by endowing them with superfluous syllables.

What interesting, what unusual persons his students were! They came from a score of lands and cultures. He had spent almost nine years now introducing immigrants to the mysteries of English. Nine years. . . . Why, over three hundred students must have sat before him in that time. Some he remembered quite vividly, others—scarcely at all. Some had been swift to learn, others so slow, even obtuse. Some students were B.K. and some were A.K. . . .

Mr. Parkhill stopped dead in his tracks, frowning. Why on *earth* was he falling into that exasperating habit again? It was absurd, perfectly absurd! Why could he not shake it off, once and for all? *Qui docet* certainly should *discet.*

The bizarre initialing had begun almost two weeks ago, when he had awakened from a dream with a pounding heart and drenched with perspiration. (Even when he played squash, Mr. Parkhill rarely became *drenched* with perspiration.) And the dream had recurred, to his dismay, at least five times.

There was nothing especially complicated about the dream; it contained no esoteric symbols (Mr. Parkhill had reread Freud carefully) such as appear in the dreams of even the least neurotic among us. It certainly contained nothing (if you ignored the ladder) which could by the most fanciful stretch of the imagination be called "erotic" or even "libidinal." No. It was just a plain, run-of-the-mill dream. This was what psychiatrists called its "manifest content":

A huge crowd was gathered before the school building, which stood freshly painted, sparkling with untrue radiance and bedecked with gay flags and carnival banners. Some sort of ceremony was taking place. In one version of the dream, Mr. Leland Robinson, principal of the A.N.P.S.A., was addressing the throng; in another, the Chief Justice of the United States, dressed in majestic, if incongruous, regalia (curled-locks wig, white ruff, a voluminous scarlet robe) was delivering the oration; and several times it had been none other than the Secretary-General of the United Nations himself who held the crowd in the dream spellbound.

But it was not that part of the dream that always tore Mr. Parkhill's sleep asunder. The part from which Mr. Parkhill regularly awakened, throat parched and temples hammering, the only part of the dream, indeed, that repeated itself in identical form no matter *who* was delivering the main oration, occurred when the festivities suddenly stopped, a hush gripped the multitude, and Mr. Parkhill found himself the target of all eyes. The entire faculty and student body of the A.N.P.S.A. were staring at him in silent accusation—until (for reasons he could never make out) he began to climb a gigantic ladder in excruciating slow motion. He mounted the rungs with moanings, for a bronze plaque was strapped to his back. The ladder seemed a hundred stories high, even though it rested just above the entrance to the school. What Mr. Parkhill seemed driven to do, from that awful ladder, was hang the bronze plaque on a gigantic hook above the doorway. Engraved on the plaque in Gothic, golden letters was this legend:

AMERICAN NIGHT PREPARATORY SCHOOL
FOR ADULTS
Founded 1910
b. 35 years B.K.
d. "?" years A.K.

That "?" always blazed like a neon sign, the ? in bright red
and the " " in blue. The A.K., however, was outlined in
green.

A horn, howling into his very eardrum, caused Mr. Parkhill to jump back to the curb just as a truck whooshed by
his nose and a hoarse voice implored God to strike him
dead. Mr. Parkhill apologized to the vacant air. The traffic
light, which he had utterly forgotten to observe, was in-
dubitably red. Or had he mistaken the red of the light for
the red of the "?"?! He felt ashamed of himself.

He replaced the briefcase that had slipped to his knees,
stepped back up the curb, and waited for the light to
change. It changed to green, of course; Mr. Parkhill swiftly
crossed the street.

"B.K." . . . "A.K." Oh, he knew what those cryptic nota-
tions signified! They stood for "Before Kaplan" and "After
Kaplan." In fact, that was the key to the whole dream,
which simply converted into symbolic form a thought that
must have been churning and churning, unresolved, below Mr. Parkhill's consciousness: *viz.*, that the American
Night Preparatory School for Adults, which actually had
been founded a good many years before Mr. Kaplan ever
entered its doors, was doomed to survive only "?" years
after Mr. Kaplan left them. Left? That was just the point.
Would Mr. Kaplan ever leave?

The question had haunted Mr. Parkhill long before he
had been hounded by that disquieting dream. For he did
not see how he could, in conscience, promote Mr. Kaplan
to Miss Higby's grade (only last week Mr. Kaplan had said
that the plural of "sandwich" is "delicatessen"), and Mr.

Parkhill could not bring himself to advise Mr. Kaplan, as he was often tempted, to transfer to some other night school where he might perhaps be happier.

The undeniable fact was that there was no other night school in which Hyman Kaplan could possibly be happier: Mr. Parkhill might be happier; Miss Higby might be happier; at least half of his colleagues in the beginners' grade would surely be *much* happier. But Mr. Kaplan? That buoyant scholar displayed the strongest conceivable affection, an affection bordering on idolatry, for his alma mater.

That was another sticky point: the A.N.P.S.A. could not possibly be the alma mater of one who had never been graduated from it; yet Mr. Kaplan had a way of acting as if it already was.

And that was yet another of the baffling traits which made Mr. Kaplan so difficult to contend with: his cavalier attitude to reality, which he seemed to think he could alter to suit himself. How else could one characterize a man who identified the most famous Strauss waltz as "The Blue Daniel"? Or who, recounting the tale of the cloak spread in the mud before Queen Elizabeth the First, had credited the gallantry to "Sir Walter Reilly"?

Every way Mr. Parkhill turned, he seemed to sink deeper and deeper into the Kaplan morass. For if Mr. Kaplan could not be promoted, or lured away to greener pastures, what *could* Mr. Parkhill do about him? Sometimes Mr. Parkhill wondered if Mr. Kaplan was deliberately trying to remain in the beginners' grade for the rest of his (i.e., Mr. Parkhill's) life. This thought had begun to worry Mr. Parkhill so much that he had brought it up at the last faculty meeting.

Right after Miss Schnepfe had reminded the faculty that each teacher was responsible for snapping off the lights before leaving the classroom, and that the sofa in the faculty lounge had broken another spring and might have to be sent out for repairs, Mr. Robinson asked if there were any other problems which ought to be brought to his attention. "Any problems," he beamed. "As you know, I do not believe in hampering discussion with rigid agendas!"

Mrs. O'Hallohan had raised the perennial problem of ventilation. On very cold nights, classrooms were stifling and classes disturbed by the clanging of radiators; and on very hot nights, the fans near the ceiling did little to relieve the teachers' discomfort or the students' torpor.

Mr. Robinson's face clouded. He said he would speak severely to Mr. Janowitz, the school's temperamental "custodian."

Miss Melanie Pflaum then raised the problem of the chairs. Was the budget really so sparse that *some* of the one-armed oak relics could not at last be replaced by wider, less rickety seats?

"The blackboards," cut in Mr. Krout, "are far worthier supplicants than the chairs!" Why, half the slates in Mr. Krout's room were so thinned by use and glazed by erasings that they now repelled chalk—"the way Moslems reject pork!" (Mr. Krout certainly had a way with similes.)

Mr. Robinson made a wigwam of his hands as he mulled these complaints over, then told Miss Pflaum that the chairs could more sensibly be reglued than replaced, and Mr. Krout that if he used the blackboards which did not repel chalk *before* he assigned students to the slates which did, he would be surprised by how much he would decrease the wear and tear on the latter and "equalize, so to speak," the condition of the former. "There is a lot of life left in those old boards!" Mr. Robinson exclaimed. "Just transfer some of the workload to the new." (Mr. Robinson meant "the less-used"; there were no new blackboards in Mr. Krout's room, nor in any other.)

Miss Higby asked whether officials of the city's Board of

226

Education (*or* the State Department of Education) had yet indicated whether they would accredit the A.N.P.S.A. Mr. Robinson firmly asked everyone to be stout in faith as long as the application was pending. (It had been pending for forty-six months.)

At this point, the colloquium flagging, Mr. Robinson turned to Mr. Parkhill. "Is there not some problem *you* wish to share with us, Parkhill?"

What Mr. Parkhill wished was that he had not replied so quickly, considering how his question would sound to someone like Mr. Robinson: "Sir, what is the school's policy toward a student who may—er—never be qualified for promotion to a higher grade?"

He would never forget the ooze of ice that froze Mr. Robinson's features. (Few knew that under Mr. Robinson's confident façade seethed emotions that led men to end up as what Mr. Kaplan called "a nervous rag.") "Parkhill," Mr. Robinson steelily murmured, "we may all profit from the ancient adage: *'Presto maturo, presto marcio?!'* Yes: 'The sooner ripe, the sooner rotten!' That applies to pupils no less than fruit! . . . I, for one, never give up hope for slow learners—for *any* slow learner. To my humble way of thinking: better several fruitful semesters in the same grade than one barren promotion to the next!"

That had certainly been a memorable answer, but it left Mr. Parkhill exactly where he had been before: What could be done about Hyman Kaplan? The man simply refused to learn. No, no, Mr. Parkhill promptly corrected himself. It was not that Mr. Kaplan refused to learn; what Mr. Kaplan refused to do was *conform.* That was an entirely different matter. Mr. Parkhill could get Mr. Kaplan to understand a rule—of grammar or spelling or punctuation; what he did not seem able to do was get Mr. Kaplan to *agree* with it. Somewhere, somehow, Hyman Kaplan had gotten it into his head that to bend the knee to custom

227

was a hairsbreadth from bending the neck to slavery. (To Mr. Kaplan, the plural of "pie" was "pious.")

Nor was that all which impeded Mr. Kaplan's progress. The laws of English, after all, have developed century after century, like the common law; and like the common law, they gain in authority precisely from the fact that men go on observing them down the countless years. But Mr. Kaplan was not in the slightest impressed by precedent. He seemed to take the position that every rule of grammar, every canon of syntax, every convention of usage, no matter how ancient or formidable, had to prove its case anew. He seemed to want the whole English language to start from scratch. It had taken considerable persuasion on Mr. Parkhill's part, for instance, to convince Mr. Kaplan that there is no feminine form of "ghost." For Mr. Kaplan argued, not without a certain merit, that since a feminine host is a "hostess," a feminine ghost should be a "ghostess."

It was most trying. Mr. Parkhill was beginning to think that the secret to Mr. Kaplan's uniqueness lay in the fact that whereas all the other students came to school in order to be instructed, Mr. Kaplan came in order to be consulted.

Not that the man was an obstreperous pupil. On the contrary. Not one of Mr. Parkhill's three hundred abecedarians (that was what Mr. Robinson liked to call students) had ever been more cooperative, more enthusiastic, more athirst and aflame for knowledge. The trouble was that Mr. Kaplan was so enthusiastic, so athirst and aflame for knowledge that he converted the classroom into a courtroom—a courtroom, moreover, in which the English language was forced to take the stand as defendant. Indeed, Mr. Kaplan sometimes acted as if English had to justify its every rule under his anointed cross-examination.

How else could one describe a situation in which Mr. Kaplan maintained that if a pronoun is a word used in

228

place of a noun, a proverb is a pronoun used in place of a verb? It was preposterous, of course; yet when Mr. Parkhill had challenged Mr. Kaplan to give the class *one single example* of a pronoun used in place of a verb, Mr. Kaplan, transported by that elation which possessed him *in statu pupillari,* beamed, "I'll give t'ree exemples. Soppoze you are on vacation, an' somebody esks: 'Who vants to go for a svim?' T'ree pipple enswer: 'I!' 'Me!' 'You!' All pronons. No voibs." (Mr. Olansky had almost had a stroke that night.)

Surely a student could not be permitted to go on the way Mr. Kaplan did, changing the tongue of Keats and Swift and Trollope to suit himself. But if a pupil refused to accept authority, the testimony of experts, the awesome weight of precedent, to what higher court could his preceptor possibly appeal? Ay, there was the rub. (Mr. Kaplan believed that modern cities consist of streets, boulevards, and revenues.)

Mind you, Mr. Parkhill reminded himself, Mr. Kaplan had never denied that English had rules—good, even admirable, rules. What he would not accept, apparently, was that the rules applied to *him.* Mr. Kaplan had a way of getting Mr. Parkhill to submit each rule to the test of "rizzon," and Mr. Parkhill was beginning to face the awful suspicion that he was no match for a man who operated with rules of reason entirely his own. Only a man with rules of reason entirely his own would have the audacity to give the opposite of "height" as "lowth," or the plural of "woman" as "married." Sometimes Mr. Parkhill thought Mr. Kaplan would never find peace until he had invented a language all his own.

In trying to grope his way through the fog of his dilemma, Mr. Parkhill had even taken Miss Higby into his confidence. "Miss Higby," he had said during a recess, "it might just be that one of my students is a—well, a kind of genius."

"Genius?" echoed Miss Higby.

"Y-yes. I mean, he pays close attention, never fails to do his homework, volunteers every time we have Open Questions or General Discussion, and yet—well—I mean . . ." Mr. Parkhill illustrated his quandary by being unable to describe it.

"And *that* makes you think he's a 'genius'?"

"No," protested Mr. Parkhill. "What I'm trying to say is that he—well, he seems to take the position that since he raises no objection to our rules, why should we object to—er—his?"

Miss Higby had made a sort of gurgling noise. "I think we're going to get an extra day of vacation this semester!" She hurried to her room.

That remark had made Mr. Parkhill quite cross. It was not at all a matter of an extra day of vacation, this semester or any other. Vacation had nothing to do with it. The trouble with Miss Higby was that, like Mr. Robinson, she could not see the forest for the trees; worse, people like that could not see the *trees* because they were so preoccupied with the forest. They refused to face facts.

They refused to face facts, Mr. Parkhill felt, just as Mr. Kaplan refused to abide by conventions. Still, that did not absolve the American Night Preparatory School for Adults of its responsibility; it only added to its burdens.

What Mr. Parkhill finally concluded was that if Mr. Kaplan refused to enter their universe, they would have to enter his. Mr. Parkhill no longer doubted that Mr. Kaplan did live and think in a universe all his own. That would explain how he had come to define "diameter" as a machine that counts dimes, or named the waterway which connects the Atlantic and Pacific "the Panama Kennel."

Mr. Parkhill passed his hand across his brow. He wondered if it might not be best to think of Mr. Kaplan not as a pupil but as some sort of cosmic force, a reckless, independent star that swam through the heavens in its own unpredictable orbit. (After all, Mr. Kaplan referred to England's titan of science, codifier of the laws of gravity, as "Isaac Newman.")

Mr. Kaplan was simply *sui generis.* Perhaps that was why he so often responded with delight, rather than despair, when Mr. Parkhill corrected him. It had taken Mr. Parkhill a long time to discover that Mr. Kaplan's smile signified not agreement but consolation. Where all the other students sank into gloom upon committing an error, Mr. Kaplan shot into the clouds from which to celebrate his originality. . . .

Ahead loomed the school building. Tonight, bathed in gossamer moonbeams, it took on a ghostly grandeur.

Mr. Parkhill removed his hat as he went up the worn stone steps. Just as he opened the door, a voice behind him sang out, "Goot ivnink, Mr. Pockheel!"

He did not have to think or turn to know whose voice that was. No one else pronounced his name quite that way, or infused a routine salutation with the timbre of Archimedes crying "Eureka!"

"Vhat's a madder? You not fillink Hau Kay?"

"I beg your pardon?"

"You vere lookink so fonny on de school."

Mr. Parkhill caught a glimpse of Mr. Kaplan's bright, benign mien, beclouded, for a moment, with solicitude.

"It's nothing," said Mr. Parkhill hastily. "Nothing at all."

But he knew that he *had* been "lookink fonny on de school." He could have sworn that for one demented moment he had seen, twinkling over the entrance:

b. 25 years B.K.
d. "?" years A.K.

They entered the temple together.

231

4

MR. K·A·P·L·A·N CONQUERS AN AD

It was with a feeling of genuine usefulness that Mr. Parkhill announced: "Your homework assignment, class, will be of special interest!" He smiled.

Mr. Parkhill found himself smiling a great deal lately— not because he was a smiling type (on the contrary, he was an earnest, unsmiling type), and not because he actually felt like smiling. He smiled because he knew how much his students appreciated it. It soothed their anxieties; it stiffened their confidence; it definitely shored up their morale. He could not help but see how swiftly the class reacted to the subtlest variation of his moods—elated by his approval, depressed by his concern, crushed by his displeasure.

"The assignment," he continued, the smile cemented to his lips, "is a practical exercise which you will be able to put to—er—practical use."

At the first "practical" the entire congregation had sat up; at the second, they leaned forward. If there was anything they hungered for, it was to wring utility from a heartless tongue.

"Take an advertisement out of a newspaper—any advertisement, for a job, an automobile, a vacuum cleaner, any advertisement at all—and answer it!" Mr. Parkhill's smile congealed; to his surprise, not joy but unease swept the faces before him.

"Answer an *att?*" someone quavered.

"In *English?*" someone queried.

"*Me?!*" quaked Mrs. Yanoff, her black dress reinforcing her pessimism.

"Now, now," Mr. Parkhill reassured them, "the assignment is not hard. After all, you have all seen the 'Help Wanted' or 'For Sale' columns in newspapers." He replaced his ailing smile with a fresh edition. "Well, over this next weekend, simply look through a newspaper, select an ad, *any* ad that interests you, and—just answer it!"

Groans of uncertainty swelled into alarums of dismay, climaxed by an "Oy!" of premature defeat. Mrs. Moskowitz was already fanning herself with her notebook.

"Remember," Mr. Parkhill quickly added, "we have already had exercises in writing letters, both personal and business. Let's say this homework involves simply *another* exercise in letter writing!"

"Ufcawss! Plain an' tsimple!" That was Hyman Kaplan, and for once Mr. Parkhill felt grateful to that dauntless spirit.

"Are there any questions?"

Minnie Pilpul raised her left hand. (Actually, Mrs. Pilpul, who was left-handed, only elevated her thumb.) "Could you be so kind to give a for instance?"

"I beg your pardon?"

"She means be so kind and give an *example,*" explained Miss Mitnick.

"Ha!" scoffed Mr. Kaplan. "Who nidds more exemples? Mr. Pockheel axplained it poifick! 'Halp vanted.' 'For Sale.' Iven a baby could unnistand!" He scowled at the widow Pilpul for flinching before what any infant could understand, and sniffed at Miss Mitnick for giving aid and comfort to a backslider.

"I only t-tried to help," Miss Mitnick stammered.

"An' *I,*" said Mr. Kaplan, "don nidd exemples of exemples!"

"Stop!" boomed Reuben Olansky, glaring at Mr. Studniczka, who had not uttered a sound. "Let *once* the class not be an all-for-free!"

"It's 'free-for-all,' " remarked Mr. Parkhill.

"Ha!" exulted Mr. Kaplan. "Olansky ken't iven *objact* corract!"

"Keplan," glowered Mr. Blattberg, "give a rest your tongue!"

"Tonight will be a three-rink circus!" laughed Nathan P. Nathan.

"Gentlemen," said Mr. Parkhill hastily. "Mrs. Pilpul's request is quite in order; I shall be glad to offer several more—er—specific examples." The Mitnick-Olansky-Blattberg patrol basked in Mr. Parkhill's favor. "You may, for instance, answer an ad that offers to rent a room, or sell a radio, or—or—" To his annoyance, Mr. Parkhill's mind went blank—totally, exasperatingly blank. He scoured the cellars of memory for those images, those classified images, he knew must be stored there by the thousands. "Or a free dancing lesson!"

It was not, alas, an ideal example.

"Dencing lessons?" gasped Mrs. Moskowitz. "At my age who takes from Arthur Murphy?"

"Arthur Murray. . . ."

"It's only *vun* exemple!" blurted Mr. Kaplan. "Mr. Pockheel also offert a room to rant!"

"My flet has already four rooms, so who needs—"

"So don't rant a room! Buy a car!"

"Class—"

"A car?" bristled Mr. Hruska. "Who affords?"

"Buy it *sacond-hend!*"

"Mr. Kap—"

"An exemple isn't a pair hencuffs!" retorted Mr. Kaplan. "Hruska, you got to use imegination!"

"I don't understand ads," sulked Lola Lopez. "They use *leetle* words wheech—"

234

"Those," said Mr. Parkhill at once, "are *abbreviations.*
And, as a matter of fact, working with them might turn
out to be one of the most useful features of the assignment!
You will have the whole weekend—"

"I hate dosa 'brevyations'!" declared Lucca Barbella.

Mr. Kaplan hurled a "Ha!" at shameless Barbella. "Ab-
brevyations didn't bodder Ban Frenklin or J. P. Morton."

"They dida not answer ads!" cracked Rome's native son.

"Dey vould thank Gott for de *chence!* To find a varm
room mit a roof over deir had! To go by car, instad on tired
fit—"

"Class—"

"Stop!" roared Reuben Olansky, groping through an outrage that only reblurred his vision. "Why do you drag in by
his shoes J. B. Moran? And where did Benjam Franklin use
abbreviations?"

"That's right!"

"Vhere?"

"Give even one case!"

"Keplen," rejoined Mr. Kaplan with hauteur, "is pre-
zanting exemples, not takink cross-exemination!"

Mr. Pinsky cried "Pssh!" and slapped his cheek.

Mr. Olansky smote his forehead, howling.

"That will be enough, class," said Mr. Parkhill crossly.
"There are many *simple* ads from which you may choose.
I suggest you copy the advertisement you decide to answer,
or—better yet, clip it out of the paper! Bring it to class with
your letter. Then, I am quite sure—"

Before he could tell them what he was quite sure of, Mr.
Kaplan's contempt boiled over. "Vhat kind students ve got
in cless enyhow? Did Mr. Pockheel bag us on banded knees
to comm to school? Did he sand ot ingraved invitations?
Did de Prazident sign a law dat averybody got to enswer
an ed or go to jail?"

The list of particulars enraged the anti-Kaplan cabal,
who raised an uproar, which triggered deafening defenses

from Kaplan's comrades. Mr. Pinsky accused Miss Lopez of jeopardizing the class's morale by questioning Mr. Parkhill's judgment; Olaf Umea fumed that Mr. Pinsky was Mr. Kaplan's spineless lackey. Miss Kipnis declaimed that Mr. Kaplan was an adornment to the grade and a model for the brave; Miss Tarnova moped that "this mon" was a wolf in cat's clothing. Isaac Nussbaum tried to mollify both legions by quoting Isaiah, but the beating of swords into ploughshares was lost in the bellow of C. J. Fledermann excoriating those "stoogies" who blindly followed where e'er mad Kaplan led. This prompted Mrs. Shimmelfarb to scourge Christian Fledermann for attacking the pygmies on the sidelines instead of confronting the champion himself on the field of honor. Nathan P. Nathan was in seventh heaven, his laughter so potent that it wakened Mr. Trabish from his slumbers.

"Class! Class!" Mr. Parkhill kept protesting. "We *cannot* go on this way! Order. Please—everyone—compose yourselves!"

In the imposed composure which followed, Miss Goldberg reached for a peppermint, Miss Lopez crossed herself, and Stanislaus Wilkomirski fired one patriotic shot of parting: "America is free country!"

"Amarica," crooned Hyman Kaplan, "did not gat freedom from pipple who are afraid to enswer an ed!"

But all that was over and done with. It was the following Monday night. Peace—and work—enveloped the scholars, who had crammed the blackboards with their homework.

The assignment was turning out to be more successful than Mr. Parkhill had dared hope. Miss Kipnis opened the evening with a rather effective, if repetitious, reply to an advertisement of the Bell Telephone Company:

Dear Telephone—

Your ad says you want young women. I am young woman.

You print "salary good." Good.

You want girls to come to office Wed. 9–1. I will come to office Wed. 9–1.

Happily yours,

Clara (Cookie) Kipnis, "Miss"

The diagnosis of this offering had been both brisk and productive: Mr. Milas Wodjik challenged the propriety of "Dear Telephone," and Mr. Tomas Wodjik promptly added that "Dear Company" would be better. Miss Ziev remarked that placing a "Miss" between quotation marks was both superfluous and misleading (on Miss Ziev's left hand gleamed the new ring with which Mr. Andrassy had repledged eternal devotion). Miss Mitnick suggested that "Happily yours" was not proper in business correspondence and might, besides, give the Bell Telephone System the impression that the applicant was too flighty to be entrusted with "calls from a long distance." Mrs. Pilpul wondered whether it was not more accurate to write "I will come to office *between* 9 and 1," instead of "I will come to office 9–1." "The way *she* wrote," observed the hearty widow, "she will be standing on her lags four hours!"

Mr. Parkhill had congratulated the critics on their acumen.

Mr. Fledermann's letter followed Miss Kipnis's; and C. J. Fledermann, Mr. Parkhill was delighted to see, had shown exceptional bravery in answering a long advertisement from the Bronx Unique Products Agency for "GO-GETTERS!" interested in augmenting their income by selling, on commission, hand-colored portraits of the Pope, which were "guaranteed to sell like hot cakes." Mr. Fledermann's salutation was correct, his text commendable, his final greeting impeccable. His downfall, alas, came *via* an unnecessary postscript:

P.S. I like to sell hot cakes.

Mr. Parkhill went to considerable pains to explain the difference between selling hot cakes and selling *like* hot cakes. Nathan P. Nathan went into a paroxysm.

Not all the students, of course, had reached the laudable levels of a Kipnis or a Fledermann. Mr. Studniczka, for instance, had answered a notice announcing the sale of "Furn., unpainted" by declaring that he was a wizard at removing paint from furnaces. Mrs. Shimmelfarb had unfortunately mistaken "Lab. Tech." for "labor teacher." Miss Atrakian had applied for a position which required "Highest refs." by stating that she heartily approved of any business firm that gave "highest refunds."

And there had been other pitfalls—mares' nests which no one, not even Mr. Parkhill, could possibly have foreseen. Mr. Umea had replied to a notice offering $25 reward for a lost dog with a letter that contained this baffling line:

Send $25.00. I found your college dog.

The class might have gotten entirely out of hand ("What kind dog is smot enough to pess even high school?" "They lost a *dog,* not a student!") had not Mr. Parkhill, in a stroke of inspiration, solved the mystery: Olaf Umea simply had thought "collie" the abbreviation for "college."

Tiny Lola Lopez had drafted an answer to "Wanted: Housekeeper" which cunningly reduced the probability of error to the very bone:

Dear Ad:
I am housekeeper.
L. Lopez

There was not much one could do with that.

Now the last platoon was at the blackboard. Rochelle

238

Goldberg was putting the finishing touches to her précis of qualifications for the post of receptionist for Juno Princess Slips. Mr. Pinsky was completing an epistle to "Zig Zag Zippers, Inc." Miss Olga Tarnova, whose throaty suspirations hinted of a time when spurned lovers had flung themselves off cliffs from Monte Carlo to Murmansk, was addressing a Hindu seer who claimed to have direct entrée to the hereafter:

Ahmed Taj' Chandra
Box 308
Eve. Post

Ah, dear Ahmed—
I saw soulful ad you wrote to help world grow in Secret Powers. Many nights I sleep awake—

Mr. Parkhill read no further; he *wished* Miss Tarnova would begin to use the definite article, and choose less exotic material.

The letter to Miss Tarnova's right was—Mr. Kaplan's. There could not be the slightest doubt that it was Mr. Kaplan's, for on the board was printed:

ANSWERING AN AD
by
H*Y*M*A*N   K*A*P*L*A*N

The author stood poised before his handiwork as if he were Leonardo—one hand holding his notebook as if it were a palette, the other wielding the chalk as if it were a brush, examining his masterpiece with narrowed eyes and a lilting hum of approbation, taking a step back or a lunge forward as the divine afflatus moved him. Mr. Parkhill sighed. How Mr. Kaplan loved a blackboard: to him the slate was no lifeless surface on which to record his homework; to him it was a golden road to posterity.

As Miss Tarnova signed her name to her letter with a

flourish, the bracelets on her wrist tinkling, the master, jarred out of communion with the Muses, scowled, "Tell me, Tarnova, vhich symphony of Mozart's you playink: de foist or de lest?"

Miss Tarnova did not deign response; she flared her fine nostrils and glided back to her seat like a Grand Duchess spurning a *moujik.*

"Please finish," Mr. Parkhill quickly called. "Take your seats. . . . We shall begin with—Miss Goldberg."

It was a good choice: Miss Goldberg had outdone herself. Her application for the post of receptionist at Juno Princess Slips was terse and telling. The only question anyone raised was whether "Dear Madam" might not be more fitting than "Dear Gentlemen" for "someone in princess slips."

Mr. Pinsky's letter to Zig Zag Zippers, Inc., ran into stormier weather. Mr. Pinsky had for some reason composed his entire communication in capitals:

HELLO.
I SAW YOUR AD FOR BUS OPERATOR
I ACCEPT $25,000, SO—

"Holy smoky!" Mr. Nussbaum, ever the cantor, exclaimed before the floor was even thrown open for discussion. "That is a telegram, not a letter!"

"Is this night school or Western Union?" demanded Mr. Blattberg.

"It's a picnic," chortled Mr. Nathan.

Mr. Kaplan dashed to aid his aide-de-camp. "Telegrams get rizzolts! Congradulation, Pinsky!"

Mr. Olansky raised his hand, glaring at Miss Atrakian, whom he mistook for Mr. Pinsky, and in caustic vocables inquired how any business in its right mind could offer twenty-five thousand dollars to a bus driver. "Not even in Tel Aviv!"

The challenge did not faze Sam Pinsky, who handed Mr.

240

Parkhill the clipping in question. The twenty-five thousand dollars was there, all right, but it had been requested, not offered. When Mr. Parkhill explained that "Bus. opp." means "Business opportunity," not "Bus operator," Mr. Pinsky looked badly shaken.

"Don't take it hod," Mr. Kaplan murmured.

"Charge admission!" gurgled Mr. Nathan.

"Gentlemen. . . . The next letter . . ."

Miss Tarnova read her letter, one hand at her throat. "Ah, dear Ahmed," she intoned, "I saw soulful ad you wrote, to help world grow in Secret Power. . . ." (Mr. Trabish yawned; the lure of the East cast no spell on Oscar Trabish, who had trouble staying awake during Open Questions, much less attuning his soul to the supernatural.) "Many nights I sleep awake—"

"You slip avake?" cried Mr. Kaplan. "Ha! Maybe you also sit stendink op?"

Olga Tarnova sniffed her perfumed kerchief in olfactory rebuff. As soon as her dulcet rendition ended, Mr. Parkhill said, "That is a most *interesting* letter. There are—a few mistakes, but on the whole you have improved in every way." She certainly *had* improved. (Miss Tarnova's previous recitation was called: "Leopold Stokowski, Don't Butcher Tchaikovsky!") "Comments, class?"

Mr. Wilkomirski recommended a comma after the unpunctuated salutation. Lola Lopez tried to persuade Miss Tarnova to *lie* awake instead of sleeping awake. Mr. Hruska asked, "Why 'Dear Ahmed'? Is not more polite 'Mister Chandra'?"

Miss Mitnick addressed herself to Miss Tarnova's final greeting, which virtually leaped from the blackboard:

> I remain,
> A soul-mat

Olga ("Panjura") Tarnova

241

"I'm sure," Miss Mitnick said earnestly, "Miss Tarnova meant to put 'e' on the end of 'mat.'"

"Da, da," moaned the soulful diva.

"Very good." Mr. Parkhill started to convert the "mat" of Miss Tarnova's soul into its "mate," when Mr. Kaplan cut in sternly: "Vhat's all of a sodden dis 'Penjura'? Is dat a name or a game?!"

"To Ahmed I am 'Ponjura'!" flared Miss Tarnova. "In Hindu spirit world we all take new names!"

"For dat you don't have to go to Hindus. *Prisons* are pecked full of pipple who used fake names."

"Pssh!" admiring Pinsky's slap on the cheek rang out.

"Koplon, where is your *soul?!*" shouted Miss Tarnova.

"Naxt to my hills," said Mr. Kaplan.

"Bodzhe moi!" cursed the "Rossian."

Nathan P. Nathan was holding his sides.

"Next! Next!" Mr. Parkhill rapped a rattling tattoo with his pointer. He shot a quick glance at the clock. Only nine minutes remained. (How he had hoped there were less.) The final letter was Mr. Kaplan's.

The room stirred like a field of wheat before a heralding wind as Hyman Kaplan rose. That careless smile, that shooting of the cuffs, that benevolent gleam to those about to share in impending revelation—then Hyman Kaplan grasped his lapels in the manner of Disraeli, and read: "'Enswerink an Ed, by Hyman Keplen.'"

Mr. Parkhill lowered himself into his chair.

Mr. Kaplan read his text with matchless fervor:

Box 701
Daily New
New York

Dear Box,
   One day was Hyman Kaplan home, feeling his blues, thinking "What is world coming to? No body happy, people worryd, we live on a vulcano."

"How a man can find peace?" asked Hyman Kaplan. How a man can escape this jongle? No way.

No way? *Stop, Hyman Kaplan!* Look. Listen. Read what is here in the paper in front your 2 eyes! A wonderful ad! What it says? This it says—

"Man with ambition. Must have ideas, imag., init., drive. Salary no object. Box 701."

O.K. Box 701, look no more! I am that man.
1. "Ideas" I have plenty
2. "Imag." I can imagine anything
3. "Init." My initials are H. K.
4. "Drive." I don't—but willing to learn.
    Y.T.

$$H*Y*M*A*N \quad K*A*P*L*A*N$$

Before Mr. Kaplan could finish his name, the wolves were baying at the moon.

"What is that 'Dear Box'?" glared Mr. Olansky.

"Important eds give only a 'Box,' " said Mr. Kaplan.

"Should be 'Dear *sir,* '" stammered Miss Mitnick. "Not 'Dear B-box!' "

"How do you know is only vun boss in dat box?" returned Mr. Kaplan.

"You were feeling your 'blue*s*'?" blustered Mr. Blattberg. "Should be singular—'blue'!"

"I falt *vary* blue, so I made plural."

" 'Daily *New*' should be 'Daily *News*'!" protested C. J. Fledermann.

"Since vhen is vun copy plural?" sniped Mr. Kaplan, reversing his field.

Now the emendations came fast and furious.

" 'No body' should be 'nobody,' " trilled Lola Lopez.

"Excellent," said Mr. Parkhill.

"That word 'drive' in ads means energy," objected Miss Atrakian, "not car-driving."

"Good!"

"What is that bandaged-op 'Y.T.'? Is Koplan too *weak* to

write out 'Yours truly'?" Mr. Olansky was so offended that he resorted to maximal insult: deliberately turning his chair so that he could turn his back on his *bête noir*.

The class swarmed across Mr. Kaplan's mistakes, not heeding Mr. Parkhill's anxious interventions, not pausing to let Mr. Kaplan reply. Had they been less drunk from the taste of blood, they would have noticed that Mr. Kaplan was not even trying to respond. He was the picture of aplomb. But such courageous forbearance was too much for the faithful, who rallied to his banner.

"Keplen, *say* something!" begged steadfast Pinsky.

"Mr. Kaplan, *answer,*" pleaded loyal Gidwitz.

"Go on, Mr. Edison," sneered Mr. Olansky to the rear wall. "Make a miracle!"

"Class . . ." called Mr. Parkhill. "We *must* speak one at a time! Those who wish to comment on Mr. Kaplan's letter —please wait to be recognized. . . . Miss Mitnick."

"I see five more mistakes," announced Miss Mitnick. "At least."

"Fife mistakes!" chortled Mrs. Moskowitz.

"At *least,*" concurred C. J. Fledermann.

The mistakes Rose Mitnick saw and named and pinned to the mat of analysis were but the beginning. Other voices sought Mr. Parkhill's sanction; other scholars leaped into the fray. The errata of Hyman Kaplan unrolled on a seemingly endless scroll.

Yet, nothing ruffled the man's sangfroid. To every blunder pinpointed, every sarcastic suggestion or sardonic change, Mr. Kaplan made no demurrer. Even the laughter of Nathan P. Nathan drew no riposte from Mr. Kaplan— save once, when he smiled with mystifying kindliness, "I see you now realize aducation can be a plashure, boychik."

Mr. Parkhill began to feel alarmed. He was placing so many corrections on the board that his wrist was beginning to ache; yet Mr. Kaplan offered not a word of defense.

244

He simply stood there, lofty, almost courtly, neither chastened nor abashed. Mr. Parkhill's scalp began to prickle. He thought he caught a gleam in Mr. Kaplan's eyes.

The longer Mr. Kaplan met criticism with such nobility, and rectification with such grace, the more Mr. Parkhill fought off a sense of panic. He could understand fortitude under fire. He was quite familiar with Mr. Kaplan's invulnerability to humiliation. But he could not help wondering when and how that virtuoso of escape would remain unscathed. Experience warned Mr. Parkhill that perhaps Mr. Kaplan's surprising sufferance was only camouflage for some unsprung trap.

The hands of the clock crawled to 9:58. Only two minutes remained, almost nothing left to correct, when Miss Mitnick raised her hand once more. "Why does Mr. Kaplan give his initials? Doesn't the abbreviation 'i-n-i-t' mean 'initia*tive*'?"

"Of course!" said Mr. Parkhill. (He had not thought anyone would catch that.) " 'Initia*tive,*' Mr. Kaplan."

Mr. Kaplan nodded politely. "But de ed *I* answered vanted my initials."

Mr. Parkhill studied his chalk cautiously. "Mr. Kaplan, there is hardly any—uh—room for difference about what 'i-n-i-t' means."

"In general, or in dis poticular ed?"

"Koplan, stop sneaking!" Mr. Olansky gloated to the ceiling.

"Admit you are wrong!" shouted one of the Wodjiks.

"Give an *inch!*" pleaded Bessie Shimmelfarb. *"Once only, give an inch."*

Hyman Kaplan spurned geometric appeasement.

"Mr. Kaplan," said Mr. Parkhill suddenly, "suppose we settle the point by referring to the text of the advertisement you answered."

"It's on de board."

"Your *reply* to the ad is on the board," said Mr. Parkhill frigidly. "I asked for the—actual ad."

"Onfortunately," said Hyman Kaplan, "dere is no ectual ed."

"Hanh?" cried Mr. Olansky, wheeling around.

"A trick!" charged Mr. Blattberg.

"Tropped, tropped!" rejoiced Miss Tarnova.

A monstrous—an unbelievable—truth began to dawn on Mr. Parkhill. "Mr. Kaplan, are you telling us that *you made up the ad?"*

"Soitinly," said Mr. Kaplan.

"No!" howled Reuben Olansky.

"Mein Gott!" moaned Isaac Nussbaum.

"Who can beat Kaplan?!" cheered Mr. Pinsky.

Mr. Parkhill put his chalk down without a word. He made no effort to calm the furor of the hoodwinked which exploded around him. Mr. Kaplan, never content with reality as he found it, had simply composed his own ad.

Perhaps it was his need to be different. Perhaps it was his need to reconstruct life to suit his heart's desire. And perhaps, Mr. Parkhill shuddered, the perverse genius that governed Hyman Kaplan had known all along that there was no higher authority on earth for the meaning of "init." than the man who had placed that abbreviation in his own ad.

5

THE G·O·O·D SAMARITAN

"Yos, it was romonteek, but trogic. How Nicolai Ilyich soffered! The day and the night, the week ofter the week, dear
Babushka prayed—"

"Miss Tarnova," Mr. Parkhill interrupted gently, "in English, we say 'day and night,' not *the* day and *the* night.'
Watch those definite articles. . . ."

Olga Tarnova's languorous lashes fluttered. *"Da.* Dear
Babushka went to chorch to pray, to find the hope for
cure—"

Mr. Parkhill cleared his throat apologetically. "I'm
afraid it's 'hope,' not *'the* hope,' and *'a* cure,' not *'cure.'* You
use the definite article when it is not required, and omit it
when it is."

Miss Tarnova's ululations testified to a confusion for
which Mr. Parkhill had the utmost sympathy. "So how we
con tell when we should use, and when we should not
use?!"

"That's a good question." Mr. Parkhill hefted his chalk
thoughtfully. "The articles in English may be definite
(that is, 'the') or *in*definite (that is, 'a' or 'an'). *'The* boy,' for
instance"—swiftly he wrote "the boy" on the board—"is a
definite, *particular* boy; but 'a boy' "—the white letters
spun under "a boy"—"means any boy—"

"I wos not reciting about boys!" protested Miss Tarnova.
"Nicolai Ilyich was soventy-four!"

247

"Oh. Well, I meant *any* person—boy or man—or any *thing:* 'The clock' is a definite clock, but 'a clock' means any—"

"So my saying *'the* hope' was definite!"

"We-ell," said Mr. Parkhill reluctantly, "when abstract nouns are involved—"

"Ooo," groaned Mrs. Moskowitz.

"—we do not use any article at all."

"Oy!"

"You see, class, abstract nouns are qualities or emotions, like 'hope' or 'fear'—"

"Movvelous!" sang Mr. Kaplan.

"—or 'pity,' 'hate'—"

"I definitely hate some people," flashed Miss Tarnova, "so why is wrong *'the* hate'?"

Mr. Parkhill's palms went moist. "Well, one *can* say 'The hate which—er—Wilbur felt for—' "

"Who's 'Vilbur'?" demanded Mrs. Moskowitz.

" 'Wilbur' was just—an example. Any name would express the point—"

"She hates Koplan!" announced Mr. Olansky.

"Thot's definite!" intoned Miss Tarnova.

Mr. Parkhill studied the door. "Perhaps we should devote our next session to a thorough analysis of articles and abstract nouns." He felt like a coward; but Recitation and Speech had just begun, and the terrain of articles and abstract nouns was strewn with such thorns. . . . "Please return to your recitation, Miss Tarnova. You were saying that—er—Babushka went to church to pray, hoping to find *a* cure. . . ."

Olga Tarnova's dark orbs smouldered. "Also prayed my dear brother, Alexonder Ivanovich, always brave, who said us—"

" *'Told* us.' "

"He *said,* not told!"

248

Mr. Parkhill wished he did not have to press on. "Then you must say 'said *to us,*' I'm afraid."

Miss Tarnova wrung her hands; she was meant for midnights and mazurkas, not for the heartless stomp of an alien grammar. "Pardone, pardone . . ." She smoothed her tresses with a gesture that would have done credit to Camille. "Alexonder Ivanovich told us all not to worry. So we tried to altogether forget."

"To forgat altogadder!" called Mr. Kaplan.

Miss Tarnova's glare could have started a bonfire. "Whot is wrong now?"

"Tsplit infinitif!"

Mr. Kaplan had, by supreme concentration, memorized three axioms of English syntax, and he clung to them as cosmic verities: "Wrong tanse," "Dobble nagetif," and "Tsplit infinitif!" (It had taken weeks for Mr. Parkhill to convince Mr. Kaplan that it was "tsplit infinitif," not "tsplit infinit*y*"; something about "tsplit infinity" rang bells of recognition in Mr. Kaplan's soul.) Whenever the opportunity arose to use one of these three *obiter dicta,* Mr. Kaplan, ecstatic, seized it. "Tsplit infinitif!"

Miss Tarnova flung out her shapely arms, tinkling all her bracelets, and stamped her foot in fury. "Article—not article—definite, indefinite—splitting finitive! I am Russian! I say what is in *heart!* English has no soul! *Nitchevo!* I stop!" She flounced to her seat in a perfectly understandable huff.

"Miss Tarnova," Mr. Parkhill said anxiously, "a student does not mean to give offense when he offers—"

It was in vain. Miss Tarnova was imploring others who had fallen before Mr. Kaplan's blade—Miss Mitnick, Mr. Blattberg, myopic Olansky—to waste no time in avenging inequity most foul.

"Won't you come back, Miss Tarnova?" asked Mr. Parkhill earnestly. "Please complete your *most* interesting recitation."

"Other time, maybe. Other time."

"Som odder time," Mr. Kaplan said politely.

A Slavic oath crossed Miss Tarnova's cherry lips.

"My!" said Mr. Kaplan in admiration.

Mr. Parkhill quickly called on Mr. Studniczka.

Peter Ignatius Studniczka trudged to the podium as if to the gallows. It was his début in Recitation and Speech. He stopped at Mr. Parkhill's desk, head bent, cheeks waxen, dripping perspiration.

"Well, Mr. Studniczka!" said Mr. Parkhill cheerfully.

Mr. Studniczka lifted his face. He looked haggard. He was a quiet student who rarely spoke a word in class, or volunteered a comment, and treated homework as if it were poison ivy.

"Er—you may begin," smiled Mr. Parkhill.

The last vestige of life drained out of Peter Studniczka's cheeks. He loosened his tie, then unbuttoned his collar. (*That,* thought Mr. Parkhill, should certainly relieve some of Mr. Studniczka's discomfort.) His eyes went glassy. He opened his mouth—and released a burst of strangling noises: "Lds gntlmns I lak N'Yrk bt nt altime becuz nt lak *wrk* s'hrd. . . ."

The words, if that was what they were, drowned in a gurgling stew. Silence swallowed the gurgle. The class sat stunned. Someone coughed. (Had Nathan P. Nathan come to school that night, he undoubtedly would have laughed, but Mr. Nathan was undoubtedly cheering his head off at Madison Square Garden.)

"A—er—little louder, Mr. Studniczka," said Mr. Parkhill bravely. "And *slower.* Do go on. . . ."

The agonized man fixed his eyes somewhere between the ceiling and the top of Miss Atrakian's head. He parted his lips. His tongue clucked dryly. No words emerged.

250

Mr. Parkhill kept smiling and nodding and broadcasting enheartenment. Mrs. Yanoff emitted the most friendly bleatings. Miss Goldberg tried to buttress Mr. Studniczka's nerves by the vicarious consumption of a nougat. Mr. Hruska grunted sounds of support. But none of these succoring efforts produced meaningful vocables from Peter Ignatius Studniczka.

Suddenly, Mr. Kaplan leaned far forward and whispered, "Mister, just talk! Ve all on your site!"

Out of the pall that shrouded him, Peter Studniczka searched for the benevolent stranger.

"Is easy! Just talk lod, clear—*netcheral*. . . . Efter all"— the Samaritan smiled—"voice den Tarnova you ken't be!"

Miss Tarnova's impure ejaculation broke the verbal logjam. In one breathless torrent, without the briefest pause or beat or intermittence, Mr. Studniczka bolted into verbosity: "Ladies gantlemans I lak Nev York but not altime. Work too hard but is fine place with good eats and I see nice movie. America is more good as Czestchova, so not sorry I come. Want to marry good lady, cook, wash. Want boy name Dinko, also girl—not care how name. Please."

And like a tornado which had roared into the room and right out, leaving a silence of desolation, Mr. Studniczka, liberated from recitation, stumbled back to his seat.

Mr. Parkhill did not stir for a moment. The class seemed shell-shocked—all but Mr. Kaplan, who was chortling in celebration of the coming-of-age of his ward.

"Er—" Mr. Parkhill spoke up at last (his voice sounded as if he was under water). "Corrections, class . . . ?"

The beginners' grade sat immobilized.

"*No* corrections?" Mr. Parkhill asked lightly. "Surely someone can start us off."

"The speech was so *fast,* who could cetch?" protested Mr. Blattberg.

"*Sí, sí,*" sighed Miss Lopez.

"Hard t'understand," grumbled Milas Wodjik.

"Hard t'understand," grunted Tomas Wodjik.

"Ha!" rang out the sustaining voice of Mr. Kaplan. "Dat spitch vas fromm de hot! A man's emotions you don't see t'rough like gless!"

"He spoke too *fast*," complained Mrs. Pilpul.

"Ve livink in an aitch of speed!" Mr. Kaplan retorted.

"I dida not hear good," complained Lucca Barbella.

"Go to an ear spacialist!" Mr. Kaplan recommended.

"Are there any *specific* corrections?" Mr. Parkhill cut in hopefully.

"Yes!" It was Reuben Olansky. "Even if was too fast, *I* noticed soitin corractions." He cast a smug sneer toward Mr. Pinsky (whom he mistook for his master, Hyman Kaplan), placed his notes within an inch of his nose, and peered through his bifocals. "Was missing lots and lots of 'the' and 'a.' Some verbs were present for past and in the past for present, and futures didn't exist at all! 'Ne*v* York' isn't 'New York' and 'Please' instead 'Thank you' in the last place isn't good in the foist place!"

"Yah! . . . Sure! . . . *Dozens* mistakes!" the pro-Olansky chorus resounded.

Mr. Studniczka stared at his palms.

"Well, class . . ." Mr. Parkhill said slowly, "Mr. Olansky has certainly caught quite a few errors. Perhaps we should—"

An irate voice cleaved the air. "*I* vant to say a few voids!" Mr. Kaplan started for the podium.

"Mr. Kaplan," said Mr. Parkhill, not without alarm, "it is not your *turn*."

"So pretend it's time for *my* spitch!" Two great strides took Mr. Kaplan to the platform. He buttoned his coat as if buckling on his armor, cast a scythe of scorn across the field of nit-pickers, and exclaimed: "Ladies an' gantleman an' Mr. Pockheel! Vhat's de minnink Jostice?"

252

The forum stirred uneasily.

"Jostice? J-O-S-T-I-S. Vhat it minns?" Hyman Kaplan ignored the possibility of another's answer. "I'll tell you. Jostice is de finest, de most beauriful idea in history! It's kind! It's sveet! It's nauble! It's liftink op all human beans!" (Mr. Kaplan, indeed, lifted up with the words, dispatching his passion from the increased elevation achieved by raised heels.) "Do *enimals* have Jostice? No! Are—"

"Mr. Kaplan . . ." Mr. Parkhill had just recovered from "human beans." "You must slow down!" It was like asking Demosthenes to put the pebbles back in his mouth.

"—Are *sevedges* havink Jostice? No! Den who got it? Tsivilized pipple!"

" '*Pe*ople,' not '*pip*—' "

"In *dis* room are soitin types who forgat de rizzon ve all came to vunderful U.S.! Vhy? Becawss here are de stritts pasted wit' gold? Ha! Becawss ve vould all gat rich all of a sodden?!" The judicial features clouded. "You might as vell try to ritch de moon wit' a toot-pick!"

"Stop!" howled Reuben Olansky (but what howl can be heard in a hurricane?).

"So vhy ve came to vunderful U.S. from all contries? Crossink lend an' cease, in trains an' sheeps—"

"*Mr.* Kap—"

"—going t'rough tarrible hodsheeps to see et lest dat beauriful Statue Liberty? Ve came for vun plain rizzon: Becawss here ve got Friddom! Here ve are brodders! Here ve are 'Vun nation, inwisible, mit liberty an' Jostice free for all'!"

Mr. Parkhill wished he could lie down. But bright was the light in Molly Yanoff's eyes, deep the glow on Mr. Nussbaum's cheek. Even Oscar Trabish had traded somnolence for admiration.

"So look on vhat heppened in dis vary room a few minutes behind me! Who vas stendink here? A fine man. A good man. An immigrant de same as you an' me. Mr. P. I. Studniczka." (Mr. Studniczka looked up, thunderstruck.) "An' ven dat svitt saul makes his *foist spitch* to de cless, his foist chence to give a semple his English ve should all halp him ot, vhat he got? Sympaty? No! Unnistandink? No! Jostice? Phooey! He got fromm *soitin* fallow students"— Mr. Kaplan froze the blood of those unnamed—"shop voids, high-tone criticizink. Batter *ashame* should soitin pipple be!" Several of them, indeed, were already writhing in mortification.

Suddenly, Mr. Kaplan smiled at Reuben Olansky and, honey on his tongue, inquired: "Podden me, Olansky. How lonk you are in U.S.?"

Mr. Olansky blinked, as confused by the question as by his failure to locate its source.

"Mine dear Olansky, it's only a qvastion," purred Mr. Kaplan. "Are you tong-tie? How lonk you are in U.S.?"

"Seven years!" shouted Mr. Olansky. "I came—"

Mr. Kaplan raised a barricading palm. "Saven yiss. ... My! *Saven* yiss! Not t'ree, not fife, but saven yiss!" Then he struck. "An' only in beginnis' grate!"

"Hanh?!" Mr. Olansky clawed at his forehead, livid, sputtering such mordant rejoinders in his native tongue that Mr. Parkhill began to hurry from the back row to the front.

"Studniczka, how lonk are *you* in U.S.?" called Mr. Kaplan.

All heads turned to Peter Studniczka; all ears pricked up; but Mr. Studniczka turned as maroon and speechless as a beet.

"Studniczka," Mr. Kaplan whispered, "you got to halp me ot. Like I'm your lawyer! Tell, Studniczka. De troot is de troot!" The clarion voice ascended. *"How lonk you in Amarica?"*

"Two year," strangled Mr. Studniczka.

Mr. Kaplan's whoop was pure rapture. "Only two yiss? *An' also in beginnis' cless!* You hoid, cless?! You hoid, Olansky?"

Mr. Olansky had not only heard, he had wheeled around in his chair, presenting his back in visible insult to Torquemada, and began hurling his chagrin at the rear window: "Should be a law against Koplan! . . . A coise on his liver. . . . The man is *meshuggeh. . . .*"

"Class—"

"Two yiss voisus *saven* yiss!" the stern advocate reminded the jury. "A mountain naxt to a moose! A new immigrant besite a man should alraddy hev his citizen papiss! . . . Olansky, hang your hat in shame! Studniczka, lift op your ice an' be prod! You—"

"Stop!" roared Mr. Olansky. "How long *are you in America?*"

"I'm comparink!" thundered Mr. Kaplan.

The bell pealed an end to the bloodletting. But the class milled around, arguing, inveighing, accusing, defending, praising Mr. Kaplan for his compassion or denouncing him for his prosecution, inflating Mr. Studniczka's prospects for progress or consoling apoplectic Olansky for his immolation. The brouhaha raged even as they collected their books and donned their coats, to file out at last, trailing farewells to their pastor.

"Good night . . ." Mr. Parkhill responded. "Good night . . ." He wanted a word with Mr. Kaplan, alone. He wanted to insist upon self-discipline, restraint, the renunciation of any more cunning wiles or crafty entrapments.

But Kaplan was halfway out of the door; and to his side hurried Mr. Studniczka, calling, "Mister! . . . Mister! . . ."

Mr. Kaplan turned.

"Mister." Mr. Studniczka fumbled with his mackinaw. "You talk good."

"Me?" Mr. Kaplan sighed. He gazed at his client. "You know how lonk *I'm* in Amarica?"

Mr. Studniczka shook his head.

"Fiftin yiss."

Mr. Studniczka blinked. "You—talk good."

Mr. Parkhill turned off the lights.

6

MR. PARKHILL'S BIRTHDAY

It was a miserable evening. All day long the rain had swept down in driving shafts, the way it used to pour on Camp Quinnipaquig, the summer he had spent there as a counsellor. Quinnipaquig. . . . That had been a pleasant summer, the lake blue-cold and ever-so-bracing. Mr. Parkhill remembered the time he—

The ormolu clock on the mantel chimed. It chimed as sweetly as the night he had first put it there, after they had read his father's will. He looked up: 5:30. It was a good time for a sherry, a Mozart record— Mr. Parkhill bolted out of his easy chair. Good gracious! He had been so absorbed in Suetonius that he had lost all track of time. Why, he had to meet his class at 7:30. Perhaps he would not go to the restaurant, after all. He could scramble a few eggs—no, he had forgotten to buy eggs that morning. Not forgotten, really; he simply had hated to brave that rain; and he had enjoyed the long day at home, and the thought of this evening's special treat.

He did not even put his bathrobe on its hanger, dressing so rapidly, wrestling into his jacket, his Burberry, tugging on his rubbers, jamming on his hat, swinging the battered briefcase off its hook (thank goodness he had corrected the homework that morning!), spearing his umbrella. He locked the door and hurried down the stairs.

257

Mrs. Mulvaney, who lived down the hall, was coming up, a yard wide, groaning under two wet shopping bags. He had to squeeze against the wall, holding his umbrella and briefcase over his head, panting, "Good evening, Mrs. Mulvaney," as she panted, " 'Tain't a fit night out for beast or man—not that the good Lord made the one different than the other!"

He tripped down the stairs ("Different than" . . . not one person in a thousand said "different from") and opened the big umbrella. The rain hammered on the dome.

It was only two blocks to his favorite restaurant. He slipped slightly on a piece of lettuce in front of the G. and R. grocery. (Someone really should report the G. and R. to the city; why, the sidewalk in front of their premises was halved by their discarded crates and cartons.)

Through the wet, fogged windows of La Belle Époque, the old-fashioned chandeliers beckoned.

"Some night, huh?" The doorman clucked.

"It certainly is."

Pierre opened the door for him, and Adolphe helped him take off his coat.

"I'm terribly late tonight," said Mr. Parkhill.

Adolphe looked astounded. "But eet is not yet even seex on clock, *m'sieur!*"

"I mean I have to be out by seven . . . my class. . . ."

"Ah, *dommage.* . . ." He led Mr. Parkhill to a table. There was no other patron in La Belle Époque so early.

He ordered quickly. And as he sipped his *apéritif,* he reached into his pocket and removed the lacy birthday card from Aunt Agatha, mailed, as it was every year, so as to arrive exactly on date, and containing, as it did each year, a crisp five-dollar bill with the tart instruction: "To be spent on something *foolish.*" Aunt Agatha always underlined the "foolish."

The other letter he had received (and what a pleasant

surprise that had been) was from Mr. Linton. He read it again:

The Tilsbury Academy
(founded 1802)
Old Tilsbury
Vermont

Office of the Headmaster

May 4

Dear Parkhill:

The other night, Mrs. Linton and I were reminiscing about past boys, and as we browsed through old school annuals together, we came upon your photograph (the year you were awarded the Ernestine Hopp Medal for School Spirit). Mrs. Linton reminded me of the time you astonished us all, as a freshman, by parsing that sentence from Cicero during tea. We laughed merrily.

The only other boy Mrs. Linton remembered so well was Wesley Collender ('38), who placed a copper contrivance in the fuse box at Farwell which expanded and contracted so that the "lights out" bell rang on and off, on and off, for a goodly ten minutes before Mr. Thistlewaite could ascertain the cause and effect the remedy! Thistlewaite is no longer with us. He is, I believe, at Claremont or Carmel or some such place in the western states that begins with "C."

Be that as it may, Mrs. Linton called my attention to the birthdate under your picture. "Why, that is next Tuesday!" she exclaimed, and indeed it was.

I extend, accordingly, our combined felicitations, and express our wishes for, in *loquendi usus,* "many happy returns!"

Faithfully yours,
Amos Royce Linton

P.S. What *are* you up to these days?

It had been awfully nice of Mr. Linton to write. The last time he had seen "Old Molasses," which was what the boys

259

privately called Mr. Linton, was six years ago, when his class had presented the school with a carved newel-post for Modley Hall.

The clams were exceptionally sweet, he thought, this season. And the onion soup was delicious. No one made better onion soup than his mother had. When did he last —yes, the spring before she passed away, wraithlike and uncomplaining. Mr. Parkhill had just turned thirty. Her last words to him had been, "Be a good boy."

As he savored the kidneys *à la Grecque,* Mr. Parkhill remembered the first time he had gone back to visit Tilsbury. It was the year after he had received his B.A. He had worked so hard at Amherst that he had not had a real chance to visit the old school. He felt guilty about that.

When Mr. Linton had asked him what he was doing now, Mr. Parkhill told him he had taken a temporary post, as a substitute "just for the teaching experience," at the American Night Preparatory School for Adults.

"Parkhill," Mr. Linton had asked in his no-nonsense manner, "what on *earth* is that?"

"It is a night school, sir."

"College entrances? Cram courses? That sort of institution?"

"Oh, no, sir. This is an elementary school."

"A *what?* Speak up, Parkhill!"

"An *elementary* school, sir," Mr. Parkhill repeated. "For adults."

Mr. Linton must have gotten very hard of hearing, for he had gazed at Mr. Parkhill stonily and mumbled something that sounded like "Good God!" But that could not have been it; that was not at all like Mr. Linton; it was probably "Great Scott!"

Mr. Parkhill often found himself thinking back to that visit to Tilsbury. He could understand that a man like Mr. Linton had no way of knowing what a fine institution the

American Night Preparatory School for Adults really was. After all, Mr. Linton had led a rather sheltered life: Exeter, Harvard, Oxford. . . . (He wondered what Mr. Linton would have said when Hyman Kaplan named our leading institutions of higher learning as "Yale, Princeton and Hartford.") Mr. Linton always taught the senior Latin course— and what a strict drillmaster he had been! He would utter the most scathing remarks about a *lapsus linguae,* and even more acid ones about a *lapsus calami.*

Tilsbury. . . . What a different world that had been. Mr. Parkhill felt a rush of pleasant memories: that lovely campus, so tidy, green, serene, composed; the broad river that overflowed its banks in the spring; the school pond on bright winter days, a burnished mirror; the path across Main Quad that none but lordly seniors were permitted to use. . . . Those were happy days in a happy world, a world ten thousand miles and years away.

Occasionally, Mr. Parkhill caught himself wondering what it would have been like if he had returned to Tilsbury as a master. (In truth, Mr. Linton had never even sounded him out on that.) Life was curious. Who would have dreamed that Mr. Brockway, the teacher for whom Mr. Parkhill had been summoned to fill in "just for one or two sessions" at the American Night Preparatory School for Adults, would never return? Why, Mr. Robinson, the principal, could never even learn what had happened to him. Mr. Robinson was livid about such an unprofessional flight from duty, and had written several scathing letters to the New York Teachers Association, but the N.Y.T.A. had not been able to help Mr. Robinson very much; the only information they could relay was that Mr. Brockway had sent them a postcard from Acapulco, saying that two months at the American Night Preparatory School for Adults had driven him to the edge of a nervous breakdown, and should he regain his health he would rather take a job in a slaughterhouse than return to the A.N.P.S.A.

"*Café, m'sieur?*"

"Sanka, thank you."

Mr. Parkhill recalled how Aunt Agatha used to ask him, whenever he visited her, if he intended to spend the rest of his life among "those people in New York." Aunt Agatha, who had never even set foot in New York, did not understand the special rewards adult students provide someone who regards teaching not as a job, but as a mission. He had once had a little fun at Aunt Agatha's expense, saying, "Why, Aunt Agatha, just as grandfather Hewitt brought God to the heathen, I bring Grammar to the alien."

Aunt Agatha never brought up the subject again.

He glanced at his watch. How nice. There was time for a second cup of Sanka.

"Foreigners?" Mr. Linton had wheezed. "You teach *foreigners?*"

Mr. Parkhill wiped his mouth. He recalled the night Mr. Kaplan, cornered by his enemies, who demanded he explain the meaning of the "R.S.V.P" he had, in a reckless burst of elegance, tacked onto a letter composition, rejoined, "It minns 'Reply, vill you plizz?' " Even the memory made Mr. Parkhill smile.

He paid his bill, put on his coat and his rubbers, stepped into the street. The rain was not letting up.

He began to walk briskly, leaning into the deluge. He could hardly wait to get to the school. Sometimes, when he entered that old, unprepossessing building, he felt as if, like Alice, he was walking through a looking-glass into an antic and unpredictable land.

"Miss Goldberg . . . Mr. Fledermann . . ."

Mr. Parkhill could not help noticing that Mr. Kaplan had not yet arrived. The seat in the center of the front row,

262

that seat directly in front of Mr. Parkhill's desk, was empty. When Mr. Kaplan occupied that place, he seemed to increase in size, until he blotted out the rest of the class; and when Mr. Kaplan was not in that seat, as now, it seemed as barren as Bald Mountain.

"Mrs. Pilpul . . . Mr. Wilkomirski . . . Miss Atrakian . . ."

It was not simply that the corporeal Mr. Kaplan was missing; the Big Dipper had disappeared.

"Miss Gidwitz . . ."

"Here."

"Mr. Nathan . . ."

"Ready for the show!" chuckled Nathan P. Nathan, sending Mr. Parkhill a disconcerting wink.

"Mr. Olansky . . ."

Mr. Olansky was nowhere to be seen. Mr. Parkhill worried about a man so near-sighted on a night such as this.

"Mr. Kap—"

Sam Pinsky cut the fateful name in half. "Mr. Keplen asked me I should say he is onawoidably ditained. But he will positively come!"

"Thank you." Mr. Parkhill put the attendance sheet to one side. "Well, class, suppose we complete our last meeting's—er—uncompleted Recitation and Speech."

"I have goose-dimples!" wailed Mrs. Moskowitz.

"From practice you will *learn*," chirped Miss Mitnick.

"I should live so long."

"Now, now, Mrs. Moskowitz," Mr. Parkhill smiled. "Nothing ventured, nothing gained." (And probably because of that letter from Mr. Linton, *"Empta dolore docet experientia"* leaped into his mind. How appropriate: "Experience wrought with pain teaches.") The hand of Oscar Trabish rose limply.

"Yes?"

"What does that mean?"

263

"I beg your pardon?"

"What does it *mean?*" Mr. Trabish repeated. "Those words you just gave. About adwentures and games—"

"Ah!" Mr. Parkhill exclaimed. "I said 'Nothing ventured' —not 'adventured,' Mr. Trabish—'nothing gained,' not—er —'games.' That is a saying. It means that if we never try, how can we hope to succeed?"

"Psssh!" Mr. Pinsky goggled. "Will Mr. Keplen be mat he wasn't here to hear that!"

" 'Mad,' Mr. Pinsky, not 'mat.' And it really would be better to say that Mr. Kaplan will be 'disappointed' or 'sorry' instead of 'mad.' After all, 'mad' means insane—er —crazy."

"Exoct worrd for thot mon!" declared Miss Tarnova.

"Wait till Mr. Keplen comes before you insult!" snapped indignant Pinsky.

Mr. Barbella gave a derisive laugh. "Ifa Kaplan scratches, Pinsky hollers 'Ouch!' Ifa you tickle Kaplan, Pinsky makes 'Ha, ha!' "

Mr. Pinsky turned on Lucca Barbella, trying to bestow upon him that glare, compounded of ice and fire, with which Mr. Kaplan froze the blood of his foes.

"You look like Cholly Chaplin, not Hymie Kaplen!" mocked Mr. Nussbaum, fingering an earlock.

"That's *right!*" laughed Mr. Nathan. "Pinsky practice—"

"Mrs. Pilpul," Mr. Parkhill called quickly. "Your recitation."

A cantata of encouragement launched the widow Pilpul on her fearful path. She moved her chair, smoothed her hair, soothed her morale, and proved her mettle by answering a question no one had asked: "So what's to be afraid?"

"Sure!"

"Soitinly!"

"So what's the worst can heppen?" asked "Cookie" Kipnis.

"The woist can happen is I'll make a million mistakes," said Minnie Pilpul.

This fusion of courage and stoicism garnered new praises from the gallery.

"Good fa you, Mrs.!"

"That's a spirit!"

"Best weeshes!" sang Lola Lopez.

Mrs. Pilpul, having marched to the front with stately tread, placed one hand on the desk (it looked for a moment as if she were reeling, but she was only twisting or stretching), placed the other hand on her hip and caroled:

> "Roses are ret
> Wiolets are blue
> Sugar is sveet
> And so are you!

"This kindergarten pome I just said," Mrs. Pilpul announced, "is learned by all the kitties in America. Just like my little goil, Hinda, age hate, from who I learned it. So why I am taking time in Racitation and Speech to say this simple nurse's rhyme?"

"Why?" asked Mr. Vinograd, who favored the literal.

"Because the woild would be a better place all around *if grown-ops behaved more like kitties!* Honist and nice! If Congriss was more like kindergarten, would maybe be less graft, crime and wiolence! . . . Everybody: Remember children!" With that exhortation, Mrs. Pilpul stalked back to her place.

She barely had time to regain it before hands were bobbing up and down like buoys in a squall. The most energetic bobbing was effected by Mr. Olansky, who had entered the room some time ago.

Mr. Parkhill called on Mr. Blattberg, who opened the postmortem by observing that Mrs. Pilpul had used "goil" instead of "girl" and "woild" instead of "world." (Mr. Blattberg had come a long way since his initiation into the beginners' grade.)

Miss Gidwitz remarked that Mrs. Pilpul "used 'hate,' which is for hating, instead of 'eight' which is for telling age!"

Stanislaus Wilkomirski deplored the fact that Mrs. Pilpul kept saying "kitties" when she obviously meant "more than one children."

Mr. Barbella electrified the academicians by challenging Mrs. Pilpul's naïve panacea: anyone familiar with either children *or* kindergartens, Mr. Barbella hotly observed, knew that our little ones would "chop off da heads" of all within reach if but possessed of the weapons and provided with the opportunity.

"Shame! Skaptic! Cynic!" hissed Olga Tarnova.

Mr. Barbella cried, "Name of the name!" in Italian.

Miss Tarnova volleyed a scorching rejoinder in Russian. *"Vryét—"*

"Class, please!" Mr. Parkhill intervened. "Let us limit our discussion to Mrs. Pilpul's *English*. There were several mistakes in pronunciation—which have not yet been mentioned. They occurred in Mrs. Pilpul's first two sentences!"

The class dived deep into memory to retrieve Mrs. Pilpul's first two sentences. Their diving produced symptoms of asphyxiation.

"The rhyme began," hinted Mr. Parkhill, " 'Roses are red . . .' "

The class reconstructed "Roses are red" without a single spotting of Mrs. Pilpul's "ret".

"The next line was 'Violets are blue . . .' "

No one seemed to have noticed how the widow Pilpul had mispronounced "violets."

Mr. Parkhill turned to the board and printed:

RED   VIOLETS
RET   WIOLETS

266

"The two top words tell us exactly how they should be pronounced. But Mrs. Pilpul pronounced them as I have written them, incorrectly, in the lower words."

To his surprise, not a single "Oh," "Ah," or "Hoo Ha!" ascended (although Mr. Nathan winked again).

"Let me show you how important that is. For example . . ." On the board Mr. Parkhill printed:

PEAS
PEACE

"Now, class, there is all the difference in the world between 'pea*z*,' which we eat, and 'pea*ss*,' which we—long for."

Now the "Ah!"'s and "Ooh!"'s ascended, crowned by a reverent "Holy smoky!" from Isaac Nussbaum.

"Now, class, concentrate on this. . . ." He stepped to the next board, on which he limned:

1. CLOSE
2. CLOSE

addressing his flock over his shoulder: "If we pronounce 'close' with an 's'—thus, 'clossse'—it is an adjective, meaning 'near' or—er—'stuffy.' 'Come close to me,' or 'It is a bit close in the room tonight.' . . . But if we pronounce these *very same letters* as 'close,' with a 'z,' the word becomes a verb, with a *wholly* different meaning: 'to shut,' as in 'Please close the window,' or 'Do close the door'—"

In uncanny dramatization (albeit in reverse) the door was flung open. A gust of cold dampness swept across the scholars. All heads swung to the doorway as one—there to behold, his face wet, his smile incandescent, his hair wreathed in a halo of mist—

"Mr. Kaplan!" cried Fanny Gidwitz.

"Et lest!" grinned Sam Pinsky.

"Mm-mnh," yawned Oscar Trabish.

Not all his peers greeted Mr. Kaplan in such joyous accents.

"About time!" scowled Mr. Olansky, consulting his watch to see what time it actually was.

"Did you had to stop on the way at City Hall?" sneered Mrs. Yanoff.

"Ara you coming or going?" inquired Vasil Hruska, the "coming" swathed in regret, the "going" fraught with desire.

The hostile sentiments roused Mr. Pinsky to a retort of pure inspiration: "Mr. Keplen isn't late; the class is *early!*"

Mr. Nathan flung his head back, transported. "Kapalan's brain is like the flu—it's spreading!"

"Good evening, Mr. Kaplan," said Mr. Parkhill.

It was just like Mr. Kaplan to enter the room that way. Any other student arriving this late would have courted invisibility, as Mr. Olansky had, opening the door like a mouse, tiptoeing in like a thief, creeping to the nearest vacant haven. Not Hyman Kaplan. He could not even arrive late without endowing it with the flourishes of a world premiere. From the smile he was now dispensing to the rabble who had taunted him, one would think his tardiness called for public celebration.

"Come in . . ." Mr. Parkhill noticed that Mr. Pinsky was signaling to Mr. Kaplan with surreptitious flippings of his hand and *sotto voce* "Psst! Psst!"'s. Mr. Kaplan nodded but made not the slightest move into the room.

"Do join us," said Mr. Parkhill dryly.

"Axcuse me," said Mr. Kaplan. "You are blocking de dask."

Mr. Parkhill could hardly have been more astonished. He had indeed moved from the blackboard to the side of the desk nearest the door; but why that should impede Mr. Kaplan's passage from the door to his seat, a path entirely unobstructed by Mr. Parkhill *or* the desk. . . . "Mr. Kaplan," Mr. Parkhill replied frostily, "you may take your seat—"

He never finished, for the moment he started to turn back to the board (where he wanted to add "Night . . . knight" as yet another example of the prickly pairing of sounds/spelling) Mr. Kaplan lunged toward the desk, whipped a large object from behind his back, plopped it on the desk, and cried, "Soprise!"

The class, which had remained unusually quiet (now that Mr. Parkhill thought of it), erupted.

"Congrajulation!"

"Happy boitday!"

"A hondritt more!"

The Messrs. Wodjik croaked in unison, "Present is from *all!*"

Mr. Parkhill flushed. So that was why Mr. Kaplan was so late . . . and why he had made so odd an entrance . . . and why he had offered no apology for so tardy an arrival. He had been shopping. . . . But how in the world had they found out it was his birthday?

Mr. Kaplan was pointing to the parcel rather like one of the prophets on the Sistine ceiling. "Plizz open op. It's a prazant."

"Let all have a look," called Lola Lopez.

"Maybe Mr. Parkhill already hos it?" Miss Tarnova intoned in typical premonitory gloom.

"Impossible!" Mr. Kaplan glowered.

"*Noh*thing is impossible," moaned the fatalist.

"Look in a mirror," purred Mr. Kaplan.

"Shah!" called Mrs. Moskowitz.

"Ze class muzt be *quiet* quiet!" commanded C. J. Fledermann.

The sounds fled into the tunnel of silence.

Mr. Parkhill glanced around. "I—uh—I hardly know what to say."

"*You* don't know what say?" echoed Mr. Studniczka in astonishment.

"Don't say. Enjoy!" called Minnie Pilpul.

Mr. Kaplan raised an imperial hand. "Attention, class. Mr. Pockheel . . ."

Mr. Parkhill tugged at the wrapping. The paper was gold, but the band of ribbon was white, tied in a bow the size of a cantaloupe, and wet, which made it very hard to rip or split or even stretch.

"Tear it!"

"*Pull,* maybe."

"Cot with a knife.!"

"From the site!"

He managed to separate the cantaloupe and the ribbon and peeled off the gold-colored paper. As the last damp strip of paper dropped away, he opened the box. There lay an attaché case.

"Take ot and hold op," whispered Mr. Kaplan.

Mr. Parkhill executed the instructions.

"Psssh!" cried Mr. Pinsky, slapping his cheek in ecstasy. "Is dat *beautiful!*"

"*Bella, bella!*" That, of course, was Lucca Barbella.

"Use in best of halth!" called the widow Pilpul.

Mr. Kaplan passed his lighthouse beam across the ranks, inquiring *sotto voce,* "How's abot mine choice?"

"Fine!"

"I gotta admit!"

"Poifict!"

Mr. Kaplan accepted their accolade.

Mr. Parkhill wiped his palms. "Class, this is—*very* kind of you—"

"Mr. Pockheel!" Mr. Kaplan's pain was unmistakable. "Your acknowledgink comms *after* my prezantink!"

"I beg your pardon."

Mr. Kaplan faced his confrères, raised his arms, inclined his head in the gracious manner of the Prince Royal distributing prizes at a rustic bazaar, and orated: "Distingvished titcher in Amarican Prep School for Adolts—" (Mr. Parkhill wondered why it had never occurred to him

270

to call the A.N.P.S.A. a prep school.) "—tonight ve have a fine occasion. Soch an occasion comms only vunce a year to eny man, only vunce a year iven to our titcher!" Mr. Kaplan paused for the applause he deemed appropriate; it came; it departed at a wiggle of Mr. Kaplan's forefinger. "So tonight ve salebrate Mr. Pockheel's boitday. Ve have no fency *program,* ufcawss. Still an' all—"

"Make short, in Gott's name!" implored Mr. Olansky.

"The Constitution didn't take so long!" laughed Mr. Nathan. "Rose Mitnick is supposed to make the speech!"

"Call Miss Mitnick!"

"Miss Mitnick!" "Rose Mitnick!" came a dozen rebellious cries.

"You'll *gat* Mitnick." Mr. Kaplan's *noblesse oblige* indicated that there is no accounting for human folly. "So, now, fallow students, to *prezant* de prazent givink our rizzons for how ve chose it, an' a full dascription of de insite, ve vill hear from de *odder* member of de Boitday Prazent Committee! Hau Kay, take de floor, Mitnick."

But Miss Mitnick had slumped so deep in her chair she was neither visible nor audible.

"Mitnick . . ." murmured Mr. Kaplan.

The wan maiden's skin had turned the color of a squirrel.

"Talk!" begged Mr. Kaplan.

But Miss Mitnick could not talk: her lips were parted but her tongue was paralyzed.

*"Mit*nick!" called Mr. Kaplan urgently.

Miss Mitnick had turned to stone.

"She has stage-fried!" cried Fanny Gidwitz.

"Swallowed her tong!" mourned "Cookie" Kipnis.

"She's just nervous," laughed Nathan P. Nathan. "Rosie, make your speech!"

Even the voice of her courter fell deaf on Rose Mitnick's ears.

"Mitnick, Miss Mitnick, stand *op,* Rose Mitnick!"

moaned Mrs. Moskowitz. It had the cadence of a dirge.

Petrified, her hair as distraught as her larynx, Miss Mitnick lay supine, a limp chrysanthemum.

"Sombody slep her hends!" cried Mr. Kaplan.

"Make on her 'Boo'!"

"Snep fingers!"

"Could be her shoes are too tight," ventured Mr. Pinsky, with professional expertise. "She nids at least a 5-B."

The contralto of Olga Tarnova ululated above the others. "Wonce I saw octress had seemilar choke-in-troat. Eight minutes. In Rossia. In weenter. By lohver's ronning away with soprano. Oh, was sod, sod." (Miss Tarnova could not utter "Hello" without conjuring up some tragic image from the frozen steppes.)

Mr. Kaplan was staring at Miss Mitnick with as much horror as she was gaping at him in terror. "Mitnick," he pleaded, "it's not for *me.* Remamber! It's for Mr. *Pockheel!"*

No other tocsin could have penetrated Miss Mitnick's benumbment. She struggled to her feet, a convulsive automaton, her glazed eyes aimed at the middle of Mr. Parkhill's chest; panting, by a heroic act of will, she staggered forward and into the fire: "On behalf of beginners' grade and all the students in it, I present this little key—" Miss Mitnick stopped. "—key—" she gibbered. "Key . . . *key*?!"

"Give her the *key!"* laughed Mr. Nathan.

Mr. Kaplan snapped his fingers in apology, and pulled a red ribbon from his pocket, a ribbon from which two tiny keys sparkled. *"Two* keys," he whispered. "Make plural."

Miss Mitnick took the ribbon and held it forth stiffly. "I present these keys, to now open the guaranteed genuine leather, full-lined, solid-brass-hinges case for Mr. Parkhill!"

Now it was done. Hurrahs. Applause. A fanfare of felicitations. A hush.

They were all beaming at Mr. Parkhill.

He coughed. "Thank you. What a thoughtful—surprise! I—am most grateful. It's very kind of you, all of you. Thank you ever so much."

"Aupen op de case!"

As Mr. Parkhill fitted one of the little keys into the lock, he noticed that the case was initialed: "M. P." . . . "M. P."? How strange: "M. P." stood for "Mounted Police" or "Member of Parliament." His initials were not "M. P." His first name did not even begin with "M."

The rain was slashing at the windows, and the distant city noises signaled their intimations of the raffish. At Tilsbury, the peepers heralded each spring in night whistlings so constant and melodious that none who first heard them could believe his ears. Some visitors simply could not believe that the peepers were frogs, not bobolinks. . . . Suddenly, Mr. Parkhill recalled the odd expression on Mr. Linton's face that time he had told him about the American Night Preparatory School for Adults. Then Aunt Agatha's prim features swam into recollection. . . .

Mr. Parkhill looked up. The faces that loomed before him were larger than life, it seemed: Mr. Kaplan, Miss Mitnick, Miss Tarnova . . . Pinsky, Olansky, Gidwitz . . . They seemed united, for once, in unfamiliar concord.

And revelation explained the initials on the case. "M. P." Obviously. The class always called him "Mr. Parkhill." The occasion had never arisen for them to know, or for him to tell, his first name.

Why, he could hardly remember the last time anyone had addressed him by it.

273

MR. K·A·P·L·A·N AND
THE INEXCUSABLE "FEH!"

"Fata viam invenient," Mr. Parkhill reflected, as he called the beginners' grade to order. "Fate will find a way." Vergil —that was who had said it. It was a consoling maxim; and Mr. Parkhill clung to it as he called the roll.

"Mr. Vinograd."

"Here."

"Lola Lopez."

"Sí!"

"Mr. Peter Studniczka."

"Yo."

"Mr. Kaplan."

No answer.

"Mr. Kaplan?" repeated Mr. Parkhill, aiming his glance directly at Hyman Kaplan, who reclined in his established site in the very kernel of the front row.

Still no answer.

Mr. Parkhill frowned. "Mr. *Kap*lan!" he called for the third time, quite firmly, forcing Mr. Kaplan's gaze to meet his own. Forcing? No; Mr. Kaplan's eyes had been waiting for a rendezvous with Mr. Parkhill's all the time. It was only when he was certain that Mr. Parkhill was observing his every movement that Mr. Kaplan narrowed his eyes and turned to throw a withering glare at the occupant of the chair at the left end of the front row. In a tone dripping

274

disdain, the thrice-named scholar intoned, "Keplen is in place."

Mr. Parkhill adjusted his glasses uneasily. "Mrs. Pilpul . . ."

Mr. Parkhill did not like the look of things; he did not like the look of things at all. When Hyman Kaplan flung the gauntlet down at the opening of an evening, in so slow and sententious a manner, a fracas surely lay in the offing. And from the buzzings and "Pss! Pss!"ings that bounced from one camp to another in the room, Mr. Parkhill sensed that the class, too, had read the ominous meaning in Mr. Kaplan's pantomime. That slitting of the eyes, that lethal stare, that doomsday tone—to anyone who knew Hyman Kaplan these signified but one thing: Hyman Kaplan had issued that deadly warning which precedes a declaration of war. There could be no doubt about it.

"But why?" Mr. Parkhill wondered. Whenever Mr. Kaplan bestowed so scorching a glare on a colleague, it was for one reason: his honor had been slurred, and demanded satisfaction.

Who was the villain at the left end of the front row? He was one Fischel Pfeiffer. He had registered in Miss Higby's class; but Miss Higby had just marched Mr. Pfeiffer into Mr. Parkhill's room, handed Mr. Parkhill a slip of paper, and whispered that, although Fischel Pfeiffer was a rare and dedicated pupil, a student of undeniable promise, he was "not quite ready" for the heady heights of Advanced Grammar and Civics.

"Why not?" Mr. Parkhill had whispered back.

"You'll see," Miss Higby rewhispered, with a cunning smile. (Mr. Parkhill wished that Miss Higby, who could be so forthright about things like "Drill, drill, drill!," would not suddenly wallow in innuendo.)

During the two teachers' muted exchange, Mr. Pfeiffer had remained standing, silent, baleful, lips tight, his expression a testament to despond. None but the blind could have misread his mood: Mr. Pfeiffer was mortified by demotion.

He was a dapper man with a foppish mustache, a polka-dot tie, a cream-colored suit the sleeves of which stood out as sharply as two razors.

"Good luck," Miss Higby murmured, tripping out of the room.

Mr. Parkhill turned to greet his new charge. "We're glad to have you with us." He offered a reassuring smile. (At least it reassured Mr. Parkhill; it made no dent on Mr. Pfeiffer.)

"Class, this is"—he glanced at the name on the transfer slip—"Mr. Pfeiffer, Mr.—er—Fischel Pfeiffer. . . . Won't you take a seat, please?"

From the miasma of his discontent, Fischel Pfeiffer surveyed the Siberia to which he had been exiled.

"There is a place right there—in the front row," suggested Mr. Parkhill lightly.

Without a word, Mr. Pfeiffer limped toward the empty chair at the left end of the front row. It was at that moment that Mr. Parkhill had felt a premonitory twinge: in order to reach the seat at the end of the front row, Mr. Pfeiffer was obliged to pass directly in front of Mr. Kaplan. And Mr. Kaplan, leaning far forward, presumably to retrieve a pencil which had not dropped to the floor, had followed every word of the dialogue between Miss Higby and Mr. Parkhill with the keenest fascination. . . .

As Mr. Pfeiffer crossed in front of Mr. Kaplan, that self-appointed protector of the homeless had sung out, "Valcome, Fischel Pfeiffer! Valcome to beginnis' grate!"

The new pupil had paused, appraised his unsolicited cicerone with glacial disesteem, and uttered a monosyllable the mere recollection of which made Mr. Parkhill's forehead dampen: "Feh!"

That was all Fischel Pfeiffer had said: "Feh!"

Now "Feh!" was an expletive Mr. Parkhill had heard before—but in the *corridors* of the American Night Preparatory School for Adults, never inside his classroom. The expression had, in fact, intrigued him as a fine example of onomatopoeia. Just as "moo" or "quack" or "coo" convey their meaning with faultless accuracy, so "Feh!" is a vivid, if inelegant, vehicle for the communication of distaste.

"Feh!" The class had caught its collective breath, then turned from Fischel Pfeiffer to Hyman Kaplan, a man renowned for sensitivity.

His jaw had dropped: "Feh?" Mr. Kaplan echoed dazedly. "Feh for de *cless?!*"

"Our exercise tonight is Open Questions," Mr. Parkhill quickly announced. Long experience had taught him to recognize the first alarums of discord, and how to canalize hostility by diverting attention. "The floor is open, class. Any questions at all. Any problems in English you may have encountered in reading, or writing, conversation. . . . Who will begin?"

Up rose the irate hand of Sam Pinsky.

"Mr. Pinsky?"

"I ebsolutely agree with Mr. Keplen!" proclaimed Mr. Pinsky. "A member shouldn't make 'Feh!' for the class!"

"That," said Mr. Parkhill crossly, "is not a question."

The unsure finger of Lola Lopez signaled for enlightenment.

"Miss Lopez?"

"Why 'sceessors' has a 'c' and 's' but not 'z's?" asked Lola Lopez. "I *hear* 'z's!" (The spelling of that dreadful word "scissors," Mr. Parkhill brooded, must have plagued every student and teacher in every English course in the land.)

"I'm afraid 'scissors' just is spelled that way," Mr. Parkhill replied with regret. "As we have often seen, many

277

words in English unfortunately do not look at *all* the way they—er—sound."

" 'Fight'!" laughed Nathan P. Nathan.

"Very good."

" 'Psychology'!" offered C. J. Fledermann.

"Excellent! . . . To get back to Open Questions . . ."

Lucca Barbella asked, with a certain bellicosity, "When doesa 'i' precedes 'e' and when 'e' precedes 'i'?"

"There is a useful little rhyme about that!" Mr. Parkhill smiled. "Don't you remember it, Mr. Barbella?"

"No."

Mr. Parkhill cleared his throat:

> "Put 'i' before 'e' except after 'c'
> Or when sounded as 'a'
> As in 'neighbor 'and' weigh'!

Remember?"

"I wasa absent."

"Sometimes you are ebsent vhen you are prazant," observed Hyman Kaplan.

Mr. Barbella damned him in Italian, which caused Nathan P. Nathan to acclaim him with laughter.

"Class . . . Miss Ziev?"

"Where is Denever?"

Deftly did Mr. Parkhill work his way through the next series of questions, a succession of sonar snares and orthographic delusions. Yet he could not shake off a sense of foreboding; for in the caverns below consciousness, the ominous, flatulent "Feh!" of Fischel Pfeiffer still reverberated.

It was hard enough to preserve decorum in a class torn by fierce vendettas, a class that included such antagonistic personalities as Hyman Kaplan and Reuben Olansky, or Mr. Kaplan and Aaron Blattberg, or Mr. Kaplan and Miss Mitnick. To add to this scholastic powderkeg a Fischel

Pfeiffer, a man foolhardy enough to affront Hyman Kaplan—Mr. Parkhill felt a surge of outright annoyance with Miss Higby.

When Open Questions ran dry, Mr. Parkhill announced, "Now, class, suppose we try a review drill on—vocabulary. Pencils and paper, please . . ."

The room rustled like aspens in the wind.

"I shall write five words on the blackboard. Simply use each word in a sentence, a—er—*full* sentence, that is. Five words, therefore five sentences," he smiled. "Compose your sentences carefully. Remember, I shall grade not just your spelling but your grammar, punctuation, use of *other* words. . . ."

Mrs. Moskowitz began to fan herself with her notebook. It was hard enough for Mrs. Moskowitz to spell one word right; to spell five correctly, and employ them in sentences in which all the other words had to be spelled right, and selected properly, and fitted into the stubborn architecture of syntax—that, for Mrs. Moskowitz, was virtually a sentence to Devil's Island.

Mr. Parkhill turned to the blackboard. In large block letters, he printed:

1. CHISEL
2. FIZZLE
3. GROAN
4. INCOME
5. CLIMAX

"Ooy!" came from unnerved Mrs. Moskowitz.

"Moskovitz," called Mr. Kaplan, "make santances, not funerals!"

Mr. Parkhill moved down the aisle. How pregnant the prelude to commitment always was. The class was scrutinizing the board as if it was a forest in which unseen snipers lurked in ambush. They reconnoitered "chisel" warily, flinched before "fizzle," hurdled guileless "groan" to reach forthright "income," pausing for second wind, so to speak, before taking the measure of the word which Mr. Parkhill, with playful accuracy, had chosen to complete the maze: "climax."

"I'm sure you all know the meaning of these words," said Mr. Parkhill.

"I," wheezed Olga Tarnova, "om not."

"Come, come, Miss Tarnova. Relax."

The sultry brunette heaved into the unknown.

Miss Mitnick had already bent her head over her note-book, the bun of her hair a doughnut on the nape of her demure neck. Beside her, Nathan P. Nathan was all admiration. Mr. Olansky had unbuttoned his vest, cleaned his bifocals, pressed his Scripto, shaken it from habit of years of struggle with fountain pens, and inscribed his first sentence. And Mr. Kaplan cocked his head to one side, repeated each word aloud in a clear, loud whisper, added an admiring "My!" or "Tchk!" of homage to Mr. Parkhill's gifts as a teacher, exclaimed, "Fife *fine* voids!" and shot Fischel Pfeiffer a glare designed to inform that churl of the riches which the beginners' grade spread before the worthy.

Mr. Fischel Pfeiffer never saw the reprimand. After one swift glance at the board, the mustached malcontent set to work with startling speed. Before most students had even cleared the troubling reefs of "chisel," Fischel Pfeiffer slapped his pencil down and announced, "Done!"

The appearance of a whirling dervish would have caused no greater astonishment.

"Done?"

"Finished?"

"So fest?"

Heads were popping up, mouths popping open, all around the congregation.

"We have here a *ginius?*" asked "Cookie" Kipnis.

"A regular spid demon?" Mr. Nussbaum queried.

"Pfeiffer expects to greduate before midnight!" rasped Mr. Pinsky, glancing toward his captain for approval. But Mr. Kaplan looked as if he had run into Beelzebub.

Before the sensation created by Mr. Pfeiffer's velocity had spent its force, that dapper gentleman had reached the blackboard, where he began to transcribe his sentences with an alacrity never before seen in the beginners' grade.

"We generally *wait* to go to the board until I—" Mr. Parkhill's voice trailed off.

Words were flowing from Mr. Pfeiffer's chalk as if from a magic wand.

All work amongst the watchers stopped. The class sat transfixed. Then a chorus of "Oh!"s and "Ah!"s and "Fentestic!"s rent the air. For on that plain, black board, in most beautiful script, Fischel Pfeiffer had written:

1. In Detroit Michigan she saw shiny Chinese bracelets in shops, ingraved by sharp *chisels.*

A hymn of admiration ascended from the seated—not only for the exquisite calligraphy, which would have done credit to a Persian, but for the mettle of a man brave enough to tackle names as prickly as "Detroit Michigan," or a phrase as exotic as "Chinese bracelets."

"Such panmanship!" marveled C. J. Fledermann.

"He writes like an artiss!" cried Minnie Pilpul.

"Like an arteest? No! He *is* an arteest!" throbbed Miss Tarnova. "This mon has soffert! This mon has soul!" (Olga Tarnova divided humanity into two unalterable groups: those with and those without "soul.")

Glee gushed from Mr. Blattberg. "Keplan, are you watching?"

"Pfeiffer makes you look like a greenhorn!" jeered Reuben Olansky, searching for the greenhorn through his bifocals.

Mr. Kaplan said nothing. He was pale, staring at the board where Mr. Pfeiffer was finishing his second sentence:

2. Soda waters are waters which they *fizzle.*

Now the "Oh!"'s and the "Ah!"'s burst like fireworks, topped by one reverential rocket: "Supoib!"

"Mamma mia!" gasped Lucca Barbella.

"Mr. Pfeiffer is raddy for college!" announced Mr. Vinograd.

"Now, now, class. Order. . . ." To tell the truth, Mr. Parkhill was as impressed as his charges. And why not? His years in the beginners' grade had taught him to expect for a sentence using "chisel," say, "I have a chisel," or "Give me chisels," or even "I like chisels." As for a word like "fizzle" . . .

Mr. Pfeiffer transferred three more sentences to the board with a rapidity and certitude that were to become a legend in the American Night Preparatory School for Adults:

3. Life is not only tears and *groans.*
4. Good *income* beats diamonds.
5. What is Man? Bird? Beest? No. God's *climax.*

To a symphony of praises as spirited as any Mr. Parkhill had ever heard in the classroom, Fischel Pfeiffer turned from the board, flecked a hair from a creamy sleeve, and returned to his seat.

"Boy!" laughed Mr. Nathan.

"Wohnderful," crooned Olga Tarnova. *"Khoroscho!"*

"Koplan," mocked Mr. Olansky, "you have nothing to say? Not one single criticize?"

Not only had Mr. Kaplan nothing to say, he seemed to

282

have no place to go. He was slumped so low in his chair that his shoulders were where his hips should have been.

"You look like a pencake!" crowed Mr. Blattberg.

Mr. Parkhill felt sorry for Hyman Kaplan. True, a man with so reckless a confidence and so luxuriant an ego might well expect to meet occasional reverses. Still, Mr. Kaplan had a certain proud flair, a daring, a *panache* not often found among the earthbound.

"Time is passing, class," said Mr. Parkhill. "Finish your assignment."

The class pulled unwilling eyes from the ornamented slate. They sighed and stirred and wrote their own humbled sentences. Soon Mr. Parkhill sent six students to the board. They copied their sentences dutifully, but the heart seemed to have gone out of them. For before all their eyes, like an unscalable summit, shone the glittering coinage of Fischel Pfeiffer.

How feeble, by comparison, seemed Mr. Hruska's "Actors give big *groans.*" How lackluster lay Miss Gidwitz's "The rain *fizzled.*" How jejune looked even C. J. Fledermann's foray into aesthetics: "Hungarian music has glorious *climax.*"

With apologetic phrases and self-deprecating shrugs, the listless six shuffled back to their places.

"Good!" said Mr. Parkhill brightly. "Discussion . . . Miss Ziev, will you read your sentences first?"

Miss Ziev, who had become more vivacious since Mr. Andrassy (in Mr. Krout's class) had repledged his troth, read her sentences, but dully—and the discussion thereof died stillborn. Not a scoff greeted even Miss Ziev's "The boy has certainly *groan* lately."

Peter Studniczka followed Miss Ziev, and not one outburst of "Mistake!" or "Hoo ha!" greeted Mr. Studniczka's "In bank are 2 doors: In come and Push Out."

Lola Lopez followed Mr. Studniczka, and Mr. Parkhill,

unable to inspirit his charges, had to carry the entire discussion by himself—even unto Miss Lopez's defiant, "Brazil has a nice, hot *climax.*"

The desultory response persisted even to Mr. Pinsky's alarming use of "chisel." (Mr. Pinsky seemed to consider "chisel" the diminutive of "cheese," hence his "Before sleep, I like a little milk and *chisel.*")

It was Mr. Parkhill alone who pointed out lapses in diction, the stumbling of syntax, the marooning of prepositions. The very heart of discussion had expired in the beginners' grade. Gone were the *sine quibus non* of debate: strong convictions, bravely held; the clash of opinions fiercely defended; the invaluable friction of a pupil certain he is right rubbing against another unaware she is wrong. . . .

Now only Mr. Pfeiffer's sentences remained to be read aloud. Mr. Parkhill teetered back and forth on his heels. "Mr. Pfeiffer, will you please read your work?"

A hush. All waited. All listened. And what all then heard, in indescribable astonishment (Mr. Pfeiffer had only opened his mouth twice, once for that unforgivable "Feh!" and then for that arrogant "Done!"), was a high, thin, squeaky sibilance: "In Detroit Missigan see saw siny Sinese braceletss in sops, ingraved by sarp tsiselss." There was no getting around it: Mr. Pfeiffer had said "Missigan" for "Michigan," "see saw" for "she saw," "siny" for "shiny," "sops" and "sarp"—

"A Litvak!" rang out a clarion voice. It was Mr. Kaplan. "Mein Gott, he's a *Litvak!*" He wheeled toward Mr. Parkhill. "Must be! From Lit'uania! He prononces a 'sh' like a hiss stimm—"

The heavens split above the beginners' grade.

"Shame, Koplon," howled Miss Tarnova.

"Can Pfeiffer *help* it he's a foreigner?" protested C. J. Fledermann.

"He's a foreigner *and* a Litvak," cried Hyman Kaplan.

"In class is no place to condemn!" shouted Mr. Olansky.

"To descripe," said Mr. Kaplan, "is not to condamn!"

The riposte only fanned the flames that swept through the battalion of Fischel Pfeiffer's admirers.

"Not fair!" charged Mr. Blattberg hotly.

"Not fair?" purred Mr. Kaplan. "If a student calls a shoe a 'soo' should ve give him a banqvet an' sing 'Hooray, hooray, he's ruinink English'?!"

"But discussion should be about the *work,*" sputtered Miss Atrakian, "not the *personal.*"

"Mine remocks are prononciational, not poisonal!" rejoined Mr. Kaplan.

Mr. Nathan was having a fit.

"Class, *class,*" Mr. Parkhill kept saying, "there's just no reason for such—"

"Keplan, you are *bad!*" blurted Isaac Nussbaum. (Mr. Nussbaum, who was pious, tended to confuse error with sin.) "Mr. Pfeiffer writes like a king!"

"Ha!" scoffed Mr. Kaplan. "He can write like a kink but he talks like a Litvak!"

*"Gent*lemen—"

"Kaplan, you jalous!" seethed Mr. Hruska.

"Who's makink poisonal remocks now?" leered Mr. Kaplan.

"Mr. Kap—"

"Stop!" boomed Reuben Olansky. "Mr. Hruska put his finger on! Koplan picks on tiny ditails!"

"A fishbone is tiny, but ken choke you to dat!"

"Mr. Pfeiffer's words are so fine, so what if he recites not perfect?" pleaded Miss Mitnick.

"A mistake," said Mr. Kaplan, "is a mistake."

"Mr. Pfeiffer needs praise, not pins!" railed the widow Pilpul.

"Are ve in cless to praise—or to loin?" flashed Mr. Kaplan.

"You don't give the Litvak a chence!" cried Mrs. Moskowitz.

"I vouldn't give an *Eskimo* a chence to wrack English!" Mr. Nathan was shaking like a man made of Jell-O.

"Kaplin, give an inch!" came Bessie Shimmelfarb's overdue plea for accommodation. "Just *vunce,* give an *inch!*"

Mr. Kaplan placed truth above measurement.

"You have to make allowance for frands!" stormed Mr. Blattberg.

"If mine own brodder made soch mistake," Mr. Kaplan retorted, "should I give him the Nobles Prize? If Pinsky makes a mistake, does Keplen say, 'Skip, skip, maybe he's a cousin Alfred Einstein's'?"

*"Gent*lemen!"

"What's Einstein got to do with Pfeiffer?" asked bewildered Milas Wodjik.

"What's Pfeiffer got to do with Einstein?" snapped Tomas Wodjik.

"Koplon, Koplon, whare is your *pity?"* beseeched Miss Tarnova.

"Piddy?" Mr. Kaplan shot up like a flagpole. "You esk piddy for *de man who sad 'Feh!' to de cless?!"*

And now Mr. Parkhill understood Mr. Kaplan's wrath, his outrage, his unyielding fusillade. "Class, there is no need for such heated dispute! Nothing is gained by passion," he said. "We are all—" The upraised thumb of Mr. Pinsky caught his eye. "Yes?"

"How do you spall 'passion'?"

Mr. Parkhill cleared his throat. " 'Passion,' " he said, regretting his impulsiveness, "is spelled 'p-a-s-s—' "

Before he could complete "passion," the bell rang its reprieve.

The platoon of warriors rose, assembling their effects, streaming to the door, arguing among themselves, calling their familiar salutations. "Good night, all." "A *good* lasson!" "Heppy vik-and." Mr. Trabish, awakened from his slumber, asked, "What happened?"

It had been a difficult evening, Mr. Parkhill thought to himself. A most difficult evening. The road to learning was so long, so hard, strewn with such sunken mines.

He saw Miss Mitnick approach the man who, responsible for all the tumult, had been entirely forgotten in the heat of battle.

"Mr. Pfeiffer," she blushed, "your writing is splendid!"

"Also your sentence structure!" laughed Mr. Nathan.

Mr. Blattberg joined them with a hearty "Pay no attention to cockamamy Keplan!" He twirled his grandsons' baby teeth with zest, and sent Mr. Pfeiffer the half-fraternal, half-subversive smile he employed when trying to recruit allies to the anti-Kaplan forces.

Then, to Mr. Parkhill's astonishment, Mr. Kaplan himself stepped up to Mr. Pfeiffer and extended his hand. "Pfeiffer, I congradulate! I hope you realize I vas only doink mine *duty*. I didn't minn to hoit your fillinks."

"You sabotaged his self-respact!" hissed Mr. Blattberg.

"You made mish-mosh from his recitation!" glared Mr. Olansky.

"You—y-you acted *hard,*" Miss Mitnick stammered.

Mr. Nathan took her hand in his.

But Mr. Pfeiffer straightened his bow tie and said, "If you esk me, Mr. Kaplan wass right."

"Hanh?"

"Who?"

*"Kep*lan?!" The Blattberg-Mitnick-Olansky task force was flabbergasted.

"A misstake is a misstake," said Fischel Pfeiffer, quoting Mr. Kaplan, indifferent to the coals he was heaping on the heads of his friends. "A fect is also a fect. My pronounssing is a scandal. My mouse is too full 's's."

287

"Pfeiffer, dobble congradulations!" cried Mr. Kaplan. "You honist! Batter an honist mistake den a snikky socksass! So you made a few mistakes. Who doesn't? Still, you made on me a *fine* imprassion. Soch beauriful hendwritink! Not iven Mitnick or Nat'an P. Nat'an writes so fency. Tell me, vhere you loined how to write like dat?"

"I am in embroidery," preened Mr. Pfeiffer.

"Aha!" Mr. Kaplan beamed. "Vitout men like you vould be a deprassion. . . . Good night, Olansky. Good night, Blattboig. Good night, Mitnick." He strode to the door, where he turned, narrowing his eyes as of yore, and in measured cadence murmured, "I vill vipe dat 'Feh!' ot from my mamory, Fischel Pfeiffer. Lat gone-bys be gone-bys! But vun t'ing you should know: You ken write like an angel, you can spall like a profasser, but ve got a *titcher*, Pfeiffer, who, onlass you prononce 'sh' like a mama to a baby an' *not* like you booink at a ballgame, vill hold you in de beginnis' grate if it takes fifty yiss!" He disappeared.

As Mr. Parkhill locked his desk, he had the uneasy feeling that Mr. Kaplan might be right, and hoped against hope that he was wrong. Fifty years . . . ! Unless—yes—*Fata viam invenient.*

8

A GLORIOUS PEST

" 'Then, amidst the breathless hush of his peers,' " read Mr. Parkhill, amidst the breathless hush of his flock, " 'Patrick Henry took the floor. All eyes turned to the fiery young lawyer, who proceeded to deliver the most scathing attack on monarchy yet heard in the Virginia House of Burgesses: "Caesar had his Brutus; Charles the First, his Cromwell; and George the Third"—'cries of "Treason! Treason!" interrupted him'—"and George the Third may profit from their example! . . . *If this be treason, make the most of it!*" ' "

Applause rocked the spellbound forum.

"Hooray!" cried Mr. Umea.

"Wonderful!" breathed Miss Mitnick.

"That's the way to talk!" crowed Mr. Nathan.

Mr. Parkhill lowered the book. He felt pleased: not only because the eloquent *démarche* always stirred his senses, but because the beginners' grade, having listened with such intensity of interest, had responded with such amplitude of emotion. "That, class, was one of the most dramatic moments in the history of the thirteen colonies from which our country was formed. And ten years later, this same patriot, Patrick Henry, delivered another speech, which many consider even more memorable. It has, indeed, become one of the truly—er—immortal orations in history." He closed the book. What teacher worth his calling required a text for that matchless peroration? " 'Is life so dear, or peace so sweet, as to be purchased at the price of chains and slavery? Forbid it, Almighty God!' " He paused. " 'I know not what course others may take, but as for me—*give me liberty or give me death!*' "

If the students had applauded Patrick Henry on monarchy, they brought the rafters down for him on liberty.

"Hoorah!"

"T'ree chiss for Petrick Hanry!"

"*Bravo! Bravo!*" Lucca Barbella was on his feet, prepared to lead a parade.

"Class . . ."

"Justa like Mazzini!"

"Ha!" Mr. Kaplan's scorn cracked out like lightning. "How you can compare a Petrick Hanry to a—vhat vas dat name you mantioned in de same brat?"

"Giuseppe Mazzini! Greata man! Greata patriot! . . . In Italia, we also have true patriot!"

"Mr. Barbella—"

"If in Italy you had a Petrick Hanry *bifore,* you vouldn't have a Mussolini later!" Mr. Kaplan intoned from on high. He raised his head toward heaven, and declaimed: " 'Give me liberty—or give me dat!' "

"True! True!" cried fierce Hruska.

"Keplen, should go in politics!" Mr. Pinsky slapped his cheek with a resounding "Pssh!"

"This mon—in *politic?!*" Olga Tarnova writhed in nausea.

"Class! Your attention!" Mr. Parkhill was rapping his pointer on the desk without a twinge of uncertainty. (When the tribute due Patrick Henry was being accorded Hyman Kaplan, who had managed to utter the deathless line as if he had made it up on the spot, it was time to call a halt.) "I shall now assign your homework."

Out came pencils to record, and notebooks to receive, Mr. Parkhill's instructions.

"During this semester," he began, "we have had occasion to discuss some of the better known episodes in American history. I have not done this in—uh—chronological order, because I have answered your questions as they arose, or explained the background of a holiday as *it* arose. American history, as such, is one of the subjects in Mr. Krout's grade." (He thought it best not to remind them that Mr. Krout was entrenched far beyond the fortress of Miss Higby.) "We discussed Woodrow Wilson, say, before we even *mentioned* the Monroe Doctrine. Or Thomas Paine before one of you brought up Pocahontas."

"I asked about Pocahontas. . . ." murmured "Cookie" Kipnis.

"Y-yes. . . . Well then, your homework assignment is: a composition on any famous figure, or any famous incident, in the American Revolution."

"Foist-class assignmant!" beamed Mr. Kaplan.

"Hard," said Mr. Wilkomirski.

"Hod but *good!* Who vants an izzy lasson? Izzy is for slowboats."

" 'Slowpokes,' Mr. Kaplan!"

Confusion wracked Mrs. Moskowitz. "Which famous figures? Which accidents?"

" '*In*cidents,' Mrs. Moskowitz, not '*acc*idents'!"

"My mind is a blenk about *in*cidents, also," mourned Mrs. Moskowitz. "Please—a few exemples. . . ."

Stalwarts rushed to help her.

"Try crossing the Delaware!"

"Take Ben Frenklin."

"Liberty Bells."

Mrs. Moskowitz wiped her jowls.

"Maybe the Mayflar!"

"Spilling that tea in Boston Harbra?"

"Don't shoot till their eyes turn white!" sang Mr. Nathan. Neither heroes, events nor historic sayings sufficed to lift Mrs. Moskowitz out of gloom's mire.

"Mrs. Moskowitz," Mr. Parkhill began, "I think you might—"

"Moskovitz, you not tryink!" scowled Mr. Kaplan.

"Vat *am* I doing—ice-skating?" snapped Mrs. Moskowitz.

"You holdink beck de cless!" announced Mr. Kaplan.

"So go witout me!"

"You sebotagink our morals!"

" 'Mor*ale*,' Mr. Kaplan, not *'mo*rals,' " said Mr. Parkhill anxiously. "Mrs. Moskowitz, the assignment is really not as hard as you fear. After you get home, when you have time to think and remember and—review your notes—I'm *sure* you will get many ideas." He was not sure Mrs. Moskowitz would get any, much less many, ideas; if an idea was to inspire Mrs. Moskowitz, it would be because the idea found a way of seizing her, not the other way around.

Lola Lopez's favorite finger wiggled in the air. "How long should thees homework last?"

"It should be . . ." Mr. Parkhill weighed his next words carefully. "I do not want a long or—er—elaborate essay, class. Let's say—oh, not more than a page and a half. Of course, one page would do nicely." He hoped he had not sounded hopeful. "That's all for tonight. . . ."

Four nights later, in the solitude of his apartment, Mr. Parkhill was correcting their compositions. It was too soon to know whether he should feel pleased or disappointed. His students' homework always contained so many *surprises*. Some were heartening, some discouraging, some paralyzing. This batch of papers contained so many surprises that it was difficult to characterize them at all. The excursion into history seemed to have carried his pupils into the most curious *personal* involvements.

Take Mr. Pinsky. Sam Pinsky was an amiable pupil who

ñever let his reach exceed his grasp. Yet this time, Mr. Pinsky had thrown caution to the winds. He had appraised the entire colonial policy of eighteenth-century England, becoming so incensed by what he called British "cold-heartiness" that he had launched into diatribe:

> Colonists were starving like flys. But all England did was make more taxis. Taxis, taxis, taxis! On food. On tea. Even on a card to a dying mother.
> I think Georgie III was a dummy!

That was not at *all* typical of Mr. Pinsky.

Or take the essay of Stanislaus Wilkomirski, whose ancestors had survived oppressions beside which the Stamp Act could be deemed philanthropic. Mr. Wilkomirski had paid his respects to that peerless seaman, "Admirable Jones." Mr. Parkhill could see how a neophyte might confuse "Admiral" with "admirable," but that Mr. Wilkomirski later alchemized "John Paul Jones" into "Jumpall Jones" Mr. Parkhill found hard to condone.

Or take Mrs. Yanoff. For some reason, the lady in black had taken personal offense at General Cornwallis, scourging him for not surrendering to Washington *soon* enough. Mr. Parkhill could not tell whether Mrs. Yanoff had meant her essay to be descriptive of, or delivered to, contemptible Cornwallis.

Reuben Olansky had penned a tirade against the Tories, whom he accused of crimes too heinous to be described, or, if described, to be spelled correctly. (It was hardly fair to blame the Tories for insulting "prepositions" when all they had done was offer unacceptable propositions.)

After these erratic fulminations, Miss Mitnick's composition was a pleasure to read. Entitled "A Hero: Nathan Hale," her essay contained this moving passage:

> They tied his hands behind to hang him. But brave, with his bare head he made a wonderful statement: "I regret I have only one life to give for the country."

Mr. Hale was not maybe so important as Washington, but he is my hero. I admire.

Why, save for the unfortunate abolition of "admire"'s transitive rights, that paragraph would have done credit to a student in Mrs. O'Hallohan's grade.

Nathan P. Nathan's commendable composition puzzled Mr. Parkhill on one point. The half-page extolled John Hancock, whose handwriting (wrote Mr. Nathan) no red-blooded American would ever "forge." It took quite a few troubling moments before Mr. Parkhill realized that only a "t" separates "forge" from "forget."

Miss Ziev, from whom Mr. Parkhill had not expected to receive any homework at all (Miss Ziev no longer wore the ring given her by Mr. Andrassy), had come through with an unusual offering:

MINUTE MEN
Farm boys with long riffles. Always ready to fight. Did.
A famous battle, with 1 shot the whole world heard, was the Battle of Grand Concourse.
Good work, Minute Men!

The only way Mr. Parkhill could explain how Concord had become "Grand Concourse" was that Miss Ziev had a relative who resided on that thoroughfare.

Mr. Studniczka—Mr. Parkhill sighed. Peter Studniczka had submitted yet another of his cryptic substitutions for prose:

1776
Best Man—G. Washington
Bad Man—King
Trators—Ben and Dick Arnold
Pattriot—*PULASKI FROM POLAND!*

Mr. Parkhill was not happy about that paper. Something in Mr. Studniczka's psychological structure made him approach English vertically. Whether it was because he actually thought in columns (which Mr. Parkhill would understand, were Mr. Studniczka an accountant, or Japanese), or whether he had a phobia about horizontal prose, which requires subject, verb, predicate, Mr. Parkhill did not know. Mr. Studniczka had a long way to go. Mr. Parkhill corrected the spelling of "trators" and "pattriot," and in the margin of Mr. Studniczka's inventory wrote: "This is not a *composition,* Mr. S. Please use whole *sentences!*" He started to put the paper aside, paused, and added: "Bene*dict* Arnold. One traitor, not two."

The next paper popped pellets of color before Mr. Parkhill's eyes.

AL X. HAMILTON VERSES TOM S. JEFFERSON
A Play!
By
H*Y*M*A*N K*A*P*L*A*N

Mr. Parkhill put the paper down and went into the kitchen for a glass of water. He sharpened his red marking pencil thoughtfully before picking up Mr. Kaplan's "A Play!" again. Before he had read two lines, he was wincing.

HAMILTON: "The government should be strong!"
JEFFERSON: "No! Be ware strong government. People must decide."
HAMILTON: "People? Ha, ha, ha, ha. Don't trust people."
JEFFERSON: "I TRUST! Also U.S. money says 'God trusts.' O.K. *How's about you?*"
HAMILTON: "You are a dreamy. Don't be so nave."

At this point, Mr. Kaplan, exhausted by the weight of long words, had dropped into abbreviations; this had no doubt lessened the strain on his fingers but played havoc with the names of his protagonists:

HAM: "Every business needs a boss!"
JEFF: "From bosses comes Kings! Don't forget!"

295

HAM: "That's my last offer, Tom S. Jefferson!"
JEFF: "Same to you, Al X. Hamilton."

Mr. Parkhill reached for an aspirin.

"Good evening, class," said Mr. Parkhill. "First, I shall
return your homework. Each paper has been corrected
and—evaluated. Please study my comments—they are in
red—carefully. I believe you can learn more from your
own mistakes than from almost any other—"

Up stabbed Mr. Kaplan's hand.

"Y-yes?"

"You *liked* de homevoik, Mr. Pockheel?"

"Well," the reply unrolled cautiously, "I think all of you
tried very hard. There were, of course, errors, many errors
—in some cases, too many. I shall now distribute—"

"Still, *som* homevoik gave you a big soprise?"

Mr. Parkhill averted his gaze. He knew exactly what Mr.
Kaplan was driving at. The man was trying to lure Mr.
Parkhill into some compliment—say, that imagination is
more important than error, and that one particular student had by sheer inspiration soared far, far above his
fellows. . . . "Mr. Kaplan," said Mr. Parkhill firmly, "the
purpose of homework is not to—'surprise.' In fact, the best
homework is the kind that contains no errors at all, thus
giving me no 'surprises.' " With that *tu quoque,* Mr. Parkhill distributed the homework. "Miss Atrakian . . . Mr.
Olansky . . ."

Mr. Kaplan looked crestfallen. How, looking crestfallen,
he exuded the pride of one who had scaled Parnassus, Mr.
Parkhill would never understand.

". . . C. J. Fledermann."

The compositions streamed back to their creators,
whose swift sounds of illumination rewarded Mr. Parkhill.

296

"I spalled wrong 'Philadelphia'!"

"Harry is not 'Hairy' . . ."

"Psssh! Was I wrong!" Mr. Pinsky's self-administered slap told Mr. Parkhill that Mr. Pinsky was determined to learn, whatever the emotional cost.

"Examine the corrections carefully, class. If you have a question, just raise your hand. . . ." He strolled down the aisle. (There is a world of difference, Mr. Parkhill had learned, between sitting at a desk and strolling down an aisle: the former is judiciary, the latter egalitarian; the one stresses decorum, the other induces relaxation.)

The next hour went so swiftly that the bell rang before anyone suspected it was time for recess.

In the final portion of the session, Mr. Parkhill conducted a spelling drill of which he felt rather proud: twenty words containing "e-i-g-h-t" (from "freight" to "weight" via "height"), and twenty containing "o-u-g-h" (from "cough" through "rough" to "trough").

He had just announced "Bought . . . thought . . . enough . . ." when Mrs. Moskowitz flung down her pen and appealed to Miss Kipnis beside her: " 'Enough'? *Enough!* Why not put in 'f' when is pro*noun*ced 'ffff'? A mind can creck from soch torture, Cookie!"

"You got to be patient," sighed Miss Kipnis.

"Don't give op!" called Rochelle Goldberg, placating her own nerves with a caramel. "Learning takes *time.* . . ."

They had reckoned without the defender of the faith. "Ha! Vhat kind students are talkink? Moskovitz," called Mr. Kaplan, "U.S. vasn't fonded by sissies!"

"I dun't want to found, I want to spall!"

"Class—"

"Nottink good is izzy!" declaimed Hyman Kaplan. *"Eating* is good, and easy!"

"You compare spallink to eatink?" Mr. Kaplan's expression set a new high for amazement. "You tritt English like lemb chops?"

"*You* make English chop suey!" jeered Mr. Olansky.

His cohorts burst into laughter.

"Class, *class,*" said Mr. Parkhill. (Mr. Nathan was choking.) "We are engaged in a spelling drill, not a debate!" He waited for combat to subside, then addressed Mrs. Moskowitz. "I can well understand how someone from another land feels when confronted by some of the peculiar ways in which English words are spelled."

"*I* am from anodder lend," said Mr. Kaplan, "an' still I don't holler 'Halp!'"

"Mr. Kaplan," said Mr. Parkhill crisply, "English *is* a difficult language. And many of our words *are* spelled in most unreasonable—"

"Moskovitz ken still make a good profit from odder pipple's semples!" intoned Hyman Kaplan.

Mr. Parkhill frowned. "I beg your pardon?"

Mr. Kaplan sat as serene as a lamb.

"I thought I heard you say that Mrs. Moskowitz could—er—'make a good profit'—"

"Like de Pilgrim's Fodder," said Mr. Kaplan.

"The Pilgri*m* Father*s*!" Mr. Parkhill tried not to sound annoyed.

"What have the Pilgrims to do with Mrs. Moskowitz?" protested Miss Mitnick.

"Yos!"

"Tell!"

"It's obvious," said Mr. Kaplan carelessly. Apparently, he considered it too obvious to continue.

"Mr. Kaplan," said Mr. Parkhill, "your comment is as unclear to me as it is to Miss Mitnick! I suggest you explain —no, no, you need not go to the *front*—"

Mr. Kaplan was already halfway to the podium he adored. There he stopped, turned, and withered Mrs. Moskowitz with his scorn. "De Pilgrim's Fodder—"

298

"Pilgri*m* Father*s!*"

"—didn't sail beck to England becawss dey had to spall de void 'enough'!" Now the patriot transferred his attention to Miss Mitnick. "Dey had beeger trobbles. Hindians, messecres, skinny hovests—"

"Mr. Kap—"

"—spying fromm de Franch, poisicutions fromm de British—"

"Stop with the lecture in American history!" howled Mr. Olansky.

"Stick to Mrs. Moskowitz!" shouted Mr. Blattberg.

"Class—"

"The Pilgrim Fothahs didn't hov to put op with Koplon!" lowed Olga Tarnova.

Triton was deaf to the minnows. "An' vhen de time came for de Amarican Ravolution, brave men like John Edems, Tom Spain—"

"Thomas *Paine*, not 'Spain'—"

"—knew dey had missink a slogan, a spok, a fire to light de lemps of Liberty! So along came Pettereck Hanry."

"It's *'Pat*rick,' not 'Pett*e*rick'—and 'H*e*nry,' not 'H*a*nry.' "

Mr. Kaplan's gaze had gone dreamy. "Dat vas a man . . . A prince! A tong like silver."

"Mr. Kaplan, it's 'tongue,' not 'tong'!"

"So *Pat*rick Hanry vent into de Virginia House of Poichases—"

" 'Burgess—' "

"—an' at vunce all vas qviet, like de gomment districk on Chrissmis Iv. So Patrick Hanry got don on de floor—"

"*Took* the floor!" Mr. Parkhill was beginning to feel dehydrated.

"—took de floor, an' in dose beauriful, parful voids vhich comm don de santuries for all Amaricans who got true blood—"

" 'True-*blooded*'—"

"—Pet sad, 'Julius Scissor had his Buddhist—'"

" '*Brutus*'!" cried Mr. Parkhill.

" 'Cholly de Foist had his Cronvall, an' if crazy King Judge got a brain in his had he *vill make a profit from soch a semple!*' "

Mr. Parkhill sank into his seat, which seemed to have had its legs shortened.

"Dat," Mr. Kaplan concluded, "also epplies to Moskovitz!" He strode back to his chair.

"All I said was 'enough' should have vun little 'f'!" wailed Mrs. Moskowitz.

"Koplen, you mad!" fumed Olaf Umea.

"Give an *inch*, Mr. Kaplan—"

"Thees mon will change heestory single-honded!" That, perhaps the truest thought yet uttered, came from Lola Lopez.

"Call a doctor! Examine his head!" Mr. Olansky had placed his own head between his hands.

"Mr. *Kap*lan—" Mr. Parkhill began. But he scarcely knew where to begin, so he began again. "Mr. Kaplan, rarely have I heard so many mispronunciations in so short a time! Charles the First was *not* 'Charley the—er—Foist.' Cromwell was *not* 'Cronvall.' And what Patrick Henry said was certainly *not* what you said he said! There is a world of difference, Mr. Kaplan, between 'George the Third *may profit from their example*' and 'George the Third can make a profit out of such a sample'! Do you understand?"

Mr. Nathan was gasping and laughing in tandem.

Mr. Kaplan had cocked his head to one side, signifying attention, closed both eyes, indicating cerebration, then opened one eye, denoting illumination. "Yes, sir. But I vill alvays edmire de glorious pest."

"Mistake!" sang out Miss Mitnick. " '*Past*' is not '*pest*.' "

One Mr. Wodjik guffawed. The other Mr. Wodjik gig-

300

gled. Miss Goldberg swallowed a Kiss from Hershey, Pa.

"Tonight is averybody an axpert?" Mr. Kaplan caustically inquired.

"Tonight," Miss Mitnick retorted, "you don't have to be an expert to know the *'past'* from a *'pest'!*"

The room rocked with merriment.

"Good for you, Miss Mitnick!"

"Bravissima!"

"This time Rose has him in a coroner!" exulted Mr. Nathan.

Mr. Kaplan ignored the petty barbs and puny arrows, turning to the one who had given him the challenge direct. "Mitnick," he said with pious pity, *"you* are talking abot prononcing; but *I* am talking abot history!"

" 'Past' *means* history!" Miss Mitnick blushed tearfully. "What you said was 'the glorious p*e*st.' "

"Koplen, give up!" advised C. J. Fledermann.

"Keplan, sit down!" brayed Miss Pomeranz.

"Kaplen, give an *inch!*" pleaded Bessie Shimmelfarb.

"Mr. Kaplan," cut in Mr. Parkhill. "Miss Mitnick is absolutely right! 'Past' refers to what has gone by. 'P*e*st,' on the other hand, refers to an annoying or irritat—" Too late, too late did Mr. Parkhill see the trap into which he, like poor Miss Mitnick, had fallen.

"To a tyrent like King Judge Number T'ree," declaimed Hyman Kaplan, "vhat else vas Patrick Hanry axcept a glorious pest?"

After that, twenty words with "o-u-g-h" seemed inglorious trivia.

BRIEF BUDDHA

No trumpets blared as the fat little man marched into the room. He was moonfaced and ruddy. His nose was tiny, his mustache reddish. The mustache was so thick it made the nose resemble a grape.

The little man reminded Mr. Parkhill of a Buddha. Buddhas, of course, do not wear mustaches; they look supremely serene, ever-so-wise, and rather jolly: this stranger radiated the gaiety of a radish. Still, he made Mr. Parkhill think of a Buddha. . . .

The stranger halted before Mr. Parkhill's desk. His left arm cradled a derby as if it was a baby. His right arm stiffened as, without a word, he thrust forth a yellow card:

VISITOR'S PASS

AMERICAN NIGHT PREPARATORY SCHOOL

FOR ADULTS

Please admit bearer: *Mr. Teitelman*
for one trial lesson.

Leland Robinson
Principal
by *M. S.*

The names were written in on the printed form, in the unmistakable scrawl of Miss Schnepfe, Mr. Robinson's factotem. Miss Schnepfe's first name was Louella, but she had fallen into the habit of signing herself "Miss S." When she was in a hurry, as she must have been in the case above, she initialed things "M. S." (Several members of the A.N.P.S.A. faculty felt that power had gone to Miss Schnepfe's head.)

As Mr. Parkhill deciphered the visitor's name on the yellow card, the entire beginners' grade appraised its prospective colleague: Rochelle Goldberg with the thirst of a maiden approaching thirty, Mr. Blattberg with the suspicion of a bill collector, Mrs. Yanoff with the expertise acquired in her search for a mate for her daughter.

"Mr.—er—Teitelman?" smiled Mr. Parkhill.

The fat little man drooped. He did not seem optimistic.

"Take a seat, please . . . anywhere." Mr. Parkhill kept smiling, for he knew how self-conscious a newcomer is. "And please consider yourself a full-fledged member of the class for the evening. Enter into our work just as if you were a regular student. . . . Indeed, I hope you *will* be, after tonight." Mr. Parkhill pumped fresh air into his smile, but not a flicker of pleasure lightened the dour countenance. The fat little man merely trudged to the first empty chair he beheld; it was in the front row. This caused considerable stirrings and murmurs amongst his peers, for new students, and certainly *visitors,* invariably sought a haven in the last row. But the stranger plumped his pudgy form into that vacant chair in the front line, between Mrs. Pilpul, on his left, and Hyman Kaplan, on his right.

Mr. Parkhill announced: "Tonight, we shall devote the first half of our session to completing the Recitation and Speech exercise of last evening. We still have to hear from —let me see"—he consulted the class roll—"Mr. Hruska, Miss Atrakian, Mrs. Moskowitz, and—yes, Mr. Trabish."

Three of the four sentenced to oratory promptly moaned.

"I'll be tarrible," soughed Mr. Hruska.

Miss Atrakian wet her lips nervously. "I wish I don't have to go."

Mr. Trabish made neither sound nor sigh, until the "Oy" from Mrs. Moskowitz roused him from slumber. "Time to go home?" he blinked.

"Time to vake op!" said Mr. Kaplan.

"We shall give our speakers a few moments to review their remarks," announced Mr. Parkhill brightly. "Meanwhile, the rest of the class might brush up on page forty-six of our textbook."

The congregation rustled through *English for Beginners*. Page 46 contained a list of transitive verbs. Dark scowls and glum mutters ascended from the ranks. The beginners' grade *hated* transitive verbs; they resented the hard-and-fast rule that transitive verbs require a definite object. (Mr. Kaplan had once complained, "I ken be dafinite mit*out* an objeck.")

Mr. Parkhill turned to the fat little man. "You may share page forty-six with Mrs. Pilpul. . . ."

The widow Pilpul pushed *English for Beginners* to her right with flirtatious intimations. But the roly-poly guest made no reactive lean to his left. His thoughts were obviously elsewhere; his gaze was fixed glassily on some ogre above Mr. Parkhill's head.

Meanwhile, the four scholars assigned to recite conducted individual rites of preparation. Miss Atrakian opened and closed her notebook—whispering a line with the book closed, opening it to check on memory, closing the book, mumbling the next line of her speech, reopening the book. . . . Vasil Hruska, who was made of sterner stuff, shunned unworthy cues and props; he rehearsed his address in silent mouthings. Mrs. Moskowitz tried to mollify fate by wailing "I'll be a dummy!" And the last member of the quartet, Mr. Trabish, began to rub his hands. (Mr. Trabish's years as a baker had taught him to clear his mind by massaging his palms.)

304

To all these preliminary orisons, Hyman Kaplan paid not the slightest attention. He was absorbed in assessing the fat little man out of the corner of one eye; his other eye remained fixed on Mr. Parkhill, like a sentry. (Mr. Kaplan appeared to possess a separate guidance system for each orb; it was uncanny.) For several long moments Mr. Kaplan subjected the rotund visitor to optic synopsis. Would the stranger prove brilliant or stupid? Would he speed up or drag down the sacred transmission of knowledge? Above all, would he be friend or foe? (Neutrality, to Mr. Kaplan, was inconceivable.)

Mr. Kaplan finally leaned leftward and, in a confidential tone, whispered: "How's by you de name, plizz?"

The newcomer twitched, but said nothing.

Mr. Kaplan cleared his throat. "Eh . . . How—is—by—you —de *name?*"

Buddha blinked, reached into his vest, and placed an impressive fountain pen on the arm of his chair. A name, stamped in gold, glittered on the barrel of the pen.

" 'F. Teitelman,' " Mr. Kaplan read. " 'F'—aha! For 'Philip.' "

The mustache quivered in the negative.

"Not for 'Philip'?" Mr. Kaplan pondered the duplicity of 'F.' "Aha! 'Frenk'!"

The nose above the mustache rejected "Frenk."

"Eh—so vat *is* by you de name?"

"Jerome."

" *'Jerome'*? But dat's mit a 'G'! So vhy is on your fontain pan 'F'?!"

The dumpling grunted, "It belongs to my wife."

"My!" murmured Mr. Kaplan.

Mrs. Pilpul's countenance darkened.

"Well, class!" Mr. Parkhill tore his attention away from the little drama which had held him in thrall. "We should be ready now. Mrs. Moskowitz, will you please recite first?"

The portly matron rose, froze, recovered, stepped on Mr.

Fledermann's shoe, blubbered remorse, tugged at her girdle, bobbled her purse, returned Miss Mitnick's encouraging smile with a Cheyne-Stokes rattle—all in the time it took her to lumber from the row in the back to the platform at the front.

"Now, you'll gonna hear mistakes!" Mr. Kaplan grinned to the fat little man. "By de bushel!"

Mr. Nussbaum, who was endowed with exceptional hearing, snapped, "They should hire you for Yom Kippur!"

"Truth is batter than veseline," rejoined Mr. Kaplan.

"You smesh a poisson's confidence!" charged Miss Kipnis.

"How ken you smesh vhat *isn't?*"

"Class!" called Mr. Parkhill. "This is no way to start off! I *must* ask for—silence. Mrs. Moskowitz, state the subject of your recitation, please."

Mrs. Moskowitz, who had been in no condition to hear Mr. Kaplan's prophecy, wiped the perspiration off her brow. "My sobject is—'Arond My Flet.'" (Mrs. Moskowitz had become fixated, in her orations, on the familiar terrain of her apartment: "Getting a New Carpet," "Cleaning Drapes," "Cooking Big Meals." Once, in reckless expansion, she had expatiated on "In a Kitchen Is Gaz a Danger!!") "Men don't know how hard is life for ladies! Housewoik is hodder than homewoik. Also hodder than being in a factory or stending behind a conter." She stopped. "Hommeny mistakes so far?"

"Not so many," smiled Mr. Parkhill. "You might be a *bit* more careful in pronunciation. It's '*hard*er,' for example, not '*hod*der.' And—a mistake many of you make—'*work*,' not '*woik*.'"

"*Soch* a titcher ve got." Mr. Kaplan beamed at the fat little man; the freshman's features remained as unanimated as farina.

"Go on, Mrs. Moskowitz."

306

The dowager swallowed air and, bosom heaving, de-claimed: "Ladies work in a shop or store all day, but still, on coming home, don't rast! They have to clinn up de house, make sopper, take care of children (if there are, which I have, two, long should they live and be halthy), then get for tomorrow morning brakfast raddy, do laun-dry, fix clothes, or—or—" The prolonged passage had ex-hausted Mrs. Moskowitz's resources. "—and so far!" She stopped.

Mr. Parkhill sent her an invigorating nod.

Mrs. Moskowitz flailed her hands. "So what more is to *tell?*"

"Abot feexing claws!" trumpeted Mr. Kaplan.

"Awright," said Mrs. Moskowitz, startled by the source of assistance. "I'll describe fixing clothes."

"Teitelman," Mr. Kaplan whispered, "don't be a shy. You ken give ideas, too!"

The sphinx sat inscrutable.

"For fixing clothes," announced Mrs. Moskowitz, "you should have a niddle, a spool of trad the same color, and also a little—"

"Time!" called the stranger.

All heads swung in surprise. Visitors *never* volunteered suggestions.

"Fine, Teitelman!" chortled Mr. Kaplan. "Dat's a boy!"

But Mrs. Moskowitz stared at the interloper with animus. "Why *time,* Mr. New? For fixing clothes you should have a niddle, som trad—"

"You nid time *also!*" Mr. Kaplan defended his protégé.

"And you also nidd a *chair,* for sitting on," shouted Mrs. Moskowitz, "and *light,* you should see, and a *roof* you shouldn't get vet! *Time?!*" she repeated hotly. "I want to tell about mending socks and shoits, and Mr. Mustache dregs in a clock!"

"You right!" called Mr. Tomas Wodjik.

"Good for you!" chimed in Milas Wodjik.

"Kaplan, sharup!" scowled Mr. Olansky.

Mr. Parkhill had been tapping his ruler on the desk for five seconds. "Class . . . *class*. . . . Our visitor simply offered —a suggestion. Proceed, Mrs. Moskowitz."

"So like I said," the aggrieved one continued, "for sewing, you should have a niddle, some trad—and something else. Because if you have a very *tick* piece goods, like a man's coat, how can you push t'rough a niddle?! So you have to put on your pushing finger a tiny, teeny cop. From tin it's made, full of small bumps, so the niddle shouldn't slip. It's called a—"

"Dumbbell," sang Buddha.

Some gasped, some goggled, some winced, but Mrs. Moskowitz snapped, "Mister-New-Student, I-don't-know-who-you-are—"

"De name is Teitelman," beamed Mr. Kaplan.

"—*I* don't mean 'dumbbell'! Maybe *your* vife uses dumbbells for sewing. *I* use a *t'imble!* Now if butt-in Mr. Teitel-bum—"

"Teitel*man,"* said Mr. Kaplan.

"—stops intropting, I'll go on. . . . If you have a niddle and trad and *t'imble,* the rast is easy. You just fill op de holes."

"Bravo!" rejoiced Mr. Barbella.

"Congradzulazion!" cracked Mr. Wilkomirski.

Mrs. Moskowitz, breathing heavily, ran two fingers through her hair. "So what *else?"*

"How about washing floors?" prompted Mr. Blattberg.

"Clean your windolls," offered Goldie Pomeranz.

"Wex the tables," hinted a cabinetmaker.

But Mrs. Moskowitz, unable to both think and hearken simultaneously, plumbed her own soul. "Cooking! Yas! Arond every lady's home is cooking! Which I love. Since I am a little girl, I am cooking. And baking . . . Baking! Oh, I—love—baking! I bake brat, rolls, cookies, even—"

308

"Pies," called Mr. Teitelman.

"CAKE!" shouted Mrs. Moskowitz. "Not *pies!* Cake! 'K-A-K-E'!"

"Mrs. Moskowitz, it's 'c-a-' "

Mr. Kaplan rushed to protect the flank of his ward. "But you make pies *too,* no, Moskovitz?"

"I—bake—CAKE!"

"Moskovitz, you too axcited!"

"Mr. Kap—"

"I bake *cake!*"

"A foist-cless cook got to make pies!"

"Corract!" concurred Mr. Trabish.

"Who asked you?!" snapped Mrs. Moskowitz.

"He's a *ba*ker!" cried Mr. Kaplan.

"Class—"

"And Mr. New? He's a Franch chaff?" flared the matron. "Teitelman vas only tryink to halp!"

"Mr. Kap—"

"Let Mr. Mustache halp *you!*" fumed Mrs. Moskowitz. *"Me* he'll drive crazy—"

"Mrs. Mosko—"

"—giving dumbbells for t'imbles, dregging in *time* all of a sodden, den t'rowing *pies* in my cake! Enoff! I'll *bust!* Good-bye!" And with that, cheeks aflame, her hair so disarranged she looked like a frantic Medusa, Sadie Moskowitz stomped back to her chair.

The sensitive tribunal seethed—with sympathy for Mrs. Moskowitz and sneers to tactless Teitelman.

"He didn't give Mrs. M. a chonce!" moaned Olga Tarnova.

"He was trying to halp!" Mr. Pinsky echoed his master.

"Help?" railed Christian Fledermann. "Zoch help iss poison!"

"I hear bees in de room agan," murmured Mr. Kaplan.

"Please . . . *class!*" Mr. Parkhill marshaled all his powers of conciliation to head off open warfare. "I *do* think Mr. Teitelman was just trying to—participate in our—"

"Soitinly!" said Mr. Kaplan.

"A new student we shouldn't poisicute," observed "Cookie" Kipnis.

"Who *pois*icuted?" flared Mr. Blattberg. *"He* was the one—"

"Class—"

"In my opinion," called Mrs. Pilpul, whose opinion no one ever solicited, "Mr. Teitelman should get a pinch sympaty."

"He should have his lips sewed up!" rejoined Mr. Olansky.

In vain did Mr. Parkhill tap his knuckles on the desk, in vain seek a truce. "Class, this is ab—"

"Everyone has right to correct," muttered Mr. Studniczka.

"But not to neg, neg, *neg* a spiker," returned Mrs. Yanoff.

"I *admire* a new man who talks his *foist time in class!"* declared Mrs. Shimmelfarb.

"I odmire a mon which knows the difference of cake and pie!" retorted Olga Tarnova.

"That will be enough!" Mr. Parkhill's severe tone squelched the broil and brabble. "Mrs. Moskowitz, I'm sure we all understand how you feel. But Mr. Teitelman is—" He might have been shooting peas at Gibraltar.

"Mr. Mustache is anodder Kaplin!" cried Mrs. Moskowitz.

"Class—"

"I suggest Kaplen *and* his pel sharop!" huffed Mr. Nussbaum, through quivering whiskers.

"I soggest you stop a vulgar word like 'Sharop'!" exclaimed Shirley Ziev.

Throughout the clash and conflict, Messrs. Kaplan and Teitelman sat quiet, side by side, comrades indifferent to

310

snipers. They paid scant attention to the next speech, by Miss Atrakian. They raised no quibbles about the oration of Mr. Hruska. They nodded absently to the words of Mr. Trabish, who had been the first to rally to their standard. The two knights just reposed in valor, bound by fraternal effort in a noble cause.

When the recess bell tolled, the chattering class started into the corridor.

Mr. Kaplan smiled at the fat little man. "You vant to stap otside a few minutes?"

The orphan of the storm shook his head.

"Hau Kay," said Mr. Kaplan. "Stay. Rast. T'ink op more fine ideas!" He headed for the throng beyond the door, gloating.

The fat little man sat quite still in his chair, gazing at Mr. Parkhill. Only the two of them were in the room.

Mr. Parkhill cleared his throat. He wanted to tell Mr. Teitelman that class sessions were not usually so agitated; that emotions had been roused to such a pitch because of the class's genuine thirst for knowledge; that there was, in fact, a certain value in heated debate. . . . Before Mr. Parkhill could phrase even the first of these propitiations, the visitor stood up, placed his derby upon his head, said "Goom-bye," and waddled out of the room.

Mr. Parkhill looked after him in distress.

Soon the gong sounded an end to recess. The scholars filed in. They took their places. Mr. Kaplan did not sit down. "Teitelman?" he called. His eyes darted right and left. "Who seen Teitelman?"

No one had seen Teitelman. No one seemed to know where or how the fat little man had vanished. (Mr. Parkhill wondered whether Buddha had ever used a Fire Exit.)

"Let us take up the list of transitive verbs on page forty-six," said Mr. Parkhill.

The textbooks rustled busily.

311

"Miss Goldberg, will you begin?"

Miss Goldberg read: "Tell . . . give . . . throw."

The hateful verbs stilled the last perturbations of the beginners' grade.

"Remove . . . choose . . . catch . . ." read Mr. Wodjik. (Since they often changed places, Mr. Parkhill was not sure which Mr. Wodjik it was.)

Heads bobbed up and down in rhythm to the litany. All heads, that is, save Hyman Kaplan's. He was inert, gloom drowning his usual vivacity. He ignored the travail of the transitive. He uttered not one "My!" or "Aha!" to verbs passive. The heart had gone out of Hyman Kaplan. Lost was the old bravado, gone the bright, irrepressible flair.

Only once did Mr. Kaplan emerge from the gorge of mourning. That was when, assessing the empty chair beside him, Mr. Kaplan sighed, "My . . . I lost a *fine* frant."

10

THE PERILS OF LOGIC

In the beginning, Mr. Parkhill had assumed that the incredible things Mr. Kaplan did to the English language were the offshoots of ignorance—ignorance garnished with originality, to be sure, but ignorance nonetheless. (How else explain Mr. Kaplan's belief that a summary is a short summer?)

But then Mr. Parkhill began to think that it wasn't ignorance which governed Mr. Kaplan so much as *impulsiveness*. (That would explain the sentence he concocted when asked to use the word "orchard": "Each Sunday he sent her a dozen orchards.") And for a time Mr. Parkhill toyed with the notion that Mr. Kaplan's startling improvisations were produced by a certain mischievousness. (How else account for the man's blithe assertion that the body of water which separates France from Britain is "the English Canal"?)

But all of these hypotheses collapsed the night the beginners' grade was running through a lively exercise on synonyms and antonyms. Mr. Kaplan placed these sets of "opposites" on the board:

slow	fast
upton	donton
rich	skinny

Most teachers would have dismissed "skinny" as a grotesque guess. But Mr. Parkhill thought it over with great

313

care. *Why,* he asked himself, would an intelligent man like Mr. Kaplan consider "skinny" the opposite of "rich"? The answer came to him in a flash: the reason Mr. Kaplan thought "skinny" the antonym of "rich" was that in his experience rich people were fat! *Ergo:* if the rich are fat, then *(mutatis mutandis)* the poor must be skinny. (He wished Mr. Kaplan had used "thin" instead of "skinny," but he had to admit that "skinny" is much more graphic.)

The more Mr. Parkhill analyzed Mr. Kaplan's peculiar solecisms the more did he become convinced that neither ignorance nor caprice nor puckishness was the key to Mr. Kaplan's airy revision of the English language. It was logic. A private kind of logic. A unique logic. A secret, baffling logic. But logic. Mr. Kaplan made mistakes because he simply ignored or refused to abide by convention. After all, human conventions do not rest on reason, but on consensus. Mr. Kaplan's malapropisms therefore arose from the fact that his logic and the logic of English just did not happen to coincide! (Mr. Parkhill had always been a staunch believer in *"De gustibus non est disputandum."*)

Any lingering doubts Mr. Parkhill harbored about the whole problem vanished when Mr. Kaplan called the instrument which doctors use to listen to the human heart a "deathascope."

One Wednesday night Mr. Parkhill gained a fresh insight into the workings of Mr. Kaplan's mind. Miss Goldie Pomeranz was reciting, recounting a frightening experience with a dog. The dog's name, according to Miss Pomeranz, was "Rax." (She probably meant "Rex"; Mr. Parkhill had never heard of a dog named "Rax.")

"Was he a wild bist!" Miss Pomeranz declaimed. "I was trying to pat him, very nice, on the head. And I was saying, 'Here, Rax, be a good boy.' And without a word, not even one bow-wow or groll or making angry his tail, Rax bite me in the lag!"

" 'Bite,' " said Mr. Parkhill, "is the *present* tense, Miss Pomeranz."

Chagrin clouded the bitten maid's countenance.

"You want the—*past* tense," Mr. Parkhill said gently. "What is the past tense of 'to bite'?"

"Omigod," bleated Miss Pomeranz.

"The past tense of 'to bite'—anyone?"

Mr. Kaplan sent up a trial balloon: "Is it 'bited' . . . ?"

"No, it is not 'bited'!"

"I agree," said Mr. Kaplan.

Miss Mitnick raised her hand, just above the head of Mr. Trabish, dozing pleasantly in the row ahead. "The past tense of 'bite,' " she volunteered, "is 'bit.' "

"Right, Miss Mitnick! 'Bite, bit.' The dog *bit* you in the leg, Miss Pomeranz. And the past participle—?"

" 'Bitten,' " blushed Rose Mitnick.

Nathan P. Nathan applauded.

But Mr. Kaplan closed one eye, cocked his head, and whispered to himself, "Mitnick gives 'bit' . . . *'Bit'* Mitnick gives? Also 'bitten' . . . ?! 'Bite, bit, *bitten'*—it sonds awful fonny."

Mr. Parkhill could not pretend he had not heard this soliloquy: the entire room had heard it. "Er—isn't that clear, Mr. Kaplan?"

"Clear, Mr. Pockheel?" The ruminating orb opened. "Yas, sir. But I don't see *why* it should be 'bitten.' . . . To me, it don't make *sense."* (Yes, he had said "why," not "vhy.")

"It *doesn't* make sense?" Mr. Parkhill echoed lamely, then glimpsed a golden opportunity: "You mean it isn't *logical?"*

"Pretzicely."

"Well, Mr. Kaplan! Let us address ourselves directly to that point! Language is not always—logical. But it has *laws,* laws which have grown and become accepted down the centuries." Mr. Parkhill was rather excited by the

315

chance to enlighten the class on so important a concept. "I'm sure you remember our various verb drills, Mr. Kaplan. Well, the verb 'to bite' is very much like, say, the verb 'to hide.' 'To hide' is conjugated 'hide, hid, hidden.' Why, then, isn't it—er—logical for the principal parts of 'to bite' to be 'bite, bit, bitten'?"

Mr. Kaplan hesitated but a smidgeon of a moment. "I t'ink de past time of 'bite' should be 'bote.' "

" 'Bote'?" Mr. Parkhill echoed.

" 'Bote.' Because, if it is 'write, wrote, written,' why not 'bite, bote, bitten'?"

Mr. Nathan laughed until the tears rolled down his cheeks. Mr. Barbella hooted.

Mr. Parkhill wished he could lie down.

"B-but there is not such a *word* as 'bote'!" cried Miss Mitnick.

" 'Not such a woid,' " Mr. Kaplan echoed, all pity. "Mine dear Mitnick, did I say dere *is* such a woid? Never! All I said is: why *shouldn't* be such a woid?!"

"Mr. Kaplan, *there is no such word,* as Miss Mitnick quite correctly observed!" Poor Miss Mitnick was biting her lips. "Nor is it 'logical' that there *should* be such a word!" This time Mr. Parkhill was determined to nip the Kaplan casuistry in the bud. He recapitulated the exercise on regular and irregular verbs. He recited the principal parts of a dozen samples. He spoke with special earnestness, for he suspected that a good deal depended on his exposition.

By the time Mr. Parkhill had finished, Mr. Kaplan was all admiration, Miss Mitnick's normal pallor had returned, Mr. Olansky smirked like a crocodile, and Miss Goldberg savored a gumdrop.

Recitation and Speech continued. Mr. Sam Pinsky delivered a brief address on the mysteries of his craft, pressing. Mrs. Pilpul followed with an eyewitness account of an altercation in a "beauty saloon." Mr. Trabish, energized by brief slumber, issued an apologia for the community of bakers, who are as fallible as any other caste of men, and confessed that on at least two occasions he had carelessly produced soggy hard "rawls." Mrs. Yanoff, her black dress shining, described a trip she and her "husbar," Morris, were hoping to make to a metropolis called "Spittsburgh." The recess bell quelled the skirmish over "husbar" and the brouhaha about "Spittsburgh."

The second student to take the floor after the session resumed was Hyman Kaplan. "Ladies, gantleman, *patient* Mr. Pockheel. . . . Tonight, I'll gonna talk abot noose-peppers, dose vunderful, movvelous—"

"Pardon me," Mr. Parkhill broke in at once. (It was foolhardy to give Mr. Kaplan free rein at the very outset of what was going to be an elegy to journalism.) "It's 'Tonight I am going'—not 'I'll gonna'—'to talk.' . . . And the word is *'newspapers,'* not 'noose-peppers.' " Briskly, he printed NOOSE, PEPPER, and NEWSPAPER on the board. Carefully, he explained the meaning of each word. (When he drove home the difference between "news" and "noose," Mr. Blattberg burst into cackling.)

"So," Mr. Kaplan resumed his tale, "a *news*paper is to me a *miracle* we have in tsivilization. What is a *news*paper? Ha! It's a show! It's education! It's tregedy! It's comical! It's movvelous! A *news*paper gives to our messes—"

" '*Mass*es,' Mr. Kaplan, not '*mess*es'!"

"—gives to our *mass*es information about de whole woild. Even advoitismants in a paper titch a lesson. An' ufcawss all odder pots of a paper: de hatlininks—"

"*Mr.* Kaplan! Headlines are *not* 'hatlinings.' "

"Denk you. Also editorials, cottoons—"

" 'Cartoons'—"

"—an' pitchiss. In *news*papers we find ot all dat's happenink at home an' aboard."

" 'A*broad*'! And it's good to hear 'what' and 'we'!"

317

"—An' *abroad.* . . . We read abot politic, abot crimes, abot all kinds *scendels* people are making—" Mr. Kaplan paused to cluck sorrow for the persistent follies of the human race. "Also a paper gives *useful* inflamation: stock mockit prices, where a show is playink in case you want to spand a fortune to go look on it, who died, who got marry—" He shot a congratulatory nod toward Miss Ziev (who, after so on-and-off a betrothal, was about to become Mrs. Andrassy) and encouraging winks to both Miss Mitnick and Nathan P. Nathan (who had not resolved the conflict between surrendering his freedom or his basketball). "Also we get wather raports, abot if it is going to be sun, snow or rain. . . . Well, dis morning I was reading a newspaper. In English!" Mr. Kaplan paused, should his colleagues care to acclaim this feat. "I rad abot de naxt elaction. So what de paper said? Foist, he said dat de—"

"Mr. Kaplan, one moment! It's *'it* said,' for a newspaper, not *'he* said.' "

Mr. Kaplan looked stunned. "Not 'he'?"

"No, of course not 'he.' *'It.'* Have you forgotten our lesson on pronouns? On gender? 'He' is masculine, 'she' is feminine. Not that grammatical gender is *always* determined by—er—sex," Mr. Parkhill hastily added. "We say 'she' for a country, for example, or a ship. But for newspapers one must use the neuter pronoun: 'it.' "

Mr. Kaplan thrashed in the coils of analysis. "Not masculine . . . not faminine . . . in de middle!"

Mr. Parkhill waited.

"Mr. Pockheel, I undistand abot masculine, faminine, an' neutral—"

" 'Neu*ter.*' "

"—but shouldn't we say 'he' abot *som* papers? I mean, when a paper has a masculine *name?*"

Mr. Parkhill frowned. "I don't see what the name of a

paper has to do with it. When quoting *The New York Times,* for instance, we say 'It said.' Or of the *New York Post,* we say 'It said.' Or—"

"Dose papers," Mr. Kaplan conceded benignly. "But when a paper has a real masculine name?"

"And which paper," asked Mr. Parkhill, slightly amused, "would you say has a truly—'masculine' name?"

Mr. Kaplan's features dripped modesty. "Harold Tribune."

•

(P.S. To the young and the British: The *New York Herald Tribune,* a most distinguished daily, expired in 1962.)

319

11

MR. K·A·P·L·A·N
CURES A HEADACHE

There were many evenings in the beginners' grade which Mr. Parkhill remembered with special clarity: the night Mr. Kaplan had delivered his surprising memorial to Jake Popper; the night Mr. Kaplan had reconstructed, in astonishing detail, the death of Julius Caesar. . . . Come to think of it, Mr. Parkhill reflected, most of the evenings he remembered—surely those he remembered most vividly—involved one or another of Mr. Kaplan's mind-boggling alterations of the English language.

He idly wondered, this pleasant night, when both windows of the schoolroom were wide open and a sweet breeze freshened the air, what conceivable feats of innovation, what monstrous flights of false logic, Mr. Kaplan could possibly extract from the simple homework assignment for this evening: a one-page composition, on any topic, which six students had already transcribed on (and five had read aloud from) the blackboard.

Mr. C. J. Fledermann had fashioned a commendable description of "Castles in the Rhine." Mr. Milas Wodjik had written a crisp letter to his twin brother, Tomas, who, standing at the board right next to him, had written a crisp letter to Milas.

Miss Lola Lopez had produced a rather fervent vignette on the noble character and historic achievements of *"El*

320

Libertador," Simón Bolívar, who had fought Spanish tyranny in such lands as Colombia, Venezuela, Peru—in none of which Miss Lopez, who came from Havana, confessed she ever had the good fortune to reside.

Mr. Nathan P. Nathan had speedily transcribed his homework (he had actually written it in the classroom, before the opening bell) with a running obbligato of private laughs. The composition was an account of the breathless last moments of a basketball game against Mr. Nathan's team's arch-rival, Ashkenazi's Aces:

> Score 72–72. The croud yells crazy. Dopey Dave got the ball. He passes to me. Nosey Prishkin is garding me and trys a steall. *He fowls!* Croud is more crazy. I go to line. Boy was I nervus! But I breat deep, take my time, and sink the ball in. Boy! Game is dun. So we win 73–72.
>
> I sure am proud of my teem.

Mr. Nathan had made remarkable progress in the months during which, at intervals, he had attended the A.N.P.S.A. If only he would subject his spelling to a portion of the discipline he expended on his foul shots, Mr. Parkhill sighed. . . .

Now, only the homework of Miss Mitnick awaited class autopsy. She had placed her composition on the board in a hand as dainty and diminutive as her personality. Blushing, stammering, she read the sentences aloud:

My Work—a Waitress

My job is as waitress in a cafeteria. It has the name "Meckler's 4-Star Famous." I am working 9 hours a day, from 7–½ in morning to 4–½ after-noon.

We are serving breakfast, lunch (also luncheons, they are smaller) and supper—or "dinner" like Americans say. But I go home before.

My work is to stand behind counter. Giving Coffee, Tea, Ice Tea, or cold Milk—as customers ask. It is not so hard.

But I get tired from standing all day. And sometime I have bad headackes.

My pay is not too good, but I am happy for having *any* job. People should be happy for having work. Because all over the world is hard times.

Thank you.

Miss Mitnick stopped. The blush had left her cheeks; she was as pale as an oyster.

"Dandy, Rose, just *dan*dy!" laughed Mr. Nathan.

"That *is* good," said Mr. Parkhill. "There are some mistakes, naturally—in punctuation, in the use of prepositions; but on the whole, Miss Mitnick, that is *ex*cellent!"

Giddied by such praises, Rose Mitnick reeled to the sanctuary of her seat.

"Now then, corrections." Mr. Parkhill smiled. "Please study Miss Mitnick's work carefully, class. Jot down any mistakes you see. In a few minutes, I shall call for volunteers."

The scholars slid into the sea of concentration, their brows a wave of furrows, their lips tightened bulkheads of resolution. Reuben Olansky (after walking up to the blackboard to examine the words, his nose almost scraping the slate) scribbled corrections on an envelope. Rochelle Goldberg chewed a Tootsie Roll to fortify her faculties. Mr. Blattberg strengthened his cerebration by fingering the watch chain from which his heirs' incisors gleamed. And Hyman Kaplan, who had been unusually sedate throughout the evening ("I can't corract about besketball because I never even saw one in poisson!"), shot one penetrating glance at Miss Mitnick's essay, uttered a premonitory "Aha!" and proceeded to ply his pen across his trusty journal.

Mr. Parkhill sauntered down the aisle. "I'll give the class a hint," he said lightly. "There's one word—only one in the entire composition, I may say to Miss Mitnick's credit— that is *spelled* wrong."

The class glanced from the board to their paragon, who turned crimson. But Mr. Kaplan did not look up; he was scribbling away in a fever.

"You need not spend too much time—er—*elaborating* on Miss Mitnick's mistakes," said Mr. Parkhill uneasily. "Just make brief notes. That will give you more time to examine punctuation . . . prepositions. . . ." (Prepositions were the Achilles' heel of the beginners' grade.)

Mr. Parkhill strolled back, up the aisle. Mr. Pinsky's squint suggested that he had spotted several flagrant errors. Miss Atrakian was crooning Armenian affirmations over her tablet. Mr. Trabish tossed between yawning and exegesis. And Mr. Kaplan, lost in some holy mission, was breathing heavily.

"Very well, class. Who will be the first volunteer? Corrections?"

To his surprise, Mrs. Moskowitz raised a pudgy palm. "Shouldn't be in Miss Mitnick's assay 'l' on the end of 'cafeteria'?"

"I'm—afraid not," said Mr. Parkhill. (Mrs. Moskowitz had the unfortunate habit of adding an "l" to nearly all nouns ending in a vowel; she once purchased a "neck tiel" for her husband, had changed the covers on her "sofal," and always asked the grocer to give her fresh "tomatols.")

"More comments?"

"Not enough definite articles!" declaimed Isaac Nussbaum. "It should be '*a* waitress,' '*the* morning,' '*the* counter'—and even 'before' *something!* You can't just be 'before'!" Mr. Nussbaum certainly was in top form tonight.

"Very good," said Mr. Parkhill, adding four articles to Miss Mitnick's offering. "We might all pay closer attention to our definite—and indefinite—articles. . . . Mr. Trabish?"

"People should be happy *to* work," announced Mr. Trabish, "not '*for*' work—"

"Correct."

"—although *I* am myself heppy for *and* to."

Approval danced across the ranks: no one had suspected baker Trabish, who sometimes slept through an entire evening, of possessing such keen perception.

"Miss Kipnis?"

"In my poisonal opinion," opined Miss Kipnis, *"lunch* is what men are eating, but *luncheons,* which Miss Mitnick says are smaller, is what ladies eat."

"Well . . ." Mr. Parkhill tactfully suggested that some men, when in a hurry, often ate luncheons, too. "In fact, some restaurants feature a 'Business Man's Luncheon.' "

"That's nice," said "Cookie" Kipnis.

"Who will be next?"

The congregation was silent.

"Come, come. There are several more mistakes . . . Mr. Kaplan?"

"Is *planty* mistakes by Mitnick, but"—Mr. Kaplan paused sententiously—"I am not raddy."

Mr. Parkhill looked puzzled. "Er—why not just give us the mistakes you have already discovered?" He nodded toward Mr. Kaplan's notebook.

"I'm only beginnink." Mr. Kaplan held up his Doomsday book. What had taken so much of Mr. Kaplan's effort was a printed legend:

Mistakes by Mitnick
(on Black-board)
by
H*Y*M*A*N   K*A*P*L*A*N

The rest of the page was blank.

At least, Mr. Parkhill consoled himself, Mr. Kaplan had learned how to spell "blackboard"; heretofore he had deformed it into "blackbored," "bleckbort," and even "blackbroad."

Mrs. Pilpul raised an imperious ruler. "It should not be by Miss Mitnick a *number* 'one-half' after the 'seven,' and also after the 'four.' That way is for *sizes*—like in stockings, or two-and-half pounds meat, or happles."

"That's a very good point," said Mr. Parkhill.

" '*Vun*-half' is for socks, not clocks," declared Mr. Kaplan.

Mr. Pinsky slapped his thigh in appreciation of this *bon mot.*

"Class, how should 'half-past seven' and 'half-past four' be written?"

For a moment it appeared that no one in the beginners' grade knew how half-past seven and half-past four should be rendered. Then Christian Fledermann said, "Wiz *numbers:* a seven-sree-zero and a four-sree-zero!"

"Excellent!" Mr. Parkhill erased "7–½" and "4–½" and, on a playful inspiration, wrote "730" and "430." "Like *this,* Mr. Fledermann?" He raised an eyebrow.

Mr. Kaplan had learned that whenever Mr. Parkhill raised an eyebrow, the answer was "No." "No!" he sang out.

"I was addressing Mr. Fledermann," said Mr. Parkhill coolly.

"*He* didn't enswer," said Mr. Kaplan.

"Perhaps you didn't give him time," said Mr. Parkhill icily. "Mr. Fledermann, are these correct?" Mr. Parkhill's pointer touched "730" and "430."

"N-no," said Mr. Fledermann warily.

"Dat's what *I* obsoived," said Mr. Kaplan.

Mr. Parkhill ignored him. "Like this, Mr. Fledermann?" He wrote "7–30" and "4–30." Again his eyebrows arched, so again Mr. Kaplan cried, "Dat looks like crecked dishes!"

Mr. Nathan shook with gratitude for so vivid a wit.

"Mr. Fledermann," scowled Mr. Parkhill.

"It ztill—don't *look* good," ventured Christian Fledermann.

"Of course not! Like *this?*" Mr. Parkhill made it "7/30"

325

and "4/30," one eyebrow arching gaily.

"Wrong!" blared Mr. Kaplan. "Mish-mosh!"

"This mon is crazy," moaned Olga Tarnova. "He has *balyéza!*"

"Soon *he'll* be the titcher!" glowered Reuben Olansky.

"Well, class," said Mr. Parkhill unhappily, "Mr. Kaplan happens to be right. . . . *All* of these signs are wrong for the representation of time." Impressed by Mr. Kaplan's rapid negations, Mr. Parkhill asked, "Can you tell the class the correct form?"

Mr. Kaplan's smile congealed. "De *corract* form?"

"Yes."

"We did not have dis subject in cless."

Mr. Parkhill blinked. "We *did,* some time ago. But—do you know?"

"What?"

"*Which* mark of punctuation to use when indicating *time.*"

"Not yat," finessed Mr. Kaplan.

Unfriendly snorts and sneers countered Mr. Kaplan's canny subterfuge.

"Some chip trick!" bawled Mr. Blattberg.

"Hoo-hoo!" hooted Mr. Hruska.

"Mr. Kaplen *edmits* he don't know something?" gaped Mrs. Shimmelfarb.

"He didn't edmit!" cried loyal Pinsky. "He avoided!"

"Oy!" smiled Mrs. Moskowitz, no easy feat.

"I'll bust!" laughed Nathan P. Nathan.

"*Class . . .* order. . . ." Mr. Parkhill felt let down by Mr. Kaplan. Not because Mr. Kaplan had canceled the achievement of knowing what was wrong by not knowing what was right: that was a common failing. What disappointed Mr. Parkhill was that Mr. Kaplan had been so cocksure in his rejections of the hyphen and the slash that he had lured Mr. Parkhill into assuming that he did know the correct answer. . . . Mr. Parkhill inserted colons after "7" and "4." He touched the "7:30" and the "4:30" with his pointer. "How about *this* way, class?"

"Poifick!" cracked Mr. Kaplan, for Mr. Parkhill's eyebrows had remained inert.

"Mr. Kaplan is right." Mr. Parkhill was both impressed and mystified. "This mark, class, is used to indicate time, and in many other ways—to introduce a list, say, or a quotation, or after the salutation, 'Dear Sir' or 'Dear Madam' in a letter." On a portion of the blackboard he made clean with the eraser, Mr. Parkhill chalked two large dots, one below the other, in a magnified colon. "What do we call this mark, class?"

Hemmings and hawings betrayed their ignorance.

"Anyone?"

No one.

"It's a very *useful* mark of punctuation, class. . . ."

"I wish I knew it!" grinned Mr. Nathan. "Rose, tell the teacher. *Guess,* even."

Miss Mitnick said timidly, "Semicolon?"

"Not *quite.* But you are close, Miss Mitnick! *Very* close. This is not a 'semicolon' but a—"

Up shot one pen of Hyman Kaplan.

"Mr. Kaplan."

"Two periods!"

A pang pierced Mr. Parkhill's spine. *"No,* Mr. Kaplan! That was a most *un*fortunate guess. This is called a *colon. "* He quickly returned to Miss Mitnick's essay, concealing his dismay, changing a tense here, a dependent clause there, making every correction, indeed, except one: Miss Mitnick's glaring "headackes." He faced his students. "I have left just one mistake in Miss Mitnick's work—the mistake in spelling I mentioned earlier. Who can find it?"

Once more, his flock mobilized their energies. Miss Mitnick stared intently at her sentences, yearning to expunge her disgrace by being first to remedy her blunder. The widow Pilpul scrutinized the board without mercy. Mr. Olansky donned a fiercer expression, as if to intimidate the distant prose. Nathan P. Nathan, knowing the boundaries of his knowledge, simply laughed. And Mr. Kaplan, invigorating his critical powers through incantation, murmured each word aloud: "My—job—is—as—waitress. . . . Aha! In 'waitress' should be no 'i'!"

"No, Mr. Kaplan. 'Waitress' comes from 'wait,' and 'wait' contains an 'i.' "

Mr. Kaplan looked wounded.

Mr. Umea rejoiced.

Miss Mitnick stammered, "I think m-my 'headaches' is spelled wrong."

"Ufcawss!" cried Mr. Kaplan. " 'Hadakes' is spalled wrong!"

"That is what Miss Mitnick said." Mr. Parkhill could not resist the deserved rebuke, nor an ironic invitation: "Perhaps you will favor us by spelling it right."

" 'Had-akes' is two woids in vun. . . ."

"Yes, Mr. Kaplan. So we spell it just as if we were spelling the two separate 'words'—not 'woids.' If you simply combine 'head' and 'aches'. . . ." Mr. Parkhill lifted the chalk to the board. "Would you spell—?"

Mr. Kaplan misconstrued the invitation and leaped to the blackboard, where, as friend and foe alike held their breath, he printed:

H-E-A-D-A-X-E

For a horrified moment, Mr. Parkhill was struck silent, as silent as his scholars, who were uncertain whether Mr. Kaplan had committed a new crime or made a contribution to orthography. At last, Mr. Parkhill shook his head, erased the gruesome HEADAXE and wrote HEADACHES in its place. Once more had Hyman Kaplan massacred an expectation he had so clearly, so recklessly, aroused.

12

DAYMARE AT WATERLOO

American Rev. Goodby England. U.S. solders died.
Civil war. Salves no more barefoot.
Solders died in North. Solders died in South.
World War. Making world save for Democracy. Solders died. Sailors died.
World War again. Solders, sailors, plain pilots died.
These are for why now we put on their graves flowers, same as anyone, May 30. This is my virgin of Memo. Day.

—Mary Atrakian

Mr. Parkhill leaned back in his easy chair. Two nights ago, he had given his students a little lecture on Memorial Day, how Arlington Cemetery is its focus and the Unknown Soldier its shrine. He had been careful to point out that every land honors those fallen in battle. He had shown the class pictures of the Cenotaph in London, the Arc de Triomphe, Red Square (at which point Olga Tarnova, a progeny of White Russia, had hissed with fervor).

Now, correcting the homework in the easy chair in his lodgings, Mr. Parkhill realized that his words and pictures had made a deeper impression than he had anticipated. He started to correct Miss Atrakian's eulogy, feeling relieved that she had written, rather than spoken, her heartfelt words. There would have been no problem in his explaining the word "version" to the class; but "virgin"—!

329

"Virgin," Mr. Parkhill could not help thinking, bristled with all sorts of dangers, given the volatile types in the beginners' grade.

He turned to the next paper. It was by Fanny Gidwitz. On the first page was printed only this title:

SOLDEIRS AND SAILORS—HURRY!

Mr. Parkhill read this three times before meaning came. His red pencil raced across the page:

Miss G—
You mean "Hurrah!"—or "Hooray!" There is all the difference in the world between "Hurray" (or "Hooray") and "hurry."

—Mr. P.

He was frankly disappointed in Miss Gidwitz.

He turned to the next paper. To his surprise (now that he thought of it, the compositions had been chock-full of surprises), a poem met his eyes:

I
Today remember
Last December
Was no place
For Decoration Days

II
Soldeirs, sailors,
Airplaners, Marines
Shouldn't stand only
By hot-dog machines
—Nathan P. Nathan

Who would have dreamed that beneath the frivolous façade of Mr. Nathan flowed such lyrical emotions?

He corrected the spelling of "soldiers," wrote " 'Pilots,' not 'airplaners,' " and added "Good effort, Mr. N!" (He did not think it wise to comment on the incongruity of "hot-dog machines.")

The next opus, a letter from Mr. Christian J. Fleder-mann to someone addressed as "Deer Heinrich," contained this thought:

> In old times, armies moved very slow, but today everything goes quack-quack.

At that moment, Mr. Parkhill decided it was time to drill the class vigorously once more on antonyms. One of the most useful byproducts of homework was that it gave Mr. Parkhill time away from the pressures of the classroom (the clash of egos, the partisan storms) to think up lessons specifically designed to remedy specific, persistent errors. "Antonyms!" he thought, as he doffed his slippers. "They are *pretty* shaky on their antonyms."

He opened the very next session of the class by announcing, "Tonight, class, we shall concentrate on our Opposites." (He would not dream of inflicting "antonyms" on his fledglings.) "Notebooks, please. Write five nouns in one column, and write their opposites—opposite." The play on words pleased him. (He could never understand why Miss Higby, according to all reports, conducted her class with such humorless rigor.) "We shall then place our lists on the blackboard for group comment."

It was heartening to see how the students welcomed the assignment. Opposites seemed to enlist their enthusiasm —unlike indirect objects, which they resented, or irregular verbs, which they loathed. Opposites were honest, open, above-board. Confidence bloomed in the forum.

Mr. C. J. Fledermann unbuttoned his vest and sharpened his pencil cheerfully. Miss Ziev set pen to paper with zest. (The banns for Miss Ziev's marriage to Mr. Andrassy had officially been posted.) Mr. Trabish even reversed a yawn in midstream, transforming torpidity to approval by a mere rerouting of breath. And Mr. Kaplan, that visionary gleam in his eye, cried, "Opposites! My!"

It promised to be a fruitful evening. Mr. Parkhill strolled down the aisle, nodding and smiling; his apprentices smiled and clucked in return. When he reached the back of the room, he raised a window. He noticed that some light bulbs in the electric sign at the end of the street, "Tip Top Used Cars," faintly flickered: the sign sometimes read "Tip Top Used Curs." (Mr. Studniczka might have written that. Poor Peter Ignatius Studniczka. He had been plunged into such despair by the past perfect tense that he had surrendered to defeat, and had never returned to the school. . . .)

Mr. Parkhill ambled back, up the aisle, glancing with interest at notebooks in which opposites were sprouting like mushrooms.

After several minutes, Mr. Parkhill announced, "One minute more . . ." and in two minutes called, "Time. . . . Are we ready? . . . Good! Will the following please go to the board? Miss Mitnick . . . Mr. Nussbaum . . . Mrs. Shimmel-farb . . ." He called six names in all.

It was a buoyant platoon that advanced upon the black-board, and a triumphant one that returned. Their chalked columns were a tribute to Mr. Parkhill's tutelage. Not a single mistake marred the quintet of antonyms Miss Mitnick had provided:

Silence	Noise
Gloomy	Happy
Weak	Strong
Fancy	Plain
Smart	Stupid

Only one tiny lapse in spelling blemished Mr. Nussbaum's counterparts: "Fresh . . . stole." Miss Kipnis had produced four excellent antonyms, tripping only on the opposite of "wet," which she rendered as "fry," and Mrs. Yanoff harbored the understandable illusion that the opposite of "freedom" is "jail." But all things considered, antonyms had gotten off to a flying start.

Soon Mr. Parkhill sent six more scholars to the board. None turned in as faultless a performance as Miss Mitnick's, but none committed a gaffe as queer as Mr. Nussbaum's either. . . .

Another sextet was dispatched to the board. Mr. Parkhill felt quite cheerful, even optimistic. Nothing so warms the cockles of a teacher's heart as progress—visible, unmistakable progress—in his flock.

He smiled at the board. From her tiptoed stance, Lola Lopez had neatly written, in tiny letters that seemed fitting for so petite a form:

baby	boy
child	man
man	woman
save	spend
hello	solong

Reuben Olansky was printing, in the mammoth hand of the myopic:

sick	normal
over	under
front	back
death	life
strong	wick

At once Mr. Parkhill saw how he would approach the correcting of "wick."

He turned to Mr. Hruska's offering. Learning came hard to Mr. Hruska. Scowling, perspiring, muttering discontents, Vasil Hruska had but partly scaled the battlements of English:

black	white
white	black

333

1	2
2	1
eat	not eat

Mr. Parkhill sighed. It was a long, hard row Vasil Hruska had to hoe—but hoe it, Mr. Parkhill had no doubt, he would.

The next pupil at the board was Mr. Kaplan. Mr. Parkhill braced himself. And after but one glance at what Hyman Kaplan had this time conjured out of the carnival of his mind, Mr. Parkhill turned his back to the board. *Frangas, non flectes:* the man might break, but he would never bend.

What *could* one do about Mr. Kaplan? It was discouraging to confront such impediments—novel, even ingenious, but still impediments—to instruction.

Mr. Kaplan was standing before the board in bliss, hand on hip, eyes enraptured, a Robert La Salle on the bank of the Ohio; and Mr. Parkhill, even from the back of the chamber, could hear La Salle humming—humming just loud enough for everyone in the room to share his ecstasy.

What induced such beatitude in Mr. Kaplan's soul was (1) performing at the blackboard, which he loved; (2) envisaging the broil and brabble of discussion, which he adored; (3) contemplating the wonders of the human brain, of which his was so scintillating a model:

H*Y*M*A*N K*A*P*L*A*N

gives

5 Opp.

The name, as always, gleamed like a banner: the bright stars relieving the loneliness between one letter and another. It grieved Mr. Kaplan that Mr. Parkhill had made him desist from using colors on the slate to outline the letters and illuminate the stars; and, in truth, the deprivation made the name anemic. Under his triumphant title, the Ariel of the beginners' grade had written:

Can Man live without Opp? No! Why? Without opp. is impossible to discuss anything.

Soppose someone hollers, "Wrong!" How can you say "Right"? Only with an opp.!

So Mr. Parkhill gives a fine lesson—5 opp.

So Hyman Kaplan is happy to presant:

Word	Opp.
1. Spic	span
2. Tall	shrimp
3. N. Dakota	S. Dakota

Mr. Kaplan was searching the ledges for a fresh stick of chalk.

Mr. Parkhill wiped his brow. It was not going to be an easy evening, after all.

"Take your seats, please." Mr. Parkhill glanced at the clock. "Miss Lopez . . ."

Miss Lopez read her words as if they were caged birds, and her opposites as if releasing them from captivity.

"Any corrections?" asked Mr. Parkhill.

"Not vun!" cried Mr. Kaplan promptly. "Congradulation, Lipschitz!" (Why Mr. Kaplan converted "Lopez" to "Lipschitz" only God could explain.)

"The opposite of 'hello' is really 'good-bye,' " Mr. Parkhill told Miss Lopez. "Mr. Olansky."

Reuben Olansky put his notebook to within an inch of his nose to read his words (he could never make out the glyphs on a distant blackboard): "Sick . . . normal. Front . . . back. Strong . . . wick."

"Mistake!" called Miss Mitnick.

"Yes?" (Mr. Parkhill could always rely on Rose Mitnick.)

"The opposite of 'strong' is spelled wrong."

"How *should* it be spelled?"

"W-e-a-k," said Miss Mitnick.

"Exactly!" Mr. Parkhill smiled; Mr. Kaplan's face fell.

" 'Weak,' Mr. Olansky, is not *'wick.'* " He wrote WEAK and WICK on the crowded slate. "You see, class, why we

335

must be so careful in pronunciation? The short 'i' is *not* the long 'e' and—uh—vice versa. That is what is at the root of Mr. Olansky's difficulty. . . . Now, who can tell us what 'w*i*ck' means?"

Before anyone could so much as make a stab at what "w-i-c-k" meant, Mr. Kaplan sang out, "Point of order!"

Mr. Parkhill frowned. He was not accustomed to hearing protocol invoked in the beginners' grade. "Y-yes?"

"Didn't you jost say de void '*vick*' is wrong?" inquired Mr. Kaplan.

"I said that 'w*i*ck' is not 'w*ea*k.' "

"So 'wick' isn't wrong!" Mr. Olansky jeered righteously. "Just different."

"Well," Mr. Parkhill said unhappily, " 'wick' is wrong as the *opposite* of—"

"Wrong *an'* different?!" cried Mr. Kaplan. "So Olansky made two mistakes instead of vun!"

"Mr. Kap—"

"But 'wick' is a real word!" protested Reuben Olansky.

"So is 'pastrami'!" observed Mr. Kaplan. "But it's not de opposite of 'ice cream'!"

Mr. Olansky fell into piteous yammerings. Mr. Nathan howled.

"Mr. Kaplan!" Mr. Parkhill tapped his chalk on the desk sternly. "We can dispense with—sarcasm. Let us return to the question I asked. Who can tell us the meaning of 'wick'?"

Earnest brows furrowed as earnest eyes focused on "wick": sixty lips tightened as thirty minds probed for "wick" 's innermost secret.

"It's quite a—*common* word," said Mr. Parkhill hopefully.

Up sailed the palm of Hyman Kaplan.

Mr. Parkhill pretended not to see it. *"Anyone?"* he asked.

No one responded to "Anyone?" save Mr. Kaplan, who began to swing his arm like a reversed pendulum.

Mr. Parkhill wrestled with his conscience, and finally sighed, "Very well. . . ."

"Savan days make vun wick!" declaimed Mr. Kaplan.

"No, no, no!" Mr. Parkhill winced. "That is a 'week'!" He was quite cross with Mr. Kaplan, and so reproachful in applying the chalk that it broke. With a fresh stick he wrote:

WEEK
WEAK
WICK

"My!" exclaimed Mr. Kaplan. "I fond a toid woid!"

" 'Week,' " said Mr. Parkhill, "means seven days. But 'weak' "—he tapped the second word with his pointer— "means not strong. And 'wick' "—he tapped the third word sharply—"is the cord or thread inside a candle, the part that burns!"

A chorale ascended from the enlightened.

"Oooh!"

"I see!"

"Haddaya like that?!"

It was ever thus: the revelation of a new word was like the establishment of another beachhead on the spiky shores of English.

"Like in a cigarette lighter, I have a wick!" exclaimed Olaf Umea.

"Wick, weak, *week*," practiced Isaac Nussbaum.

"W*ea*k . . . week . . . w*i*ck," intoned Olga Tarnova, a weary whippoorwill.

Mr. Parkhill next called upon Vasil Hruska.

Mr. Hruska clutched his necktie. " 'Black . . . white. White . . . black. One . . . two. Two . . . one. Eat . . . not eat.' . . . I hope." His shoulders sagged.

Before Mr. Parkhill could offer a therapeutic word, Mr. Olansky, smarting under his wounds, lashed out, "What kind of opposite is 'not eat'?"

"Emoigency kind!" retorted Mr. Kaplan, who would defend anyone Mr. Olansky attacked. "You axpact a hongry man to use poifick gremmer?"

"Who said anything about diet?" yowled Mr. Olansky.

Mr. Kaplan averted his eyes piously.

"But 'not eat,' " stammered Miss Mitnick, "isn't an opposite."

"Why not?"

"Because—"

"Ha! 'Because' isn't a rizzon; it's a conjonction!" Before this unexpected feat of grammar from Mr. Kaplan, Miss Mitnick flinched.

"*Mr.* Kaplan!" Mr. Parkhill made no attempt to conceal his displeasure. "Mr. Olansky and Miss Mitnick are quite right. 'Not eat' is *not* an opposite. It is, I'm sorry to say, not a good phrase in any sense." He erased "not eat" with one firm swipe of the eraser. "Mr. Olansky, what is the opposite of 'eat'?"

Mr. Olansky blinked blankly. "Eh . . . ah . . . kh . . ."

"Ai-ai-ai," crooned Mr. Kaplan. "Hruska at least didn't sond like he's gargling!"

Furious, Mr. Olansky searched for Mr. Kaplan through the wrong half of his bifocals. "Maybe *you* know the opposite of 'eat'?"

"I," said Mr. Kaplan with dignity, "vasn't called on by Mr. Pockheel!"

"Stop!" roared Mr. Olansky. "You wiggle-piggle out of every—"

"The opposite of 'eat,' " announced Mr. Parkhill loudly, "may be one of several words. . . ." He wrote FAST and STARVE on the board. (He wished he could reprimand Hyman Kap—but one can hardly tell a full-grown man to

338

stand in the corner.) "And Mr. Hruska, since 'black' is the opposite of 'white,' then 'white' is obviously the opposite of 'black.' And 'one' and 'two' are *numbers,* not opposites. Can you think of any other words?"

Mr. Hruska pondered dolefully. His face reddened, but his cerebration froze.

"Just look around the *room,*" suggested Mr. Parkhill. "You will see many—opposites." He lifted his eyes to the ceiling, then lowered his head to the floor. He touched his head, then lifted his foot. He touched his chest, then turned his back. (Would Plaut and Biberman—Professor Samish had drowned, most unexpectedly, a year ago, and Dr. Luther Biberman had co-authored the new, sparkling edition of *Teaching English to Foreigners*—approve?)

Mr. Hruska had been following every move of Mr. Parkhill's pantomime in fascination.

"Now, can you think of a pair of opposites?" asked Mr. Parkhill.

"Yos! 'Butter . . . bread'!"

How on earth Mr. Hruska associated ceiling-floor, head-foot, chest-back, with butter and bread, Mr. Parkhill could not imagine.

"Mr. Hruska, 'butter' and 'bread' certainly *go* together, but I think it is stretching the point a bit to—er—call them opposites. . . ."

Mr. Parkhill glanced at the clock. He hoped that no time remained, for Mr. Kaplan's opposites were next. But the hands of the clock overlapped at 10 minutes to 10, and Mr. Kaplan was already rising and smiling. "Mr. Kaplan," Mr. Parkhill quickly said, "before I call upon you, *may* I remind you that the assignment calls only for five words and five opposites? We—er—do not want a speech, nor a lengthy introduction!"

How often had Mr. Parkhill tried to restrain Mr. Kaplan, who approached the most routine assignment as if it

339

might lead to the Legion of Honor? Mr. Parkhill had never been able to check that exuberant imagination. It was like asking a gladiator to strike only one blow, or Magellan to cross only one sea.

Already a few students, scouting Mr. Kaplan's work in anticipation with that hawklike zeal they reserved for the weasel in their midst, were chortling. A cocksure sneer sped from Mr. Olansky to Mr. Barbella (it was intended for Mr. Blattberg beside him); a knowing gloat winged from Mrs. Yanoff to Mrs. Pilpul. Miss Tarnova plied an inscrutable smile along her inscrutable lips and honed her handkerchiefed dagger for the carnage to come.

For once, Mr. Kaplan did not respond to criticism as if it were decapitation. He was too busy alerting his small band of acolytes. "Trabish! Wake op!"

"Just read your words from your chair!" Mr. Parkhill ordered.

Mr. Kaplan flinched. "Not go to the bort?"

"You can see the words quite clearly from your chair! And that's all you need read: the *words!*"

Mr. Kaplan lamented man's inhumanity to man, summoned support from the arsenals of faith, and read bravely: " 'Fife opposites by Hyman Keplen'!" (The title, apparently, could be smuggled into the category of "words.") " 'Spic . . . span,' " recited the hobbled bard. " 'Tall . . . shrimp.' 'Naut Dakota . . . Sot Dakota.' 'Talk . . . sharop.' 'Nightmare . . . daymare.' "

Mr. Parkhill wheeled toward the board in astonishment. There it was, all right, in Mr. Kaplan's unmistakable script: "Nightmare ***** daymare."

"Hanh?!" cried Mr. Blattberg.

A malediction came from Miss Tarnova.

"Pssh!" Mr. Pinsky slapped his cheek in admiration.

Miss Mitnick's mouth was a circle of horror. Mr. Nathan was doubled over.

Mr. Parkhill debated how to proceed. "Nightmare . . . daymare."

Fists, fingers, pencils, rulers were waving wildly, supplemented by pleas and petitions: "Mr. Parkhill!" "Titcher!" "Mistake! Mistake!"

"Class . . ." he said in a bit of a daze. "You may lower your hands and—er—other objects. Everyone will have a turn. . . . We shall take up Mr. Kaplan's mistakes one at a time."

Mr. Kaplan's jaw dropped. Not "Mr. Kaplan's mistake" but "Mr. Kaplan's *mistakes.*" And "Everyone will have a turn. . . ." And "one at a time. . . ." Mr. Kaplan started a deep-breathing exercise.

"Mr.—Fledermann," called Mr. Parkhill.

C. J. Fledermann declared pettishly that since "spic" was not the opposite of "span," "span" could not masquerade as the opposite of "spic." " 'Spic *and* span' can't be broken op!"

This *caveat* inspired Lucca Barbella to cry: "There isa no 'spica' by himself and no 'spana' also!"

"It's one *phrase,*" announced Miss Atrakian. "Like twins from Siam!"

This pleased the brothers Wodjik.

"*Cats* also come fromm Siam," purred Mr. Kaplan.

The *non sequitur* went unheeded.

So felicitous was the phrasing of Miss Atrakian, so vivid her imagery, that the entire Olansky-Blattberg-Nussbaum phalanx burst into applause. Miss Mitnick mustered up enough courage to titter.

The exultation scarcely thinned before Stanislaus Wilkomirski thundered that "shrimp" could not, by the most generous canons of usage, be accepted as the opposite of "tall." A shrimp, Mr. Wilkomirski shouted, was a fish, and no fish could be an opposite—"even a shark like Mr. Kaplan!"

Horselaughs certified the brilliance of the simile, and

341

guffaws vented the sweetness of revenge from those who had long suffered at Mr. Kaplan's hands.

Now Olga Tarnova—feline and mysterious—crooned, "Is not true thot to aducated people, North Dakota and South Dakota—both spelled wrong!—are *names?* So how can be one an opposite other? Can Pinsk be opposite of Minsk?" (Never had the milliner displayed such irony.) "Can Christmas be the opposite of New Year's? *Nyet!*"

"New York is opposite Brooklyn," flared Mr. Kaplan.

"Mr. Kaplan!" Mr. Parkhill was running out of patience. "Geography is not diction!"

"Good for Mr. Parkholl!" laughed Isaac Nussbaum.

"Kaplen, take asprin!" leered Olaf Umea.

Nathan P. Nathan covered his eyes and tossed about in his chair.

Miss Mitnick dropped her penguin air and entered the lists. "Nightmare . . . *day*mare?" Her cheeks were flushed. "I can't believe! Who ever heard such a word—such an *idea*—as a 'daymare'?"

The ranks rocked with new jubilation. Mr. Blattberg twirled his watch chain gleefully. Mr. Olansky bared his teeth in redemption. Miss Goldberg celebrated with halvah.

Mr. Parkhill was so busy replacing Mr. Kaplan's mistakes with antonyms fit for their duties that he did not notice what effect the merciless barrage was having upon its target. "Miss Mitnick is absolutely right, Mr. Kaplan! There is, strictly speaking, *no* opposite for 'nightmare.' I mean, when one does not have a nightmare, one simply has pleasant, untroubled sleep." He drew three implacable lines through "daymare," and asked, "Are you clear about all these corrections, Mr. Kaplan?"

Mr. Kaplan did not respond. He was gaping at his handiwork as if both he and it had been clubbed. So many corrections on what had seemed so spic-and-span a text. . . . So much ridicule, from such plebeian souls. . . . Mr.

Kaplan was horrified. He was mortified. He was crushed. There could be no doubt about it: Mr. Kaplan was at Waterloo. Defeat—massive and incontestable—had quashed Hyman Kaplan at last.

"Mr. Kaplan," Mr. Parkhill repeated, "is everything *clear?*"

Mr. Kaplan was as bereft of speech as he seemed to be of hearing.

Mr. Parkhill felt a twinge of remorse. Perhaps he should have spoken less sharply. Perhaps he should have stopped Mr. Kaplan's foes from slashing him to ribbons. He felt a pang of guilt, too: he *could* have intervened, and saved Mr. Kaplan's face. At the moment, that face looked ready for an embalmer.

The bell, for once merciful, chimed along the corridor.

At once, Mr. Parkhill called, "That will be all for tonight."

He had never seen the class so happy. They were chuckling and chortling—riding the rare rollers of revenge. Some students mouthed choice morsels from Mr. Kaplan's absurd antonyms; others bade him farewell—condescending or amused. Only Mr. Pinsky, fealty undimmed, glared defiance at those who had undone his prince.

"Koplon"—Miss Tarnova leaned over the prey like a presence out of Gogol—"you made enough mistakes tonight for whole year!"

"You learned a lesson?" mocked Mr. Blattberg.

"Next time don't confuse opposites and shmopposites!" Mr. Olansky resembled a malicious owl. "Agreed?"

Only then did some last, faint ember flicker in Hyman Kaplan's heart. "Agreet?" he echoed, all disdain, a man who might lose a battle but never a war. "No, Reuben Olansky. Naver, mine dear Tarnova. I'll give you all a prazant, a new opposite to remamber: de opposite of 'agree.' . . . 'Nuts!' "

Mr. Parkhill felt as if he was having a daymare.

13

MR. K·A·P·L·A·N, EUMOIROUS
TO THE END

It had all begun so innocently, thought Mr. Parkhill. Only
when the fume and foam of conflict had settled, many
hours later and away from the seething scene of battle,
could he organize his recollections.

Yet, how could he have known? Perhaps the time had
something to do with it. The school year would soon be
over; and when any semester approached its end, tempers
grew tauter and patience wore thin. But where had things
gone awry? With whose rash word? Whose brash quip?
Which—

Perhaps it had started with the homework of Mr. Isaac
Nussbaum, Orthodox cantor but unorthodox student,
who had transcribed his composition on the blackboard:
"Why Horses Die All Over." The opening was as electri-
fying as the title:

> Horses who have four legs are slower than autmobiles,
> and whose use makes horses die all over.

"Mr. Nussbaum," Mr. Parkhill had begun, "when you
say 'horses who have four legs' (incidentally, we use 'who'
for human beings, and 'which' or 'that' for animals) you
imply that some horses do not have four legs."

Mr. Nathan burst into laughter. "Only fareaks!"

"Do you see my point, Mr. Nussbaum?"

344

"Yes, yes," the bearded one nodded. "How should it be changed?"

"Very simply," smiled Mr. Parkhill, "just—"

"Take the lags off the horses!" called Mr. Kaplan.

"Y-yes." Mr. Parkhill was pleased that Mr. Kaplan had improved so rapidly in recent months; that he was actually saying "the" instead of "de," and had even learned to use "off" instead of "from," which he had always pronounced "fromm." "I think the best thing to do is simply"—he drew a chalk line through "who have four legs"—"eliminate these four words! Now read the sentence."

" 'Horses are slower than—' Of course!" Mr. Nussbaum shook his head so happily that his skullcap slipped askew. "I don't *need* the 'who have four legs' at all!"

"Exactly." Mr. Parkhill then ran his pointer along the sentence, deliberately ignoring the misspelling of "automobiles," and stopped at the first word in the dependent clause: "and." That "and" was a perfect example of the superfluous conjunction, the grammatical fault Plaut and Biberman so aptly called "thwarted subordination."

Mr. Parkhill tapped the errant "and" three times. "You do not need this 'and' at all, either, Mr. Nussbaum. If we simply remove it"—Mr. Parkhill suited action to thought with one stroke of the eraser—"the proper relationship between the two ideas is preserved." He paused. "Automobiles do not 'make'—that is, *cause*—horses to die, Mr. Nussbaum.... Did you not mean to say that the automobile has *replaced* the horse?"

Mr. Nussbaum had no qualms about conceding that automobiles had replaced, rather than murdered, horses.

"Now, class, does anyone see a misspelled word in that sentence?"

" 'Automobile'!" That was reliable Miss Mitnick. "There should be an 'o' between 't' and 'm.' "

345

"Very good!" Mr. Parkhill inserted an "o" between the "t" and the "m."

And that, as he looked back upon it, was the fatal moment! Yes, that innocuous "o" was where the deplorable succession of events had begun. For "automobile" offered Mr. Parkhill a perfect opportunity to tell the class a bit about etymology—an exciting domain to students who knew languages other than English. Etymology could offer new and priceless clues to adults from abroad.

"Can anyone tell me *why* there should be an 'o' after the 't' in 'automobile'?" Mr. Parkhill smiled broadly.

Up went two fingers belonging to Hyman Kaplan.

"Yes?"

"There should be an 'o' efter 't' and before 'm' in 'automobile' because that's the way it's spelled!"

Mr. Parkhill did not try to disguise his disappointment. Circular reasoning had always been Mr. Kaplan's *forte,* and downfall. (But how Mr. Kaplan's pronunciation had improved! He had said "because" rather than "becawss," "spelled" instead of "spalled"; why, he was even saying "and" and "way" instead of "an'" and "vay" these days!)

" 'Because that's the way it's spelled'?" Mr. Parkhill echoed. *That* does not help a bit! That is simply— uh . . ."

"Because we need a vowel to squeeze in de sond 'o'?"

"N-no." With a stroke of the chalk, Mr. Parkhill separated "auto" from "mobile." He stepped back. "Notice, class: 'Automobile' consists of two parts—'auto' and 'mobile.' Now, the first part happens to come from Greek, the second from Latin. And each of these has a specific meaning. 'Mobile' means moving. 'Auto' is Greek for—"

"Yos! Yos!" Miss Atrakian was overjoyed. " 'Auto' means —myself!"

"Exactly," said Mr. Parkhill. "So 'automobile' means 'self-moving,' moving under its own power, the 'auto' from Greek—"

346

"Now we stodying *Grik?*" cried Mrs. Moskowitz in horror. To Mrs. Moskowitz, the one thing English did not need was foreign aid—and enlargement—from yet another tongue.

"Did Greeks invent automobills?" blurted Vasil Hruska. "I thought it was Henry the Fourth."

"Henry 'For*d*'!"

"No!" Miss Atrakian snorted. " 'Automobile' is the word —Greek! 'Airplane' is Greek! 'Telephone' is Greek! All, all, all are Greek!"

Nationalism, which never lay more than a sliver beneath the simmering surface of the beginners' grade, bubbled through the room.

"Atrakian, don't be a hug! Leave a few screps for other nations!" charged Mr. Pinsky.

"Telephones came from Alexander Grayhound Bell," averred "Cookie" Kipnis.

"Airplanes are from U.S.," chirped Miss Lopez.

"Class . . . Miss Atrakian did not mean that the Greeks actually *invented* all these wonderful devices. She meant that the words which we use to *name* them are Greek—uh —in origin."

"Aahh . . ." drifted through the room.

"Oohhh," many murmured.

"Aha!" cried Hyman Kaplan, who scorned half measures.

Respectful glances showered upon Mary Atrakian, tendering her, as surrogate, the admiration her forebears richly deserved. (The fact that Miss Atrakian was Armenian, and bore as little love for Greeks as she did for Turks, was not known to her peers.)

Suddenly, the baritone of Lucca Barbella blasted the air. "Who giva da world Art?" he demanded. "Music? Paved roads? Roman arch? Galileo? Marconi? . . ." Mr. Barbella might have gone on cataloguing the genius of Rome had

347

not even this brief sampling stung Olga Tarnova to the quick.

"Rossia! Rossia!" Miss Tarnova protested. "Tolstoy. Lermontov. Chakhov."

"Michelangelo! Leonardo! Rossini!" retorted Mr. Barbella.

"Ladies, gentlemen . . ." Mr. Parkhill was tapping his pointer on the desk. "We *must* dispense with such heated dialogue!"

"Also Greek!" cried C. J. Fledermann.

"Mr. *Parkhill* is Greek?" Mr. Wilkomirski, who was a riveter, could not trust his ears.

"'Dialogue' is Greek," snorted Mr. Fledermann, "not teacher."

"How come you know so much Greek and so little English?" laughed Nathan P. Nathan.

"He is a man of high culture!" snapped Mr. Olansky.

"Ha!" That was Kaplan. "Atrakian was *born* in Greece—"

"I was born in Bulgaria," protested Miss Atrakian.

"—so for dat she desoives a monument? T'ink, Olansky. Everybody got to loin *some* language. Greek is just her modder's tong."

"Her father spoke Grik, too!" retorted Mr. Umea.

Miss Atrakian had been trying (to no avail) to inform the class that her knowledge of Greek came from neither parent, but from her fiancé, whom she had met in Roseland, the mecca of ballroom dancing on Broadway.

"*Averyvun* in this room can talk a foreign tong!" Mr. Kaplan turned to Mr. Pinsky. "Pinsky, spik a few woids Rumanian."

"Mr. Kap—"

Mr. Pinsky uttered a few words in Rumanian.

"Wodjik!" Mr. Kaplan summoned a second underling. "Give a semple Polish."

Both Wodjiks, who were not Polish, promptly babbled

348

syllables from some indecipherable, but no doubt worthy, tongue.

"Nussbaum, say 'Hello and goodbye' in Hibrew!"

"No, no!" Mr. Parkhill drummed his pencil on the desk resolutely. "That will do, Mr. Kaplan." (He estimated that at least five other languages awaited Mr. Kaplan's summons.) "Let us return to the word 'automobile.' I was merely trying to point out that English is a living language. It is not fixed, unchanging. It grows all the time, adding new words, new shadings—"

"Oooo!" Poor Mrs. Moskowitz. To her, words were as immutable as mountains. To suggest that new words were being spawned right and left around her—that was opening the gates to bedlam.

"Let us take another word," said Mr. Parkhill quickly. He turned to the board and printed:

AUTOGRAPH

"Now, class, we saw that 'auto' refers to self. Does anyone know what 'graph' means?"

"Atrakian," Mr. Kaplan sighed, "you de only Grik in de cless."

"I—am—Armenian!"

"Close inoff."

Mr. Fledermann blurted, "I studied in Choiminy some Greek! So, 'Graph! . . . 'Grapho'! That means 'write'!"

"Very good, sir!" said Mr. Parkhill. "Therefore, 'autograph' means one's own handwriting, or signature. Now do you see, class?"

They not only saw; they were staggered.

"Wohnderful . . ." crooned Miss Tarnova.

"Haddaya like that?"

"Please, give more examples!"

"There are many, many more examples," said Mr. Parkhill gaily. He meditated for a moment. "Here is a word

349

which may strike you as—er—hard. I know it *looks* difficult—very difficult; yet I'm sure all of you have seen it
dozens of times!" He printed:

HOMOGENIZED

Mr. Hruska fell off his chair.

"That's a *word?*" wailed "Cookie" Kipnis.

"What's a word?" asked Mr. Olansky, blinking with a
ferocity that added nothing to his vision.

"Ooy," gasped Mrs. Moskowitz.

All around that intent forum, murmurs of uncertainty
accompanied expressions of pain as the gruesome
HOMOGENIZED defied their fathoming.

"Here is a hint to the ladies," said Mr. Parkhill. "Whenever you go into a food market, I am sure you see—" He
rested his pointer on HOMOGENIZED.

"That?" sniffed Mrs. Yanoff. "Never."

"Who shops in a zoo?" asked the widow Pilpul.

"How can we buy something we can't pronounce?"
asked Miss Goldberg.

Mr. Parkhill was not at all disheartened. "Now, now,
ladies. *Think.* I can assure you that you have all seen this
very word! Many times. . . . Does anyone have a clue?"

The blushing hand of Rose Mitnick rose. "Doesn't this
mean a certain kind of milk?"

"It certainly does!" said Mr. Parkhill heartily.

"Good girl, Rose!" laughed Nathan P. Nathan.

"Meelk?!" gulped Lola Lopez.

"Goodness sek!" Miss Ziev scribbled a note that would
enliven many a dinner after she was Mrs. Andrassy.

"I knew you would recognize it!" beamed Mr. Parkhill.
"Now, 'homogenized' milk will take on a *much* richer
meaning once we understand what its separate parts
mean."

He raised his chalk and with one swift stroke bisected

HOMOGENIZED. " 'Homo' means 'like,' or 'the same.' 'Genos' refers to 'type' or 'kind.' Homogenized milk, therefore, is a milk which is the same throughout, milk in which the cream has been thoroughly distributed—"

"You mean I am drinking *Greek* milk?" Miss Atrakian was scandalized.

"No!"

"Greek milk is from goats!" smirked Olaf Umea.

"I am not a goat!"

"You are not a cow eider," said Mr. Kaplan, "but you drink Amarican milk!"

At this point, Lucca Barbella, who was becoming increasingly hostile to Hellas, broke in to ask Mr. Parkhill whether Greek was the *only* language which had enriched the Anglo-Saxon. Had not a certain other noble tongue endowed English with rare linguistic treasures? Through both his question and his intonation, which suggested an overheated diplomat delivering an icy *démarche,* Mr. Barbella practically accused Mr. Parkhill of playing favorites among the nations.

"Latin," Mr. Parkhill promptly agreed, "has probably contributed even more words to English than Greek has."

"Bravo," said Mr. Barbella.

"We have to learn still *anodder* lengvidge?" quaked Mrs. Moskowitz.

"My nephew writes Latin," Mr. Wilkomirski announced.

"What?!"

"You teasing?!"

"He is doctor," said Mr. Wilkomirski.

"Class, suppose we now try a few words with Latin roots. It is extremely interesting!" Onto the board sprang:

POSTPONE

"Now, 'post' means 'after,' and 'pone' comes from 'ponere' —to 'place.' So 'postpone' means—"

351

"Tea!"

Mr. Parkhill stopped short. "I beg your pardon?"

"Tea!" It was Reuben Olansky.

" 'Tea'?" echoed Mr. Parkhill, somewhat bewildered. " 'Tea' is not a Latin—"

"It's Chinee!" boomed Mr. Olansky. "You asked for foreign words in—"

"Oh, I see what you mean. Yes, 'tea' is, I believe, from the Chinese—"

"Zwieback!"

Mr. Parkhill coughed. "What?"

"Zwieback!" Mr. C. J. Fledermann insisted. "From Cherman."

"Oh, yes!"

"Man alife!" exclaimed Mr. Kaplan. "Aren't any woids in English fromm *England?*"

"Englond? Bah!" Olga Tarnova flicked her handkerchief at Albion. "Englond is not romahnteek. Englond is foodball, sail-boys. *Whare is Englond's soul?* . . . Rossia! Rossia has most beautiful worrds. *Zvezda,* that means 'star.' *Syértse*—that is 'heart'! *Píshushchaya mashína*—'typewriter'!"

That was all that was needed to rouse those who carried the Mediterranean in their blood.

"Those wordsa are *Russian!*" snarled Mr. Barbella.

"Give examples of Rossian in *English!*" demanded Olaf Umea.

"Class—"

"I give honderd examples!" flashed Olga Tarnova. "Vodka! Caviar! Borscht!"

"Dose are foods, not woids!" gibed Mr. Kaplan.

"Borodin! Dostoevsky! Pushkin!"

"Zeez are *names!*" objected Christian Fledermann.

"All Rossian!"

"But dose woids *stay* Rossian!" exclaimed Mr. Kaplan.

352

"We want woids which pass into *English*. Kip your borscht an' blintzes, Tarnova! Push away Pushkin! *Homogenize* somting in Russian! Did Rossians give us a name for automobills? Talaphone? A hot drink? Iven a cold sneck?" Mr. Kaplan was waxing indignant.

"Mr. Kap—"

"You are prajudiced against Rossia!" railed Miss Tarnova.

"He'sa jalous Italia, too!" alleged Mr. Barbella.

"We must all be *broad*minded," cut in plaintive Miss Mitnick. "Mr. Kaplan, you are not international—"

"Ha! I didn't objact to Chinese tea!"

Mr. Parkhill was rapping his pointer so sternly, and frowning so frostily, that he stilled the factions by sheer force of will. "Nothing is to be gained by these heated exchanges! We are here to study, not argue." Stigmata of shame spread across the faces he beheld. "Since some of us seem to feel so intensely about this, I suggest that those who wish to—may bring to our next session a brief list of words, *English* words, which you recognize as—being of foreign origin!"

That was how it had begun. Just that simply. Who could have foreseen that Mr. Parkhill's suggestion would open the dikes to a flood?

For that was precisely the way Mr. Parkhill felt now— flooded, inundated by wave upon wave of words, names, roots, prefixes, suffixes, rolling across the room from distant and exotic shores. No sooner had he finished calling the roll than Lola Lopez, who must have consulted half the Spanish-speaking population of New York, rattled off words of Hispanic vintage, beginning with "arena," ending with "tobacco," and including four extrapolations of "cigar."

Miss Lopez had scarcely run out of breath before Miss

Atrakian, who seemed to have plundered her fiancé's knowledge of Homer and Euripides, began flinging gems from the Aegean before the barbarians. And no sooner had the dust settled in Miss Atrakian's path than Mr. Barbella was pouring out melodious syllables culled from the Tyrol to Calabria. And before his last, ringing echoes had expired in the fervent air, Olga Tarnova, bosom heaving, eyes smouldering with strictly retroactive love of Holy Russia (civilization had been throttled there in 1917, as far as Miss Tarnova was concerned), began to intone a Slavic litany.

Mr. Parkhill had never heard anything like this before. Christian Fledermann followed Miss Tarnova with proud loot from the Rhineland, ranging from "edelweiss" to "kindergarten" to "pumpernickel." Mr. Wodjik donated several vocables from some Balkan clime, which, since no one could understand them, joined the ranks of English without challenge. Mr. Nussbaum offered three words which bore the proud, albeit intermediary, *imprimatur* of Israel: "shlep," "kibitzer," "mish-mosh." To this, "Cookie" Kipnis, a fastidious spirit, added "bagel," which inspired the widow Pilpul to toss in "lox."

Mr. Wilkomirski, who often misunderstood an assignment, rose above the call of Poland to present words from three languages in which he had not the slightest vested interest: "carnival," "whiskey," "kimono." Even Oscar Trabish, fatigued from his work before the ovens, yawned, " 'Chef'. . .'menu'. . .'omelet'—all Franch!"

"Pistol!" cracked Mr. Hruska, tapping the Czech. To which Mr. Barbella, beside himself with piqued patriotism, flung " 'Bank'! 'Sofa'! 'Pepper'!" into the teeth of his colleagues.

The room was beginning to resemble the Olympic games.

Mr. Kaplan had remained surprisingly mute throughout

354

the etymological parade. Now he sought to catch Mr. Park-hill's attention. He did this with mooings, hummings and "Psst! Psst!"'s which reinforced a beseeching expression that implied he would die on the spot unless recognized. It proved unnecessary for Mr. Parkhill to do so, because Mr. Kaplan, divining the intent, anticipated the act. He leaped to his feet, announced, "I have woids from all over de seas!" and strode front and center.

All the other students had recited from their seats, of course; but Hyman Kaplan was not the man to forfeit the advantage of an erect speaker over a recumbent audience.

"Frands, fallow students, all-Amaricans!" Mr. Kaplan paused. "I say 'all-Amaricans' because only in a school in wonderful Amarica can we show soch pride in the conter-butions from foreign nations! In this megnificent etmos-phere—"

"Mr. Kaplan," Mr. Parkhill broke in, "this is *not* an exer-cise in Recitation and Speech. Simply present your words."

"I shouldn't give beckground remocks?" Mr. Kaplan might have been Apollo, asked to discard his lyre.

"No," said Mr. Parkhill stonily. "There is no need what-ever for background—re*marks.*"

Mr. Kaplan hefted a piece of chalk with a sigh that wed-ded injury to innocence, and printed nine letters on the board:

EUMOIROUS

Spots floated before Mr. Parkhill's eyes.

"What?" That was outraged Olaf Umea.

"Is that a word or a disease?!" guffawed Mr. Nathan.

"Some people got a noive like gallstones!" That was Mrs. Yanoff, heaving in black.

"What is the word?" Mr. Olansky asked frantically. "What did he do to the board?"

355

"Mr. Kaplan," frowned Mr. Parkhill, "I—"

"He wrote 'humorous' with 'e-u'!" Miss Gidwitz informed Mr. Olansky.

"The woid is not 'humorous'; it's 'eumoirous,' " remarked Mr. Kaplan.

"Fake!" howled Mr. Olansky. "A fake word!"

"Watch this mon's treecks!" warned Miss Tarnova.

"Eumoi—' Oy?!" oyed Mrs. Moskowitz.

"Class . . ." Mr. Parkhill floundered in misery. In all his years as a teacher, no pupil had ever brought a word into the classroom which Mr. Parkhill could not explain; Mr. Kaplan had bagged a specimen Mr. Parkhill could not even recognize. His eyes bored into the nine letters on the blackboard. What an ungainly—an outlandish—word! A Grecian word (that was clear); but what a freak: Mr. Parkhill wondered whether any Greek had ever used it.

"Eumoirous . . . eumoirous. . . ." It raced through Mr. Parkhill's head. The prefix, of course, meant "good," and "moir"—from "moira"?—perhaps had something to do with destiny. "Euphorious!" popped into his mind. Could Mr. Kaplan possibly have meant "euphorious" instead of "eumoirous"? There was, after all, a good deal about Mr. Kaplan that was emphatically euphorious.

"Where *did* you get such a crazy word?" he heard Mr. Olansky roar.

Mr. Kaplan pointed a regal finger at the stand in the corner on which Webster's Dictionary reposed.

"Pssh!" Mr. Pinsky slapped his cheek, chortling.

Mr. Nussbaum clutched his beard and prayed.

"Mr. Kaplan," said Mr. Parkhill carefully, "suppose you tell us what that word—means."

"It's from Grik."

The laconic reply only fanned the wrath of the forum.

"Answer Mr. Parkhall!"

"Don't play pick-a-boo with the question!"

356

"This beats Barnum and Paley!" laughed Nathan P. Nathan.

"Mr. Kaplan," said Mr. Parkhill drily. "I do not doubt that your word is—or comes from—Greek. But that is not what I asked you. I asked: What does the word mean?"

"Don't *you* know?" asked Mr. Kaplan in astonishment.

Mr. Parkhill stared at the blackboard glumly. He would not dissemble; he would not evade. "No." The moment the irretrievable negative left his lips, Mr. Parkhill regretted it. The entire grade was staring at him—their teacher, their Solon, their Solomon—in horror. The very foundation of education was crumbling before their eyes.

"Teacher don't know a word?" Milas Wodjik was thunderstruck.

Tomas Wodjik asked the same question; but backward: "A *word* teacher don't know?"

"A foreigner can stump an American-born?" Miss Ziev was so aghast she fingered her engagement ring to remind herself that not all was lost.

"Mr. Parkhill . . ." Miss Mitnick, wan, bewildered, could say no more.

They were like passengers on a storm-tossed ship whose captain confesses a total ignorance of navigation.

"Class . . ." Mr. Parkhill adjusted his glasses, smoothed his tie, teetered back and forth on his heels, forced a vapid smile upon his lips—all the while fighting for time. "Let us not make mountains out of molehills. No one can know —or use—all the words in English. There are, after all, half a million words in the language"—a heart-rending *"Gewalt!"* came from Mrs. Moskowitz, whose nerves collapsed at the prospect of half a thousand—"and no one can possibly keep all of them in his head. That, in fact, is one of the reasons we have dictionaries! . . . Now, Mr. Kaplan, suppose we come directly to the point. Define 'eumoirous'!"

Strangely enough, Mr. Kaplan did not appear pleased. He did not even look contented. He looked flabbergasted, even apologetic, a Boswell who had accidentally sent Dr. Johnson sprawling in the dust.

Mr. Kaplan lifted a blue slip of paper from his pocket. Dolorously, he read: " 'Eumoirous. Adjective. . . .' It means, says the dictionary, 'Happy'; also 'fortunate from good intantions or good actions.' " He lowered the blue slip contritely.

"Shame, shame on such word!" hissed Miss Tarnova.

"Crazy!" mumbled Mr. Hruska.

"*I* wouldn't make Mr. Parkhill such trouble!" announced Rochelle Goldberg through her lozenge.

"Give Koplan a diploma!" lashed out Mr. Olansky. "Greduate him! Now! Good-bye!"

"Good-by-y-ye!" echoed Olaf Umea.

Not a retort or riposte came from Hyman Kaplan. He stood in silence and (could such a thing be?) regret.

"Well, class," said Mr. Parkhill. "Mr. Kaplan has certainly brought us a—uh—most unusual word."

"That woid is not unusual; it is unbelievable!" bellowed Mr. Blattberg.

"For that blame Grik, not Keplen," said Mr. Kaplan.

This gambit so enraged Mr. Blattberg that he began swinging his watch chain as if it was the sling not of David but of Goliath, yearning to kill David with his grandsons' baby teeth.

"Kaplen, give an *inch,*" pleaded Bessie Shimmelfarb.

"Class!"

"You are not fair, Mr. Kaplan!" blurted Miss Mitnick, verging on tears. "Mr. Parkhill wanted words that would help, not confuse—"

"Som people," sighed Mr. Kaplan, "can drown in a gless of water."

"Now he gives swimming lessons!" raged Mrs. Pilpul.

358

"Gentle—"

"Everyone else in the class brought in useful words!" cried Miss Mitnick.

"Does aducation have to be useful?" rejoined Mr. Kaplan.

"In a hundred *years* we wouldn't use a word like 'eumoirous'!" Miss Mitnick wrung her hands in despair.

"Could come an occasion for *som* student in this room to use 'eumoirous,' " Mr. Kaplan murmured.

"Mr. Kap—"

"The day you use that cockamamy word," stormed Mr. Olansky, "snakes will fly and elephants sing!"

"Keplen," said the name's owner, "is not responsible for the animal kingdom."

"*Mr.* Kaplan!" Mr. Parkhill did not try to soften his annoyance. "I entirely agree with Miss Mitnick and Mr. Olansky! Your word is *most* obscure. Good English is simple English. The purpose of words is to communicate, not to impress. And a word such as 'eumoirous'—"

Mr. Kaplan's features sagged like wax in the sun. He had obviously expected Mr. Parkhill to praise him for discovering so exceptional a word as "eumoirous," perhaps even hold him up to the class as a model of ambition and courage. Instead, Galahad saw King Arthur leading the Saracens.

"Now let us proceed to dangling participles!" Mr. Parkhill picked up the textbook. "Page seventy-five . . . Mr. Kaplan, you—may return to your seat."

For the remainder of the evening, Mr. Kaplan sat silent, wrapped in desolation. The man had retired to the tent of hurt pride, and within it—who knew his thoughts? Only as the hour of departure drew nigh did Mr. Kaplan bestir himself—and then only to bend head over notebook and, without sound or sign, begin to write.

At long last, as Mr. Parkhill himself was becoming sated

with dangling participles, the final bell chimed its signal of adjournment.

The exhausted scholars collected their notebooks, stuffed their brief-bags and satchels, cleared the hook-slat of coats and hats and scarves, donned their garments, and streamed to the door.

"Good night, Mr. Parkhill."

"Good ivning."

"So lung."

"See you next time."

Mr. Parkhill returned the parting phrases as he sorted out his books and papers. He reached for his attendance record—and frowned. Mr. Kaplan was still in his seat, still writing. Mr. Parkhill made more noise than necessary in closing the desk drawer.

Mr. Kaplan rose. "Goot night," he said, pausing before Mr. Parkhill, then closed the door as he went out.

Mr. Parkhill sank into his chair. Rarely had he felt so tired. His neck was stiff. He leaned back, irritated anew by the squeaking of the chair's unoiled spring. He began to massage his temples.

He had harbored such high hopes for "words from foreign sources." He remembered an admirable article in *PARSE,* the journal for English teachers, some months ago, an article by Dr. Helmut Ganshmeier of M.I.T., titled "Cognates: Vital Clues from Foreign Tongues." . . . Dr. Ganshmeier was a linguistic wizard who had become so fascinated by word-roots in culture diffusion that he had moderated a symposium on "Psycho-Linguistics." What novel, what challenging ideas that issue of *PARSE* had contained. But Dr. Ganshmeier had never been forced to deal with a student like Hyman Kaplan. . . .

Mr. Parkhill rubbed his eyes. On the desk he saw a sheet of foolscap. It was folded. He reached over and unfolded the page. Something was written on it, but upside down. He turned it right side up.

Dear Mr. Parkhill—

Tonight I disagreed with you. Still you are the best teacher.

If I dont learn from you, I wont learn from anyone!

(singed)

Hyman Kaplan

p.s. You should feel eumoirous.

Mr. Parkhill tossed the paper on the desk with impatience. That was just like Mr. Kaplan—to find a way, however canny, however pertinacious, to prove his point, to have the last word whatever the ruse. . . . "Eumoirous . . . Happy from good intentions or actions."

Well, Mr. Parkhill told himself, he did not feel at *all* eumoirous!

He put on his hat and rubbers before a delayed awareness of incongruity made him pause. "(Singed) Hyman Kaplan." Why, Mr. Kaplan had spelled his name without stars!

Mr. Parkhill picked up the note again. It was true. "Hyman Kaplan" lay in gloomy black. Without crayoned colors. Without red letters outlined in blue. Not garnished with a single star of green.

Then a gleam of color caught his eye. On the underside of the fold, which he had not seen before, was printed:

TO MR. P*A*R*K*H*I*L*L

As he switched off the lights, Mr. Parkhill wondered whether he would ever again be so honored.

He felt eumoirous.

The End

361